Waldwick

Waldwick...War of My Brothers

Kenneth Linde

Waldwick Books
www.waldwickbooks.com
McHenry, Illinois

Waldwick...War of My Brothers

Copyright © 2021 Kenneth Jon Linde

Waldwick Partners, Inc.
dba Waldwick Books
www.WaldwickBooks.com

April 2021

Printed in Wisconsin, United States of America

Library of Congress Control Number: 2019900114

ISBN: 979-8-9852613-3-2

ISBN: 979-8-9852-6133-2

9 798985 261332

This book is dedicated to all the passionate people in theworld and the belief that the right to passion does not belong to one gender, race,religion,nororientation.

Passion is the inherent right of all humans to believe in something, strive for and achieve something that is honorable, noble and kind. To find a passionate person is a rare gift for those who are passionate can open your mind and heart to something you've never seen or felt before simply because they sincerely believe that mountains have no meaning without the valleysbelow.

Who Am I, What do I know, When Will I Stop, Where Will I Go?

My name is Henry Terrill. Most people call me Hank. I was a farmer my entire life as was my father and his before him. Now, before I get too deep in the muck, I need to tell you that I'm not what you would probably call the 'average farmer,' more like a square peg in a round hole, I guess. Most farmers are pretty conservative. I think that comes from being alone so much and reliant on yourself.

When I was in high school, my favorite subjects weren't industrial arts or physical education like my friends. It certainly wasn't farming. I only became a farmer because Ma and Pa needed help back then. I loved English class especially writing stories and then music and that's probably why I'm punching these keys today as my long-lost interest reappears. I never intended on writing a book and don't know if I really am. It's just that my mind Is full of all kinds of things that have happened and I want to share them with my kids and grandkids before I, too, am just a memory who slowly fades away.

I'm 59 years old and was married to my wife Ann for nearly 40 years. It was a good marriage, filled with love and laughter. Nothing fancy! Nothing exciting! Just a good solid union of two people who loved each other, respected each other, and shared this thing called life. No one has any idea what the next day will bring. Even the next instant, when a life can change forever. If it's fun or exciting, you're standing on top of the mountain. If it's bad, you're down in the valley. It can be pleasant or something violent and brutal, people never know. All that is real is the fact that when it's you whose life changes, rearranges or perhaps even ends, you're no longer a spectator, but a participant.

Two years ago, I was out bailing hay. Ann had gone into town and was late returning, which wasn't like her. I sensed something was wrong and saw Sheriff John Plover pull in the driveway. By the look on his face, I knew it was bad news. It seems Ann was on her way home on Highway 23 when she hit a deer, ran off the road into a tree and was gone. First it was shock, then denial and finally profound sadness as my life changed in that instant and I was all alone. How do you tell your kids their mother is gone? How about the grandkids and Ann's family? That night was the worst of my life, calling and telling, trying my hardest not to break down. My brother, Tom, and his wife, Sue, came to help, but what can anyone do? As the week prevailed, I learned who my friends were as they took care of the chores and I took care of saying goodbye to my wife. I cannot properly express my sadness, nor sorrow! When you live in a small town, it doesn't take long for the news to spread.

What was the most devastating was the reaction of some folks. For most, it was a true expression of their condolences. For others, it was as if I had some disease and they were afraid to look me in the eyes. Those are the ones I'll never forget! Ann and I lived in the house my great grandfather built. It isn't much, but was always filled with love and kindness. The day she died, the cold, dark reality of her memory chilled the house and I simply couldn't stay there anymore.

As sadness became reality, I realized my time had come to give up what I'd always been - a farmer. It took a while to get everything straightened out in terms of belongings and all the legal stuff. I finally went to our kids and told them I wanted to retire. Milking 200 head twice a day was too much and the passion was gone.

In May, I sold the Terrill family farm to my brother Tom, as neither of Ann's and my two kids were interested in it and I wanted to keep it in the family. We did what was called a Quick Claim Deed without lawyers or anyone involved. When your next-door neighbor is your brother that you grew up with and someone who had been your pal for 59 years, it was good enough for me.

Tom agreed to pay me so much per month until the day I died. He didn't need to borrow money and pay the bank interest and I didn't need to pay capital gains taxes. Burt Warren, our accountant, said the tax advantages of selling like this versus inheritance were incredible. Our family had already been down the tax road when Pa died without a will and we had to pay lawyers and the government for land we'd been working for nearly twenty years.

In our agreement, I stipulated that the spit of land called Skunk Hollow where we went to grade school, where the trees stood tall and a small stream trickled from beneath the earth couldn't be changed. Tom knew what these ten acres meant to me and agreed. He's always been a man of honor and so, once again, it was done on a nod and handshake and I knew that the land would always be. When the 'sale' was completed, I moved out of the house and into Mineral Point. The old house had seen better days and was in need of a lot of repairs, if anyone was ever going to reside in it again. Instead, it became an empty shell as photos and memories were removed and our auction saw the furniture I no longer needed scattered to neighbors and strangers throughout Southwestern Wisconsin. It was a sad day and yet it was what was needed. Life does go on!

The house that had been my home was haunted by the love and laughter of my dear Ann who'd gone away and I just couldn't live there anymore. After living my entire life on the farm, except for four years in Madison at the University, living in town was going to take some adjustment. I wanted to find a house but elected to take my time by renting an apartment on High Street above the Red Rooster Restaurant.

The move was simple in terms of the furniture and clothes. The only tough part was hauling over 500 LP's up the outside stairs and deciding where to put them. With all the time in the world, I did what I'd done in Madison. I bought some concrete blocks and some pine boards and built some heavy-duty shelving. I then sorted the records based on genre and then within each genre by artist. It took over a week, but was worth it.

On one shelf were my big band albums from the forties. On another were all my folk records like the Christy Minstrels, Peter, Paul and Mary, Led Belly, Dylan and others. On the next shelf was my folk-rock collection that was just beginning to grow. Finally, on two shelves were my rock records of all the groups from the sixties. I sent a change of address card to Columbia Record Club and sure enough, two weeks later, I got my first letter and the choice of selecting a new group called Crosby, Stills and Nash that I bought. At first it seemed strange living in town and in an apartment. I wondered if I'd made a mistake. The peace and tranquility of nothing but a summer's breeze, was replaced by the sounds of trucks and cars rolling past my front window all hours of the day and night.

The apartment was small and yet suitable. The living room faced High Street and I could watch the world pass by. The bedroom was in the middle, somewhat insulated from the clangs and clamor of humanity. The kitchen and bath were in the rear. It was clean and freshly painted and for one person it was fine.

In the morning, the sweet smells of breakfast from the Red Rooster below came wafting up and served as my alarm clock, reminding me that another day was upon me. As my eyes opened and reality set it, the realization that I had nothing to do and nowhere to go would slide through my veins like ice water, chilling my soul, while reminding me that the world was certainly passing me by.

One certainly is the loneliest number! As first, I thought my malaise would be temporary, but one can only look at a TV Guide so many times before that highlight of the day went away. As my routine set in, I'd get up, get cleaned up and saunter downstairs for breakfast. The food was great and prices reasonable and the social network gave me a break from being all alone.

Night time was the worst. You can only watch so much television or read for so long and then you need to go to bed. No matter what I did, there were dreams of Ann and the farm, the family and the woulda's, coulda's, shoulda's of regret. The dreams prevailed and on many nights were, quite honestly, nightmares. Folks told me I needed a break and I finally agreed. Sadness has a way of taking the warmth out of sunshine. I'd always wanted to travel, but the cows had always kept us on a leash. I used to joke and say they were my mistresses and when they called, I came running.

Now that the cows were gone, I wanted to see the world, because, quite honestly, I hadn't seen much. In fact, other than Mineral Point, Madison and the State Fair in West Allis, I rarely left Waldwick and, other than Dubuque, had never been out of Wisconsin. As I settled into the routine of my new life, I finally agreed that I needed to simply get away.

Having never been anywhere, I had no idea where to go. Those who had 'been there' told me, "If you've never been out West, nor seen the majesty of the Rocky Mountains, they're quite the sight. Then you can go to Las Vegas and do some gambling." I thought, "hell, they certainly were never farmers where every day is a gamble! If the weather or the bugs don't get you, the government will and when you finally do have the one 'perfect' year with just the right temperature and moisture, you realize so did everyone else and the price of your crops fall simply because the supply exceeds demand, even when you're a member of the co-op."

From the photos of the Rockies I saw in magazines, the glimmering peaks looked like they almost touched the sky. Some of them were even covered in snow in July. While this caught my eye, like life, I realized that it was the valleys below that gave those mountains meaning. Without the valleys, there would be no mountains. Peaks and valleys are just the exceptions to the everyday life that we all have and what we need to be able to live with. I just needed to climb out of the valley.

I was intrigued by the Rockies, but also had an inclination to go out East because of all the history and my interest in our family heritage. After a little studying, I decided there were three places in the east, I'd visit – Washington D.C., Philadelphia and New York City. God only knows why. I didn't have the slightest idea how to begin and so I called one of those travel agencies in Madison that had one of those new '800' telephone numbers that didn't cost long-distance and asked the lady to send me some brochures.

When the brochures arrived, I went to the Mineral Point library and looked at atlases and decided I couldn't go East and West in one trip and so I took out a quarter and flipped it. Heads meant East and tails meant West.

On the flip of that coin, my fate came into being and the decision to explore the East became my destination. The travel agent lady asked a lot of questions about what I wanted to see, where I wanted to stay and how long I intended to be gone. Traveling alone meant there was no timetable. It was just me and what I wanted to see. I didn't need anything fancy just clean, safe and quiet. In the end, she was nice enough to make all the plans and did it all for free, including the telephone call.

I decided to wait until after Neil Armstrong walked on the moon. I guess I thought my trip was a little less dramatic than his. While his was "one small step for man, one giant step for mankind", mine was simply a few small steps for an old farmer from Wisconsin who'd never been anywhere.

I'd never been on an airplane and thought I really didn't need to make the trip that way. Airplanes are for those in a hurry and that's one thing I certainly wasn't – in a hurry that is. I bought a new suitcase from the Sears Roebuck catalogue and made plans.

The first leg would be by Greyhound to Madison. I hoped John Kepler would be driving, as he was Mineral Point's favorite who would take care of all the kids and make sure they were safe and secure coming or going to and from home.

The day arrived and I went to the Ben Franklin and bought a spiral notebook, two #2 pencils and one Bic pen. My goal was to write down as much as I could, as my Kodak camera would only freeze sights and not memories. I was sitting on the porch of the Hotel Royale when the Greyhound came into view and there was John, big smile and all. He'd already been to Dubuque and was on his way back to Madison, yet his broad smile made me feel welcome.

I climbed the stairs and noticed that the front row was empty and that meant I could talk to John if he had the time. I put my suitcase in the overhead rack and settled in. John asked me where I was going and I laid out my itinerary. He asked me how long I'd be gone and I told him I didn't know, as there was only a beginning and no end.

We stopped in Dodgeville, Ridgeway, Barneveld, Blue Mounds, Mount Horeb and Verona with John calling out the towns along the way, greeting each passenger as if they were old friends and thanking those who had taken the ride with him. As we neared downtown Madison, we rode across the new John Nolen Drive which had been created by filling in a small strip of Lake Monona that was adjacent to the railroad tracks that had traversed the lake for over one-hundred years. Remembering back to my Wisconsin history class, I recalled that John Nolen was an American landscape architect and founding member of the American City Planning Institute. Nolen was hired by John Olin who was an entrepreneur, conservationist, and philanthropist in the city and the first president of the Madison Park and Pleasure Association who persuaded community members to contribute over a quarter million dollars to the development and maintenance of the parks.

In 1908, Olin contacted Nolen for advice in laying out Madison's city parks including what became Tenney Park with its lagoons and all. Without money to pay Nolen, Olin enlisted the support of the city, University of Wisconsin and the state and they worked with Nolen to develop the entire Madison Park system.

Everyone was so impressed by Nolen's ideas that he was commissioned to develop a plan for the entire Wisconsin state park system. Having seen the rapid deforestation of northern Wisconsin, the depletion of mineral resources in the southwest, and increasing urban development, the State hired Nolen to not only to find locations for the parks but also provide a reason for their existence.

Nolen recommended the creation of four state parks and provided guidelines for the establishment of the entire state park system. I'm glad he did or I don't know where all the folks from Illinois would go on the weekends. As the Greyhound crossed Lake Monona, the Capitol, in all its splendor, stood like a giant against the summer sky.

John Kepler drove the big bus north on Broom Street to West Mifflin and then the two blocks until he entered the Greyhound terminal that was in the lower level of some large grey office building just one block off the Capitol square. I shook hands with John and thanked him, pulled down my suitcase and asked directions to the Milwaukee Road train station, which was six blocks away.

I could have taken a bus to Columbus and met the Northwestern Train, but felt it would be closer to change stations in Chicago than go through all the nonsense in Wisconsin. With that, I had four hours to kill and so I dropped twenty-five cents in one of those 'secure lockers' and walked the block to the Capitol building. I'd always marveled at its majesty and knew that going up in the rotunda and out on the walkway still represented the highest point in any building I'd ever been in my life. I made my way up the marble stairs and looked south at Lake Monona and then walked around and looked north at Lake Mendota. Part way back, I stopped and looked west down State Street at the mishmash of buildings and big signs for the Orpheum and Capitol Theaters.

I killed an hour and walked back down West Washington Avenue and stopped in the Rennebohm Drug store located in the Hotel Lorraine where I went to the ice cream counter and ordered a banana split. It was my going-away treat and, while not as good as Tom and Ethel Tradinicks' at the Sweet Shop in Mineral Point, it still tasted really good on an early August day. I kept a close eye on my Timex and when it was 90 minutes to departure time, walked across the street and turned the key in the locker and was relieved to see my new Sears Roebuck suitcase right where I'd left it. As I walked outside, there was a taxi cab waiting and the driver offered to give me a ride. I'd never ridden in a taxi before and the thirty-five cents for the six-block ride seemed like a lot, but then this was rip to be filled with firsts and so I said "OK".

Five minutes later, we were at the former Chicago, Milwaukee and St. Paul station and I gave the driver fifty cents and told him to keep the change. He thanked me and said, "Goodbye". The travel agent had mailed my train tickets and so I simply stood on the platform and looked at the beast before me. This was to be my first train ride. The engine was diesel. The last time I'd been this close to a train was one of the black monster steam trains that burned coal. My, times sure had changed.

The conductor, leaned down from one of the cars and hollered, "All aboard!" and I entered the second car behind the engine. I was directed to my seat and was asked for my ticket, as the conductor took out a paper punch and poked a hole indicating that I'd paid to go to Chicago and then on to Washington D.C., only changing trains in Chicago. For the next two hours, I was mesmerized by the passing sights of cities and towns, fields and forests, all with cars stopped simply waiting for us to go by. We arrived in Union Station in Chicago and I was bewildered. Gone was the tranquility of the clickity-clickity-click beneath my feet, replaced by the rush of humanity, all in a hurry to go somewhere else.

I asked for directions and some man pointed at the sign and went to track number seven and waited with others. Soon the call came to board and I walked down the smoke-stained, darkened concrete way until I was met by another conductor who informed me that my reserved seat was in car number five, which I'd already passed. He took me for a rube. But then, I guess I was. I boarded the train and found my seat by the window. It was in coach. Had I known they had little rooms, I think I'd have paid more and sat in one of those instead.

'Kah-Rin'

I sat looking at the darkened walls of Union Station, still covered with soot from steam engines of a time gone by while somewhat oblivious to those boarding. It startled me when this young woman came aboard and threw her backpack in the rack above my row. Indifferent to me, it seems she'd been awarded the seat next to mine. This young lady was probably twenty-one at most, with long, bleached blonde hair and wearing those super low-rise jeans that I learned later were called hip-huggers, that seemed more like barely butt-covers to me. The front had no pockets and only two exposed buttons with a big peace sign belt buckle at the end of her thick leather belt. I wondered why her pants didn't fall down. Perhaps it was because the legs were skin tight, all the way to the knees and were stuck in place, before they flared out into enormous bell bottoms that covered her boots which had thick soles that added probably six inches to her height.

My new riding mate was wearing one of those skin-tight, tie-died shirts that looked like somebody painted it on and then splattered paint all over the front of it. Like half the girls in college and even some in Mineral Point, she was without a bra, probably done as a measure of protest or perhaps to get the attention of every single set of eyes that passed her way.

My new seat mate sat down with a thump and I could tell that the last thing she wanted was to sit next to some old farmer from Wisconsin for the next fifteen hours. There was a deep sigh as she opened the cover of "Rolling Stone" magazine and snapped the pages to make sure I was paying attention.

As she perused the mid-section, she came to an article about the fifth anniversary of some French clothing designer named Rudi Gernreich who introduced the topless bathing suit. When you're hauling cow manure all day, I guess it had slipped my attention. This young lady, who I later learned called herself

"Kah-Rin" looked at me and flashed the image in my face asking, "What do you think of this?" She had broken the silent barrier as I looked at the photo and replied. "Bet she's gonna be cold in January in that getup."

'Kah-Rin' looked at me in disdain as she pontificated, "Rudi Gernreich designed the monokini as a protest against the repressive society of America. Our society is so – so blatantly sexist – I'm going to move to France, where they're more liberated and treat women as more than objects. Why is it that men can walk around with no shirts on and no one cares, but American women don't have the same rights?"

Before I could answer 'Kah-Rin' continued. "When the first photograph of Peggy Moffitt wearing this design was published in *Women's Wear Daily,* it generated a great deal of controversy." 'Kah-Rin' stared at me in all earnestness and asked, "what's wrong with a woman's breasts?" Adding, "Do you know that when a woman wore one of these suits on a beach in Chicago, she was arrested?"

My God, what did I get myself into? 'Kah-Rin' continued. "Let's talk about sex." My eyes must have widened as I thought she meant with me until she continued. "In America a man has sex with several women he's considered a lover while a woman is considered a whore. This, too, is a double standard! This too is wrong! A woman should be able to do with her body what she wants to – free love for everyone!" Even in my advancing age, that didn't sound too bad, except of course, for our daughter.

We were just pulling out of Union Station and I already had been shown naked breasts, told I lived a double standard and was sitting next to a girl who felt she should have sex with whomever she wanted. I should have taken the plane! The conductor came and punched our tickets and that seemed to calm things down a bit.

I sat there and watched as 'Kah-Rin' opened her purse, took out a small mirror and re-applied her lipstick, which was already almost as thick as the soles on her shoes. For the next hour, all was quiet and then, when 'Kah- Rin' had completed "Rolling Stone" and noticed that I was writing in my spiral notebook, she asked me what I was doing. I explained that Ann had died, I sold my farm to my first brother and this was my first trip outside of Wisconsin. My plan was to keep a journal of all the things I saw and people I met along the way.

My seat-mate asked me what I'd written about her and I explained that I'd written that I was sitting next to a nice young lady named 'Kah-Rin' who had expressed her feelings about the roles of women in American society.

'Kah-Rin' asked me what my wife did when she was alive and I told her she helped run the farm to which she replied, "In other words just a glorified farm hand?" "No, she raised our two kids, did all the bookwork, kept the garden and helped in the fall when it was harvest time."

"Like I said – just a farm hand." I was insulted, but knew better than to express my feelings when there were still twelve hours of sitting side-by- side in front of us.

"Women deserve the right to do what they want and that means more than JUST raising kids and being farm hands," 'Kah-Rin' announced, to anyone and everyone. As we were rolling through Indiana and the clickity click had almost put me to sleep, 'Kah-Rin' spoke in a very determined tone. "I'm going to Washington to demonstrate for equality for women. I cannot and will not accept the cultural and legal validity of patriarchy and the practical validity of social and sexual hierarchies being used to control and limit the legal, physical and social independence of women in our society."

I wondered if she'd read that on the back of a comic book or perhaps one of those wrappers that came inside Double Bubble bubblegum, as she continued, "American men have participated in legalized formal and informal forms of sex-based discrimination since the beginning of our country, predicated on the existence of the social constriction of gender."

"Women want – no make that demand - total equality in the workplace and society and we reject the idea that piecemeal equality will eliminate sexual discrimination against us. We want to foster a government and society that emphasizes the value and agency of human beings, individually and collectively – especially, as they apply to the human rights of all people by defining our socio-economic position and political roles in this country."

I took a deep breath and realized I wasn't in Waldwick anymore. As the day wore on so did she. I politely listened and then couldn't handle anymore. I had to pee and excused myself. As I walked back towards the rear of the train, I noted a bar car and stopped for a beer. I almost pooped my pants when I saw the sign that said, 'Budweiser $5.00'.

I had my choice, spending a percentage of my vacation budget getting drunk while staying away from 'Kah-Rin' or going back and listening to her rant and rave about how bad a person I was simply because I was a man. I decided on option two and went back to my seat only to find that my neighbor wasn't there. I hoped she'd found some other victim, as I slid into my seat and closed my eyes.

A few minutes later 'Kah-Rin' returned with glassy eyes and the sniffles. She slightly smiled at me, took her seat, closed her eyes and before long was breathing deeply – thank God. Darkness fell, the lights dimmed and the rolling countryside became a diorama of twinkling lights as those within our rail car reflected off the glass and I could see my next-door neighbor's head droop in silence.

Around eleven, the inside lights were turned off and soon, my eyes closed and I slithered into the abyss called sleep, which I welcomed after such a long day. I was startled awake by the bright lights of tomorrow gleaming in my face and learned we were about an hour from Washington DC. I was surprised I slept so well. I think it was the clickity-clickity-click of the wheels on the tracks, whose sounds of silence was only punctuated by the call of the conductor announcing we would be in Washington in 30 minutes.

As my mind cleared, I realized that I was all the way to Washington

D.C. and it had been less than one day since I smiled at John Kepler in Mineral Point, Wisconsin. After getting my bearings, I stood and gingerly climbed over the still zonked 'Kah-Rin' and made my way, toothbrush in hand, to the phone booth they called a bathroom, whose redolence reminded me of our old outhouse. I did what I needed to do and got the hell out of there. You can only hold your breath so long.

As I was returning to my seat, I noticed that my neighbor had departed. I hoped for good. A few minutes later she returned, now wearing knee high boots and one of those micro-mini skirts that barely covered her butt with an American flag bandana in her hair. If her skirt got much shorter, she'd have two more cheeks to powder and she smelled like cheap perfume, which seemed a little better than the train's bathroom. Within a few minutes her diatribe began again.

According to 'Kah-Rin', Ann had wasted her life and being a farmer was a worthless way to spend your days when you could join the Peace Corps and save the world. She told me that I'd held Ann back from reaching her potential and, for all intents and purposes, personally impeded the life, liberty and equality of all women in the world.

I'd had enough. I'd been polite. I listened to her crap and never responded to her insults, accusations or innuendos. As she opened her mouth one last time, I stopped her and asked her if she had ever been on a farm. She looked at me and admitted she was raised on one outside Kewaunee. She wanted to make Kewaunee sound bigger and more *contemporary* and did so by explaining that it was a suburb of the booming metropolis of Green Bay, home of the Green Bay Packers.

I looked at her and asked her if she knew the difference between a horse, cow and deer. She looked at me incredulously and said, "Of course". "They all eat grass, correct?" She nodded in the affirmative as I continued. "When a cow eats grass and relieves itself, it comes out looking like a pie. When a horse eats the same grass and relieves itself, the grass comes out as looking like apples. When a deer eats the very same grass, and relieves itself, the grass comes out like little balls. Why is that?"

"I don't know," was her response.

"In other words, you don't know shit! Yet, for the past fifteen hours you sat here and demeaned me and what I chose to do with my life. You've insulted the memory of my wife and the life she chose and told me that I was wrong. You said you were coming to Washington to demonstrate for women's rights and yet your attitude, demeanor and belief is that the way to change people's ideas and values is to insult them and denigrate their way of life."

I was on a roll and kept going. "You DON'T change opinions by insulting people! You don't get them to believe, by repeatedly telling them they're wrong, especially when you don't have a clue whether they were in love, happy or satisfied with the lives they lived. Finally, you certainly don't come to Washington to change the world looking like you got on the wrong train and should be on the one going to Sarasota, Florida to audition for Ringling Brothers Clown College."

'Kah-Rin' sat stunned and before she could respond, I continued. "Karen" - as I pointedly called her. "If you want to create change, you need to be an example of what you want the change to be and right now all you have done is shown me exactly why my opinions, beliefs and intents are steadfast."

I stared directly at her so that she could see that I was serious. "If, and that's a BIG IF, the day comes and you grow up, remove that chip on your shoulder and five pounds of make-up from your face, perhaps, just perhaps, you'll begin to accept that change comes slowly, person-by-person, one-by-one and the only way to have it happen is when people accept you, identify with you and agree that your ideas, opinions and beliefs are right. This comes from example and WITHOUT ever telling them, their ideas, opinions and beliefs are wrong. That's leadership and not intimidation."

I was in a tizzy and kept on pounding. "Rather than focusing on what women don't have, you must accept the challenge of elevating them, by helping increase their knowledge and confidence thereby positioning women to exceed their own expectations. You can't demand it! You can't legislate it! If you want true change and true liberation, you need to change everyone's opinion regarding what's right and what's wrong, including women. Only then, can you create change."

Karen stared at me with a look as if she didn't have a clue what I was talking about and so I continued. "Have you any idea what social elevation is?"

She was becoming intimidated and meekly shook her head 'no' and so I added, "Social elevation is an emotion you don't hear much about and yet it's all around us. It's created by witnessing virtuous acts of remarkable moral goodness which is what heroes do to become heroes and true leaders have the ability to exude. Psychologists say that social elevation is experienced by people as a feeling of appreciation and affection for the individual whose exceptional conduct has been observed, where the observation motivates those who experience it to open up to, affiliate with and assist others to the point that it makes an individual feel lifted up and optimistic about humanity and also tomorrow."

I wasn't going to stop now and so I added, "Karen, social elevation is a part of leadership and leadership involves relationship building, where a strong relationship starts with trust and evolves into respect that comes from the consistency of doing what you say you're going to do. It's not about carrying signs and telling people they're wrong. It's not about diminishing and degrading others simply because they have a different outlook on a subject than you do. It is about the slow, gradual evolution of thoughts and feelings until they align with yours."

I looked Karen right in the eyes and added, "A friend of mine once said, "You can't motivate people, but you can inspire them, and every great leader must be inspirational and have the innate ability to push the right buttons to get the most out of those who believe in them. This is a difficult task, because every person is different and responds to a different style of leadership. However, true leaders understand and accept the fact that change only happens from within, one person at a time and not on a train from Chicago where you offend and insult the person sitting next to you simply because you think they're different than you and therefore wrong, while you blatantly exude any sense that you don't trust them, their beliefs or their history."

I looked at this young girl who was still sitting, mouth agape, in shock that someone had finally told her the truth instead of quietly absorbing all her pontifications. I added, "If you want to change a person, you have to trust that person and understand their motivation simply because their motivation comes from within, based on how they were raised and what they experienced. It's not something you can do to someone else. They have to want to change! They have to want to see the difference and be willing to make the right amount of sacrifice, as they recognize and appreciate their own strengths and weaknesses and accept who they are. That's the reality of life and the beauty of leadership. I'm not a leader, nor, unfortunately are you."

"You're just a little girl with all kinds of ideas in her head about what's right and wrong who thinks she has all the answers when she doesn't even know what the questions are. Now, if you don't mind, the train has stopped and I'm getting off. I wish you luck because, unless you remove the chip on your shoulder, you're REALLY going to need it."

I guess we'd had an audience as those around us began to applaud. As my feet hit the aisle, I turned one last time to Karen and said, "Oh by the way, that topless bathing suit you attempted to shock me with was something my wife would **never** wear, simply because she wore **nothing,** when we went swimming. Now, where does that fit in your description of liberation?"

As I was entering the vestibule between the cars, the porter was smiling a huge smile out of acceptance for what I'd said and tipped his hat as I slid a ten-dollar bill in his hand. My train ride was over and I had a lot to write about, stopping for an instant to mentally apologize to Ann for sharing a little-bit of our private lives. There's a spring-fed pond on Waldwick and when no one was around, it was our way of cooling off on a hot summer's day where skinny dipping can be one of the true advantages of being a farmer.

<u>Oh Washington Where Nothing's Done and Politics is No Joy</u>

I guess I wasn't prepared for what I was about to experience. First, the rush of people was immense, with no one smiling. Second the heat and humidity was as bad as any that besieged Waldwick on the worst summer day. The taxi driver wanted two dollars to take me to the hotel. I thought, 'No way.' I'd done that and walked the twelve blocks, getting soaking wet in sweat along the way.

It was 12:05 when I arrived at the hotel. The desk clerk looked at me with disdain and asked what I was doing there. I told him I had a reservation. He said that check-in time wasn't until three and that if I wanted a room, I'd have to pay for an extra day. Imagine $28.00 for three hours! Instead, I sat beneath one of the big fans in the lobby and scowled at the desk clerk until the hands read three and went back to the desk and checked in. It was then I realized I wasn't in Mineral Point anymore.

I went to my room and opened my spiral notebook and wrote my first day, including John Kepler, Madison and my first taxi ride, Chicago and then Washington D.C., with my thoughts and comments about all that had transpired. As I looked out the window, I noticed that darkness was falling, and I hadn't eaten all day. I went downstairs and asked at the front desk where I could go to get something to eat. I was told that the neighborhood, "Wasn't really that safe at night," and he recommended eating in their dining room. My God, where was I? "Not safe in America's Capitol?"

I went into the dining room and ordered a hamburger and a glass of lemonade. The bill was four dollars! Four dollars, I just shook my head. Imagine four dollars for one hamburger and a glass of lemonade!

I spent a week in Washington visiting all the museums and memorials and watching the anti-war demonstrators. I'd seen them on TV at home, but this was different. I was there and realized it wasn't nearly as dramatic as it seemed on television. I tried talking to a couple of them, but they had no interest in an old man with a farmer tan, who didn't have a camera aimed at them.

As I was about to give up, a young girl came up to me and asked where I was from. I said, "Wisconsin." She asked me what I thought of the war, and I didn't really know what to say. I thought about Madison and all the demonstrations there and how every night it was the same message. What was different was those involved in protesting seemed to be growing in number and getting more like me.

At first, I thought it was just kids trying to avoid the draft and then I began seeing moms and dads and then veterans who had been 'over there' and began to wonder. The peace sign, which had been the "V" for victory sign from Winston Churchill in World War II had matriculated down to little kids. The peace symbol began to appear on cars and trucks and I was beginning to wonder if there wasn't something I was missing.

Here I was in Washington D.C. – the center of our national politics and no one seemed to care, except those who were demonstrating. It was business as usual even though, every single day, more American soldiers were dying in a war that most Americans didn't want.

As I wrote in my notebook – I realized I was a square peg in a round hole in many other ways. I didn't fit in with the young crowd in terms of attitude, dreams and desires and certainly didn't feel *that old.* While other farmers liked country-western music, mine was rock and roll. At first it was just the harmony that got me, then I started listening to the words and what I heard was people crying out saying enough is enough!

I really enjoyed watching boxing on TV. Mineral Point wasn't very good in high school football, but was always great in wrestling and perhaps because I wrestled and from what dad taught me, I got the boxing bug. We listened to it on the radio as the Badgers were always a powerhouse and Verne Woodward was a great coach who even had a TV show on Channel 33 called 'The Little Badger Boxers' consisting of little kids in oversized boxing gloves that was always fun to watch.

I was listening to the NCAA Championship matches from the UW Fieldhouse in 1960 when, in the second round, some fella from San Jose landed one punch that was described as a classic right hand to the left temple of a Badger boxer named Charlie Mohr that people say ended varsity college boxing forever. Charlie collapsed in the dressing room and prayers were said for his recovery. Charlie died the following Sunday and that was the end of college boxing.

Life goes on and boxing fans turned to the pros with Cassius Clay being one of my favorites during the Olympics. I laughed at all his antics and loved his saying, *"Float like a butterfly, sting like a bee."* Clay changed religions and then his name to Mohammed Ali and refused to be drafted, for which he was sentenced to five years in prison and stripped of his heavyweight title for three years.

A lot of people didn't think much of him, and at first, I was one of them. We all need to serve our country in one way or another. Heck, he wouldn't have gone to battle. They would have used him in some sort of special forces. I did give him credit though for standing up for what he believed in. It's amazing how anti-war demonstrators made me think of Charlie Mohr and Ali, but then we're all for something and against something else, including war.

During my seven days in D.C., I visited everything I could get into. Besides the Smithsonian, my favorite was the National Archives Museum, where I stood in silence and read every word of the Declaration of Independence and Constitution. To me, the most important line was the first line of the second paragraph. *'We hold these truths to be self-evident, that all men are created equal, that they are endowed by their Creator with certain unalienable rights, that among these are life, liberty and the pursuit of happiness.'*

The security guard must have thought it strange that an old man would mingle with hordes of school kids, who would glance at the documents simply to say they'd been there, before moving on - not realizing what they had seen, nor feeling what was written on those pages and how it gave every American the freedom we have. Sadly, those documents today, are all taken for granted – nothing more than pieces of paper. So sad! So very, very sad!

After spending the morning with the national archives, I went to the Library of Congress and read that when Jefferson wrote *"all men created equal"*, he wasn't talking about individual equality. What he meant, at that time, was that the American Colonists, as a people had the same rights of self-government as other peoples of the world and hence could declare independence, create new governments and assumed their 'separate and equal station' among other nations.

After the Revolution succeeded, Americans began reading that famous phrase another way and it became a statement of individual equality where everyone, that every member of a deprived group could claim for themselves. With each passing generation, our notion of who that statement covers has continued to expand and it is that promise of equality that has always defined our Constitutional freedom.

As I read those words, the thoughts of those demonstrating began to ring true. The right to protest, when one felt something was wrong. The right to equal opportunity and not unequal treatment, either for against a person, because of their gender, race, religion or creed.

I went to the mall and stood below the Lincoln Memorial and looked to the west. The memorial was much taller than it looked on my Philco portable television. My mind went back to 1963 and Dr. Martin Luther King's *'I Have A Dream'* speech and how it made me feel as he looked across the reflecting pool toward the Lincoln Memorial and into the hearts and souls of so many Americans.

When you're a farmer in Waldwick, Wisconsin, you don't get exposed to colored folks that much. The one's I'd met in Madison all seemed like good people and I guess, because it was Madison and things weren't as bad as a lot of other places, I really had no idea what it was like. That sure was a great speech and I remember watching it on Walter Cronkite with tears in my eyes. Great words presented by great people can do a lot to change the minds of others. I stood for a moment and took a deep breath. I was at the very spot where history was made.

I then walked to the other side towards the Capitol and looked at the grassy area and imagined 100,000 protesters gathering there in October of 1967 and simply shook my head in disbelief. So many people! So much passion! So much anger! I remembered 1965 when I still supported the administration on Vietnam. It was then that we began hearing about a small minority of anti-war activists who were making their voices heard, including students, as well as prominent artists, intellectuals and members of the hippie movement.

Quite honestly, I didn't know what to think as we heard about a growing number of young people who were rejecting authority and embracing the drug culture. They couldn't have been anymore opposite than what I believed in or stood for and I just shook my head in dismay.

The way they dressed! The way they looked! The way they acted were all totally against what I believed to be normal. Like so many others, I looked at those first anti-war demonstrators and considered them leftists, cowards and hippies. I didn't have much in common with them as I proudly stood by the flag of the United States of America and what it stood for. As things evolved, it seemed as if the kids running the program were getting that much more anti-American and therefore against everything I believed in.

Members of some leftist organization called the Students for a Democratic Society or SDS began organizing 'teach-ins' to express their opposition to the way in which the war was being conducted and how our government worked. I remember watching Channel 15 in Madison in October, 1967, when the newscaster reported on the demonstration at the University of Wisconsin against the Dow Chemical Corporation. Dow is the company that makes a flammable gel called napalm that the U.S. government uses in Viet Nam to burn and destroy anything and everything that gets in its way. Burning to death has got to be a terrible way to go.

Dow Chemical was on campus trying to recruit new employees at the School of Business. The anti-war protestors were having, what began as a peaceful demonstration against Dow's attendance. Suddenly everything turned violent and Madison police went after the crowd with clubs and shot teargas cannisters into the Commerce Building. Incredibly, there were about 200 accounting students taking their six-week exam in room B-210. The tear gas cannisters exploded in the lecture hall and the dazed and bewildered kids came tumbling out of the building coughing and wheezing, crying and sneezing. These kids had done nothing more than try to get an education, only to be engaged by police who came after them with the same anger they'd attacked the demonstrators - clubs in hand and revenge in their hearts.

The past few years have been really tough in Madison and yet, you could see people's minds changing as they began to see that the Vietnam war wasn't what it was being presented to be. After watching 100,000 people march on Washington, Ann and I stayed up late one night and watched Chet Huntley and David Brinkley report that 30,000 of the marchers who decided to go to the Pentagon and express their opinions, were also exposed to a brutal confrontation with soldiers and U.S. Marshals with clubs and teargas.

We watched in horror as hundreds of demonstrators were beaten and dragged to the ground, only to be arrested. These were Americans and the First Amendment that I'd read the day before, gave them – gave me – gave us - the right to peacefully express our opinions. When I saw, what I saw and felt back then, changed my feelings regarding the Viet Nam war.

Living in Wisconsin, we already know what taxes are all about and when President Johnson announced that he would ask for a 10% increase in federal taxes to fund the war, I'd had enough. If the money and lies weren't bad enough, the anti-war movement really hit home when you could watch the death and destruction every night on NBC in living or would that be dying color.

When you've got little kids giving the peace sign and bumper stickers saying get out of Vietnam, you know people are getting fed up. The president even went so far as to have General William Westmoreland, commander of U.S. forces in Vietnam, address Congress. This calmed things down for a little bit, but last year's Tet Offensive destroyed much of Johnson's credibility concerning the Vietnam War. We weren't winning! All we were doing was killing people – ours and theirs. I shook my head and looked at the ground, regretting I hadn't been one of the 100,000 people who stood where I was standing.

Sadly, I sincerely don't think our government has any idea how to keep peace around the world, when it can't keep peace at home. What I thought would be a marvelous destination was quickly turning into one filled with disappointment and cynicism. Those I looked up to as leaders, were no different than you and me except they had the need for power and prestige that most folks never feel.

I wanted a break from Washington and so the next morning, I took a side-trip to Baltimore. I wanted to visit the spot where 1.5 million people, including my ancestors from Cornwall, set foot on America. There's a strange feeling being where someone before you had once been. I walked around and read all the little signs and looked at the few displays there were. Sadly, I failed to find anything to connect me to those who made my life possible.

At least I could say I'd been at the very spot where the Terrill American heritage began – filled with hopes, dreams and simply tomorrow. On my last day in Washington, as I was walking through the national Capitol building, I saw an empty wooden bench and took my place, at first to simply rest and then observe. As I sat there, I began to see what Washington politics was really all about and the difference between leaders and politicians.

I took out my Bic pen and began writing in my spiral notebook. I wanted to harvest my thoughts and observations of that day so that I could rationalize why it was that my beliefs were changing regarding our country and why we were going askew. I remembered back to my conversation with ''Kah-Rin'' and wondered where she was and what she was doing. I thought about her and pondered whether she too felt as disappointed as I did, not in the government, nor the institutions, but the people running the government.

I began to realize how many of them really weren't in it for us, but for themselves where the money, power, prestige and perks they'd acquired were so great and so narcotizing they were willing to virtually sell their soul simply to hang on to what they had. I shook my head as I concluded that politicians are what ruined politics. Many of them appeared to be an inbred, corrupt, venal, shallow, power-hungry cabal of elites who only cared about enriching themselves. I never realized that six out of the nation's ten wealthiest counties surround the Washington, DC area, where politicians have a chokehold on politics.

Perhaps that little girl had been right! I wished I could run into 'Kah- Rin' again and tell her this. "Great leaders understand that you can't micromanage everything. You can't wave a magic wand and everybody is going to be dialed in. They realize they're working with a human element. However, there's a huge difference between being a leader and a politician."

"Politicians use their rhetoric and common themes to develop political positions in terms familiar to the voters that they believe their constituents will agree with. Many times, it's not what the politician believes in, but what he thinks will get the vote. All the negative advertising about an opponent makes me sick. The falsehoods and rumors have taken the desire to serve and made it the need to win."

I know that rumor has always played a major role in politics and negative rumors about an opponent are typically more effective than positive rumors about one's own side. Sadly, so many promises stated before an election become lost after the tally is done where the words "middle class" only appear at election time. I know it's not always the politician's fault, but it still hurts.

Once elected, these politicians become government officials and have to deal with the permanent bureaucracy of non-politicians. I know, there's always a subtle conflict between the long-term goals of the elected and the ordained bureaucrat who knows that those chosen are only temporary employees they've seen come and go time after time after time.

Tragically, in the American system, at all levels, winning politicians replace the bureaucracy with those who formed their base of support. This 'spoils system' has seen administrations once designed to protect and defend common folks like me turned into mouthpieces for the organizations they were supposed to protect us from.

While civil service reform was supposed to eliminate the corruption of government services, that's simply not the case. All that's happened is they've become more sophisticated in how they distort the structure to match their needs that all start and end at one point – money. Money for re- election! Money for personal convenience! Money that creates more power and more exclusivity than was intended."

Going to the Library

I'd warmed the Capitol bench long enough, but wanted to add more to my imaginary conversation with 'Kah-Rin' and went to the library to study the different types of politicians. From a few hours of sitting alone, frantically scribbling in my notebook, I began to realize there are two main career paths which are typically followed by politicians in America.

First, are the career politicians who work in the political sector until retirement and then pocket all the perks they've voted for themselves and live happily ever-after. Only in politics do those who participate retain their title after leaving office, even though they're no longer in that office, no longer serving America and no longer making decisions intended to help those they represented.

The second group, are what I labeled the 'political careerists' who are politicians who gain a reputation for expertise in controlling certain bureaucracies and then leave politics for a well-paid career in the private sector making use of their political contacts. Normally these are lawyers who join special interest groups taking the concept of 'what's good for all' and add the word 'except' at the end, whereby they bend and shape rules and regulations, laws and policies to fit the group who's paying the highest fee to get what they want done.

I'd met enough politicians to realize that they're 'different' than the rest of us. The really good ones know how to make you feel important by remembering your name. They have the knack to remember thousands of names and faces and recall personal anecdotes about their constituents. I have a hard time remembering my own name, let alone thousands of others. As I was digging through the files at the library, one of the librarians noticed me and came over and in a quiet whisper inquired what I was doing, while asking if she could be of assistance. She was a bit younger than me – probably about 50

I'd guess - had brown hair tied up in one of those buns, black glasses, no make-up and was conservatively dressed in a long dark grey skirt with a white blouse, small gold necklace and stud earrings, all adding up to what I'd call the "plain Jane" look back home.

I told her that I was from Wisconsin and on vacation. I shared that I'd been touring Washington and had some questions about politics. When she asked what I thought of Washington, I was polite enough to point out what I'd enjoyed. She looked at me and inquired "And?".

"Well, I guess I'm a little disappointed in the people." "You mean the politicians?" she inquired.

I nodded in the affirmative. "Not as dynamic as you thought?"

Again, I nodded in the affirmative as she added, "There have been some great men who've come through this town, but there have also been a lot of scoundrels too."

"How can you tell the difference?" I asked. "By their eyes," the librarian replied.

"Their eyes?" I inquired as I peered into hers and sincerely felt I could feel her soul.

"Those who are sincere will look you in the eye and you can tell that they're telling the truth. Slick politicians look at your face instead of your eyes and flash a phony smile. It doesn't take long and you can tell."

"Have you ever met any of them?" I asked. "Great ones?"

"Yes, great ones."

"Three" was the response, as the librarian had a soft smile on her face reflecting back to a time and place when she experienced greatness.

"May I ask who?" I inquired.

"Ronald Reagan, Dr. King and Bobby Kennedy" was her reply.

"What about President Kennedy?" I asked.

There was a slight pause and then a forlorn look as she replied. "There's so much people don't know. If they only knew - he was the consummate politician."

"Wow!"

The librarian looked at me and I could tell she was sizing me up. I wondered if it was social or political and, also, to see if she could be a little more forthright as she added, "The biggest challenge of my job is when some young, wet-behind-the-ears, staffer is sent over here from the Dirksen Building and told to get some information."

"They think that just because they work for Senator Blowhard, they're special and start demanding this and that with the justification that they're SO important and whatever it is that the Senator asked for will save the world from teetering on the brink of global calamity. We've heard it all and do our best. The one's that really get us are those who start dropping names and making demands and we simply let it go in one ear and out the other."

With that, the librarian took me to a rarely visited corner and pulled out a book and paged through it until she found an article that summarized the different types of politicians a lot better than some old dirt-poor farmer from Wisconsin ever could.

As she handed me the book, she did so in a manner that her hand brushed against mine and I felt the softness of her heart ricochet through my entire body. This wasn't what I expected, nor intended and yet it was there.

I took a quick breath as if to expel the emotion, but it was too late and I couldn't let go. My intent was to take the book back to the table and write down what it said, but the librarian said that for ten-cents a page she could make a copy for me. I was amazed, I'd never used one of those copy machines before.

Here's what the article said: *"There are four pathways by which a politician's personal history could influence their leadership style and abilities. The first component is how they were raised or what they experienced may influence their core beliefs, which are then used to shape their basic beliefs that cannot be proven and are typically argued from rather than argued for. These can be anything from religion to opinions of people of color to different nationalities, to the role of government in our lives."*

"The second component is the politicians' skills and competence that are influenced by personal experience. The areas of skill and competence can define where they devote resources and attention as a leader."

"The third component revolves around the value of the elected position not only financially, but in terms of perks that allow the politician to receive special benefits the rest of us simply aren't given."

"A leader's previous profession may also be viewed as higher importance, causing a disproportionate investment of leadership resources to ensure the growth and health of that profession, including former colleagues. Other examples beside profession include the politician's innate characteristics, such as race or gender."

"The fourth component is how a politician's personal history affects their public perception, which can, in turn, affect their leadership style. War heroes receive a higher rating than a typical lawyer. Those who have served in lower elected positions are seen in a different light than those just starting out as most people still value service and experience. Female politicians, for example, may use different strategies to attract the same level of respect given to male politicians."

"Many of us attack politicians for being out of touch with the public. Areas of friction include the manner in which politicians speak, which has been described as being overly formal and filled with fancy words and false promises that are quickly forgotten when the person is elected."

I spent the next two hours reading and writing. As it was time for the library to close, I wanted to thank the lady for her help. I went to the counter and nodded my gratitude. 'Plain Jane' had deep brown eyes that simply captured my attention and her smile was almost effervescent in a professional manner where she made me feel as if she enjoyed her job and helping others.

I noticed that the ring finger on her left hand was bare. It had been nearly two years since Ann died and I had no ulterior motive other than having someone to talk to and so I explained that Ann passed away and I was in town alone. Being a gentleman, I asked her if she would like to have dinner with me, assuring her, it was all above board. I just needed someone to talk to. It had been a week alone and I was leaving Washington the next day.

A gentle smile crossed her face and she noted that she would need to call home and ask her mother. I thought she was joking until she explained that her 85-year-old mother was living with her and the librarian needed to make certain her mother would be all right.

Cucina Rosa

As the library lights dimmed and the doors were about to be locked, I asked the librarian what her name was and she said Katherine Johnson, but everyone called her Kat. I asked her if it was all right to call her Katherine as I loved the sound of her name and she smiled.

I took an empty page from my spiral notebook and wrote: _"Katherine Johnson is going to dinner with Mr. Henry Terrill, 158 High St, Mineral Point, WI 53565, phone (608)255-2185._ Then, I took out my driver's license and asked Katherine to make a copy of the note and license and put it someplace where someone could find it in case she didn't show up for work the next day.

A smile of gratitude crossed Katherine's face. She knew I was trying to be a gentleman, and my intentions were sincere. As we walked out of the library, I asked where a good restaurant was and Katherine indicated she knew just the place – a small Italian restaurant named Cucina Rosa with great food that had Chianti bottles with candle drippings on them strategically placed on tables that were covered in white linen and butcher's paper, all ensconced in an environment quiet enough for small talk and leisurely enough for an extended meal, which she said, was difficult to find in D.C.

We walked a few blocks to the restaurant and when we arrived were immediately seated. Katherine excused herself and went to the lady's room. When she returned, she looked like a different person. Gone were her black horn-rimmed glasses, replaced by contact lenses. She let her hair down, put on some make-up and joined 'Kah-Rin' regarding fashion-political-social statement attire or lack of.

Katherine had gone from 'Plain Jane' to somewhat, make that, a very attractive woman, in the matter of minutes. I was virtually in shock and I guess my smile must have given it away as I stood when she returned and slid her chair in for her as we spent the next half-hour sharing our life stories. I told her all about Waldwick, Mineral Point and Ann and that this was my first trip outside Wisconsin.

Katherine noted her husband had died, for which I said I was sorry. She added he'd been a pilot and Colonel in the Air Force who was killed in a training accident in 1965 as he was preparing for a mission in Viet Nam. She noted they had two grown sons. One of who was in the military and the other living in New York. She noted that when her mother had a stroke two years ago along with the onslaught of dementia, she became her caregiver, moving into her mother's house in McClean, Virginia.

I asked her if her husband worked in the Pentagon and she said, "No" and reluctantly added that his last assignment was at Andrews Air Force base. I felt I was digging a little too deep and wanted to change the subject, but Katherine continued, sadly saying. "Ron was a great guy, who loved to fly and died doing what he loved best."

I didn't know if she was referring to his death or her belief that he loved flying more than her as I shared that I'd never been in a plane. She asked how I got to Washington and I told her by train and it was a long story that she coaxed out of me.

There was a long pause as we both collected our thoughts, then Katherine added, "The military isn't for everyone. Between the political games you're forced to play if you want to move up in rank, to constantly relocating, there really isn't much stability. I get Ron's pension and took the job at the library simply to keep my sanity. I love my mother and will do anything for her, but I needed someplace to go simply to have a break and different life."

"Did you go to college?" I inquired. "I have degrees from Yale in Art and Art History, which is where I met Ron," Katherine replied. "I went there because my dad had a law degree from Harvard and I wanted to show my independence and Yale also has one of the finest Art departments in the country."

"Why aren't you working in your field?"

"First, times have changed. Second, I could never really have a career, because we never knew how long we were going to be in one place.

Right now, I'm the most educated, lowest paid person on the library staff," she added wistfully.

Katherine took a sip of wine and lamented as she slowly shook her head, "I once believed politicians were there for 'us'. Today, I sincerely believe many politicians are clueless, selfish, manipulating liars, who are incompetent and corrupt, taking money in exchange for goods or services, rather than working for the general public good. They'll only tell you what they think you want to hear and not what's right or wrong."

I realized that her opinions were in total agreement with my conclusions and that made me comfortable with what I'd seen as Katherine took another relatively large sip of wine.

Carefully putting the glass down she added, "As my life has progressed, I've become more cynical and sincerely feel that we're on the wrong road to greatness where the word 'we' has been replaced by the concept of 'me' and we've become a nation of selfish people only concerned about themselves and not willing to make sacrifices for the good of others." "Sure, there are those who stand out for their bravery or generosity, but most don't care about anyone or anything except themselves. I can only hope and pray that tomorrow will be a better day when those who are elected are real people and not those who are only in it for their own benefit, who wear Teflon clothes intended to deflect the bad, while attempting to simply acquire the good so that they can be re-elected and retain the power, prestige and perks they've become accustomed to."

Katherine continued, "Government has become too big and too lucrative. It's no longer for the good of the people. It's one huge business where citizens pay admission simply because we have to, for which we have a majestic court of princes and princesses who dillydally in a world of puffery with one goal in mind, sustaining their power for power's sake, such that the money earned and benefits reaped go beyond anything and everything common citizens can even comprehend."

I sat, totally enamored by what Katherine had elicited and then confidentially added, "As a child, I stood and saluted the flag of the United States of America – 'one nation, under God with liberty and justice for all'. Today, I looked at that piece of cloth - tattered and torn by strife and injustice and grieve that the only thing that remains true is *under God* who must be looking down with tears in his eyes, simply asking *How did I go wrong?*"

Katherine's glass was empty and she didn't resist when I filled it again. I felt the conversation was getting too deep and so I changed course and asked, "Other than helping old farmers find out about politicians, what do you do at the library?"

A somewhat embarrassed smile crossed Katherine's face. "My main responsibility is editing the magazines that come in."

"What do you mean edit?" I asked.

She continued. "We have the First Amendment, but we also have a policy concerning images or articles that don't meet the social, legal or ethical standards of the community, particularly when it comes to those under the age of eighteen."

"My job is to review the magazines for images and articles that are deemed discordant with those standards and either remove them from the magazines or sequester the entire magazine from general public consumption so that it can be seen only upon special request by adults only."

I must have had a quizzical look on my face as Katherine added, "As an example, I take each month's issue of Playboy, remove the centerfold and clip out any photos that would be considered offensive by the general public. In addition, I review the different articles for content to ensure they're not too – uh – descriptive."

"Just Playboy?" I asked.

"Heavens, no. There are dozens of magazines I edit each month- 'Penthouse, Hustler, you name it."

"Oh my God. Does it ever bother you?"

"Not really. First, you get used to it and second, what they show or write about has never been anything that has offended me. With my art degree and living in Germany for four years, I'm quite used to the perspective on what the American media sells."

I thought I'd better change the subject. "So your mom's healthy enough to take care of herself?"

"No, I have Maria, who came from Guatemala with her husband and helps out. Maria stays with mom during the day. When I called home, it was to see if Maria could stay a little later and thankfully she could."

As we opened our second bottle of wine, I asked Katherine more about her life.

"So you've lived in a lot of places?" "Seven," was the answer.

"Any favorites?"

"Germany! That's where our boys were born and the Germans definitely have a better lifestyle than Americans."

"Really?" I seemed incredulous.

"Yes, most Western Europeans do. They aren't as money-oriented as Americans and live at a slower pace. People aren't out to impress each other with cars and houses and material possessions the way Americans are. They're just not as materialistic."

"Anywhere you really didn't like living?"

"We lived in California for three years," was her quick response. "I thought it was the cool place to live these days," I replied.

"Californians are pretty lonely. They don't know their next-door neighbors and everyone seems to be out to impress everyone else and everything is so – so materialistic and that's just not me."

"Where did you grow up?" I inquired.

"New York" Katherine replied. "When World War II broke out, we moved here and dad went back to work for the government."

"Back to work?"

"He'd worked for them when he was young and they called him

back."

As even more wine flowed, smiles came easier and comfort levels

settled in. I began sharing the entire details of my life, focusing on Waldwick and Mineral Point and then 'Kah-Rin' or Karen, as I called her.

"So you're against women's liberation?" Katherine inquired quite seriously.

"Not at all," I strongly responded.

"I was just upset by the way she dressed and how she demeaned me for being a farmer. However, what really irritated me was the way she insulted the memory of my wife. Ann and I loved each other and were happy with what we did and how we did it."

"What was wrong with how she was dressed?" Katherine questioned. "Well, I thought it was a bit, uh, extreme."

"We've all gone through phases. Didn't you?" I thought for a moment and realized I had, as Katherine continued. "Kids today are just going through theirs. It's a form of rebellion against their parents and society and all the rules they've been forced to follow for so many years. They'll grow out of it. Every generation does."

I thought of all the bra burning demonstration and asked, "So you think it's all right to run around not wearing underwear?" I replied.

"It's certainly a lot more comfortable," Katherine answered.

I could tell I hit a tender spot, as she continued. "Perhaps, if I hadn't lived in Europe and saw how they perceive the human body, I wouldn't be so – so liberal. However, the Germans and French don't correlate the human body with sex. There are nude statues in museums and nude beaches in many European countries and no one seems to be bothered by it. In America, all we have are statues of politicians and soldiers who are famous for killing people, with little celebration of the beauty of life. In Europe, it's just the opposite."

"When we lived there," Katherine paused for a moment to measure her words and then added, "the boys and I visited Paris, Rome, and Florence and saw most of the world's greatest artwork. Michelangelo's 'David' in the Piazza della Signoria, is beyond compare for its beauty and detail and no one ever balks at the fact that he is totally nude."

"Antonio Canova's, 'Perseus with the Head of Medusa' is the exactly same, as is Aristide Maillol's, 'L'Air'. They're all explicit, yet their beauty and mastery are so profound that few if anyone complains about what they see and if they do, they should either not go or simply close their eyes. "

She continued, "Religious statues such as Gi Bernini's, 'Ecstasy of Saint Teresa' are still prevalent. Sadly, if it weren't for people like Pope Pius IX who had so many defaced or destroyed in the name of modesty by cutting off or covering the statue's genitalia, the churches and religious world would be alive today with nude statues and paintings that communicate both innocence and purity."

"I thought the church just covered everything with fig leaves," I said.

Katherine smiled and replied. "The first mention of a fig leaf is in the book of Genesis and that's where it all started. Then, the Catholic Church got involved and decided that modesty was closer to Godliness and various Popes such as Paul IV began requiring coverings. However, it wasn't until the Council of Trent in the 1500's that the Catholic Church took a staunch position and virtually everything was removed or covered. As is the case with so many rules and laws made by others, the Council condemned nudity in religious art, yet the bishops and cardinals maintained their own personal collections of what, even today, would be considered pornography."

Katherine was on a roll and I felt it wouldn't be polite to interrupt as she added. "Paintings such as Goya's, 'The Nude Maja', or Courbet's, 'Sleeping Nude Woman', or Matisse's, 'Souvenir de Biskra', or Modigliani's, 'Reclining Nude' are exceptional and recognized today for their beauty as works of art and not some form of pornographic representation. Most of them were created in the early 1900's when they style was in vogue."

"Today, you click a camera and boom, you've got the same thing in living color. No effort imagery and certainly no modesty when you see what I see every month."

Katherine slid back in her chair, took yet another relatively large gulp of wine and added, "I took the boys all over Europe and had them examine the beauty of not only the art, but the human body so that they would learn that a human being can be honored and respected and not objectified or sullied in the name of commerce. Sadly, in America, we create printed social peep shows that correlate nudity with sex, simply because, in doing so, it allows a huge entire industry to exist."

"You mean pornography?" I stammered in an embarrassed way.

Katherine shook her head 'no' and added. "That's only a small part of it. I mean the entire advertising industry that drives our economy! Look at how advertising has taken virtually every product and correlated it to sex. Do this and have sex! Buy this and have sex! Be this and become sexy! Americans are just so hung up on sex and by correlating it with nudity, the ad industry has the cause-and-effect it needs to sell more beer, cars, houses, perfume - you name it. In Europe, there's a more mature and sensible separation of the human body and emotions."

I was about to say something when Katherine stopped for a moment and looked in my eyes and inquired, "When you were talking about your wife and the farm, you said you a pond right?

I nodded in the affirmative.

"Did you and your wife ever go skinny dipping?" I nodded in the affirmative again.

"Was it a sexual experience?" "No, it was swimming," I replied.

"In other words, you weren't aroused by being naked or seeing your wife naked in your pond?"

"Not at all."

"What would have happened if someone saw you?" "We probably would have been embarrassed," I replied. "Why?"

"I don't know, because that's the way we were brought up, I guess." "When you were telling me about growing up you said you didn't

have indoor plumbing."

Again I nodded in the affirmative. "How did you bathe?"

"In a bug tub mom filled with warm water." "Where did she put the tub?

"In the kitchen in the winter and out in the yard in the summer." "Did anyone see you?"

"Sure."

"Did your mother bathe you alone?" "No with my little sister."

"Did that make you uncomfortable?"

"No it made me clean." I said trying to add a little humor to the conversation.

"How old were you when it stopped?" Katherine asked. I thought for a moment and replied "Seven".

"Why then?"

"Because my sister came down with polio." "You weren't ashamed or embarrassed?" "Not at all." "

Had she not come down with polio, would you have continued?" "I guess so."

"To what age?"

"I don't know – ten, twelve perhaps" "Why then?"

"Well, I guess it would have been different if I was beginning to 'mature'.

"So in other words, reaching puberty would have changed everything?"

"I guess so." "Why?"

"I don't know, I guess it just would have." "Any regrets?"

"Only that she had polio." I replied as Katherine took yet another sip of wine and added. "You see, all the Europeans have done is taken that attitude and made it commonplace. Did you know that Winston Churchill walked around his house naked and thought nothing of it, while the Duke of Windsor and his fiancé, Wallis Simpson, were the first famous couple to swim nude in public and did so in Croatia which started the whole clothing-optional environment that is prevalent in Europe today?"

Katherine looked at my empty wine glass and slowly filled it again. We were getting blasted, but neither seemed to care, as she stated. "It's all just socialization which determines right and wrong and therefore our morals. When we lived in Germany and toured Europe, we did as the Europeans did."

"You mean you were naked in public?"

"Sure, why not? We went to Montalivet Beach, along with St Tropez."

"The kids were with you?" "Sure!"

Katherine added, as if surprised I'd even ask.

"I don't know." I replied, slowly shaking my head from side-to-side that must have caught Katherine off guard as she added. "I'm not an exhibitionist, but also not ashamed or embarrassed by my body and who sees it. I think our society would be a lot safer if we differentiated nudity from sex."

There was a pause and all I could do was think about Ann and the pond and my sisters and how it all seemed so 'normal' back then. I felt I needed to re-direct the conversation and blurted out, "I believe in equal pay for equal work."

"What about equal representation?" Katherine questioned. "What do you mean?" I inquired.

Katherine looked at me and responded, "Our current 90th Congress has a grand total of twelve elected women in it, twelve! Of that, all twelve are in the House of Representatives and none – none, mind you, are United States Senators. In its entire history, there have only been ten women who have held that office and four of them served for one year, simply to finish out the terms of their deceased husbands."

"The politicians talk about glass ceilings in business, where women can look up at senior management, but never get there. Yet, only having six women in history become elected Senators? What about that glass ceiling? What about equity? What about true representation?"

"From the first visible public demand for women's suffrage in 1848 to the introduction of the Equal Rights Amendment by Alice Paul in 1923, the fight for gender equality is still not over. The Equal Rights Amendment is a proposed amendment to the United States Constitution designed to guarantee equal legal rights for all American citizens regardless of sex by ending the legal distinctions between men and women in matters of divorce, property, employment, and other matters that's been pending for nearly 50 years."

The conversation was getting a bit heated, especially when Katherine caught my inadvertent glance towards her now somewhat unbuttoned blouse.

"What about a woman's right to choose to do with her body as she desires?" Katherine inquired.

"You mean intimacy?" I asked in a sheepish way.

"Yes! Another one of the tenants of Women's Liberation is the premise that women should be able to choose the physical activities we desire and not be objectified as nothing more than a repository for a man's urges."

"You mean, recreational sex?" "Yes," came the firm response.

"Wow! I wasn't raised that way." I responded.

"None of us were. We were all taught that, unless you're married and there was the probability that your intimate activity could result in a pregnancy, it was a sin."

I nodded in the affirmative thinking back to high school and conversations about this girl or that girl *'getting in trouble'* with no mention of the guy.

Katherine paused and filled her glass yet again as she looked at me and added. "I believe that the messages of most religious training doctrines were developed simply to increase membership in churches and not because God wanted us to be so – so frustrated and feel so guilty about our normal inclinations. Why should the physical expression between two consenting adults be religiously sacrosanct?"

My God! I thought my conversation with 'Kah-Rin' had been in unplowed ground. Katherine was certainly coming with the harrow. I'd never had a discussion like this before in my life and wondered how many people in Washington talked about sex like this. Did this mean that the quiet, proper, librarian that I took to dinner, simply because I needed someone to talk to, was actually one of those liberal Democrats?

Still another sip of wine for the two of us and yet another wave away to the persistent waitress and Katherine questioned, "Why is it that a man who sleeps with several women is considered a great lover, while a woman who sleeps with several men a whore?"

As the words wallowed in my brain I remembered that Kah-rin had said virtually the same thing as Katherine added. "I'm not saying we should all jump in bed with anyone and everyone and do this or that. I'm just saying that two consenting adults should have the right to express themselves physically in any way the desire and without any form of ostracization by religion or government."

"By consenting adults, you mean man-and-woman, right?" Katherine looked at me and shook her head 'no' and continued,

"Who are we to say what is right and wrong, good and bad? Why should the government, which consists primarily of egotistical, horny, old, white men, establish morals for everyone else, when half of them are out breaking their own rules? It's not the 1500's and certainly not the Council of Trent, therefore, why should our government tell us that what's right and wrong for people of the same gender or different races who love each other?"

I sat back in my chair, somewhat in dismay. What had started out as a nice, quiet dinner that broke seven days of solitary *definement*, was quickly turning into the next chapter of the 'Kah-Rin' saga and yet, Katherine was making so much sense even to someone who was half, blasted.

I looked through my slowly glazing eyes at the now somewhat inebriated woman sitting across from me and inquired, "So you believe gender equality means equal pay, sexual freedom and racial justice? What about Viet Nam?"

"My husband was a soldier. My husband defended our nation. My husband died, while training to go and burn people alive in a war that makes no sense. If Ron was still alive and was off the record, he would say that what's going on is simply wrong. He's not alive because he was loyal to our country and followed orders, which is what a good soldier does."

It was getting too intense and so I shifted back to personal liberty by inquiring, "Do you still go to Europe?" I really didn't know if I was trying to satisfy my prurient interests or moving away from the sadness and anger I heard in her voice when we spoke of the war.

Katherine looked at me and her tone softened as she replied, "Ron and I went a couple of times, but he was always too busy. I'd go to a nude beach tomorrow if I was in the mood and could find one. The only one I know of in the States is Black's Beach north of San Diego. I guess I could go to one of the French Islands in the Caribbean."

There was a pause and then a slight smile as Katherine whispered,

"Would you go with me?"

Jesus, Mary and Joseph! I thought it was time for some levity in an otherwise very serious conversation and so I added, "You can go skinny dipping with me in the pond out on the farm anytime you want. The mosquitos aren't too bad. The pigs won't mind and the frogs won't tell the neighbors."

This molded a sheepish grin on my lips and a broad smile on hers as she looked at me, not knowing if I was being serious or speaking in jest. I sat for a moment as Katherine's foot brushed against my shin. Electricity slithered up my body.

I took a deep breath and agreed on the equal pay and sexual freedom, but the question of homosexuality was still of concern and so I inquired. "So you think it's all right for two people to – to have sex with each other?"

"If they care for each other, why not?"

I must have grimaced as I looked at the table and then at her wanting to make certain my answer was what I really felt.

"I've never thought much about any of this. It's just not something we see or talk about in Mineral Point."

"They're there, you just don't realize it. Nationally, about 5% of all adults are gay, lesbian or bi-sexual. You said there were about 2,000 people in Mineral Point, right?"

I nodded in the affirmative.

"Then, if it's an average community, there are about 100 adults who aren't quite as conservative as you think."

"Really?"

I was incredulous, thinking about Mineral Point and trying to identify just one who might fill the bill and countered with, "Well what about Waldwick, they're twenty people that live there?"

Katherine smiled and replied, "Then the sheep had better be careful."

I almost spit out my wine in laughter adding, "There aren't any sheep in Waldwick."

Katherine looked at me and inquired, "It really doesn't matter, does it?"

"Not really, as long as they don't try to convert me."

She smiled and shook her head. "It's not some form of religious cult.

No one's going to try and convert you," as she un-crossed her ankles and brushed my shin again as another jolt of lightning slithered up my spine.

"Do you know any gay people?" I asked quite seriously.

"Yes, there were several in the art department at Yale and three who work at the library and they're some of the nicest and most generous people I know."

"How do they act?"

This brought strange look to my guest's wine-induced, blushing face as she shared her words carefully. "As I told you earlier, part of my job is editing the magazines. In so doing, I've seen thousands of photos. Instead ofbeing offended, I find some of the women beautiful and attractive as well. I don't have any inclination to – to try *that,* but don't think two people who care for each other should be judged because they do."

There was a long pause and then my new, very liberal and quite inebriated friend, leaned across the table and touched my wrist and slurred, "you're not offended by that are you?"

I'd really never thought about it and didn't know what to say. I guess its all right what people do, but how am I to know if I've never been around gay people in my life or anyway, none that

I knew of.

There was a pause as reality set in on both sides as she looked at me and whispered. "Hank Terrill, you're a gentleman and I thank you for that. However, if it wasn't that Maria needs to go home, because her husband has to go to work, I might want to sleep with you tonight – that is – if you wanted to."

Wow! I think she realized she'd gone a bit too far as her hand released my wrist, her posture became erect and I could tell her next statement was going to be somewhat more formal.

Catching her breath and herself, she added, "Hank, I just want to thank you for a wonderful evening and allowing me to talk to someone above a whisper. I'm honored that you asked me to dinner and we've been able to share 'so much'. I really needed a night like this and deeply appreciate the fact you haven't judged me, condoned me or thought less of me, while providing a wonderful evening I'll always remember."

The waitress came and I gave her a nod indicating it was time to leave the now-empty restaurant. Katherine wanted to drive. I knew neither of us was in any condition to do so. The new metro system had only been proposed and so I hailed a taxi. As one arrived, Katherine gave me a hug and deep kiss on the lips. It was the first time in over two years that I'd felt the soft lips of a woman and it felt wonderful, hoping Ann wouldn't mind.

I opened the back door of the taxi as Katherine got in and leaned forward and gave the driver her address of 8354 Alford Drive, McLean Virginia. I gave the driver $20.00 and told him to take her home. He nodded and smiled. I looked down at my new friend and kissed her one more time and closed the door.

The temptation was so great to pull her out of that taxi and take her back to the hotel or go home with her. Instead, I carefully closed the door as she looked at me, smiled and then was gone, quickly departing into my memories. I stood for a moment and tasted her lips and shook my head reflecting on what had been an unforgettable evening, before making my way back to the mall.

As I arrived, I stood for a moment watching the demonstrators still parading, still dressed in their tattered clothes and still carrying hand-made peace signs and the American flag. While my day was ending, the war raged on with ten more dead soldiers than the day before and with their demise, the anger and frustration of so many people that now was beginning to include me.

As I crossed the mall, I nodded towards the demonstrators in affirmation. Not brave enough to join them! Not strong enough to participate! Not sincere enough to shout out what I really wanted to say – one - simple - word – FREEDOM before realizing, I really had to pee!

Gettysburg

The next day, I arose early and was packing when I felt something in my back pocket. It was Katherine's address, 8354 Alford Drive, McLean Virginia 22101. I took the time to write a quick note of thanks for the wonderful evening and asked the front desk to mail it for me.

At 11:45 am, I reluctantly left Washington on the train to Philadelphia. I thought about staying and voted myself down, thinking that any further contact would only minimize what had been a very special night. It was a short train ride and, after coming all the way from Chicago, it meant nothing more than a couple of hours to sit, reflecting on Katherine and the night before.

It all seemed like a dream, and yet there was so much to think about. Perhaps I should have stayed longer. There was no phone number. Perhaps I could find her in the phone book. Perhaps someone who made me think, made me feel, made me wonder, was gone forever. How sad! How incredibly sad, as I peered out the train window, not at towns and villages, but junk yards and trash, yearning to turn back time just a few hours to the euphoria of the night before.

After Washington D.C., I didn't think much of Philadelphia. Sure, I went to Independence Hall and saw the Liberty Bell, but there wasn't too much else to see other than the shipyard. But it's a city I'll never forget.

I hadn't realized that Gettysburg was so close and you could actually take a metro bus out there instead of one of those expensive guided tours filled with blue-haired ladies and old men whose pants came up to their arm pits. I got up early and took the two-hour metro ride and then the park tour where I learned a lot!

I knew that Thomas Terrill, one of my ancestors, had died at Gettysburg. I knew that he had been with the Confederate Army, but was actually a spy for the North who was tried and executed before a firing squad before the battle even began and, because of that, was not considered a war casualty. It had been 106 years since the Battle of Gettysburg which was fought July 1–3, 1863. Over 45,000 soldiers from both sides were casualties in the three-day skirmish, making it the deadliest battle in U.S. history.

I had my choice between the canned tour with special headphones or a park volunteer – a woman in her sixties who had a furrow in her brow - that made me feel her pain. After what I saw in Washington, I didn't want the canned version; I wanted the unvarnished truth.

Someone in our group asked what the difference was between a war and battle. It was a good question, and the volunteer had a profound answer as she responded. "A battle is a small part in a war while a war is made up of several battles which is the actual fighting that takes place. War is more of strategy and planning the battles for territory, but more important for attitudes and beliefs.

Normally, the outcome of a battle does not decide the winner of a war simply because war is an intense armed conflict between states, governments, societies, or paramilitary groups such as mercenaries, insurgents and militias. It's generally characterized by extreme violence, aggression, destruction and mortality, using regular or irregular military forces."

Wow!

The volunteer continued. "America has been and continues to wage war. Some large! Some small, but all with the same objective, exercising our will on that of others or protecting our way of life from those who would take it away."

"We cannot think of war without addressing the number a casualties, where just one is large enough to impose an obligation to consider the cost represented by that number - not just one life, but one circle of life-shattering bereavement - and we must ask ourselves for what purpose should that cost be borne by those on whom it falls, and whether it's been justified."

"In America, it's now conventional wisdom that societies like ours have become "casualty-averse". It was assumed after World War II and Korea that public support for military operations in Viet Nam would collapse as soon as soldiers started dying in any significant numbers. This always seemed a strange lesson to draw where over 30,000 Americans and over one-half million Vietnamese have been killed so far and we still haven't given up."

The volunteer stopped for a moment before continuing. "Today, we see a backlash against what's going on. It seems that societies like ours will no longer support military operations involving significant casualties unless we can see both a clear and vital strategic purpose for the war and at least a reasonable chance of achieving that purpose."

"Today, public support for the war in Vietnam is not being destroyed by the casualty lists themselves or by those who demonstrate, but by the sense that the purpose of the war is unclear and our chance of success is minimal. It's not so much the loss of soldiers' lives as they're mostly strangers to us all, but the sense that their lives are being wasted."

"We, as Americans are guaranteed certain rights and one of them is to oppose the actions of our government. Today, we see intense and passionate debates about the conflict with careless public acquiescence to our mounting losses. There has been little public opposition to our commitment by those who can do something about it until recently and hardly any discussion by those who could make a difference."

"This would be less remarkable if the reasons to fight in Viet Nam were clear and compelling and success was assured. But our purposes have never been clear, and there has never been more than a slim chance of achieving even the most modest of aims that have been suggested to explain what we are fighting for."

Our volunteer lady, looked down at the ground and then at the assemblage who remained standing in rapt attention as she added, "The day will come when America will leave. Sadly, other than lives lost, there will be very little difference in Viet Nam from the way it was before we went there."

I could feel her pain as she expounded, "It will become clear over the next few years, as we compare what our political leaders were saying and what actually happened. The conviction will grow that this war was misconceived and purposes for which we were fighting will never justify the lives lost, and there was never any serious chance of them ever being achieved."

A few people began walking away shaking their heads in disagreement as she continued. "To anyone who chooses to ask the questions, it will be clear enough that, all along, this is how it would end. Voters and taxpayers might have assumed the government was carefully considering these questions on their behalf, but all the evidence points the other way. The occasional actions of leadership have made it obvious that our government has never been able to explain either its purpose or its confidence in success. Yet we, the public, have been willing to see the commitment drag on and the casualties mount. Why?"

Once again, there was a pause and then she continued. "This seems to be an important question, for two reasons. When we look back on the war and the catastrophe we leave behind, it will be clear that the lives of the soldiers killed on both sides were wasted, and we should want to understand how that happened."

Once again, the volunteer looked at the ground and pause to collect her thoughts before continuing. "Looking ahead, our attitudes towards these people, just as we look at the battlefield upon which you're currently standing, may tell us something about war in general. By learning we can begin to simply understand 'why' which is very important, since we may all find ourselves thinking much more about the next war than we have for many decades. For both reasons, we need to focus carefully on the purpose of war and how we think about the idea of war, which will be unsettling because none of us like to admit that going to war is something we choose to do."

The volunteer looked at me and added, "Sadly, we prefer to say, as political leaders so often do, when going to war, that 'we have no choice'. But going to war is always a deliberate choice as is the use of anonymous lethal violence to achieve what might be called a 'political' purpose. Without political purpose, violence is not war, but violence for its own sake is a form of piracy and plunder."

The volunteer looked directly at the others and added, "Most of us accept that there are some purposes for which making war can be justified. For us, deciding whether to go to war, or even to stay at war, is all about deciding whether the purpose of the war justifies the probable costs where the lives of our own soldiers are not the only cost to be counted, but simply one of the primary factors."

With that, she looked at me again while stating, "In conclusion, there are two questions that need to be answered in reaching the decision to declare war, here, there or anywhere. The first question is whether the objectives are worth the costs if those objectives are actually achieved. The second question is whether there's a reasonable chance of those objectives being met. Lives lost in military operations that never had a reasonable chance of achieving their objectives are wasted lives, even if those objectives are worthwhile in themselves. Lives lost in a futile attempt to achieve objectives that do not justify their cost, even if they are achieved, are doubly wasted."

The park volunteer's soliloquy about Viet Nam was over as she slipped back into her formal mode and told the story Meade's Union army repelling attacks by Robert E. Lee's

Army of Northern Virginia, thereby halting their invasion of the North. I couldn't write fast enough and so I bought one of the park brochures for a dollar that said…*'After Lee's success in Virginia, in May 1863, he led his army through the Shenandoah Valley to begin his second invasion of the North, in what he called the 'Gettysburg Campaign'. With his army in high spirits, Lee intended to shift the focus of the summer campaign away from war-ravaged northern Virginia, and hoped to influence Northern politicians to give up, by penetrating as far as Harrisburg or even Philadelphia.'*

The volunteer pointed out that the two armies began fighting on July 1, 1863, as Lee concentrated his forces to engage the Union army and destroy it. A group of low ridges, northwest of town were being defended by one Union cavalry division. When the generals saw Lee's plan of attack, they soon reinforced the ridges with two additional corps of Union infantry.

Sensing defeat, General Lee had two large Confederate corps assault the Union infantry. This collapsed the line, sending the Union defenders retreating through the streets of Gettysburg to the hills just south of town.

On July second, the Union line was laid out in a defensive formation. Late in the afternoon, General Lee launched a heavy assault on the Union's left flank, and fierce fighting raged at Little Round Top, the Wheatfield, Devil's Den, and the Peach Orchard. On the Union's right flank, the Confederates attacked both Culp's and Cemetery Hill, all of which I found on the map that was included.

On July third, fighting resumed on Culp's Hill, and cavalry battles raged to the east and south, but the main event was a dramatic infantry assault by 12,500 Confederates against the center of the Union line on Cemetery Ridge, also known as Pickett's Charge. The charge was repulsed by Union rifle and artillery fire, at great loss to the Confederate army. General Lee sensed defeat and retreated. Historians say it was the turning point of the Civil War as Lee went from an aggressive posture to one of defense, against the never-ending onslaught of Union soldiers throughout the south.

As the tour ended, I went to the lady and thanked her. I inquired about her passion as she replied. "My son died in Viet Nam and I cannot justify why."

I bowed me head in reverence and thanked her for all that she said. I also expressed my condolences as others murmured what they had overheard. The volunteer looked straight into my eyes and added. "On November 19, 1863, at the dedication of the military cemetery here, President Lincoln delivered one of the most memorable speeches in American history. In 275 words, Lincoln reminded a war-weary public why the Union had to fight, and win, the Civil War."

'Four score and seven years ago, our fathers brought forth on this continent, a new nation, conceived in Liberty, and dedicated to the proposition that all men are created equal. Now we are engaged in a great civil war, testing whether that nation, or any nation so conceived and so dedicated, can long endure. We are met on a great battle-field of that war.

We have come to dedicate a portion of that field, as a final resting place for those who here gave their lives that that nation might live. It is altogether fitting and proper that we should do this. But, in a larger sense, we cannot dedicate -- we cannot consecrate -- we cannot hallow -- this ground. The brave men, living and dead, who struggled here, have consecrated it, far above our poor power to add or detract. The world will little note, nor long remember what we say here, but it can never forget what they did here. It is for us the living, rather, to be dedicated here to the unfinished work which they who fought here have thus far so nobly advanced. It is rather for us to be here dedicated to the great task remaining before us -- that from these honored dead we take increased devotion to that cause for which they gave the last full measure of devotion -- that we here highly resolve that these dead shall not have died in vain -- that this nation, under God, shall have a new birth of freedom -- and that government of the people, by the people, for the people, shall not perish from the earth.'

The volunteer looked at me with saddened eyes and asked, "What has changed?"

I wanted to return to Washington D.C. see Katherine and get the demonstrators and the politicians to sit down, shut up and listen. Tragically, the valleys were too deep, passions too intense and distrust too great to ever imagine people from either side sitting and listening, while reasoning with each other.

I'd come to Washington to see America at its finest and left Washington feeling completely different. Gone was my blind allegiance! Gone was my sincere belief that the government was for the good of everyone. I didn't like the way the demonstrators looked, nor how they acted, but by God, I was beginning to understand what they were talking about. Not from their actions, but from the words of a man written so long ago that burned into my heart the belief that goodness does not always prevail.

Where am I?

My visit to Gettysburg was done, and I needed to travel back to Philadelphia. I caught the last bus of the night and slid into my seat. Alone, I thought of all that I'd seen and felt and curled up and fell fast asleep. I don't know how long I was there, but when I awoke, I wasn't where I thought I'd be. I missed my stop and was at the bus terminal somewhere in Philadelphia, and it was nearly midnight.

I walked out of the bus station and realized I had no idea where I was. In Mineral Point, you really couldn't get lost. In Philadelphia, it was quite easy. I looked around and realized that I was the only white person there. Those who looked at me were of a different color, and from their expressions, it appeared as if they really didn't welcome people like me in their neighborhood.

For the first time in a long time, I was concerned. I was just an old farmer from Wisconsin who got off at the wrong stop. I could only imagine the consequence. I felt the only 'safe' place was back inside the bus station and so I retreated back inside. The look on my face must have said it all, as those within read the confusion and fear in my eyes.

A young colored man came up to me and stared for a moment. I was simply afraid until he smiled.

"Looks like you missed your stop!" he announced. "Yup! I fell asleep," was my reply.

He stood for a moment and scratched his head before looking up at me again.

"Where were you supposed to get off?" "Downtown."

"Well, you're not downtown anymore," he said. "How far a walk is it?"

"It's a couple of miles, but not at this time of night." "Why not?" I asked.

"It's not safe," he replied.

"Taxi?" I inquired.

"They won't come here after dark, due to all the problems we've been having around here."

I was perplexed.

"Tell you what, why don't you come with me? I've got a place where you can stay tonight. It's safe and no one's going to bother you."

I must have had a look of concern on my face as he assured me it would be OK as he stuck out his hand and introduced himself. "I'm Reverend James Washington and my parish is only two blocks from here."

A smile of relief crossed my lips as I shook James' hand.

He nodded, and we began walking. I could see the steeple and sure enough, it was only two blocks away.

"I visit the bus station every night, trying to help out the homeless," James offered. "How about a cup of coffee?"

"That's sounds good," I replied.

We went down in the church's basement and I saw a group of cots. On several of them, men were already sleeping. James told me to stay by the stairs as he went to each man and told them something. I learned later they were warned that any altercation against me would mean he would ban the perpetrator from using the church ever again. Just because I was of a different color, didn't mean I meant any harm.

James and I went into the kitchen where a colored lady was washing dishes. James introduced her as his wife, Jean. She smiled a shy smile as James offered me a chair and went to get the coffee. We spent the next few minutes talking about where I was from and all I'd seen, and then James shared how he and Jean had dedicated their lives to those less fortunate. The goodness and generosity of these folks truly impressed me aa I told them the story of Waldwick and how my ancestor, for whom they named me, Henry Terrill, married a former slave and moved to Wisconsin.

As the conversation evolved, I became comfortable enough to ask James why the people hated me.

James looked down at his coffee cup and then up at me and said that most people needed someone to blame and tonight it was me.

"But why?" I asked.

"Have you ever heard of the Black Power Movement?" James inquired.

I shook my head 'no'.

There's a lot of distrusts in our world, and some black folks feel they've just had enough. They started a group called the Black Power Movement. Unlike Doctor King, who we aspire to be like, the Black Power Movement is a political and social movement that believes in racial pride, self-sufficiency, and equality for all people of Black and African descent."

"Racial equality?" I replied.

James nodded in the affirmative, but went a little further. "Three years ago the Student Nonviolent Coordinating Committee began representing a generation of black activists who are participating in both Civil Rights and the Black Power movements. While we all have the same goals, sadly, some of these people no longer see nonviolent protests as a viable means of combatting racism. Because of this, new organizations, such as the Black Panther Party, Black Women's United Front, and Nation of Islam have developed and with them, they've created new cultural, political, and economic programs."

"While, the initial goal was desegregation of schools and where we can live, these organizations don't feel that it's enough. Today, they feel that, only through the deconstruction of white power structures can they can make space for a black political voice to give rise to collective black power."

James stopped for a moment and looked deeply into my eyes. "Hank, they don't represent a large percentage of the people of color. Most us only want to be judged by who we are instead of the color of our skin. However, because of the beliefs of some extreme members of these organizations, the entire racial justice movement is often represented as violent, anti-white, and anti-law enforcement and that simply isn't the case."

"Sadly, on the other side, many extremists in government have used the acts of a few to question the intent of many and today, because of the color of our skin, we're under constant surveillance where we are questioned, challenged and judged as guilty for simply wanting one thing – dignity – to live our lives in peace for the betterment of our children. Instead, we're photographed, stopped, interrogated, and investigated by the police or FBI and are victims of political manifestos aimed at limiting our freedoms and rights."

"In other words, the government?" I inquired.

"Yes!" James answered. "Not all people in government and certainly not all police officers are bad. Most of them are really fine people, who only want to keep the streets safe for everyone."

"So you're doing what you can, to help these folks?"

"Yes, but hopefully more. We're here to protect the neighborhood from the extremists on both sides. You shouldn't be afraid to walk the streets of my neighborhood, just as I shouldn't be afraid to walk the streets of yours."

James didn't realize that the only threat in my neighborhood would be to step in a fresh cow pie, slip and fall, and break your neck, as I nodded in agreement and tried to hold my yawn, but to no avail.

"You better get some sleep," James offered, as I took my spiral notebook, put it under my pillow and lay down on one cot, while listening to the rhapsody of twenty snoring, homeless men.

At 5:30 I awoke to the smell of bacon cooking. I stretched and used the bathroom and went into the kitchen. Jean was already making breakfast.

"Can I help?" I asked.

I think I surprised her and smiled, saying, "Most certainly," nodding at the white aprons hanging on the hook behind the door.

For the next two hours, I functioned as server and busboy, loading up plates for the men, women and children who came through the door, wanting nothing more than a little food and a brief respite from reality. Over 100 people were served, with all of them expressing gratitude for the old white man who gave each and every one of them the thing they wanted most - a pleasant smile and a sign of respect.

I cleared the dishes and helped Jean dry the plates and put them away just as James appeared and Jean announced with a smile on her face, "Bout time you got here!"

Looking at me, she added, "He does this every day. Like magic, as soon as all the work is done, James appears."

It was time for me to go back to the hotel. I thanked them for their generosity and offered to take them out to dinner that night.

"Really?" James inquired. "Sure! Why not?"

"It would have to be early." "That's fine with me," I replied.

James looked at Jean and replied "OK. Where are you staying?" "The Holiday Inn near Independence Hall"

"Five O'clock?" "Fine!"

James called a cab, and I went back to the hotel and spent the day writing about Gettysburg in my notebook.

At 5:00, I went downstairs to the lobby and James and Jean were standing outside. I went out and greeted them, not realizing why they hadn't come inside. I'd heard there were some great Italian restaurants behind Independence Hall and suggested we walk there. Jean looked at James with a level of concern as he replied in the affirmative.

We walked two blocks and found a series of what appeared to be converted row houses, some of which had been turned into restaurants. One caught my eye and I suggested we give it a try. Again, Jean's expression was one of consternation.

We climbed the few steps and entered the restaurant. Along one wall was a long bar with a few folks sitting, having what would probably be the first of many drinks that night. Along the opposite wall were tables with white tablecloths covered with white butcher's paper just like Cucina Rosa, but without the candles. We waited to be seated and when no one approached us; I walked back and offered the table to my new friends.

sat for a few moments and then a man, about my age, came out and slapped menus on the table and left. A few minutes later, I asked if James or Jean would like something to drink. Learning that neither of them consumed alcohol, I asked if they minded if I had a beer and went to the bar and ordered a glass.

The bartender said nothing, simply pouring the beer and setting it in front of me saying, "Three dollars!"

I knew I was getting screwed, but slid four singles on the bar and told the bartender to keep the change.

The waiter returned and curtly asked what we wanted. We each ordered spaghetti and meatballs. A few minutes later, the food was presented, except it was cold. I looked at the server and said, "This is cold!"

"That's the way we serve it."

"No, it's not. Take it back and warm it up, please."

A few minutes later it came out, burned around the edges, as I sternly said, "Take it back and make it right!"

James looked at me and said, "Perhaps we should eat elsewhere."

I sternly replied, "No, we're eating here, Reverend."

A few minutes later the food came out properly prepared, and we ate our meal as those at the bar watched every mouthful, gazing at our reflections in the backbar mirror.

Jean needed to use the restroom which was at the back of the restaurant. James knew better than to allow her to walk back there alone and escorted her. As they were gone, one patron stood up and came over to the table, picked up my beer glass and poured it in my lap, seething, "Nigger lover!"

I looked at the jerk and said. "What that woman just put in the toilet has more class than you, as I reached for the serrated knife we used to cut the bread, in case I needed a weapon. With that, I stood and was about to show this clown some of my Minnie Point badass brawling when James and Jean returned and realized the situation.

"We better leave," James said.

I examined the bill and put the exact amount plus one penny on the table. I wanted to make certain the waiter realized I hadn't forgotten the tip - only giving him what he deserved.

As we walked out into the summer air, James turned to me and said, "Well, now you know what it feels like to be black."

I'll never forget that night. I'll never forget that feeling! I'll never, ever forget those fine people, who made me feel welcome into their lives.

New York, New York

Riding trains was now commonplace for me, and so my visit to the William Gray 30th Street Station in downtown Philadelphia was just another journey. The 98-mile Philadelphia-to-New York train ride offered the same gloomy look at America I'd seen before at its worst. My God, how sad! Instead, I took the picture postcard from Gettysburg and wrote a note to Katherine that read

Dear Kat:

"Four days and seven hours ago, our fate brought forth on this continent, a new friendship, conceived in Liberty, and dedicated to the proposition that all of us are created equal. Hope to hear from you soon. - HT"

I hoped she didn't mind me calling her Kat, but there wasn't much space on the postcard and it was a way to send the message I wanted.

We stopped in Newark and then slowly made our way under the Hudson River and into Grand Central Station. Getting off the train found me surrounded by hordes of travelers all hustled and bustled to get somewhere, and it was in the middle of the afternoon. I could only imagine what it was like in the morning and afternoon rush hours.

Last year Penn Central Railroad, who owns Grand Central, announced a plan to erect a 55-story office tower above the Terminal. New York City Landmarks Preservation Commission deemed the plan inappropriate and the political war began. No one knew who was going to win, but city leaders, including President Kennedy's wife, rallied against proposed changes and wanted to clean the station and restore it to its former beauty. The dirt and grime of New York had certainly taken the shine off what was once a majestic building. As I looked around at all the details, I realized why people were fighting so hard to save the building, as it was worth restoring to its former grandeur.

I walked to the Americana Hotel near Times Square but saw a sign that said "if eligible, ask for the senior rate" which shaved 15% off my bill. I had to tell a little fib in that you needed to be 60 to get the discount and my birthday wasn't until October and was concerned when the front desk clerk looked at me and asked for some identification. There was a smile on his face as he said, "Happy birthday", with a wink and a nod.

The clerk asked if I wanted a lower or upper floor and I responded that upper would be fine. I never realized that the Americana was one of the 100-tallest hotels in the world as he gave me the key to room 5110, meaning that I was going to be on the fifty-first and top floor and higher than I'd ever been in my life.

There's always a cheap thrill to doing something new. Looking out at Manhattan from such a high perch certainly was that. Everything looked so small and so far below. I unpacked my suitcase and decided to go for a stroll. Times Square sure was glittery and, yet, there were an awful lot of people that I don't think I'd really like to know.

As I walked through what they called the Theater District, I got the notion to see a Broadway play. Having just been to Washington and Philadelphia, the play 1776 caught my eye. I didn't know it was going to be a musical until I paid my $12.50 for a nose bleed seat up in the last row of the balcony for the matinee. After visiting the National Archives, it was sort of cool to see a show based on the events leading up to the signing of the Declaration of Independence that told a story of the efforts of John Adams to persuade his colleagues to vote for American independence and sign the document.

As the play ended, I decided to get a bite to eat. While the hotel was fancy and all, so were the prices. My goodness! They wanted $15.00 for a steak and then and extra dollar for a potato. I couldn't imagine paying a dollar for a potato.

I was told to try Lindy's or Sardi's, but they were as expensive as the hotel. I'd have loved to take a bite out of some of Lindy's cheesecake to see if it tasted as good as that in Mineral Point. Instead, I found a place called Tony's Restaurant, where the food was good and coffee great. On the back of the menu there was a joke I'll never forget. *"Why are there so many Italians named Tony in New York? Because they wrote their name on their foreheads on the boat coming over from Italy!"*

I filled up and went back to the hotel with a satisfied smile on my face – a Broadway play and dinner – the folks in Waldwick should see me now. As I entered the hotel lobby, I waved at the desk clerk who had 'upgraded' me as he called it, and went to the bank of elevators. As I stood there, three fellas came up behind me and when the elevator door opened, we all got in. I pushed the 51 button and moved out of the way for them to do the same, but they didn't move.

I glanced at them and they all had poufy hair, earrings and, sure-as- shootin, eye make-up on. They were wearing those tight, bell-bottom pants and high-heel shoes like 'Kah-Rin's'. Now I'm not one to judge another, but it was a little uncomfortable for me in my tan wash pants and checkered shirt and these three guys, especially when they didn't push another button on the elevator.

We rode in total silence and when we stopped; I got off and sure- enough, they did, too. I turned to the right and so did they. I turned left to go down the hallway, and so did they. Now, I was getting concerned. I ambled and so did they. As I looked down the hall, I saw this very large man sitting on a chair near my room. To say I was feeling relaxed and comfortable, would be like saying Wisconsin was going to beat Ohio State in football.

As I approached my room, the very big man stood up. He had to be at least six feet, six inches tall with huge arms and a tattoo – something I hadn't seen in years. I stopped and fumbled with my key as he looked at me, only relaxing when I turned and unlocked my door. I glanced back and the big guy nodded and the three who had been following me, continued to the double doors at the end of the hall. Whew!

I turned on the TV and watched the New York news. A lot of crime and more arguing, I could have been at home. The weather said it was going to be a nice day tomorrow and that meant it would be a good time to go sightseeing. In New York, that meant the Statue of Liberty, Empire State Building and all the rest. I spent awhile writing in my notebook so that I could remember everything that happened and when it was ten o'clock; I went to bed. As I turned out the lights, the noise hit me. The sounds of loud music interrupted my thoughts. I tried putting a pillow over my head, but that didn't work. Finally, at eleven, I got up and went to the door and listened. The loud noise was coming from behind the big guy and the double doors. This was not what I expected in a fancy hotel.

I pulled on my pants and put on my shirt and went out in the hall with the door closing behind me. I wanted to ask the big guy to ask the guys in the funny clothes, not to play their music so loud. I politely went to him and he looked at me and I asked him if he could be so kind as to ask. He nodded, and I turned to go back to my room when I realized my room key was on the dresser. I was locked out of my room and was barefoot on the 51st floor of the swanky Americana Hotel.

The big guy looked at me, and a soft smile crossed his face. He could see my predicament. "Just a minute," he said as he wrapped on the double doors. With that, one of the three who had been on the elevator, stuck his head out and saw me. I was shocked at the way he looked. Gone was the poufy hair, make-up and earring, and he was wearing blue jeans and a tee shirt with the word 'Pearl' on it.

Instead of simply telling the big guy something, this fella came out into the hallway and apologized. He said he didn't realize how loud the music had been and thought that the three rooms beyond theirs were vacant. He promised to turn down the music.

I said thank you and was about to return to my room when he asked, "Where are you from?"

"Wisconsin," I replied.

"Lots of cheese," was his retort. "Lots of cheese," I confirmed. "And lots of beer," he offered.

"Yup, lots of beer," I said, shaking my head with a smile on my face. "Interested in having a beer with us?" he asked.

I thought for a moment and realized that I was being invited into the biggest and probably fanciest suite in the one of New York's finest hotels and, after removing all his silly get-up, he looked like an all right type of guy to me.

"What kind do you have?" I inquired, as if it made a difference. "Miller, Bud, Heineken and I think there's some local beers left, including some pale ale, if you like the taste of that," adding, "Do you prefer liquor? The bar is fully stocked."

"Brandy" was my reply. "Other than cheese and beer, it's what made Wisconsin famous."

"I think we've got some of that, too."

This was a real guy and I could tell he was incredibly intelligent.

"I need to get my shoes and that means going down to the lobby."

"Aw, come on in, we'll call down and they'll run another key up for you." As he beckoned me through the door.

"Really?" I inquired, relieved to think I didn't need to go barefootin through the lobby.

"Sure! You hungry?" he asked.

"Not much," as I looked at a table covered with all kinds of seafood including lobster, shrimp, crab and scallops all covered in ice. My God, it looked good.

"Help yourself," my new friend offered, as the other two amigos came out and were also looking like normal people. Whew! A relief, I thought. I looked at the suite, and it was unlike anything I could have imagined. It had a huge fireplace, fancy chandeliers, and even a grand piano by the windows.

Off the living room was a separate dining room with a glass breakfront filled with what looked like fancy china. There were four other doors. Three led to the bedrooms, and the fourth was the door to a separate bathroom.

I introduced myself as Hank Terrill and shook hands with each of them. I'm not too good with names, but remembered Richard, John and Brad. Richard was the one who invited me in, but John and Brad were good fellas too.

"You like music?" John asked. "Sure," I replied.

"Suppose Lawrence Welk?" Brad jokingly asked, inferring that I was too old to like rock music.

"Heck, no!" I countered. "Country?" John inquired.

"Nope, I love folk music and rock-and-roll." I answered, making certain they realized I was being serious before adding. "I've got over 500 albums from the Columbia Record Club that include everything from the Dorsey Brothers and Benny Goodman from the 40s to today's music."

"Like who?" John asked.

"Well, I'm into all kinds. I got tired of the three-minute pop-go-the- Beatles and was about to give up on them and what do they do, come out with the *'White Album'*, which in my opinion, is simply masterful, especially *Norwegian Wood*. I simply can't believe their transition from pop-to-rock-to-incredible music. It's so creative and I've heard they've got another album coming out this fall that's supposed to be even better."

I was excited talking about something I loved and I guess it showed as I added, "Blood Sweat and Tears really hit home with the messaging on their new album. There are times I buy an album simply for the lyrics, and this was one of them. We played *'And When I die'* at my wife's memorial."

I was getting on a roll and it shocked these guys that I could list the albums and groups as I continued, "Blind Faith is supposed to be releasing a new album this fall that has some really heavy hitters in it. I heard that Steve Winwood, Eric

Clapton, Ginger Baker, and Ric Grech are putting the finishing touches on it now."

I wasn't letting up. "In terms of pure rock, I love the power of the music of Led Zeppelin. I mean that opening riff of '*Whole Lotta Love*' is about as classic as could ever be. Now add in the Doors, Cream, 3-Dog Night, and Pink Floyd and, my God, you've got a night full of rock-and-roll right there."

The three amigos seemed impressed and so I kept talking while they poured me some fancy brandy. "If you want to listen to true music, you have to go with The Who and "*The Rock Opera Tommy*". Who woulda' thought a rock band could create something like Tommy?"

"What about folk music?" Brad asked.

I replied. "Now you're in my sweet spot. Like I said, I love the lyrics as much as the melody. I have all the Peter, Paul and Mary albums and the Christy Minstrels, even the Smothers Brothers."

"I really enjoy listening to Odetta. I love her folk, blues, jazz, and gospel. I think she's really one of the founders of folk music and I consider her to be one of the primary voices of the Civil Rights Movement. I know she's the one who has inspired Bob Dylan, Joan Baez, and Harry Belafonte."

The guys shook their heads in disbelief that a farmer with good old Wisconsin dirt under his mails could rattle off the founding fathers of fold music as I continued. "Add in Pete Seeger, then throw in Simon and Garfunkel and you've got the base" as I shook my head and added, "'*Bridge over Trouble Waters*' showed the music world how good acoustic folk music can be."

"What do you think about folk-rock?" Brad asked.

"Oh, I love it. Adding a beat to words that have meaning and wow!"

"Any favorites?"

"While Dylan wrote it, the Byrd's version of '*Mr. Tambourine Man*' is my all-time favorite song because it has a message and truly created folk- rock. Then to take Pete Seeger's *'Turn, Turn, Turn'* and create the ideal marriage of folk-rock with a social conscience. Wow!"

I continued, "Buffalo Springfield's *'For What It's Worth'* will probably go down as one of the most memorable protest folk-rock songs ever. I sipped the last of my second brandy and began singing…*"There's somethin' happenin' here But what it is ain't exactly clear There's a man with a gun over there A-tellin' me I got to beware"*

And all three joined in…

I think it's time we stop Children, what's that sound?

Everybody look what's going down. There's battle lines being drawn

And nobody's right if everybody's wrong

Young people speakin' their minds

A-gettin' so much resistance from behind I think it's time we stop"

Richard went to the piano and started playing the melody as we continued singing.

Hey, what's that sound? Everybody look what's going down

What a field day for the heat (ooh-ooh-ooh)

A thousand people in the street (ooh-ooh-ooh) Singin' songs and a-carryin' signs (ooh-ooh-ooh) Mostly say "Hooray for our side" (ooh-ooh-ooh) It's time we stop

Hey, what's that sound? Everybody look what's going down Paranoia strikes deep

Into your life it will creep."

The guys were loving it - some old guy who could communicate with them about music.

The song ended, but I continued. "How about Jefferson Airplane? I know, half folk-rock and half psychedelic. Now throw in Judy Collins with *'Both Sides Now'*, which was the track that enabled Joni Mitchell to become popular." I just shook my head and added, "Now add Donovan and *'Mellow Yellow'*, Led Belly and Van Morrison, and you've got another day of music delight."

These guys couldn't believe what they were hearing. A 59-year-old farmer from Waldwick, Wisconsin, listing all kinds of music they were shocked to think he could list, let alone explain why he enjoyed what he heard and how it felt.

I took another sip of my re-filled brandy glass and added, "I forgot Bob Dylan as an artist! Not the greatest voice, but one of the greatest poets, in American history. His new album *'Nashville Skyline'* with Johnny Cash is out of this world. *'Lay Lady Lay'* is incredible. I just learned they wrote the song for Barbra Streisand. Then there's *'Girl From the North Country!'*"

My God, Dylan could be talking about Mineral Point. Add songs from his other albums like *'Blowing In The Wind'*, *'Like A Rolling Stone'* and *'The Times They Are A Changing'* and you've got some of the greatest folk lyrics of all time."

Brad added. "Dylan's good friend is a musician named Tony Glover. They both broke in at Minneapolis coffee houses and have kept in touch. We know him, "

"Dylan?" I asked incredulously. "No, Glover!"

"Finally, the one group that I'm eager to hear is Crosby, Stills and Nash. I just ordered their album and read in *Rolling Stone* that they've blended the harmony of folk with gentle rock and included lyrics that will knock your socks off. Now the rumor is that they're adding Neil Young from Buffalo Springfield and I can't wait to hear that."

"What about classical?" Richard asked.

"I've never got into it that much," I admitted.

Richard beckoned me over to the piano and said, "Let me show you something". With that he began playing a few chords and they sounded familiar as he said, "You mentioned BS&T."

I nodded favorably.

Richard added, "This is the lead-in from Erik Satie Gymnopédie No1 that's on the 'A' side of the album and labeled *'Variations On A Theme By Erik Satie (1st And 2nd Movements).'*

I shook my head in amazement, and Richard continued. "Classical music is where it all began and represents the actual structure for all music types. Edvard Grieg created *"Peer Gynt"* which is also called *'Morning Mood'* and is one of, if not the best classical songs ever created. The initial piano cords set the mood, followed by the delicacy of flutes and then the violins. It's simply masterful"

At this point Richard played the first few bars of the song and asked, "See how the music pulls you in?" That's what a great song does regardless of its genre. Great music allows you to escape your own reality by playing with your emotions."

I smiled at the revelation as Richard continued. "Beethoven, Bach, Tchaikovsky, Wagner, Vivaldi, Mozart, Debussy, Verdi, Massenet, Strauss, Grieg and Brahms were all gifted creators who understood that music and math are integrated as one."

"Math?" I pondered out loud.

Richard nodded in the affirmative and added, "It may sound absurd and paradoxical, but Beethoven, who's one of the most celebrated music composers of all time, was deaf most of his life. However, he had an incredibly profound mathematical understanding of piano notes. A splendid example would be his famous musical piece, the 'Moonlight Sonata' where the notes are grouped together in triads and contain an interval which, when graphed, is geometric. As you listen to the simple repetitive fingering, you're lured into the actual sonata while the base notes hold your attention. It's sounds so sad and yet, it's simply incredible. "

I must have had one of those 'huh' expressions on my face as Richard continued. "Music involves creating patterns of sound. Mathematics is simply the study of patterns. Research has found out that all popular pieces of music have definite mathematical structures that are then less prevalent in songs that aren't as popular. These structural patterns appeal to our innate desire for rhythm that parallels those within our bodies, created by the internal electrical system that keeps us alive."

"Wow!" I exclaimed and Richard continued, "The entire match of music-to-math isn't new. Greek philosophers like Aristotle and Pluto believed in the existence of a solid connection between music and mathematics to where they included music as a genre of mathematics."

"Let me show you." Richard's fingers flew across the piano keys and chords were played. "The beats which make up music are periodic. The development of appealing beats involves the creation of notes with the right mathematical combination that change frequencies and periodicity in a distinct pattern where periodicity is simply the recurrence of a sound at regular intervals."

Richard played a few more bars so that I could hear what he was talking about, and I closed my eyes and simply listened to the simplicity of what he was playing and how beautiful it was. After a few moments, Richard added, "A musical scale comprises a discrete set of pitches, having a repetition interval known as an octave." Richard played middle 'C' and then the 'C' above adding, "It's the relation between the pitches that is the important factor in creating music instead of noise and is called harmonics." Richard stopped playing and looked at me. He was the teacher, and

I stood next to him sipping my brandy, totally fascinated, as he continued, "There's a mathematical concept called the Fibonacci sequence that follows as: 1, 1, 2, 3, 5, 8, 13, 21, 34, 55, 89, ... and so on. In the sequence, all you do is add the preceding number to your selected sum to achieve your next number. As an example, $5 + 8 = 13$, $8 + 13 = 21$, $13 + 21 = 34$ that you can continue infinitely. With this, what do you think the next number will be?"

I thought for a moment and said, "55+89 or 144," smiling at my mathematical wizardry "And what would be next?"

"89+144 or –" I had to think for a moment and then responded "233" "You got it! In music, the Fibonacci sequence can be seen in piano scales and appears in the foundation of art, beauty, life and music." Richard intently replied as he quietly continued playing the four notes from Beethoven and the boys handed me another glass of brandy.

Brad added. "The word 'octave' comes from the Latin word for 8, referring to the eight tones of the complete musical scale, which in the key of C are C-D-E-F-G-A-B-C. There are 13 notes in the span of any note through its octave. A scale is composed of 8 notes, of which the 5th and 3rd notes create the basic foundation of all chords, and are based on a tone which are a combination of 2 steps and 1 step from the root tone, that is the first note of the scale."

"The music you said you enjoy correlates with the biorhythms of your body to parallel the patterns of the music you're listening to and does so by having repeating choruses or bars, performed in similar patterns, which is why you like some types of music and not others. In mathematics, we look for patterns to explain and predict the unknown. Music uses similar strategies. When looking at a musical piece, you look for notes that are less familiar, yet harmonically relate to what's called the fundamental harmonic which makes it appealing to the listener."

I stood amazed as Richard's fingers caressed the keys as he could play a myriad of tunes that I quickly recognized. I asked him, "How do you know so much about math and music?"

Richard looked at me and smiled. I have a master's degree from MIT in advanced mathematical theory and took up the piano simply to relieve stress. I got to where I realized the correlation and was good enough to audition as a classical pianist for several major orchestras. The problem was financial. I had to borrow a lot of money to go to school. I looked at the bills and what needed to be paid and realized that, as a classical pianist, it was going to take years to establish myself and earn enough money to pay off my student loans."

"I realized, I could make more money wearing weird clothes, earrings and make-up to not only pay off my college debt, but earn more in one weekend doing what I do, then I'd have made in a year as a classical pianist."

"So it's about the money?"

"Not really! It's about doing what I like. Right now, I enjoy music. When the day comes that this lifestyle doesn't work anymore, I can go back and do what I want. I've saved and invested enough that, in two years, I'll never have to work again, unless I want to."

"What about becoming a super-star?" I asked.

"No way!" Richard replied. "I leave that for those willing to become captives of their own fame. I make a good living and blend in. Once you reach a plateau, you become a brand like a can of soup and are managed by the record companies and your days of freedom are gone. You can't go anywhere or do anything because people think you're there for them."

"To escape, so many super-stars turn to drugs and alcohol, and that's simply not the three of us. We all agreed that we would rather be in the back light than the limelight and keep our freedom to do what we want, when we want, without the rush of fans taking away everything we've worked for. We're a back-up band and that's why we know so many people. We're the ones behind the stars. They get the glory and the pressure while we get to do what we enjoy, which is make music."

Brad sat silently listening to our conversation. John had gone to bed. Brad finally spoke. Again, "That's why we call him the boss. He's got it all figured out and we're along for the ride. While others are doing their thing getting high, we're watching the stock market and examining our investment portfolio. We know this gig won't last forever. However, when it's done, we all want to be able to ride off into the sunset on our terms and no one else's."

I looked at the clock and it was nearly 2:00 AM. "What are you doing tomorrow?" Richard inquired.

"Sightseeing," I replied.

"Want to hang with us?"

"Sure. Do you have to wear those funny clothes?"

Richard smiled. "Those are our costumes. We'll be in regular clothes. How about knocking on the door at 9:00? We can go from there."

"Will the big guy let me in?" I asked.

"He will, I promise." Richard replied with a smile and then said, "One last question. What about Janis Joplin?"

"Man, she sings with a passion," I replied. "Do you like her?"

"Sure, I like anyone who's passionate about what they do. Art, music, theater, even farming. When a person is passionate, then they're in love with what they do and it's no longer work, it's simply something they love to do. Until my wife died, I loved being a farmer. I loved watching things grow and also loved the sense of accomplishment and the feeling that what I'd done was mine."

I sipped the last of my brandy and tilted my glass.

"See you in the morning, Pops," Richard said with a smile.

'Pops?' No one had ever called me that before.

Magical Mystery Tour

I guess I really didn't know what to expect, but I was looking forward to seeing the sights and not doing it alone. One certainly is the loneliest number. I woke up and quickly took a shower and went to their door at exactly nine. Mr. Big had been replaced by Mr. Bigger, but he just nodded and I wrapped on the door.

As it opened, Richard was there with Brad and John behind him. Just the way I liked it, prompt. No waiting! It was all smiles as we walked down and got on the elevator.

I wondered how we were all going to fit in one taxi. I was surprised when we walked outside and there was what Richard called a 'stretch limo' waiting for us. I'd never ridden in a regular one in my life. You talk about a cheap thrill! There was an attractive young lady up front with the driver. Richard pointed out that her name was Amy who worked for the record company and would be with us for the day.

"This is cool!" I announced.

"Compliments of the record company," John offered.

We went about six blocks and headed for a wharf, which surprised me. The look on my face must have shown my concern.

"We're going to see the Statue of Liberty and it's on Liberty Island. We had our choice, going with the crowd on the shuttle or hire a boat to take us there." Brad had a big smile that matched the one on mine.

"If we went public, we would need to get in line for the next ferry and when we got to the statue, wait in another line. We've got too much planned to wait that long." Richard said,

"With the boat, we'll be there in 15 minutes and the boat will wait for us and bring us back unless you want to go Ellis Island."

I explained that I went to the center in Baltimore because that's where my ancestors came in. If any of the amigos wanted to go to Ellis, it was OK with me. None of them wanted to and so it was straight to Liberty Island.

When we got to the island, the line snaked around the outside of the building and I thought, 'My God, we'll be here all day.'

As we disembarked, Amy called on her walkie talkie and a guide came to meet us and said, "Follow me, please." We followed Amy and the hostess and went into an office where the park ranger opened a side door and we were on the inside of the statue. The amigos, or the record company, knew somebody who knew somebody, and we were in.

We had a personal guide who began by saying 'The Statue of Liberty Enlightening the World' was a gift of friendship from the people of France to the United States and is recognized as a universal symbol of freedom and democracy. The Statue of Liberty was dedicated on October 28, 1886. It was designated as a National Monument in 1924. Employees of the National Park Service have been caring for the colossal copper statue since 1933.

She added that *La Liberté éclairant le monde* is a colossal neoclassical sculpture designed by French sculptor Frédéric Auguste Bartholdi and built by Gustave Eiffel or the same guy who built the Eiffel Tower adding, "The statue is a figure of Libertas, a robed Roman liberty goddess. She holds a torch above her head with her right hand, and in her left hand carries a *tabula ansata* inscribed JULY IV MDCCLXXVI (July 4, 1776 in Roman numerals), the date of the U.S. Declaration of Independence. A broken shackle and chain lie at her feet as she walks forward, commemorating the national abolition of slavery. After its dedication, the statue became an icon of freedom of the United States, seen as a symbol of welcome to immigrants arriving by sea."

The lady continued. "Bartholdi was inspired by a French law professor and politician, Édouard René de Laboulaye, who's said to have commented in 1865 that any monument raised to U.S. independence would properly be a joint project of the French and U.S. peoples.

The Franco- Prussian War delayed progress until 1875, when Laboulaye proposed that the French finance the statue and the U.S. provide the site and build the pedestal. Bartholdi completed the head and the torch-bearing arm before the statue was fully designed, and these pieces were exhibited for publicity at international expositions."

"The torch-bearing arm was displayed at the Centennial Exposition in Philadelphia in 1876, and in Madison Square Park in Manhattan from 1876 to 1882. Fundraising proved difficult, especially for the Americans, and by 1885 work on the pedestal was threatened by lack of funds. Publisher Joseph Pulitzer, of the *New York World*, started a drive for donations to finish the project and attracted more than 120,000 contributors, most of whom gave less than a dollar. The statue was built in France, shipped overseas in crates, and assembled on the completed pedestal on what was then called Bedloe's Island. The statue's completion was marked by New York's first ticker-tape parade and a dedication ceremony presided over by President Grover Cleveland."

As we climbed the interior stairs, the Ranger added, "The statue was administered by the United States Lighthouse Board until 1901 and then by the Department of War; since 1933 it's been maintained by the National Park Service as part of the Statue of Liberty National Monument, and is a major tourist attraction."

"Public access to the balcony around the torch has been barred since 1916. However, gentlemen, I've been given instructions to temporarily employ you as members of the Park Service. Would you mind wearing these small badges?"

With that, we did what few people ever get to do. We looked out the door of the balcony, and only for a moment and just long enough to take a snapshot with Manhattan in the background my picture was taken with the biggest possible grin you can imagine on my face.

With that, the twenty-minute tour was over and we went back to our waiting boat who took us back to Manhattan. In less than 90-minutes memories were made, never to be forgotten. As we reached the dock, I saw the limo waiting. This was getting ridiculous, but I was LOVING it.

We rode a few blocks and stopped, and I looked up. The amigos had planned to go up into the Empire State Building. I was getting spoiled! Once again, Amy called ahead and we were met by an employee who escorted us to a private elevator and we had our own personal tour guide who gave us all the insight into the building. She said, "The Empire State Building is a 102-story Art Deco skyscraper designed by Shreve, Lamb & Harmon and built from 1930 to 1931 as a symbol of America's ability to overcome adversity."

"Its name is derived from "Empire State", the nickname of the state of New York. The building has a roof height of 1,250 feet and stands a total of 1,454 feet tall, including its antenna, and is the world's tallest building."

The guide added. "The site of the Empire State Building, in Midtown South was originally part of an early 18th-century farm that was developed in 1893 as the site of the Waldorf–Astoria Hotel. In 1929, Empire State Inc. acquired the site and devised plans for a skyscraper there. The design for the Empire State Building was changed fifteen times until it was ensured to be the world's tallest building. Construction started on March 17, 1930, and the building opened thirteen and a half months later on May 1, 1931. Despite favorable publicity related to the building's construction, because of the Great Depression and World War II, its owners didn't make a profit until the early 1950's."

"The building's Art Deco architecture, height, and observation decks have made it a popular attraction. Around 4 million tourists from around the world annually visit the building's 86th and 102nd floor observatories."

"The building is an American cultural icon and has been featured in TV shows and movies since the film *King Kong* was released in 1933. The building's size has also become a global standard of reference for the height and length of other structures. A symbol of New York City, the tower has been named as one of the Seven Wonders of the Modern World by the American Society of Civil Engineers and ranked first on the American Institute of Architects' List of America's Favorite Architecture."

As we reached the observation deck, the guide pointed out that there were skyscrapers on the south end of Manhattan and some on the north end, but none in the middle of the island. I asked why and she informed me that skyscrapers need to be anchored to bedrock and the bedrock beneath Manhattan dipped down in the middle of the island to where building tall buildings would be very difficult compared to both ends of the island.

Once again, obligatory snapshots and total disbelief on my part. In an hour, we'd been to the top of the world and back again, with Amy waiting with the limo.

Take Me Out to the Ballpark

"You like baseball?" Richard asked. "Used to," I responded.

"What happened?" "Carpetbaggers!" "Carpetbaggers?"

"Yup! Came to Milwaukee from Boston in 1953 - stole our hearts and then got a better deal in Atlanta and left us in 1965, making us all feel like fools."

"You sound bitter!"

"I am. We used to sit out on the porch and listen to Blaine Walsh and Earl Gillespie call the games. Spahn or Burdette pitching, Crandall catching, Adcock or Torre at first, Red Shoedienst at second, Johnny Logan playing shortstop; Eddie Mathews covering third and then the outfield of Wes Covington, Billy Bruton and the Hammer – Hammerin Hank Aaron."

Richard just shook his head, letting me know how impressed he was that I remembered who played each position on the 1957 Milwaukee Braves.

"Want it by batting order?" I asked.

"That's all right. You remember Don Larson's perfect game?"

"Sure, do!"

"So do I," Richard said with a smile. "My dad let me stay home from school because he knew we were watching perfection. It's Monday, October 8, 1956 and game five of the World Series. Don Larson gets 27 in a row against the Brooklyn Dodgers and the Yankees win two to nothing. Perfection!" Richard said, shaking his head, "Perfection!"

I looked at him and smiled. This was a brother in arms as far as I was concerned. My head bowed in respect as I outlined the 1957 World Series with the Milwaukee Braves versus the New York Yankees.

"Game One, Warren Spahn against Whitey Ford and the Braves get one run and lose. We win the second game and it's even up. Larson's pitching game three and they clobber us 12-3."

"Game four and Adcock is at bat. It's a low pitch and called a ball in the dirt. Adcock grabs the ball from Yogi Berra and shows the ump the shoe polish from where the ball hit him in the foot. He gets first base for being hit by a pitch and the Braves score two. The game goes into extra innings with Spahnie on the mound and the Braves win 7-5.

"Game five Burdette comes in and shuts them out 1-0. Game six, the Yankees come back and win 3-2. It's Thursday, October 10 and everybody in Wisconsin is home watching game seven on TV. The weather is perfect with a high in the upper sixties. Burdette is on the mound and the Braves crush the Yankees' 5-0 with Burdette going 3-0 for the World Series. Wisconsin goes crazy! We went into Mineral Point and people were tooting their horns and celebrating. The bars were packed with people hugging each other. We were all so happy! We were all so proud! We beat the Yankees – Berra, Mantle and Richardson! Whitey Ford and Don Larson! We beat em!"

"Man, you loved baseball," Richard lamented.

"The Braves took us for a bunch of rubes and left town in the middle of the night and we still hate their guts! Except Arron and Mathews of course!"

"Want to go to Yankee Stadium and watch a game?" My eyes were as big as silver dollars, "When?"

"We're on our way! The game starts at 2:00 and we should just about make it. They're playing the Twins."

"Minnesota, huh? Guess I'll be rooting for those Damn Yankees today!"

With that, we got in the limo and headed for the stadium. The crowd was small, but it didn't matter, arrangements had been made and we pulled into VIP parking right next to the stadium. I breathed deep. I was about to enter the house that Ruth built. Amy picked up the tickets at the will call window and we headed in and it all came back to me.

The green grass, the sounds and excitement of man-against-man, dueling to see who was better pitcher or batter, knowing that if the ball was hit, it would be like watching the movements of a fine clock as the fielders moved in unison with only one goal, to get the runner out.

As we entered, we kept walking down, down, down until we were right behind the Yankee dugout. My God, we could hear them talking and see their faces. "Ball! "Strike!" I could hear the ump. Who's in the on-deck circle, Mickey Mantle – THE Mickey Mantle. Richard smiled and said, "Are the seats OK?"

"Oh, my God!" I thought. Then I played smart ass asking, "What, no room in the dugout for us?"

I offered to buy the beer, but was simply told to keep my wallet in my pocket. Between innings, we drank beer and talked about a lot of things. Richard asked me if I was ever in the military and I told him no. I told him I tried to volunteer to serve my country, but they wouldn't take me.

"Your health?" Richard asked.

"Nah! I was too old for WWII. I wanted to go and was in shape and could have easily made it through basic training. When we were kids, we began doing 100 push-ups, 100 sit-ups and 50 pull-ups each day, jumping rope and running two miles. I was in pretty good shape and knew that I could do more than the PT instructors if they would have taken me."

"You did all that in one day?" Brad asked.

"Still do, except for jumping rope and running here in New York." "Holy shit! Let me see your guns."

"With that, I flexed my biceps."

"My God! You're in better shape than I am," Brad responded.

"If you could, would you volunteer today?" Richard asked.

It was a loaded question, and so I paused before answering. "At first, yes. Now, I don't know." The answer seemed to suffice, and fortunately the next batter came up.

Going to Yankee Stadium and watching the game was special for me. For the two teams it was just an everyday game with the Twins winning 5-2.

I still think they should have stopped at 154 games and not added those eight more in 1961 for the American league and 1962 for the National league. Baseball is a summer sport, and now they're playing in the middle of the Packer's season.

It didn't matter that the Twins won, I'll never forget it. I'd been at Yankee Stadium and had my picture taken with Mickey Mantle in the on-deck circle behind me and couldn't wait until everyone back in Waldwick saw that.

The game was over at four and Richard said, we needed to hurry. We had one more sight to see. My God, I thought, I'd already stuffed enough memories into my Kodak to last a lifetime as we walked out, got into our waiting limo and headed back into Manhattan where we arrived at 30 Rockefeller Plaza just before five.

"Come on, the show's about to begin," Richard said as we all rushed inside. I had no idea what was going on.

We got to the studio doors just as they were about to be closed and took our seats in the first row. We were at the *Tonight Show.* My God, the Tonight Show! Richard waved at Doc who was directing the band and Doc nodded back. Out comes Johnnie and he does his monologue. I watched his eyes dart around the studio audience. He was a master communicator just like Dr. King, but in a humorous way and I was thrilled to be there.

The show was being videotaped, and they had to leave space on the videotape for local commercials. During one of the breaks, Doc came over and gave Richard a big hug. Richard introduced me and then Doc was gone, back to the band and the show. Incredible! Just incredible!

"You know him?" I inquired.

"Sure, I auditioned for his band, but I wanted more than he was willing to pay. He gave me a standing offer and so we keep in touch. Musicians are a brotherhood, Pops – a brotherhood."

After the show, Richard insisted that we go to Lindy's for that cheese cake I'd missed. Amy called ahead, and we went. It was great. However, I was exhausted and went back to the hotel. The three Amigos were going down to Greenwich Village to listen to some jazz. They wanted me to come along. I was simply too tired.

When I got back to the room, I wrote down everything in my spiral notebook and slid a note under the amigos' door, thanking them for an incredible day. I'd purchased three postcards and addressed them all to the same person.

The Empire State Building card simply said: "Kat. I've been to the top of the world and seen the view and it's incredible. Details to follow. *HT,* "

The Yankee Stadium card simply said: "Kat, take me out to the ballgame. Got to see the Yankees and Twins and sat right behind the Yankee dugout and actually heard Mickey Mantle talking — details to follow *HT.*"

The Statue of Liberty card said: "Kat, we had the VIP tour of Miss Liberty and actually got to get inside her. Noticed she must be a libber as she wasn't wearing a bra – tee hee! *HT*"

I went down to the front desk and my friend Andre assured me that the cards would go out in the morning mail and then went to bed.

When I woke up in the next morning, there was a note under my door saying "You're welcome" instructing me to call after 10:00 as they had arrived very late.

New Shoes

The following morning, around eight, the phone rang, and it was Richard. "Heh, Eddie's wife is about to give birth to their first kid and he can't go today, do you want to come with us to the gig?"

"Sure!" I replied.

"You got any 'younger' clothes?" "Like what?"

"Like jeans and perhaps different shoes?"

"Nope, but I can go buy some."

"OK, we need to be ready to go at three. We've got a tee shirt for you to wear, so you don't need to buy any of those. By the way, if anyone asks, you're part of our security team."

"I'll be ready," as I figured I'd run out and buy some jeans and shoes and it would be cool. I went down to the front desk, and they told me that a new store called the Gap had just opened about three blocks away. I walked down there and WOW. All I'd worn for years were Roebucks and bib overalls, and they had all kinds of styles. I think they thought I made a wrong turn when I entered. I hadn't! They had a dressing room, and I tried on about four different styles. My favorites were Levi's 501's with a button fly. I couldn't believe $20.00 for a pair of jeans, but it was New York.

Next it was shoes, and I went to a large shoe store and picked out a pair of black Converse All-Star high tops. The sales clerk said they were cool. I went back to the hotel and found a black tee-shirt with the words 'Pearl Security' embroidered on it. The size said large and seemed a little tight. I changed and at exactly three, knocked on the door of the suite. Richard opened and welcomed me in, while announcing that, due to traffic, the limo was running about 20 minutes late, offering me more brandy or a beer.

Brad asked me if I could really do 100 push-ups. In order to show him that I wasn't bullshitting, I got down and pressed 90 military style push-ups as they counted.

Then I said, " Here's what separates the men from the boys," as I did five one-handed push-ups with my left arm and then five with my right. These guys couldn't believe it. I didn't even break a sweat, and it was time to go and so we went down and got into the limo.

Bethel, New York

"Where are we going? I asked.

"Some little town called Bethel, New York," Richard replied.

"Where's that?" I asked.

"About 100 miles north of here."

"Wow, how long will it take to drive there? "We're not driving. We're flying!" "What?"

"Yah, we're just taking the limo to the Pan Am building."

"Then what?"

"We're going by helicopter." "What?" I said incredulously.

"Sure! The weather's clear and Pearl couldn't handle being in a car that long."

"Pearl?"

"Yah, Janis!"

"Janis? Janis who?"

"Joplin!"

"THE Janis Joplin?"

"Yah! And you're part of her security detail and we're part of her back-up band."

I just shook my head. It was all making sense. "But why Bethel, New York?"

"We just found out, this is some big deal they're calling Woodstock and there's going to be a lot of people there."

"Holy shit!"

It only took a few minutes to get to the Pan Am building, and Amy was waiting to escort us to the roof. There was a VIP waiting room and this skinny 5'5" woman in bell bottoms and silk shirt was sitting there with her friend, Peggy. The helicopter sat and waited, as did we. The lounge doors opened and in walked Joan Baez, who was pregnant. Richard introduced me to all three ladies. I was thrilled. They could have cared less. Just another roadie security guy.

Richard told me before we left the hotel to leave my wallet and camera in the hotel safe, as there would probably be pickpockets. I followed his instructions and couldn't snap any pictures, which was probably the right thing to do. Richard had been right, these were cans of soup who only wanted to be left alone. The sky was clear, and the flight was uneventful until we neared Max Yasgur's dairy farm and I looked down at a sea of people. I learned later that the sea had around 500,000 squirming people, all interested in the same three things – sex, drugs and rock-and-roll.

As we flew, I kept an eye on Janis who was drinking Southern Comfort straight from the bottle and sharing it with Peggy. Here I was, riding with a celebrity known for her heavy-drinking, outspoken, rebellious nature, but I could see in her eyes that she also had a sensitive side. I later learned that her interests included painting, reading, and writing poetry. When she appeared on *'The Dick Cavett Show'* with actress Raquel Welch and the amigos in July, she encouraged Welch to read F. Scott Fitzgerald. Now who recommends one of the most beautiful women in the world to read novels depicting the flamboyance and excess of the Jazz Age?

There were 32 acts scheduled over four days at the concert. When we arrived, it was day two and the music was already in full gear. I hung around and pretended to be in the security detail, but it was pure mayhem. It wasn't long before I was alone and totally insignificant to everyone. The skies darkened and light rain began during Ravi Shankar and before Melanie, Arlo Guthrie and then Joan Baez.

Because it had drizzled almost all Friday night and Saturday morning, things were a mess. When John Sebastian came on stage around four o'clock, he had to quit doing anything electric and went acoustic with his last song being *'Younger Generation'* which I enjoyed, with what little I could hear.

The promoters had expected 50,000 people and close to a half- million showed up. At first, they took tickets and when the fences came down and anyone who wanted to could simply walk in. Take half-million people and put them in a cow pasture and have it rain all night and you end up with a muddy mess, highlighted by cow shit. Incredibly, people just didn't care. It had been sunny and hot on Friday, and no one came prepared with rain gear. As time wore on, their clothes were wet, their sleeping bags were wet and they were soaked!

Janis wasn't used to waiting, and so she and Peggy disappeared. Richard warned me that my badge was the only thing that allowed admission backstage, and if I went out front and lost the badge, there would be no way to get back.

I sat in back as the amigos went through their paces with three other guys who played the saxophone and trumpet and drums. I felt like a fifth wheel and with Janis and Peggy gone; I was standing all alone, trying to enjoy the music. I decided to go out and listen as Canned Heat did a six-song set, followed by the Grateful Dead and then Creedence Clearwater Revival who ended up with *'Suzy Q',* to which those of us who were sober enough, sang along.

It was 2:00 in the morning on Sunday when the stage cleared and Janis took over. A lot of people were either asleep or too stoned to listen, but not me. The boys played their hearts out for ten songs. Janis was stoned, drunk, high or something and very giddy. The quiet little woman on the helicopter was as nervous as a whore in church, while having a hard time even standing up. Between *'Kozmic Blues'* and *'I Can't Turn You Loose',* she stopped for a minute and looked out at the audience which now included me, and asked if everyone had everything they needed and were staying stoned. The audience begged for an encore and the band let them have it with *'Ball and Chain'.*

When the set was over, Janis wanted to stay and so did I, but the band wanted to leave. I tried to make my way back through the throng and didn't realize someone had lifted my backstage pass. I thought I'd be OK, getting backstage again because I'd talked to the gate security people to make sure they would recognize me. Little did I realize there would be different people at the entrance and there was no way the new people were going to let me in.

I was in deep shit. I had no ID! No pass. I No money and no one. I was in with the masses. An old man in a young person's world – straight, sober and, yes, somewhat scared. It was totally packed. If you moved your leg, an arm would take its place, and that spot was gone. People were encroaching and pushing closer together until the crowd was shoulder-to- shoulder as far as I could see. I tried sleeping standing up and woke up cold and wet—and wouldn't dry out for the next three days.

On Sunday afternoon, a brutal thunderstorm swept in. I saw the ominous dark clouds amassing and made for the makeshift vender booths in the woods known as Bindy's Bazaar. There, huddled under a tarp with dozens of other refugees, I watched the carnage unfold and couldn't believe what I was seeing. Imagine, waves upon waves of torrential water hitting hundreds of thousands of people who had nowhere to go. It was pathetic! 500,000 people had worn away the protective grass and lay bare the earth that mixed with the rain so that there was not only mud, but cow manure, as well, that was so dark and runny it looked like chocolate syrup."

I decided to head back 'up front' by the stage to see if any of the security people I knew had returned. The quagmire was so bad, it sucked my right shoe off my foot and I stood in the pudding, feeling the mess ooze between my toes. Realizing that my left foot was soaked, I looked at my bare foot and my ruined Converse All Stars and said, "Fuck it," and off came the other shoe.

I had to pee and looked for somewhere to go. A trip to the port-a- potties meant an hour each way, and once I moved, my spot was lost forever. The half-dozen official food vendors ran out of supplies the very first night. I couldn't get backstage and so I finally wandered back up the hill for plates of macrobiotic, something being served up by volunteers from the Hog Farm collective.

They airdropped tons of sandwiches, but the arms of others were longer and hands faster than mine and it just wasn't worth fighting over a sandwich. Besides, the air was so full of the marijuana smoke I was breathing; I didn't get very hungry, anyway. There were people all around who brought picnic baskets and coolers who were sharing what they had.

A guy asked me if I'd like some coffee and I gratefully said, "Yes".

"Cream and sugar?"

I nodded in the affirmative, as he put one of those little cups of fake cream and then two sugar cubes and I drank it. At first, everything was fine and then my world went haywire. I began 'seeing' and 'tasting' the music. Not only were all the people around me distorted with mouths too big and bulging eyes, but the stage began to sway. Needless to say, I was scared as the music invaded my head and ricocheted in my soul as brilliant colors swirled everywhere.

For several sets, I couldn't function. The music rattled every bone in my body and the flashes of different color light appeared before my eyes and deep within my brain all wavering in cadence to the thump, thump, thump of the drums of whoever was playing. Those around me were laughing with me and sadly, at me.

I was beyond myself – totally out of control, enveloped in the music and the masses, aware that I was unaware, within me and without me only trying to hang on to the ride that took me somewhere, everywhere, nowhere. Then paranoia set in and I was afraid that I'd never return from the rabbit hole.

Finally, I began to feel myself again, gradually returning to Earth and what had been profound, became normal once again, with jagged points of awareness that were finally rounded as my extremes lessened in intensity. I was tired and wanted to sleep, but had nowhere to go and my Converse All- Stars were simply gone.

My head was finally back on straight just in time for Crosby, Still and Nash to begin with Neil Young on stage and a circle of performers surrounding them, including Janis. My God, what a rush! *'Suite: Judy Blue Eyes'* came first, and I knew it was for Judy Collins. They played nine songs, with Young joining in on *'Mr. Soul'* and *'Wonderin'* before ending with *'You Don't Have To Cry'* as Janis as all kinds of musicians madly cheered them on.

I joined the masses begging for more as they switched to electric and played four songs, ending with number five being *'Woodin Ships'* that completely made the mud and mess worthwhile. What I'd wanted, came true and, like a little kid at Christmas, who got the present he dreamed about, I was filled with joy, as we all pleaded for more.

The group came back and did two acoustic encores – *'Find The Cost of Freedom'* and *'49 Bye-Byes'*. Still, they, we, I – all of us - wanted even more, but they were gone. My God, what an incredible performance! 16 songs, never to be forgotten.

From Saturday to Monday, I swam in the sea of humanity. I was part of the biggest rock festival ever held and yet I was alone. While thousands left, I stayed until the end and watched as the sun finally come out when Sha Na Na began singing.

While thousands, no make that millions say they were there, I was actually one of the few people who witnessed Jimi Hendrix's *'Purple Haze'* and experienced the *'Star-Spangled Banner'*. As Jimi hit that last long note, it was over and the only sounds consisted of the silence of humanity being slapped across the face by reality. Gone was the euphoria! Gone was the arousal! Gone was any sense of unity, replaced by one reality – the need to leave, but how?

No shoes!

No money!

No transportation!

An old man, alone, covered in mud and cow shit and a hundred miles from anywhere.

Whoops!

Take Me Back Where I Belong

The show was over, and I was all alone. I had no money, just a pocketful of memories. Reality slapped me across the face as I realized I had no way back to New York.

I saw a group of kids and they saw me and I guess they felt sorry for me as they let me ride with them in the back of a rental truck with New York license plates. The back door closed and the only light was the dim little bulb of the auxiliary light in the cargo area where we rode, enveloped by the profound smell of 20 unwashed companions.

For four hours we rode with me trying to get some sleep, trying to vacate the pungent odor of humanity and trying to reflect on all that we had seen, heard and done. When the truck doors opened and I stepped out, I looked for the Manhattan skyline, but it wasn't there. The rental truck with New York license plates had driven to Boston. Boston!

Here I was, filthy, without shoes in Boston. I had no idea what to do or where to go. I finally went to a police station and explained what happened. They didn't believe me until they saw my 'Pearl Security' t-shirt and one of the younger police officers began to believe I wasn't some homeless guy on the take. I think they thought it was funny to see a barefoot old man in mud covered clothes who obviously had made a BIG mistake somewhere along the line.

The police were kind enough to let me take a shower next to a jail cell and wash off my clothes and let them dry. I think they did it because I was stinking up the place. Then they took me to the Salvation Army, who fitted me with two different size nine shoes and gave me enough money for a bus ticket to New York. When I got back to Mineral Point, I sent them a check for the bus fare and the unmatched shoes.

I'll never forget boarding the bus in Boston's Central Square. My mis- matched shoes and 'washed clothes' were still mud and poop-stained, and I looked like a poster for the homeless.

I walked to the very back of the bus, watching the other passengers scatter as this dirty old man in stained Levi's 501 and *'Pearl Security'* t-shirt, tried not to be too conspicuous.

The ride to New York seemed to take forever, but we finally made it. I was happy to see the skyline and 'home'. It was a fifteen block walk from the bus station to the hotel, and I certainly got a lot of looks along the way. As I entered the hotel, all those in the lobby simply stopped, thinking I didn't belong there. Fortunately 'my guy' was at the front desk and welcomed me.

"Looks like you had a pretty rough time"

I only shook my head as he continued, "Your friends checked out and are gone, but told me you got disconnected and they couldn't find you."

"I listened to some really splendid music, but what an ordeal!" I said, shaking my head in disbelief.

My hotel friend turned and retrieved my key. The embossed number 5110 never looked so good as he noted, "Just as you left it."

"Thank you," I said with a smile.

"By the way, here's an envelope for you."

I took it and went to the elevators. It was a note from Richard apologizing and saying how sorry they were. I shook my head. It wasn't their fault. I'm the idiot who did what I was told not to. At the bottom of the page were instructions to call Amy at the record company and her phone number. I was reluctant, but knew she could pass along a message to Richard that I made it back to the hotel.

I went to my room and got cleaned up. My God, a hot shower, shave and clean clothes really felt wonderful. I looked at the note and decided to wait until morning to give Amy a call. I opened the little safe and got out my notebook and wallet and checked my funds. I could only stay a couple more days and then needed to head home.

I went down and had dinner in the hotel bar and went back up and began writing all about the escapade. When I was done, it was four in the morning and my notebook was almost full.

I went to bed and awakened at ten and called Amy and told her the whole story. She assured me she would contact Richard and let him know all that had transpired. I thanked her for all that she had done and told her I'd be catching the train the next day for home. I'd been gone long enough, and it was time to go home. Amy asked me if I'd prefer flying, knowing that the helicopter ride was my first time. I told her I really didn't have the budget for it. She said the record company had already approved paying for it. Needless to say, I was excited.

To kill time, I wandered around Times Square and went back to the hotel and packed my suitcase. When I returned to the hotel, the message light in my room was on. I called the operator, who told me there was an envelope for me at the front desk. My airplane tickets had arrived.

It was time to write some more, and this is what I wrote. I simply couldn't believe I was 59 years old and had lived through the 1960s. It was an era filled with so many aspects of social, cultural and political change that it is almost impossible to comprehend! None reflected the growing changes more that the Viet Nam War brought to our homes in living and dying color. Our battles in Viet Nam made us challenge our government and our leadership and took us from being a people who trusted, respected and obliged authority to one who challenged, disregarded and simply disobeyed those who had established the system to their benefit. In the end, success is measured as antitheses, where bad was good and good was bad, victory means defeat and our social heart and soul is being shredded into thousands of pieces, each representing a life, a thought and an intention, well meant, but gone asunder.

Compound this with the social revolution that brought about action without consequence in a liberated world, and the table has seen set for profound modification of our own definition.

What an incredible time! This is definitely a period of revolution - social, political, ethical, sexual - all intersecting at one point we call 'now' when we are in our most formative state. At this point many of our kids, the post-war baby boomers, stand defiantly, believing that Newton's Law does not apply to them, taking everything and pushing it to the limit.

These really are times of intense excitement, fear, frustration, fornication, experimentation and revelation and we all truly believe we are important and can 'change the world - rearrange the world'.

For those of us who are parents, these are times of distrust, disbelief and fear. For those generations to come, I believe that 'this' time will be reflected as a period filled with stories and acceptance of what was and what is and the realization that these times are truly changing the world, opening many doors, good and bad, that had never been opened before.

I wonder why so much is happening in such a short period. It would be difficult to go back and piece together all the different parts of the puzzle that are making everything happen as it is. I guess to make sense of it all, I'd need to look at all the pieces - baby boomers, television, birth control pills, the cold war and the threats of nuclear holocaust, Viet Nam, race relations, women's liberation and even the Interstate Highway System and try to inter- connect these dots to see how each has affected our existence, expectations and relationships with each other. It wouldn't be easy, but it could be done. In the end, it probably isn't really necessary because we're here and that's really all that matters.

I sincerely believe that you can trace many of the events through the music of the time and see how this form of communication not only reflected upon, but helped perpetuate the upheaval that is being created, took part in, and seems to survive.

I summarized my thoughts and, when I was done, took out a sheet of hotel letterhead and repeated the entire summary, neatly folding it and addressing it to Katherine Johnson, reminding myself to drop it off at the front desk in the morning and went to bed. Eyes blurry, my mind was vacated of thoughts, emotions and conclusions, all mitigated by fourteen days that opened my eyes and showed me a slice of life I'd never seen before.

As morning came, I went down to check out and was presented with the folio. I was expecting the worst. At the bottom, the net sum of the bill was zero. I looked at the front desk clerk and she said that it had already been paid. I was incredulous.

"Should I take the bus, subway or taxi to LaGuardia Airport?" I inquired.

"Neither," was the response. "Anthony will drive you."

From walking fifteen blocks with two different shoes in shit-stained clothes to a limo ride to the airport. I'd come a long way in 48 hours as Anthony took me out to Queens and dropped me at the first-class door.

As I went to the United Airlines ticket counter, a young lady in a red coat appeared.

"Mr. Terrill, will you follow me, please?" "OK?" I thought I was in deep do! "Also, are you left or right-handed?"

"Left," I responded, not having a clue why she asked. "Do you prefer a window or aisle seat?"

"Window would be nice," I replied, thinking I could look at the scenery all the way to Chicago.

As we walked past the gate, the young lady opened a somewhat non- descript door and announced, "Mr. Terrill, I want to welcome you to United Airlines and hope that our private executive lounge meets your needs. Help yourself to the food, drinks and magazines and make yourself comfortable. The room was small but had a big window overlooking the tarmac and I could see the plane right next door. There was a full spread of sandwiches, fruit, vegetables and desserts, along with beer, wine, soft drinks and bottled water at my disposal.

"When should I go to the gate?" I asked.

"I'll come and get you when the time comes. If you would like to call anyone in the United States, please use the courtesy phone on the desk."

This was a long way from taking a shower in a police station as I sat and began reading my notes. My God, I'd done a lot!

About ten minutes before departure, the door opened and my gate was right there. The girl in the red coat asked me to follow her, taking my ticket and handing it to the gate agent, who nodded and gave me a pleasant smile.

As we entered the plane, everyone else was already seated, and I was shown to 4F. I was in first class, even though I'd never been in the back of a plane in my life!

"Mr. Terrill," the flight attendant asked. "After take-off, do you prefer something to drink?"

It was mid-afternoon, and she offered me a cocktail, I thought 'Why not?'

"Do you have any brandy?" I asked.

She nodded in the affirmative, inquiring, "straight-up, on the rocks or with a mix?"

"Straight-up is fine with me."

"For dinner, we have your choice of prime rib or chicken."

"Prime rib sounds fine."

"We want to thank you for choosing United Airlines, Mr. Terrill. It's an honor to have you on board."

I had no clue what was going on or who they thought I was, but I really didn't mind.

After the seat belts were tightened and the table set in the upright and locked position, we took-off and I looked down on Manhattan and saw the Americana Hotel below. Memories flooded my brain, and I shook my head in disbelief. The flight attendant brought my drink and one for my neighbor.

"Cheers!" I said, as we lifted our glasses.

As we slipped through the clouds, there was nothing to look at and I pulled out my spiral notebook and put down the tray table. My neighbor looked at the scribbles and commented, "Looks like you've been busy!"

I nodded and explained everywhere I'd been. The 90-minute flight and conversation was certainly more pleasant than going out. Not because I was flying, but because I had someone from my generation to talk to. As we were nearing Chicago, the seat belt light came on and my tray table was locked in place. I looked down at the city and thought about 'Kah-Rin' and the train ride and all that had transpired as my neighbor inquired. "Are you writing a book?"

The thought had never crossed my mind and for an instant thought I'd say no, but then replied, I was thinking about it.

"What's its name?"

I thought for a moment and replied, *'War of My Brothers'*.

Back to Reality

We landed at O'Hare where I learned the initials were ORD, as the airport was originally called Orchard Field. My God, what a difference! I mean people everywhere and no one seeming to mind that it was total chaos. I looked at my ticket and got the red ink from the back on my shirt. It said North Central Airlines. I went to the big board and got my gate and realized I had three hours to kill before my flight to Madison. I walked around and went into the Seven Continents restaurant and had a light meal. After the food on the flight from New York, I wasn't starving, but didn't want to sit in the chairs by the gate.

I waited until 30-minutes before departure and made my way to the ramp. There wasn't any special room for me and certainly no one in a red coat making me feel important. North Central is a 'local service carrier,' flying to cities in one region and feeding passengers to larger 'trunk airlines' like United, that fly nationwide. The plane was an older DC-3 prop-job with a brown cloth ceiling and old seats. I made my way back, back, back to my seat in the second-to-the-last row and realized I certainly wasn't in first class anymore.

The schedule said it would take an hour. The flight was actually only about 20 minutes and I was happy for that. As we were landing, I looked out the window, and it certainly didn't look like Madison. I asked the stewardess what was going on and she said we had to stop in Janesville to pick up the mail. We weren't on the ground 20 minutes and took off again landing at Truax Field where I caught a taxi to the Hotel Lorraine. I didn't want to let on that I was actually going to the Greyhound bus station across the street. Not me, the savvy, sophisticated global adventurer – sure!

When I arrived at the hotel, I walked across the street and learned I just missed the afternoon bus and it would be another three hours before the next bus to Mineral Point.

I stuck my suitcase in the twenty-five-cent locker and took a walk the two blocks to State Street and looked in all the store windows. I came to Browns Bookstore and saw a Smith-Corona electric portable typewriter in the front window. Because the Americana had been free, I had money in my pocket and walked into the store. If I was going to become a writer, I needed a typewriter. Even though I was a hunter-and- pecker, I thought I could learn.

The clerk showed me the machine, and I was set to buy when she showed me a used IBM Selectric with a little ball instead of all the keys and a correction ribbon that would 'erase' my many errors. Even though it was more money, I plunked down the cash and entered the world of a literary genius, or anyway that's what I thought I was going to be.

She put it in a box and the sucker was so heavy I had her call me a cab and took it back to the bus station where I pulled out my suitcase and waited for my ride, proud of my latest acquisition. Finally, it was time to go home.

John Kepler wasn't making the run, and the driver informed me that I needed to put the typewriter in the lower compartment with my suitcase. I took out my spiral notebook as it was the most important possession and climbed aboard, sitting right above where the driver had placed my goods so that I could make certain they weren't accidentally unloaded at one of the stops.

Ninety minutes later, we pulled onto High Street and I disembarked, collecting my suitcase and thirty-pound Selectric, sighing a long expression of relief. It was fun traveling, but also good to be home. Like an old pair of shoes, it was comfortable.

I looked at my Timex and it said 9:00 PM. It had taken twelve hours to get from New York City to Mineral Point, and I was tired. I hauled my suitcase and typewriter to the Red Rooster and then took them up the stairs one-at-a-time to my apartment. I was too tired to unpack what few clothes I had with me and so I simply put them on the kitchen table and went to bed. They'd be there in the morning!

Next day, I got up and went downstairs and had breakfast. Madge was working and asked how my trip went. I filled her in on all the details as she shook her head in disbelief. I asked her what happened in Mineral Point while I was gone and her response was, 'Nothing,' which is just the way we all like it.

After breakfast, I went across Chestnut Street to the Ben Franklin and bought a ream of paper – 500 sheets and asked Mary to order a couple of IBM typing ribbons and also one of the correction ones as well. I then re- evaluated my typing skills and told Mary she'd better order two of the correction ribbons instead of one.

Mary asked me which font I had on the Selectric ball. I didn't have a clue, not even knowing what a font was. She explained a font represents the different styles of letters and sizes. She noted that Times Roman was her favorite because it looked delicate and yet allowed for more words per page. Which meant I'd use less paper to write my story. She reflected that it had been created in 1931 for some London newspaper called The Times and not for the New York Times as I would have guessed.

"Get me one of those, too, will yah?" I requested as I thought it would make what I wanted to say seem that much fancier. I also bought an extension cord so that I could work at the kitchen table and went back to the apartment and looked at my spiral notebook.

I sat down at the table to open my mail and realized I'd missed sending back my postcard to Columbia Records and was getting some obscure record album. There was also a somewhat puffy envelope which I opened. Inside was a white bra with one of Harvey Small's smiley faces drawn on each cup and a quick note tucked inside that said "mosquitoes, pigs and frogs, I'm on my way", which made me grin and wonder if it were true. I certainly hoped so because that woman, would certainly get the folks of Mineral Point talking.

I took the time to respond and walked it over to the post office so that it would go out that day. Little did I realize that this would become a regular event. Here's what I replied.

Dear Katherine:

Thank you for the wonderful gift. It was a very pleasant surprise. Because of its potential versatility I examined multiple applications including earmuffs for our farm dog and an athletic supporter for Billy our Goat.

In the end, I realized your gift would find more use as a carry-on bag. Initially, I considered using it for bowling, but was concerned that the little snaps wouldn't be strong enough to handle my balls.

Instead, I realized that your gift would be a perfect container to transport produce home from the grocery store. Initially, I tried oranges and apples, but they were too small, which I should have noticed when we were together. I then tried bananas that were the wrong shape, anyway, for a bra. Next it was cantaloupes. However, I felt they were too solid and would make your gift stretch and sag and no one likes saggy bras. In the end, I switched to Honey Dew melons and have found them to be the right size and texture for conveyance.

After bringing the Honey Dew's home, I carefully opened them and enjoyed both their sweet juices and wonderful texture as well. Unfortunately, Honey Dew's are seasonal and so I've taken the liberty of hanging my new melon carrier on my bedroom wall where I observed your smiley faces which now resemble :-) which I'm honored to have you smiling down on me each night as a climb into bed.

Sincerely *HT*

Beginning the Beginning

As I unpacked *all* my belongings and setup my Selectric in the kitchen and set it on the table I never ate at, I knew it was time to begin. First, I had to give my typewriter a name. I looked at the IBM logo and concluded that Irving B. Motivation would be appropriate, concluding that it had to be a male as it had balls. The motivation was overcoming the problem that I really didn't know how to type and then tell my story. The first blank sheet of paper slid into the machine and I sat dumbfounded. How do I tell my story? Why would anyone want to read it? Would it make sense?

I thought and then outlined all that transpired and realized there was a pattern to my life, just as there is to everyone's and regardless of who we are, there's one thing we all have in common–time. We can't increase it or decrease it. We can't make it go away, nor can we add to it. All I needed to do was figure out how to fit all the pieces together so that what I wanted to say made sense.

No matter how I put it down, it all came back to the same thing– seven. The seven decades of my life. It was then that I remembered Shakespeare and what we learned in high school. High school! My God, that was a long time ago. Mrs. Marksman made us memorize Shakespeare's seven ages of man–infant, schoolboy, lover, soldier, justice, pantaloon and second childhood, where we learned that a pantaloon was a silly old man and the stage I sincerely felt I was in.

It was then I summarized what I wanted to say by the decades I'd lived in, what I did during those ten years and how I felt. I hoped the kids would read what I wrote and understand that my pantaloon was upon me. However, at one time there had been a little boy who became a child and then a young man who married and became a husband and father and now grandfather and so this is where I shall begin.

It was then that I received the first of what was to be a series of neatly printed letters that piqued my interest and made me smile. Over the next several months, one would appear and I'd respond. At first I was going to type my response, but felt that it was personal enough and so I kept printing. The first letter said:

Dear Mr. Terrill

It has come to my attention that you recently had dinner at the Cucina Rosa restaurant in Washington DC with Ms. Katherine Johnson. During that time, you and Ms. Johnson consumed a sizeable amount of Alterego Wine, during which Ms. Johnson expressed certain personal opinions and inclinations that might have been construed as somewhat more revealing than normally expected in an initial dining experience.

Please be advised that Ms. Johnson's expressions, while probably outside the normal realm in traditional social dining, do reflect her true inner feelings and she wanted to make certain that you were aware that the Alterego wine played no part in her expressions or opinions.

Sincerely   Wanda   Duit
Alterego Wine Corporation

I read the letter and read it again and realized all the double-entendres that were included. This was going to be a fun experience as I wrote back.

Dear Ms. Duit

Thank you for your explanation. I found the evening with Ms. Johnson to be one of both pleasure and insight and look forward to meeting with her in the near future to share more of the wonderful Alterego wine and continue our meeting with the goal of sharing deeper thoughts and emotions.

Sincerely *HT*
FFA - Former Farmer of America

A Cup of Coffee

Living above a restaurant has its advantages AND disadvantages, particularly when you're a terrible cook. I realized that over-eating and little exercise would mean I'd be putting on the pounds, which I certainly didn't want to do.

My morning regime included arising when I woke up, doing my 100 push-ups and sit-ups and 50 pull-ups and then taking my shower. After that, I'd get dressed and go downstairs for breakfast. Madge, and her husband Frank, could hear the water running in my shower and knew it wouldn't be too long before I'd be down for breakfast. With that, Madge would put on a fresh pot of coffee and have the Wisconsin State Journal 'State Edition' neatly folded and at 'my' place at the very end of the dead-end side of the counter.

I enjoyed sitting in the same spot for several reasons. First, there was a wall with rooster wallpaper above the old wood paneling behind me, which meant no one would walk by. Second, the soft drink machine and the kitchen were to my left, so there was no reason for anyone to come back into 'my' corner.

Now, I'm not some sort of curmudgeon, I just like a little peace, and the spot provided that. Across from me were identical stools with the always- filled pie display proudly sitting next to the cash register enticing anyone and everyone to go off their diet, if only for a mouthful, to eat one of Hank's incredible pies.

I also enjoyed sitting in 'my spot' because I could watch who came and went and even kibitz across the island to anyone sitting on the facing stools, who was in the mood to talk. Along the wall and behind those stools were tables that ran down the west side of the building and adjacent to the stairway up to my enclave.

Up front and near the corner door was a big, round table that was reserved for families or the local yokeless who came to complain about this or that. It had been that way forever. It was convenient, functional and comfortable, just like Madge and Frank and just the way I liked it.

Every morning meant the same, the typical, "Hello," and, "How are you?" along with all the local gossip from Madge, as I perused the news and sipped my coffee, watching the regulars and irregulars saunter in for a home- style breakfast. Some mornings, I'd be hungry and even treat myself to a belly buster of two pancakes, two eggs, two pieces of toast and hash browns. Other days, it would just be coffee with two creams and a teaspoon of sugar.

Instead of paying every day, Madge kept a tab and at the end of the month, I'd settle up. The system worked and the only time there would be a hiccup is if someone came in and sat in MY seat, which wasn't very often because no one else enjoyed sitting next to the humming pop machine.

I wasn't planning on renting the apartment above the Red Rooster forever. When you can't cook to where you're accused of burning water, it was convenient to simply walk downstairs. However, one thing I missed most of living on the farm was being able to go for my walks out in the pastures and down into the forest. I guess all the years of walking the mile to and from Skunk Hollow School from our farmhouse, got me in the habit and so I wanted to keep doing it, even while living above the Rooster.

With little need for a car, I kept my old Ford truck out in the equipment shed on the farm. Tom didn't mind, and it made no sense keeping it in town when I wasn't going anywhere. After breakfast, I'd walk out the front door and make the day's biggest decision–Left? Right? Straight ahead? Or down Chestnut street? That decision would determine my 'route' for the morning and where I was going to have lunch.

For the next three hours, I'd walk the streets of Mineral Point. My favorite route was walking west on High Street to Doty Street and then left past the Methodist Church that my grandfather helped build. I'd head west on Doty Street to Ridge Street and the Jones Mansion, where I wondered from all the stories I'd heard, if they were ever thrilled.

The Jones house is a spectacular building with a glass cupola on the roof and a huge porch. It was built in 1906 by William A. Jones and was the first house in the town with electricity and indoor plumbing. Jones grew up in the area and got an education over in Platteville to become a teacher, but never taught. Instead, Jones made his money by starting the First National Bank of Mineral Point, then serving as mayor and finally a state assemblyman. I really can't tell you where he made the most, banking, business or politics, as people make money in all three.

Mr. Jones and his brothers purchased the Mineral Point Zinc Co. in 1883 when times were bad and sold it in 1897, when times were good for a huge profit. They took their profits and made extensive land purchases in southwestern Wisconsin for mining and got rich. When Mr. Jones died in 1912, his family moved to Chicago, but the family has maintained the house to this day and I'm told its spectacular on the inside.

Other days, I'd cut across and go up Doty Street to Wisconsin Street and then Madison Street and look at the beautiful restoration of Orchard Lawn. It was built by Joseph Gundry who emigrated to Mineral Point in 1845, then returned to Cornwall in 1847 to marry Sarah Perry and returned with her to Mineral Point in 1848.

Joseph was a merchant and miner who made a fortune and completed the mansion in 1868 as an eleven-acre working estate on a hill overlooking Mineral Point. Orchard Lawn had gardens, an orchard, tennis court and outbuildings including a barn, carriage house, woodshed, icehouse and even a greenhouse, surrounding the Italianate style mansion that was made of locally quarried sandstone that matches that of Pendarvis. Three generations of the Gundry family lived, worked and played at Orchard Lawn and did so in grand style.

When the last Gundry to live in the house passed away in 1936, heirs tried to sell or even give the estate away, but to no avail. In 1939 they were forced to hire a demolition contractor. After most of the outbuildings fell and the wrecking ball was poised to destroy the house, eleven local citizens intervened and raised $800 to buy out the demolition contract and took ownership for one dollar, while forming the Mineral Point Historical Society. Thank you!

In order to reach my ultimate destination, from either route, I needed to cross Ridge Street, which can be a real challenge because of all the traffic going from Madison to Dubuque, but rarely stopping in Mineral Point. Because I'm never in a hurry, I just wait until the coast is clear, cross the highway and walk west to Ross Street. There I turn left and go south to Fair Street, because the Fair Grounds are located just to the west, on the edge of town. After two blocks I turn into Graceland Cemetery and visit with my Ann and relatives before heading back to the apartment.

Taking a different route back, I like to walk east on Fountain Street past the Moses Strong Mansion who also made his money in land speculation and was in cahoots with Judge Doty on the development of Madison, I'm told. Mr. Strong was selected by Judge Doty to represent Iowa County in the State's first convention to draft a constitution and his house, which was built in 1839, remains solid as the day it was constructed as it's made of sandstone from the area.

There's a gap in the ostentatious "scenery" on Fountain Street with regular homes where common folks like me live, die, laugh and cry and this is where I'd always ponder what impressed me that day on my walk. Some days it was a person. Other days it was an event or circumstance which can be as insignificant as a clear blue sky or the cool breeze of autumn. On this day, it was the fancy houses, as I thought about those who got rich and how utterly unappreciative of the good fortune they appeared to have been. It was then that I surmised the profound sadness that it was wealth and material possessions that defined their lives and not love, laughter and goodness.

I'm not rich, but certainly not poor, either, and truly accept that money isn't everything. Money does not bring happiness! Happiness only comes from having a purpose in life. After walking by the fancy houses and seeing all those 'important' people in Washington DC and New York City, I've also concluded that wealth doesn't mean a person is living a good life, just that these 'important people' have more options than the rest of us, as I ask myself, at what cost? Are they ever happy? Do they have worries like everyone else? For those who have died, are they fondly remembered and truly missed, now that they are gone?

Some folks get a thrill out of buying things. Personally, I'm not interested in spending money. I never have been and hope I never will. I can't understand how people equate spending money with enjoying themselves. I think spending money is the opposite of enjoying myself. I'm not cheap, but there's no thrill in spending money.

I'm going to assume that when I die, God is going to ask me, 'What are you doing here?' as he lists all the sins – or supposed sins that someone decided, I'm supposed to have committed. What we're calling a sin here on earth might not be a sin in God's eyes at all. We'll never know until we get there, will we?

I remember back to Sunday school and the seven deadly sins we had to memorize that were somewhere changed. What started out as avarice, envy, gluttony, lust, pride, sloth and wrath, changed to pride, covetousness, lust, anger, gluttony, envy, and sloth. According to someone somewhere, taken together, they contain all the Bible's principles, commandments and sins in a condensed form. But who made these changes, and why?

Is pride a sin? Shouldn't a person be proud of what they worked hard to accomplish? Shouldn't people be a rewarded for the time, trouble and effort it took to accomplish their goal? Why was avarice dropped? Isn't it wrong to have excessive or insatiable desire for wealth or gain when the only replacement is the word covetousness, which means almost the same thing? Is it now all right to impugn one's wrath on another when they've wronged you? Isn't wrath just a more intense level of anger? We all get angry. It's natural and isn't a sin. What's a sin in my eyes is intentionally hurting someone simply because you cannot control your anger.

This old farmer, out for a walk, had a lot to think about as the route had me walk down Fountain Street and just past Jerusalem Park, where a small red brick house resides with white lace curtains on the windows and flower boxes that always make me think of the Crosby, Stills, Nash and Young song, *'Our House'* and the lyrics.

'Our house is a very, very fine house with two cats in the yard. Life used to be so hard,
Now everything is easy 'cause of you and our la, la, la…'

I've always wanted to stop and see who lived there, but never had the courage. The National Register of Historic Places says the house was built in 1844, which means it has a lot of history behind it. Instead, I always maintain my pace to the corner, go up what I call Chestnut Hill and back to the Red Rooster for lunch, before either climbing the stairs to my apartment or going down and sitting on the porch of the Hotel Royale to kibitz with all the other old-time farmers who didn't want to sit in a tavern all afternoon and complain about this, that or everything.

This was my route one early September morning right after my 'vacation'. I was planning on making the trip and having lunch while sitting in my favorite corner spot at the Rooster. Fate had a different plan.

When I returned and went in for a sandwich, I found a family with four kids sitting in MY spot, directly across from the glass pie display. It seems the kids thought the stools were neat because they could spin on them and made them laugh as if they were on some sort of carnival ride.

I uncomfortably sat on the other side and to this day am glad I did as I overheard folks sitting at the table behind me, talking about one of those small houses down on Fountain Street I just told you about. Without eavesdropping, I heard them discussing the fact that their mother wasn't in good health and they wanted to sell her house and have her move in with them.

Needless to say, their conversation piqued my interest and before I knew it, I was bold enough to approach the folks and tell them I'd overheard their conversation and wondered if the house was listed for sale.

They said, "No".

They were polite enough to inform me, they were from California and had just met with their mother and discussed the matter. I explained my situation and said I was interested in looking at the house, if they were interested in showing it to me.

At first, I think they thought I was putting pressure on them, and therefore their mother, and I sensed their reluctance. Instead, I explained that Ann had passed away and I was renting the apartment above the Rooster and had just walked by their mother's house and had always loved the way it looked.

As our discussion continued, I offered to inspect the property, see if we could come to a fair price and provide a security deposit, with an option to buy. I also told them I was in no hurry and would let their mother take as long as she needed to relocate. I'd keep renting the apartment upstairs until her affairs were settled.

When they realized I was sincere, there were smiles all around and so the three of us walked down to the house. As they opened the side door, I looked in and fell in love with the place. Small, neat and tidy! As I introduced myself, I realized that the woman in question was Mrs. Gordon, who had been my high school history teacher.

While she had obviously aged, she still wore her hair in a bun and her long, thin fingers included a thin gold band that had been a part of her life forever. What hadn't changed was the twinkle in her eyes and, for the first time, there was a soft smile on her face instead of the stern look that is required by teachers to ensure that students never forgot who was in charge.

She looked at me and she shook her head reciting, "Henry Terrill, did you ever understand why what I was trying to teach you was so important?"

"Sorry, Mrs. Gordon, I didn't. It wasn't the teacher's fault. It was the student!" I said with a smile as I remembered the slogan on the top of the blackboard.

"You won't know where you're going unless you know where you've been. And all the pretty girls you had your eye on," she replied.

"Caught one!" I said with a somewhat desolate smile.

"Ann Thomas, if I remember correctly."

"Yes," I concurred.

"Sorry to hear she's no longer with us. She was a pretty girl and smart, too. What did she ever see in you?"

"I don't know, but we had almost forty wonderful years together," I replied.

I could see the twinkle in Mrs. Gordon's eyes as she replied. "That's a good life and you're a good man, Henry. Mrs. Gordon motioned for me to sit across from her at the kitchen table as the California couple stood by our side. "Now let's talk some business." Nodding towards her daughter- and son-in-law, she continued. "It seems my kids think I'm too old to keep this place and too stubborn to move. This has been my husband

Charlie and my house for over fifty years and its filled with a lot of memories, I just don't want to just give it up."

The little old lady I was going to learn to love continued. "I haven't been upstairs in a long time because I just can't climb the stairs anymore and those two," again nodding at her daughter- and son-in- law, "are afraid if I get up there, I won't be able to get back down. There are two bedrooms with closets. Down here, I've got the living room, which we turned into my bedroom, the dining room and kitchen, and Charlie put the bathroom down here as well."

"We did just fine with the privy. However, in 1956 Congress passed a bill that extended the Federal Water Pollution Control Act. It was a carrot and stick legislation that meant Mineral Point had to install sewers or face a fine. However, if the town did it in a certain period, they would receive a large Federal grant to help defray the cost of adding sewers to the town."

Mrs. Gordon looked up at me and smiled. "I remember the mandate and grant being publicized in the Democrat Tribune on July 26, 1956, with quotes from the city mayor. The reason I remember the date is that it was Charlie and my 50th wedding anniversary and I was looking for the article about us when I saw the notification as Charlie made some smart remark about our wedding anniversary and sewers being mentioned on the same day."

"Like everything else around town, it was an off-again on-again proposition with people upset on both sides. We all had gotten along just fine. Then, in the fall of 1958, the City Council passed a resolution to build the sewer system and sell bonds to pay for it. There was quite a ruckus as everyone thought their property taxes were going to go sky high. The mayor, calmed everyone down when he reminded everyone that we had no choice and would receive the federal grant. He also noted that if we didn't start the project, the federal government would make us do it anyway, and we'd have to pay the entire bill by ourselves."

Mrs. Gordon's expression changed as she added. "I remember the work began in spring of 1959. Instead of a nice peaceful summer, we lived with dug up streets and mounds of dirt. The sewers were completed in 1960 and so, the entire plumbing system in the house is pretty new, if you ask me."

I nodded in agreement as Mrs. Gordon continued, "Charlie liked to keep things top notch and so, that summer we had new shingles put on, so the roof doesn't leak. We also put those Anderson thermo-pane windows in, and there isn't any draft. With all the changes, I was afraid my little garden would be a goner, but it wasn't affected at all. In fact, even when the streets were dug up, I kept planting. Until a few years ago, it used to keep me busy in the summer. Now I'm just an old lady who talks about yesterday instead of tomorrow."

There was a pause and then Mrs. Gordon continued, "Why don't you and the kids look around? I'll just sit here and wait for you."

With that, the Californians and I went on a house tour. The two upstairs bedrooms were small, but nice and looked as if time stood still. There were black and white family photos from the 1940s on old Mahogany dressers that had white doilies underneath, and the beds were highlighted with handmade crochet quilts on the foot of each of them. I was told that they had a cleaning lady come every week to keep house, as Mrs. Gordon couldn't do it anymore.

My mind was a whirl as I realized the back bedroom could be turned into my study, with a window overlooking the garden, which would be nice and quiet, although Fountain Street was never that noisy anyway, even when something was going on in Jerusalem Park.

As we finished our five-minute tour and went back downstairs, my former teacher was sitting in her rocking chair with her eyes closed. As we entered the kitchen, Mrs. Gordon smiled and looked at me. "Henry, I'm an old lady and all alone. I've lived in Mineral Point my entire adult life and the kids want me to move to California, but I want to stay here with my memories. The house is too much for me, but I'd need some time to find someplace to go." "Mrs. Gordon, you can take all the time you want. I've got my apartment above the Red Rooster and I'm in no hurry. I'm willing to create what's called an *'option to buy'* if you like. This will provide the earnest money and, when the day comes you're ready to relocate, we can close on the house then."

"How long would I have?"

"As long as you need." I responded, which brought a sense of relief to her face.

"Would that be in the agreement?" Mrs. Gordon asked.

"I'm a man of my word, but yes, it would be in the option to buy." I could see that the fear of change that had been bothering her was departing and the knowledge that she could remain in her own house for as long as she wanted, was bringing a sense of permanence and security. At the same time, it was also removing the pressures of relocating to California out of the picture.

Mrs. Gordon's daughter- and son-in-law saw the hidden logic. Their mother could live out her life in her house and they wouldn't have to worry about any details when she passed away. While still in somewhat good health for a woman of 93, it meant that everyone was getting what they wanted, including me.

"Well, let's talk a price. I don't want to give it away, but I know this town isn't growing. Would $10,000 be too much?"

I almost peed my pants - a brick house for eight grand - as I responded, "I was thinking $12,000."

"$11,000, but there's one more thing," she replied.

"What's that?" I asked.

"You'll need to mow the lawn and shovel the sidewalk and make minor repairs until I move."

"That's no problem," realizing this little old lady was lonely and was actually looking for someone to come and chat with her each week.

"Let's shake on it," Mrs. Gordon said, as she put her soft hand out for me to grasp. "Better yet, how about a toast to the new owner? Sarah, up in the cupboard, over the sink is some brandy. I think we should each have a toast."

With that Sarah's husband, whose name I learned was John, went to the kitchen and pulled out what had to be a thirty-year-old somewhat dust- covered bottle of Korbel brandy and poured four small shots and brought them back into the dining room. We toasted our new agreement and agreed to have the paperwork drawn up where I'd make the earnest payment of $1,500.

Two days after my house purchase commitment, I received a second small note that read:

Dear Mr. Terrill

Thank you for your quick response. Ms. Johnson has indicated that she too would like to continue the conversations and looks forward to sharing more of the Alterego, as she found it both refreshing and compelling.

Ms. Johnson indicated she was particularly impressed by your dedication to physical fitness and wondered if your regimen included development of all critical muscles that have a tendency to atrophy if not regularly exercised. If not, she would like to recommend that you consider adding these activities to your daily workout that will not only increase your stamina, but allow you to enhance your overall self-confidence.

Sincerely   Wanda   Duit
Alterego Wine Corporation

My reply went as follows...

Dear Ms. Duit

Please thank Ms. Johnson for her recommendation. After several years of avoiding the proposed exercise regimen, I've begun incorporating it into my daily routine and hope that within the next few months to achieve the level of stamina and performance needed to meet all expectations.

Sincerely *HT*

Regarding my purchase of the house, every Wednesday from then on, I came, got the reel mower out of the shed and mowed the lawn.

With each week, the 'visits' with Mrs. Gordon seemed to get a little longer.

I had nowhere else to go, and I began looking forward to my duties.

October

My brother Tom called one Tuesday and asked if I wanted to go to Madison to watch the Badgers play Iowa in football. The Badgers hadn't won a game in about three years, but it wasn't all their fault. First, they couldn't recruit because kids were afraid to come to a school torn by demonstrations. Second, the facilities were simply terrible where everything was outdated and the field was a joke.

The football team's grass practice field had been just north of Camp Randall and the land was 'owned' by the Engineering Department, who notified the Athletic Department they needed the land and the football team was screwed! The Athletic Department installed the same type of artificial turf they had in the Astrodome in Houston, which had never been installed outdoors.

Based on that, they paved the field and put down fake grass, not knowing that the tar in the asphalt would leech through creating big black blotches where one false move and your bare skin would be ripped to shreds. Combine the anti-war demonstrations with outdated facilities, topped off by a field that was like playing on a highway, and it's no wonder why even Wisconsin kids didn't come to Madison to play football.

In 1967, the Badgers didn't win a game and only tied Iowa. In 1968 they were 0 and 10 and started out 1969 with three straight losses, meaning they hadn't won in 23 consecutive games. Things were so bad that people weren't even watching the replay on Channel 21 at 10:30 that night.

Going to a game wasn't really that special when your team has a reputation like that. However, it sure beat sitting home alone listening to Jim Irwin explain the game on WIBA with nothing else to do. After my trip 'out East", I had the wanderlust, and it was a way to get out of town and so I said, "Yes".

Tom was given the tickets by the manager at Harker, Mahr and Gordon, the John Deere dealer who said they were great seats. In all honesty,

I think he gave them to Tom because he couldn't find anyone else who wanted them because Tom hadn't bought a new tractor in over twenty years.

How unpopular were the Badgers? The story was, people would put their extra tickets under their windshield wipers before the game and come back afterwards to find even more of them there placed there. No one wanted to go.

Saturday, game day, was one of those gorgeous October days and Tom drove. Along the way, we talked about the farm, crops, the hundredweight of milk, winter and everything else. The towns passed by and soon we were on Monroe Street, heading for the stadium. We found parking on Spring Street, two blocks from Camp Randall, that cost two-dollars. Imagine two-dollars to park your car!

We went into the stadium and purchased cold hot dogs and twenty- five cent cokes, to which Tom pulled out the first of two flasks and added a little brandy elixir after we found our seats. Mr. John Deere wasn't exaggerating! We were right on the fifty-yard line, 27 rows up. They say there were nearly 54,000 fans in the stadium. That's how many tickets were sold, but you could see the white fiberglass bleachers peeking out in every section.

Sadly, over half of the fans that were there were Hawkeye fans and probably half the Badger fans were too inebriated to know any difference. The seats were great. The problem was our red-and-white outfits didn't mix too well with the bumble bees from Iowa, who laughed at us for even being there and gave us a really hard time in our own stadium.

Iowa was a 10-point favorite, even though the Hawkeyes hadn't won in Madison since 1958 and had provided the lone highlight during the victory drought with a 21-21 tie. To say the game was unimportant would have been an understatement.

Let's just say it wasn't what you would call a must-win situation for the woeful Badgers, unless your name was John Coatta, who was head coach.

With 4:11 remaining in the third quarter, Iowa led 17-0, and it didn't look good. Tom asked me if I wanted to leave and hit some bars on State Street. You can only take so much verbal abuse, even if it was in good fun, and our flasks were empty.

I said, "No" I could endure that pain, as if I was feeling any after Tom opened the second flask. Magically, the momentum changed as the Badgers scored 23 unanswered points with Randy Marks catching the game-winning touchdown pass from quarterback Neil Graff with 2:08 left in the fourth quarter and Neovia Greyer intercepting the final Iowa pass to put the punctuation mark on the victory.

The Iowa fans around us were stunned as we joined the students storming the field, before marching to State Street to party. We were like kids again, stopping at the Brat Haus for a steak sandwich and more beer. I can still remember Elroy Crazylegs Hirsch, the Athletic Director, dancing on the top of the Grotto Bar's roof on State Street and telling everyone to celebrate, but do so with no damage or violence, as the heavily armed National Guard was stationed on every intersection just a block away and there was barbed, concertina wire ready to be unrolled if there was any trouble.

We had a blast cheering with the students and laughing our butts off. There's nothing more exciting than a football upset, especially when you spent the afternoon being told you were fools for even coming to the game. Around ten, I looked at my brother and realized he had cows to milk in the morning and we headed home. We'd been a part of history with 0-23 gone, and we were part of it! Amazing!

As we headed home, I shared with Tom what had happened in Washington and that I'd been 'corresponding'. I asked if he thought it was proper and he replied that Ann had been gone for nearly two years and I needed to move on with my life. He asked what my new friend did in Washington and I told him, she was a reference librarian at the Library of Congress. I didn't share with him what some of her duties were.

Monday, another note showed up that said:

Dear Mr. Terrill;

Ms. Johnson has reported that, based on your commitment to her proposed exercise program, she, too, has implemented a daily regimen that incorporates a similar goal of increased stamina and greater depth of activity, and she hopes to demonstrate her dedication and sincerity soon.

Sincerely Wanda Duit

To which I respectfully replied:

Dear Ms. Doit:

Thank you for the update as it allows me to visualize the activities Ms. Johnson is taking part in and do so with a greater level of anticipation. Please communicate with Ms. Johnson, I would like to compare results and determine their effectiveness at her earliest convenience.

Sincerely

HT

Henry Terrill
FFA - Former Farmer of America

Surprise

As late October arrived, it was time to cut back the flowers and rake the leaves. I asked Mrs. Gordon if she had a rake as I hadn't seen one in the shed with the mower and she replied she thought there was one in the garage and the key for the lock was on the peg next to the back door.

I took the key and walked to the back of the lot and unlocked the garage doors. You could have knocked me over with a feather when I saw what was sitting inside. There, in pristine condition, other than years of dust, was a 1958 Chevrolet, Silver Blue Metallic Bel Air Impala which was one of the most beautiful cars Chevrolet ever made.

Mrs. Gordon didn't know what was in her garage! I knew because it was one of my all-time favorite cars. I remember the first one I ever saw sitting on the showroom floor at Hult Chevrolet in Madison with the salesman telling me that the 1958 Impala was only built in Sport Coupe and convertible models and was a departure from typical Chevys with its shorter cabin, longer rear deck and was built lower to the ground.

Gone were the sharp fins of the '57 Chevy, replaced by deeply sculptured "gull wing" rear quarters. Also new, were dual headlights and parking lights and two sets of three glowing tail and brake lights with dummy rear fender scoops, front and rear fender louvers and dummy exhaust ports, to mention just a few! Whenever I saw a 58' on the street, I'd look at the taillights. One light meant Biscayne. Two lights meant Bel-Air and three meant Impala.

Mr. Gordon had purchased the top-of-the-line Impala that included really neat, roof simulator extractor vents along with a two-spoke steering wheel. Under the hood was a 348-cubic-inch Turbo-Thrust V8 engine that General Motors labeled a 350, that simply purred when it was running. There's no sweeter sound than the dub-dub-dub of a well-tuned engine!

I paused for a moment, shaking my head and the reality struck as I found the old rake and did my clean up before putting the rake away and locking the garage door, taking with one last, longing look at what would someday be a classic. When I was done, I opened the kitchen door and smelled fresh coffee brewing and, as we sat in the dining room as we always did, I inquired about the car.

"It was Charlie's." was her response. "He bought it a few months before he died. He loved that car and I just can't part with it."

"Does anyone ever drive it?" I asked.

"It's hasn't been out of the garage since the day he died, eleven years ago."

I took a deep breath. "Mrs. Gordon, do you want me to check it out. It's not good to have a car sit that long."

"Really?"

"Yes, it's bad on the tires and mice sometimes make nests in it and the battery probably is dead."

"Is it expensive to have it fixed?" she inquired.

I didn't know and asked, "Would you mind if I check it out?"

"That would be nice. Charlie really loved that car."

The next week, I brought a new battery and some carburetor starter spray as I was certain that gas had shellacked and tried it. After a couple of cranks, the baby started right up and I pulled it out of the garage. The fuel gauge read full, and all she needed was a good cleaning. I got out the hose and gave her a bath and gave the interior a thorough vacuuming with my Hoover cannister I brought from the apartment.

When I was done, I knocked on the kitchen door and Mrs. Gordon came to the window and looked out. I saw a tear trickle down her cheek as memories of her husband came to light as she reflected on the last day the car had been driven, before he had his heart attack.

"I'll put it back in the garage," I noted.

"Do you want to take it for a drive?" she asked. "I can't, there's no insurance on it," I replied.

"Oh, sure there is, I don't think I ever let it expire."

"You mean, you've been paying car insurance for eleven years on a car you haven't been driving?"

"I think so," was her reply. "Let me see if I've got the papers." Mrs. Gordon went to the kitchen and pulled out the documents. It seems her 'trusted' insurance salesman had been charging her for car insurance every year when he could have placed it in what was called a 'storage class' at a lower premium.

"Do you want to go with me?" I inquired. "Not today," she answered.

I got in and slowly pulled out of the driveway. Looking down, I noticed the car had 1186 miles on it. I drove down Fountain Street to Commerce and then out Highway 23 towards Darlington. I didn't want to go too far. I wasn't confident that all that sitting hadn't done more damage than I realized.

After a few miles, I turned around and headed back into town and went to Mitchel's Garage. Keith came out, shook his head and whistled his approval, exclaiming, "Snazzy!"

"Charlie Gordon's," I replied. "Been sitting in their garage since the day he died. Can you give it the once over? Also, you better check the tires."

Keith nodded and asked if I wanted a ride home.

"It's only a few blocks" I told him and walked, going instead to Mrs. Gordon and informing her it appeared the vehicle was in excellent condition. However, I was having Keith check it over, before I brought it back and assuring her, Keith would keep it indoors at night until I got it back."

The next afternoon, I called Keith, and he said that all the car needed was a tune-up including spark plugs, air filter, hoses, distributor rotor and spark plug wires. Other than that, it was like new. I told him to replace the parts and please call me when it was done, asking that he never mention the bill to Mrs. Gordon should anyone ever ask.

The following morning, Keith called and said it was ready. I walked down to the garage, picked up the car and drove it back to Mrs. Gordon, telling her that it had been checked over and all was fine, never mentioning the $83.00 cost for the parts and labor.

I think she knew there had been a bill, but the topic never came up. Instead she asked, "Do you think it needs to be driven more?".

I told her that cars were driven and having it sit too long wasn't good for it. She said, "Then why don't you drive it now and then?"

"I can't do that!" I countered.

"Why not?"

"Well, because it's your car."

"A car that I can't drive," She replied.

"I'll make you a deal," I countered with a smile on my face.

"What's that?"

"I'll take it out and keep it in shape, if you let me take you out to dinner once a month."

A shy smile came across the old lady's face. "You mean, like on a date?"

"Yup! On a date, where two good friends, who enjoy each other's company, simply sit and chat and have something wonderful to look forward to."

Her smile broadened as she nodded in the affirmative. It was agreed that we would take the Impala and go to dinner and give each other something to look forward to.

On our first 'date' we went to Thym's which was Mrs. Gordon's favorite restaurant, in Dodgeville. She said she hadn't been out of Mineral Point, except to go to the doctor in over a year and chuckled when she said she liked Thym's because of the tractor wheels out front, as they made her feel like a 'big wheel' too.

We had a nice dinner and talked about family. She and Charlie had two children, Sarah whom I met and David who was killed at Anzio in Italy in World War II. Mrs. Gordon noted she had four grandchildren and seven great grandchildren and they all lived in California. Sarah and her husband visited when the grandchildren were young and sent pictures, but that was about it. Mrs. Gordon made me believe she thought little of California, as she said Sarah 'changed' after they moved out *there.*

I told her Ann, and I also had two children. Jane, our daughter, who married Frank and moved to Flagstaff, Arizona, where Frank worked for the post office. I mentioned Frank had asthma and allergies really bad and so they never came home and, because of the farm, I never went to visit them.

Our son, Scott, went to school in Madison and joined the ROTC program and had been in the Navy for over twenty years and was making it a career. We were never really close, and I thought he was stationed in Hawaii with his wife, Debbie, and three kids and were expecting their first grandchild.

Like Mrs. Gordon, they all seemed to have 'walked away' and we never got to see much of them. Neither made it home for Ann's funeral. Jane couldn't afford it and Scott was somewhere in the South China sea, or that's what he said. They pitched in and sent a floral arrangement and condolences and both called to say they were sorry. I was in such a mental state, I barely remember talking to them.

I didn't mention that we had a second son named George Terrell IV who passed away at birth. I felt that there was no need bringing up death when we were talking about life.

All the correspondence with Katherine since my August visit had been via mail. When the next note arrived it stated:

Dear Mr. Terrill:

Ms. Johnson has requested an extended period prior to your next meeting, as she has several personal issues that need her attention. She hopes you understand and will not construe this as any form of a reduction in her enjoyment of corresponding, nor diminish her desire to meet again. She did note that when you meet again, she would like to consume more of the Alterego wine you shared to eliminate any reticence she might have of showing how much she's missed you.

Sincerely Wanda Doit

My mind was running rampant as I replied,

Dear Ms. Doit:

Please inform Ms. Johnson I understand the need for time and while I look forward to receiving her letter, I also look forward to seeing her again and can assure her that consumption of the Alterego will be offered but won't be necessary.

Sincerely

HT

Hank Terrill
FFA

Thanksgiving

Thanksgiving was approaching, and I asked Mrs. Gordon what her plans were and she said the ladies from the Methodist Church had invited her to their houses, while those in the Eastern Star had done the same. Tom invited me to have dinner with his family and I asked if it was OK if Mrs. Gordon join us and Tom said, "Fine."

I walked down to the house and inquired, "Would you like to have dinner with us out at the farm?" I asked.

A warm smile came across Mrs. Gordon's face as she nodded in the affirmative. "I'd like that. You feel like family to me."

Plans were made for Thanksgiving Day with Tom, Sue and their three kids and I walked down to the house, pulled the Impala out, warmed it up and helped Mrs. Gordon into the car. She said it had been years since she'd been to Waldwick and was looking forward to it. We had a splendid meal with all the trimmings and discussion turned to Skunk Hollow School. We couldn't remember if the school closed in 1954 or 1955. Mrs. Gordon said that most of the kids who went there were better educated and easier to work with than those in Mineral Point. She noted, however, there were some exceptions, as she looked at Tom and me with a wry smile on her face.

When our bellies were full, the Packers were getting ready to play the Lions, and I assumed she'd have no interest. Instead, I learned that this little old lady knew her football and loved Bart Starr. She wondered if Donny Anderson would ever be the halfback that Paul Hornung had been, noting that Anderson was a good runner, but couldn't punt or throw like Hornung could. She also noted that Paul Hornung was the only player to ever win the Heisman Trophy, while playing on a team with a losing record the year they won it. I guess her history expertise wasn't limited to Mineral Point.

We all sat in the living room and watched the game, cheering when the Packers scored and moaning when Errol Mann, who had been cut by the Packers, kicked his third field goal to beat the Packers 16-10. Even with the Packer's suffering their third loss in a row, our full bellies and lots of laughter made it a great day.

That night, I wanted to talk to Katherine. I enjoyed the word games, but needed to hear her voice. I had her address, but no phone number, and so I called 411 information. I noted Katherine's name and address and was told there was no one listed. This surprised me until I remembered she lived in her mother's house and it would probably be under her name. I didn't know what Katherine's maiden name was and no way of contacting her. For the first time in the four months since we met, I was disappointed. That night, I sat down with Irving and typed a quick note.

My Dearest Katherine:

Happy Thanksgiving, albeit late. As we sat at the dinner table today and quietly expressed our gratitude for what God had given us, my mind focused on meeting a certain woman in August who rekindled the spark that had gone out in my life. Over the past three months, you've made me feel alive again and I can only share my gratitude in writing instead of allowing you to hear the emotions in my voice, simply because I only have your address but not your telephone number. I hope the challenges of life are circumvented by the game we have by playing and that your life is filled with the joy of the season.

Sincerely
HT
Hank Terrill
FFA

The following Tuesday evening, the phone rang and a smile crossed my face.

"Hello"

"No phone number?"

"Nope!"

"Did you call information?"

"Yup, and they said you didn't exist."

"Damn, I forgot it's in my mom's name"

"How have you been?" I inquired.

"Pretty good."

"What's going on?"

"Mom's not doing well."

"I'm sorry!"

"Maria and Hector were here for Thanksgiving and mom didn't know who Hector was."

My head shook in sadness as I asked, "Anything I can do?"

"Keep being my friend"

"You don't need to worry about that."

"Thank you."

"Anything else?"

"Understand that there might be some delays in my writing. I've got a lot on my plate right now."

"No problem."

"Can I have your phone number?"

"Sure, but only in an emergency. Mom gets all riled up when the phone rings."

"Understood. Let me get a piece of paper."

With that I wrote down Katherine's number and taped it to the inside of the kitchen cupboard door.

"Do you really have my bra hanging on your wall?"

"Yup!"

"Are you really doing those–those exercises?"

"Well, I think that someday you'll need to find out."

"What were you doing when I called?"

"Writing in my journal."

"Still planning on writing a book?"

"I'm separating everything into decades so it won't be that many sections. Do you mind that I call you Kat?"

There was a pause, and I could sense her smile. "My dad called me that and I like it."

"Will there be any more messages from Wanda Doit?"

Another pause and then a giggle. "Having fun?"

"Yup!" I replied with a somewhat embarrassed grin on my face.

"Do you have any snow yet?"

"No!"

"How about sending me a picture of the pond? I want to see where we're going to go skinny dipping, mosquitos, pigs, frogs and all."

"I'll go out tomorrow and take some pictures for you."

"I'd like to stay on, but mom's calling me. Can I call you again?"

"I'll look forward to it."

"Thank you, Hank! Thank you for caring! Thank you for understanding and thank you for giving me something to look forward to. Right now, it's one of the few things I have and I'll always thank God for the day you came into the library and found me."

I took a deep breath and added, "As I thank God you were there."

With that, the call was over, and she was gone. All I craved was to be with her and yet, I knew it couldn't be. All I wanted was for the naughty fun to continue, but understood there were challenges. All I cared about was a woman I'd only met once who brought me back to life, and I thanked God for that.

The next day, I went to the farm and walked to the pond. It had been an exceptionally warm fall, and so there wasn't any ice. As a joke, I quickly took off all my clothes and laid them next to the shore, skivvies and all. I took my snapshots of the pond and clothes, took them in and had them developed and mailed them to her.

A week later a quick note came.

Dear Hank:

"Love the pond and the 'decorations' which piqued my imagination. Wish it was summer and I was there. Sorry, mom's having problems and I want to get this out in the mailbox before the mailman comes."

Love and kisses

Kat

"Boom"

It was tough having two 'girlfriends'! For Kat, the challenge was her mother. For me, the next several months consisted of planning my 'dates' with Mrs. Gordon around the weather, as she wasn't too confident walking on snow. Speaking of the white stuff, when it snowed, I'd walk down Chestnut Hill and take her shovel and clean the walk and then 'visit' with Mrs. Gordon. She filled me in on her life and some kids she'd taught at Mineral Point High along with cookies, brownies and cake that she made for me. It got to where I'd watch Bill Brown and *'Whatever the Weather'* on WKOW-TV to see if it was going to snow and look forward to our 'visits' where she'd fill me in on the history of the town I loved.

While her body was frail, Mrs. Gordon's mind was still sharp, and she really knew her stuff regarding all the 'little things' about Mineral Point, ranging from City Cemetery to why the park down the block was called Jerusalem and even why Burgess Battery opened a factory on High Street.

As I sat with a cup of coffee, warming up after moving six inches of snow off the walk, she began. "Mineral Point! The name says it all, doesn't it, Henry? The town began and survived for nearly 150 years, not because of what's grown here, but what lies beneath the surface...minerals. First, it was lead, and that's what everyone thinks about when you say Mineral Point because the lead brought miners from Cornwall in good times and made them leave when things went bad."

"The sad part was, all those miners could do was dig. Someone else decided how much they would be paid for an honest day's work. They called it the market. I call it gambling! There were good times and bad times, happy times and sad times. By the 1870s all the easy surface lead was gone, the market collapsed and there was a period of true depression when many thought our little town would simply die and go away."

I looked at Mrs. Gordon and nodded in the affirmative. When you thought of Mineral Point, you thought of lead as she continued, "Do you remember me talking about Thomas Chrowder Chamberlin in your history class?"

It had been over 40 years and I hardly remembered the names of the kids I went to school with, let alone someone she talked about in eleventh grade, and so I shook my head 'no'.

"Hand me that last book on the top shelf over there, will you please?" With that, Mrs. Gordon pointed to the white bookcase along the wall where I dreamed of putting my Zenith TV some day and watching the Packers on Sundays. Doing what was asked, I retrieved the old book and handed it to her.

Mrs. Gordon thumbed through the book until she found what she wanted to read and looked up at me to make certain I was paying attention. "Mr. Chamberlin was the chief geologist for the Wisconsin Geological Survey. Let me read what he wrote and then and it will tell you why this is so important to the history of Mineral Point. Here's what he said, 'I incline to the judgement that this region, in which the annual zinc product already surpasses that of lead, and which should rather be called the zinc district than the lead region, will continue to develop an increasing importance in the resource.'"

Mrs. Gordon looked up at me and I politely nodded as if I had a clue what she was referring to as she continued. "You see Henry, in 1882 things were tough in Mineral Point. Chamberlin's report added, 'The mineral industry, when compared with earlier mining days presented a sadly decayed appearance. The abandoned mining machinery lay rusting in pastures and fields; many of the old shafts had been filled to give free passage to the farmer's plow, and both the mining farmer and the farming miner had become just farmers."

"Like my grandfather," I added.

Mrs. Gordon nodded and concurred, "Like your grandfather and hundreds of others." She added. "When Chamberlin's geological report was published, the folks of Mineral Point and the surrounding area still remembered the good old days of prosperity, even after twenty years. The key conclusion Chamberlin came to was the fact that the zinc had been formed elsewhere and was carried here by the waters of some ancient sea where it was concentrated in the fissures and rocks. This meant there was plenty of zinc to be mined and as Chamberlin said 'while lodes have been mined in the upper measures of the Galena sandstone, and work has been suspended by water or other practical difficulties, there's a strong presumption of valuable deposits below.'"

I still didn't understand where Mrs. Gorgon was going, but listened intently as she continued. "Chamberlin added, 'The progress of the mining seems to indicate that zinc ores are more widely and abundantly distributed in the lower beds that has heretofore supposed.' In other words, there were minerals still available that could re-start the town and get it back to some point of self-confidence in its future."

Now, I was starting to see why this was so important. Instead of lead, it was zinc as Mrs. Gordon continued. "At first, zinc was used simply to keep white paint white, replacing the lead that had been used for over 80 years. Through innovation and invention, zinc galvanizing also came into play, which added thin layers of zinc to iron or steel to help prevent rusting, for which the demand for the mineral began to grow."

"For centuries, zinc had been combined with copper to form brass, but the world was changing and new ideas and technologies were appearing such as steam pumps and engines, automobiles and electricity. All these products needed components that included the mineral that had always been here, but was never taken. Finally, a third significant use of zinc came about with the development of zinc oxide that is created simply by running an electric current through a solution of sodium bicarbonate and the zinc powder."

Mrs. Gordon shook her head and smiled a wry smile as she added. "All you needed was electricity and when it became available, you could create zinc oxide used not only in manufacturing such things as rubber for hoses and tires for automobiles but as a health supplement and skin ointment."

A smile crossed my face as my class in Economics at the UW had shown the whole concept of supply and demand and how a change in one could cause a change in the item's price. I smiled and looked at my teacher and inquired, because of the report of one geologist, the entire economy of the region exploded?"

Mrs. Gordon smiled and nodded in the affirmative, adding. "Because of that one report, men who had maintained for years that ore was no longer plentiful hauled out their old mining equipment and began digging, realizing that Chamberlin was right. From Highland alone, two trainloads of zinc ore arrived every day and Mineral Point began an economic boom that lasted for over ten years as other companies like the Mineral Point Woolen Mills opened and offered even more jobs."

Mrs. Gordon nodded at the bookcase and instructed me to pull down a dusty binder. I did as instructed, as she opened to a yellowed-page, dated September 1891, reciting "Business was so good, the Iowa County Democrat, printed this eight-page special edition that reported, 'Mineral Point is on the eve of a season of advancement and improvement and her more energetic citizens are bestirring, themselves preparing for the boom that is now almost upon them.'"

"A lot of folks in town made a great deal of money in 1891 and 1892, and the town spent a lot of it improving the community. First, they agreed to get rid of the mud paths that served as streets and applied what was called macadamized surfacing where they spread a compacted layer of small broken stones mixed with concrete.

In addition, they enlarged the Second Ward School, laid new sidewalks and replaced the old kerosene street lamps with electric lights. As the town improved, new buildings also began to spring up, including the Primitive Methodist Church, while all the stores on High Street were remodeled, using plate glass for windows to bring light and customers into their stores."

Mrs. Gordon glanced over her glasses and slowly shook her head, "As had been the case so many times before. People got too excited and too confident, and the national panic of 1893 saw every business in Mineral Point severely affected, with many simply fading away. For four years, the city languished and with it went all the dreams of building a diversified industrial city. Instead, Mineral Pointers put aside their dreams and settled into what most people would have called reality–pinning their economic hopes on farmers, supported by their mines and the zinc oxide factory that carried them through that depression."

Mrs. Gordon looked at me and once again slowly repeated the two words, "Mineral – Point, where minerals created dreams and nightmares, made men rich and destroyed them, as well. For many towns, this would have been the end of the story, but not for our little town, but that's a story for another day."

I sat quietly as she shared the reality, realizing her passion and accepting that for every great reward, there is also a significant risk. She was weaving a wonderful tale of the town I loved, and I wanted more. As I walked up Chestnut Street to my little apartment above the Red Rooster, I decided and crossed over and went to the library. Mrs. Gordon's history lesson piqued my interest, and I wanted more.

The following Wednesday, it snowed again and time to have my hometown history lesson. I walked down the hill and pulled the shovel from the shed. When I was done, I wrapped on the door and Mrs. Gordon made her way. I smiled, she smiled and asked me if I was ready for my next history lesson, to which I nodded yes.

It appeared as if Mrs. Gordon had been preparing as we at in the dining room and she began as if we'd never stopped. "It was 70 years ago that the miracle everyone prayed for actually happened as the miners went back to the zinc mines and the entire region stirred with excitement and activity."

"Zinc prices were high and there was money to be made. At first, all the labor was local and done by hand. Then, as reality set in, outside investors took note and a period of speculation, espionage, violence and fraud overtook the entire area as it was covered with a thick cloud of greed. It was not a proud time. However, even with all the troubles, the ability to have modern machinery allowed the local zinc industry to expand rapidly, particularly with the addition of pumps that solved the problem with the water tables. In a matter of months, steam engines replaced horses and were replaced by gasoline engines with more power and greater capability. Soon, electric power plants were being erected near the smelting sites to allow for the use of more efficient electric motors and the new mills could refine the ore into zinc concentrate to allow for the shipment of pure ore in its finished form instead of what had been shipped before."

"For five years there was consistent growth and demand and then, in 1904, demand increased even more and with it, all the advances from the early 1900s were upgraded once again. Mining fever took hold unlike never before and Mineral Point was booming gloriously with all kinds of changes, including telephone service to Waldwick, a new high school and a railroad spur between Mineral Point and Highland. If the excitement wasn't already big enough, the newspapers reported on new discoveries and more success as all seven concentrating mills began working seven days a week while their biggest problem became finding enough workers."

"For the next five years, Pointers revived the old dream of building a great inland mining metropolis with an improved infra-structure, new buildings and hundreds of new residents all clamoring for more, more, more. For five years, there seemed to be no limit, but there always is and always will be."

Mrs. Gordon stopped for a moment to catch her breath. I'd never seen her so enthused and she continued. "There were stores with the finest clothes west of New York City. There was the Mineral Point Electric Light company bringing power to homes, along with telephones, new banks, new houses and new excitement and they paved High Street with asphalt."

"Things were booming, and no one believed it would stop until October 1909, when the First National Bank of Mineral Point, whose depositors considered it to be more secure than the banks of Madison, abruptly closed its doors. It seems that sixteen years of speculations by Vice President Philip Allen Jr., finally caught up with the enterprise as Mr. Allen had been investing outside Mineral Point and doing so in risky businesses from Maine to California, while using bank funds to do so."

"When the law finally caught up with Mr. Allen, he owned over two- million shares of stock in over 100 companies. It was estimated that he had stolen over $400,000 by falsifying records, forging notes and embezzling bank funds while selling phony notes to customers, stealing funds from the bank vault and from the estates which he administered."

Mrs. Gordon sadly shook her head as she continued. "Hundreds of customers were left with nothing and investors who had already paid for something were forced to pay again."

"What happened to Mr. Allen?" I asked.

"He was sentenced to ten years in Leavenworth, while Frank Hanscom, Allen's relative and apparent accomplice, went to Graceland Cemetery and committed suicide at his father's grave. Hanscom's mother-in- law died of shock upon hearing of his death."

"Wow! I had no idea!"

"When the bank went into receivership, it owed $700,000, mostly to folks here in Mineral Point."

"And Waldwick," I added, "Including my dad!"

Mrs. Gordon wistfully continued, "In the end, the lucky ones got forty-five-cents for every dollar they had in the bank. If it weren't for the zinc, the entire town would have collapsed. The processors began merging which put all the mining wealth and power in the hands of a few, but also saved Mineral Point."

"There's a reason our town is called Mineral Point. You need to always remember that minerals started the town and minerals saved the town, while in between, it was also minerals that nearly destroyed it."

After so many years, I finally understood what it all meant, why my father distrusted the banks, why he refused to dig holes in the ground on land where he could plant crops and why Mineral Point meant so much to him. It was the beginning of our family and almost its end.

I looked at Mrs. Gordon and took a deep breath as she concluded. "For the past seventy years, our little town has quietly held on, filled with good people who live here because they love it here—not to get rich in terms of money, but be rich, in terms of love and laughter, warmth and friendship."

She paused for a moment and then added, "You know Henry, it's been so long since I locked the front door, I don't even know where the key is anymore. This is why I can't move to California. Mineral Point is my home and is where Charlie is buried. When my time comes, I want to be next to him forever."

I finished my drink and put the books back up on the shelf from where they came. My mind was a tither in all that Mrs. Gordon had shared. Our routine was set, and I enjoyed our visits. Mrs. Gordon would mention this or that and, when I left her house, I'd go to the library and do research on what she mentioned. I really wanted to learn about what it was like in Mineral Point when I was born.

Christmas came, and I helped decorate Mrs. Gordon's little table-top tree with the metal base and pointy lights, which meant that when one burned out, they all went out. Communication with Washington had become sporadic. The somewhat obligatory cards had been shared between Kat and I with a promise that next year would be better. I knew things were difficult and so I didn't push it.

New Year's eve was always amateur night in town with too many drunks, punks and weirdos. This meant dinner at Thymes with Mrs. Gordon and then back to the apartment. I sat watching TV, counting down to eleven o'clock when the phone rang. A smile crossed my face as it was a call I'd hoped for.

"Hello."

"Happy New Year! I didn't know if you'd be home."

"I took Mrs. Gordon out for dinner and was home by seven o'clock." "Sounds like mine. Mom's not doing well, and Maria and Hector had plans. Mom only functions with Maria and me, and I just got her settled and hope that she's down for a while."

"How are you doing?"

"Fine," was the reply which I knew was a great big lie.

"How are things with your mom?"

"The Sundowner's Syndrome is the worst part. If things were predictable, it would be one thing, but you just never know. One day she's fine. The next day she's off the wall. Then she accuses me of all sorts of things and goes into fits of rage. I can't leave her alone for a minute because she wanders and I can't control her. I have a bell on her bedroom door so that if she opens the door, it rings. I haven't had a good night's sleep in two months."

"I'm sorry. Is there anything I can do?" "I could use a good back rub."

"I don't think my arms will reach that far. How about some music?"

"Music?"

"Sure, let me think what I could play for you over the phone that would help you relax." I paused for a moment and knew what she needed as I added, "Hold on, I'll put on the Victrola" With that I went and pulled Satie Gymnopédie No.1 from my collection.

"I think you're going to like this. It's being used for relaxation and peaceful times in hospitals. The first of the set is perhaps the most famous of the collection, and it really invites you to close your eyes and float away for the night. Pretend you're here and we have a fire going in my pretend fireplace and it's just you and me snuggling beneath a warm down comforter as we watch the snow fall outside the window."

With that, the music began and seven minutes of some of the most relaxing music you could imagine filled my apartment and ears. As it ended all I could hear on the other end was zzzz, zzzz, zzzz I'd put my special friend to sleep.

I whispered "Happy New Year" and quietly put the phone down to the silence of the night as midnight neared.

Broken Heart

In February, I sensed something was wrong and took out the emergency number and called Kat. Instead of her answering, Maria answered the phone. Even though we had never met, nor spoken, I knew it was her by the Spanish influence in her voice. I explained who I was and Maria indicated that Kat said she had a special friend in Wisconsin as I asked for Kat. Maria told me Kat was at the hospital with her mother and that things didn't look good.

I made Maria promise that if anything happened, she would contact me. Two nights later, the phone rang. It was Maria. Mrs. Stimson had passed away.

I knew I needed to attend if there was a funeral. I remembered back to Ann's and how important it was that family and friends mourned with me. I remembered how "alone" I felt, tearfully isolated in a time of tragedy and how I needed - no craved - the consolation of companionship as I asked Maria, "Will there be a funeral?"

"Yes. Thursday at 1:00 PM."

"In McClean?"

"Yes, at McIntosh Funeral Home."

"Burial?"

"Arlington National Cemetery."

Holy shit!

I called the travel agent lady in Madison and asked her to make an early morning flight to Washington DC. She asked which airport and I indicated the one closest to McClean, Virginia. She indicated it was National Airport. She said that if I drove to Milwaukee; the airfare was half that from Madison. I agreed, especially when the same Madison plane stopped in Milwaukee to pick us up on its way.

Thursday morning I woke up the roosters on my way to Mitchel Field in Milwaukee and caught North Central Airlines flight 537 that arrived in Washington at 10:42 AM. I had lunch, caught a taxi and made it to the funeral home a little before one.

As I entered, Katherine looked at me with incredible shock as tears exploded from her eyes. "You came!"

I nodded in the affirmative.

"You came for me!"

Again, affirmation.

"My sweet, sweet man!"

I shrugged and added, "isn't this what friends are for?"

I viewed the body and expressed my condolences to Maria and Hector and was about to leave. Sadly, there wasn't anyone else there.

I looked at Kat and shared her sadness and said how terrible it was to be a victim of such an insidious disease.

Kat looked at me and said something I'll never forget, "Life is a just temporary state during which we need to make the most of it. Death is going to happen to us all and it was her turn to go! The last few days, mom was different. Gone was her cold, selfish demeanor and she told me she loved me and how proud I made her."

"She was lucid and I think she knew her time was near and the face of death was replaced by the face of love and this is what I'll always cherish. What's sad about mom is that she was a victim of life because never really knew how to live."

I was a bit shocked by the statement but realized that Kat was right. I paused for a moment and then was going to hug Kat goodbye when she asked, "Where are you going?"

"Back home." "When?"

"My flight's at seven."

"Don't go, please" Kat begged.

"I just wanted to express my condolences."

"Can't you change your flight and stay a little longer? Please!"

"Let me see."

I called the travel agent and there was a ten PM flight and I changed

"Will you go to the cemetery with me?" Kat inquired. "OK."

A few friends and neighbors showed up and some of Katherine's co-workers from the library who Kat introduced me to. At three, they had the closing of the casket and procession to Arlington.

Kat asked me to ride with her in the limousine. I'd never been in one before that wasn't rented and enjoyed the experience. As we exited the limo, Kat slid her arm in mine and we walked to the ceremonial funeral spot. As we stood arm-in-arm, the Lord's Prayer was recited and then seven soldiers fired three rounds in unison, indicating a twenty-one-gun salute.

With that, life was officially over for Kat's mother as Kat went and touched her mother's casket one last time, dabbing her eyes in sorrow as we walked, hand-in-hand, back to the car. I looked over my shoulder and the cemetery crew was already moving the casket and taking it to be buried next to her father. It was all so – so calculated and seemed so unreal. The funeral team had to prepare for another grieving family. It would be their fifth of the day.

"You must have dinner with us!" Kat urged and so I said, "Yes". We went to the Westwood Country Club and entered a private room. Everyone at the club knew Katherine and called her Mrs. Johnson. It was a quiet time filled with stories about her mom and dad. It was a sensitive time that comes about when something so permanent as death takes place. It was a genuine time when Katherine and I, who only had dinner once, had shared some silly letters, finally, truly bonded. I'd been down her road and knew that she was very fragile. I came out of respect for her friendship and my only goal was to provide support.

As the clock neared eight, I looked at Katherine and she at me and I indicated it was time for me to go. She offered to have the car take me. I said no and asked the valet to call a cab.

We stood hand-in-hand in the lobby until the cab came.

Katherine looked at me with her soulful eyes and whispered "Thank you".

I looked at her and could only say "You're welcome" as the cab arrived.

We kissed a polite kiss and hugged a polite hug and I whispered, "call me when you're settled." To which there was a quiet nod and a squeeze of my hand.

Once again, I reluctantly left someone I wanted to stay with, be with, laugh with and cry with. I was heading home to the reality, realizing that in one day I'd left Mineral Point, Wisconsin, driven to Milwaukee, flown to Washington DC, attended the funeral of the mother of a woman I cared for, observed a burial at Arlington National Cemetery with a twenty-one-gun salute and returned home to wonder if or when Kat and I'd ever regain the emotional traction that filled our lives in the fall.

The letters didn't come for several weeks, and I was concerned. I missed their excitement, but also knew that closing an estate was a challenging task physically, financially and emotionally and she needed space. I only hoped that Katherine missed me as much as I missed her.

Spring

I was slowly giving up, believing that Kat was gone forever. Fortunately, Spring came early, and I asked Mrs. Gordon if she wanted me to plant the garden and her eyes lit up in excitement. For a few days, I worked outside while she watched. I planted her vegetables and flowers and made sure the rows were straight. When it was time to mow, I got out the old reel mower from the lean-to shed and did my task and then went back in the house where Mrs. Gordon would have homemade lemonade for me, just like my mother used to make. In a few months, this lonely old lady and I became dear friends.

Kat and I began communicating again, but it was very formal and I hadn't heard from Wanda Doit in a long time. Pain has a way of taking the fun out of life. As the days lengthened and the warm weather returned, so did the sunshine that had left our lives.

One day, one of the small 'Wanda' envelopes arrived. I had a wry smile on my face as I climbed the stairs from the mailbox and anxiously sat down at the kitchen table.

Dear Mr. Terrill:

Ms. Johnson has a meeting scheduled in Chicago, Illinois for Tuesday, June 9, 1970, and is inquiring as to your schedule and whether you could meet with her at 2:00 PM that afternoon at the Drake Hotel. Please RSVP and, if possible, please leave the following two days open as Ms. Johnson's schedule is clear.

Sincerely   Wanda   Doit

Alterego Wine Corporation

I smiled and knew my Kat was back. I was going to type a response and thought better. Instead, I got out paper and pencil, as I'd done on personal notes before, and composed:

Dear Ms. Doit:

I have reviewed my extensive business schedule and cleared the entire week by simply cancelling everything. Please inform Ms. Johnson that I look forward to seeing her and revisiting our previous conversation.

Sincerely *HT*

A week later, I received the following note.

Dear Mr. Terrill:

Ms. Johnson has made reservations at the Drake Hotel 40 East Walton Place Chicago, IL 60611 Phone 312.787.2200 for Tuesday, June 9, 1970 and, subsequent to her meeting, she would like to ask if 2:00 PM that afternoon is amenable to meet for cocktails. For convenience, simply calling the hotel and leaving a confirmation will suffice.

Sincerely   Wanda   Doit
Alterego Wine Corporation

I circled the calendar and made a point to have back-up personnel in terms of lawn mowing and overall attentiveness to Mrs. Gordon. It seems I'd become her caregiver just as Kat had been with her mother.

I counted the days, asked for permission to take the Chevy to Chicago as I didn't think it would be too cool taking my sixteen-year-old Ford pick-up with the battered fenders and rust around the wheel wells to the big city. Permission was granted, and I looked forward to my first drive to Chicago.

When June 9th arrived, I climbed into the Impala and headed for Beloit and the Northwest tollway - twenty-five cents, twenty-five cents, twenty-five cents. Jesus!

Even with all the toll booths, the drive was easy, and I made it to the Drake Hotel 30 minutes early. I didn't know whether to ring the room or wait. I waited and walked across the street to observe Lake Michigan and the funny-looking shelter that looked like a boat. At exactly 2:00 PM, I walked into the bar and there stood my Kat, looking gorgeous!

I smiled. She smiled.

I held out my hand, and she pulled me in and gave me a hug, whispering, "I missed you SO MUCH!"

I responded, "Me too—missed you, that is."

She nodded, and I joined her at a table. Our eyes were locked into each other, as were our smiles. I really can't explain how I felt. Relief? Joy? Pleasure? It was like a Christmas on steroids when I was a kid. I didn't think it was possible to have missed someone you'd only met two times before in your life.

The waitress came and asked if we wanted a drink. I just wanted to drink in the feelings of being with her. Kat ordered a glass of Pinot Noir, I ordered a Seven-Up. After all the wine we drank that first night, she looked at me with a slight chagrin. I noted I wanted nothing to cloud my mind or numb the feelings that I had right then. She blushed. I smiled.

We had casual chit chat about drives and flights and how well each other looked. I was profoundly engrossed in just her presence and we could have been discussing cattle futures for all I cared.

I reached for my glass, and Kat's hand touched mine. A bolt of electricity shot through my body as it had when we first met and I looked in Kat's eyes and simply smiled. Kat pulled back and nodded with her head, indicating we needed to leave. We went to the elevator, and the doors opened and we entered. We were the only ones onboard, but at that moment, I don't think it would have mattered as she pushed number five and emphatically kissed me, whispering "I missed you."

The fifth floor was quiet as she slid the key in and unlocked the door. She had a suite with fresh flowers on the living room table that was larger than my entire apartment with a table the size of my bathroom.

Almost before the door closed, our lips met again and there was the spark of ignition we'd both been building for so many months. For the rest of the afternoon we simply made up for lost time. At first we talked and then we kissed and then we became enmeshed in each other until there was exhaustion. Then we recovered and began again. Never had I imagined we could sustain what we did for as long as we did.

The frustrations dissipated. The loneliness evaporated. The profound sense of singularity that had been so prevalent in both of us faded as we melded into one - physically, emotionally and spiritually. By dinner time, we had reached the point where the physical aspect was literally impossible and so we ordered room service and I had lobster for the first time in my life.

That night as we sat in the living room with candles flickering, I smiled and looked at her asking, "What about the Alterego wine?"

Do you think I still need it?" "Nope!"

I was exhausted and needed sleep. I looked at the extra bedroom and thought that was for me. Instead, we crawled into bed at ten o'clock. It was nice sleeping with someone again. I was awakened Wednesday morning by soft kisses and a sweet smile. We took our time and then our showers and finally got dressed.

"I have a meeting at ten. Did you bring any dress-up clothes?" Kat inquired.

I shook my head, indicating I had not, never admitting I didn't have any. With that, Kat went to the phone and dialed zero. "May I please speak with Steven?"

There was a pause and Kat began again. "Good morning to you, too. I need you to take my dear friend to Brooks Brothers and have him fitted for a suit that we'll need delivered by 5:00 PM today. Also, please have him pick out a navy-blue blazer along with some comfortable dress shoes."

Another pause.

"Thirty minutes? Yes, have them added to my account here. Thank you, Steven."

Kat turned to me and said, "Steven will escort you to Brooks

Brothers and everything is taken care of. We have a dinner tonight and it's somewhat formal."

"Jesus! With whom, may I ask?"

There was a pause as Kat looked down and then at me. "I'm on the Board of Governors of the Chicago Art Institute and we're having our annual dinner tonight."

"The Board of Governors?"

"Yes, our family has donated several pieces of art to the Institute and I was elected."

"You want me to go with you?" "Of course, Ninny!"

It was all beginning to make sense about why she'd visited all the museums in Europe and knew so much about art.

"What about the library?" I asked, not knowing what was going on. "I was sick and tired of all the phonies in Washington and needed a change in my life. Mom had her lifestyle because of dad and they lived their life. It's just not for me. I took the job at the library simply to have someplace to go. After Ron died, the boys leaving and taking care of my mother, I needed to do something besides go to the country club and be phony. When the library learned that I had degrees in art and art history, they assigned me to the section of the library that focuses on the arts that includes not only art, but publishing and general reference."

All the pieces were falling into place.

Kat was dressed to the nines in a tan business suit with a knee-length skirt and matching blazer that covered her white blouse and pearls she said had been her mother's. She looked beautiful and noted. "My meeting this morning won't take too long, and then we can go sightseeing. Now go down and meet Steven and he'll escort you to the tailor who's coming in early to assist you."

I did as directed and got fitted for a navy-blue pin-stripe suit with a white shirt and red striped tie. A Navy-blue blazer was also selected, and the tailor made certain everything was just so. The manager assured me everything would be delivered to the Drake by the middle of the afternoon.

Dinner Is Served

The clothes arrived, and I modeled my new duds. Kat thought I looked "debonair" whatever that meant, while it made me feel good, even though I still felt like a sow's ear pretending to be a silk purse. The dinner that night was a VIP affair at the Art Institute and anyone and everyone who was who's who in Chicago was there. The mayor, governor, both Senators, you name it, along with a myriad of donors who wanted to make Chicago more than it was. I never met so many phony baloneys in my entire life where I felt like a square peg in a round hole.

Kat played their game as the dirty old men ogled at her in her low- cut, backless black gown and diamond necklace. I'd wondered how she could fit into the dress and not be sans-a-bra as I'd began calling it when the fashion trend took hold, or should I say let go. Kat filled me in, noting that Rudi Gernreich had released the 'No Bra' which, as Kat explained, was a soft-cup, light-weight, seamless, sheer nylon, elastic tricot bra where the 'No-Back' long-line version featured the deep plunging front and a contoured stretch- waistband that allowed women to wear backless dresses.

My God, it was like trying to explain the design of the Impala and so much for the enticing thoughts most men were imagining. We walked through all the exhibits and when we got to the Stinson Room, it all made sense.

Kat's parents had funded the entire room and donated the artwork,

including two Monet's that were displayed elsewhere. The total donation had been well over five million dollars before the fancy pictures on the wall. I tried to be on my best behavior and took the role of supporting actor and yet there were still the glances, not only at her for obvious reasons, but at me. They knew I didn't belong and were whispering.

Kat introduced me to everyone and when they asked what I did, Kat announced that I was a successful agri-businessman who retired early to enjoy life. It was the truth, other than the successful part. It didn't matter, I didn't fit the part, and they knew it. After dinner and handshakes, Kat realized my discomfort, made eye contact with someone by the front door and a few minutes later, the Drake Hotel limo was standing outside waiting for us.

As we were riding the few blocks on Michigan Avenue, Kat whispered, "I'm sorry if you were uncomfortable." I didn't know what to say. I just felt out of place and the folks certainly knew how to make you feel that way, making me think you can take a boy off the farm, but you can't get the farm off the boy.

As we entered the elevator at the Drake, Kat whispered, "I can't wait to get out of this dress and my feet are killing me. Will you give me a massage?" I turned to say "Yes" as she stuck her tongue in my mouth and reached for my crotch. Yiikes!

Sightseeing Serenade

We spent Thursday touring Chicago. I thought we'd be going casual but Kat came out in a white silk blazer with matching knee-length shorts, red blouse, gold necklace and earrings, all enhanced by delicate tan sandals. Geez! I sound like one of those guys talking about the movie stars walking the red carpet at the Academy Awards. I was wearing jeans and a white Polo shirt with the Drake Hotel logo on it that magically appeared and realized the blue blazer was provided to create a little class. Once again, something about silk purses and sow's ears rattled in my brain.

At least I didn't have both judge and jury staring at me. The first stop was the Wendella Boat tour which I learned, had been a familiar sight in Chicago harbors for over 25 years. We had our choice and elected to take the architectural tour which provided both the sights and history of Chicago. You would have thought we were royalty as we were given VIP seats on the boat.

With politics being a spectator sport in Illinois, it was interesting to learn about how the city solved its problems of the 1800s. In 1854, a cholera epidemic in both Chicago and Mineral Point was attributed to bacteria in the water. Chicago didn't have sewers, so the human waste of 30,000 residents was dumped into the Chicago River, which then flowed into Lake Michigan that was also the city's source of drinking water, bringing deadly contaminants to every household.

In 1855, Chicago's city engineer, Ellis Chesbrough was given a mandate to fix the problem. At first, he intended to install a sewer system, which would have been the first in the country. The problem was that Chicago's streets were barely above lake level, so sewers dug under them wouldn't drain into the lake or river. Instead, Chesbrough laid sewer pipes on the existing streets and covered them with soil, some of which were ten feet higher than before.

After the sewers were installed and soil added, new streets were constructed. The problem was, the buildings in the loop were now lower than the street level. To resolve this, the Loop property owners had their buildings jacked up to Chicago's new ground level. While the sewer system moved sewage efficiently, it was still being dumped into the Chicago River that emptied into Lake Michigan.

In 1866, Chicago suffered another cholera epidemic. To compensate for the river run-off, Chesbrough proposed digging a five-foot diameter tunnel, two miles out into Lake Michigan to harvest fresh water. Residents thought he was nuts, but went along with his "folly".

While the tunnel helped, the cholera epidemic of 1873 led Chesbrough to conceive an engineering feat even more audacious than laying sewers on top of streets or tunneling under Lake Michigan when he proposed reversing the flow of the Chicago River. If his plan worked, instead of having the river flow into Lake Michigan, the river would flow south and take all of the city's waste with it, simply by having the canal deepened. Gone would be Chicago's problems, dumped on other towns along the river, reminding me that not much has changed in the past one-hundred years.

The river was dredged and the flow reversed in 1879. Unfortunately, downstream towns now watched Chicago's sewage flow by causing all sorts of health problems to the point that a group of mayors demanded meeting with Chesbrough and Carter Henry Harrison III, who was Chicago's mayor.

With Chicago politics being what it was, the politicking and cronyism became so intense that Chesbrough resigned and left Chicago that year after determining that widening the canal would increase the water volume and move the sewage-laden water faster. More than a decade later, digging began and in January 1900 the canal opened under the auspices of the Chicago Sanitary and Ship Canal which operates it today.

After the river cruise, we went to the Museum of Science and Industry, which I loved. Once again, VIP treatment meant going in through a side door and not waiting in line. Everything had been arranged by the Mayor's office and I felt like it was New York all over again.

We were escorted to the north end of Grant Park and the Prudential Building where their famous Observation Deck was next. I learned that, from the time it opened in 1955, the deck was a major destination for its fabulous views of Grant Park, Buckingham Fountain and Lake Michigan and over a million people each year made the trek.

When we arrived, we had an escort who took us up to the top of the 41-story building on what was then called the "world's fastest elevators and highest escalators in the world". The glass-enclosed observation deck was neat and I put two dimes in the telescope by the window and looked down at the world below.

After the Empire State Building in New York, it wasn't the big thrill some people got, but it was still pretty neat to be able to say I'd been in the tallest building in the world and also the tallest in Chicago, especially when before the visits, I thought I could touch the stars from the top of our silo.

When time ran out on the telescope, we went down one floor and had a sandwich at Stouffer's *"Top of the Rock"* restaurant where they had reserved a window-side table just for us. I wasn't really hungry, but realized the trouble all the folks had gone to and didn't want to make it look like I didn't appreciate what they were doing for us.

Kat had another surprise for me and took me over to the all-new John Hancock Building a few blocks away that was just about to open. The Mayor or some big shot, made arrangements for us to go all the way up to the 94th floor and I got to ride in what was soon to become the world's fastest elevator that made your ears pop on the way up and down.

The Otis Elevator sign said that we had the option of climbing the 1,632 steps from the main lobby up to the "Observatory" or taking the elevator that would be traveling at 1,801 feet/minute or 20.5 mph while climbing to a height of 1,129 feet in just 38 seconds. I looked at Kat and she at me. I thought of the sweat and panting hard from that many stairs and decided we'd done enough of that the night before and so we rode the elevator.

Whoosh! We were there! We landed at the top and were over a 1000 feet in the air. They were just putting the finishing touches on the interior and the telescopes weren't in place yet, but you could still see Illinois, Wisconsin, Indiana and Michigan and that was neat. I just shook my head realizing I could see four states from one set of windows or five if you included the State of Confusion created by the traffic below.

Kat noted they were going to open a restaurant one floor below and promised the next time we came to Chicago, we'd have dinner there if I wanted to. It was neat having her talk about "the next time" as it made me feel confident that this was meant to be and not a one-time experience.

When we were done, we went back to the hotel and Kat tried apologizing for the dress code, but it all made sense. We had to make the right impression and she certainly did that as she changed into civilian clothes of faded jeans and black tee-shirt. Once again, in tune with the times, in terms of being "sans-a-bra" as she called it, while I tagged along in my New York Levi's and Drake Hotel polo shirt as well.

Country Roads Take Me Home

We checked out of the Drake and put the suitcases at the bell stand, walked over to Wells street and had an early dinner of deep-dish pizza, which Kat had never tasted before. Everywhere we went, eyes were on Kat and that sort of made me both anxious and proud. With our bellies full, we walked back to the Drake and had the valet retrieve my car. "This is your car?" Kat asked almost incredulously.

"Yup! 1958 Chevy Impala" Kat probably thought I'd be driving a Ford pick-up and I didn't want to tell her, it was home in the barn. "Hank Terrill, I didn't know you had it in you. This is a classic. The lines are incredible and the silver blue color matches your eyes. Thank, God, General Motors finally decided to put some form back into the function. What we have now are simply boxes on wheels."

I'd hit one of her hot buttons as she continued, "If you go back and look at the cars from the 1920's and 30's, they were true art forms. My favorites are the 1925 Rolls-Royce Phantom One, Jonckheere Coupe, in black with the red leather interior and suicide doors. I also love both the 1930 Mercedes 710 SSK Trossi Roadster and 1936 540K Special Roadster plus the 1935 Auburn 851 SC Boattail Speedster and then my all-time favorite - the 1928 Duesenberg Model J, that Al Capone drove around town here in Chicago.

Your Chevy is the first car in a long time that is even coming close and even the 1965 Mustang can't compete with your Impala. However the 1967 Shelby Mustang is a real ride"

Any thought I had of her being too high brow, just went out the proverbial window as Kat got excited about cars. She really would have knocked my socks off is she had the same discourse about tractors like the Ferguson Type A or John Deere 4020 or even the Caterpillar Diesel Sixty.

Before departing for Chicago, I really didn't even know if Kat would be coming to Mineral Point and what we would talk about during the long drive. As insurance, I decided to create a tape of music I thought librarians might like and chose some of the classical stuff I'd collected. As we drove out of the city, I slid an audio cassette into the sleeve.

"What's that?" Kat asked.

"Audio cassettes. I buy them blank at Radio Shack and record my own albums," as if she'd been living on Mars. "I thought you might like some relaxation music on our way to Mineral Point and so I created a tape just for you."

Kat seemed honored and I was relieved, having worried that it was too corny as I continued, "The first song is Eric Satie's – Gymnopédie No.1 that I played for you on New Year's eve."

"And put me to sleep if I remember" Kat said with a smile.

"It has luscious chords, a slow tempo and a gorgeous, drifting mood."

"You sound like an art critic."

"I only included the first set that really invites you to close your eyes and float away."

We listened while we slowly snaked our way out of the city. Two cars at a stop sign is a traffic jam in Mineral Point and this was crazy!

As the song ended, I announced, "The second cut is Gustav Holst's – 'Venus the Bringer of Peace' from the symphony known as 'The Planets'. After being introduced to astrology in 1913, Holst was inspired to create a suite based on the planets of the solar system and their corresponding Roman deities. I only recorded the second movement called 'Venus' which I've dedicated to you."

A broad smile creased Kat's face as her eyes closed and she reported, " The statue of Venus de Milo is commonly thought to represent Aphrodite, the ancient Greek goddess of love, beauty, pleasure, passion and procreation.

The statue was carved from marble by Alexandros, a sculptor in Antioch, Greece on the Maeander River about 150 BC. She was found in pieces on the Aegean island of Melos on April 8, 1820, and was presented to Louis XVIII who donated it to the Louvre in 1821 where she stands today. Next to the statue of David, she is the second most famous statue in history."

Kat leaned back in her seat as hands began slowly massaging the tops of her thighs. When the song ended, she came back to reality as I introduced her to Chopin's 'Nocturne No.2'. I noted. "Chopin wrote this when he was 20 years old and it overflows with delicate beauty and is perfect for relaxing. This is one I like to listen to when I drink some late night Alterego wine at home."

Again, Kat's eyes closed and I could tell she was enjoying the music as I announced that the next track was Ingolf Wunder playing Chopin's Nocturne Op.9 No.2.

"This is wonderful." Kat exclaimed.

As it ended, I announced, "Maurice Ravel's Boléro is his most famous recording as a one-movement orchestral piece. It was originally composed as a ballet commissioned by Russian actress and dancer Ida Rubinstein, which premiered in 1928."

"You put this all together just for me?" Kat inquired, as I nodded in the affirmative with a light smile of satisfaction pursing my lips.

"I'd be remiss if I hadn't included "Beethoven's Moonlight Sonata's first movement. Here you'll experience the gentle repetition of his right hand accompanied by sustained notes in the left, that create alluring harmonies. This was pointed out to me by my buddies in Janis Joplin's band that got me hooked on neo-classical, piano-oriented music."

As it ended, I highlighted Bill Evans, who was one of the greatest jazz pianists to have ever lived. "'Peace Piece' comes from his album *Everybody Digs Bill Evans* that shows jazz can also be a perfect way to relax, if given the opportunity."

"Or make love" Kat added and I smiled a not too lecherous smile.

As we reached the Wisconsin border, Bach came on and I outlined that I felt he was undoubtedly one of the all-time masters of classical music. "His heavenly Prelude No.1 is famous around the world for being a piece of simple beauty, consisting of broken chords that are blended together for harmonic consistency."

Kat was simply shaking her head in disbelief at the acoustic beauty that expanded before her. As we cut through Beloit, Massenet's 'Meditation' began. I noted that it came from the second act of the opera *Thaïs* by Jules Massenet.

"In the opera, the previously hedonistic courtesan, Thaïs, decides to follow a life of piety. The soft piano's broken chords perfectly accompany the flowing violin melody, to create the epitome of beauty in this piece."

The ride west on Highway 81 found Elgar's - Salut d'amour reaching Kat's ears and hopefully, her heart as I noted. "Elgar finished this piece in 1888, when he was romantically involved with Caroline Roberts. He called it *"Liebesgruss"* or 'Love's Greeting' which, he gave to her *Salut d'Amour* as an engagement present.

Kat's eyes were closed as she listened to the music and I saw a soft smile on her face. Great music has a way of doing that to people. We made it to Monroe and hit highway 23 as darkness was falling and I outlined that Debussy's – Rêverie which means 'dream' came on. I looked over and Kat's eyes were closed. I didn't know if she was asleep of simply listening to the music. With her head down and her hands pressed between her legs, she was either profoundly relaxed or in some sort of orgasmic trance. I just shrugged, smiled and shook my head and listened to the music as the sun dipped below the horizon.

Next came Rota's – *'Love Theme, from Romeo and Juliet'* inspired by Shakespeare's famous romance that is so affecting and purely emotional. I noted that I loved the strings and how they were able to control their dynamics to create a sense of power and sensitivity at the same time.

Mascagni's - Intermezzo, from *Cavalleria Rusticana was playing* as I weaved my way through Argyle. I looked to my right and noted that Kat's head swaying from side-to-side in tune to the music that continued as Rusticana was followed by Handel's - Ombra mai fù, from *Xerxes.*

Kat's trance broke as we pulled out of Darlington and Mozart's – 'Concerto for Flute and Harp' began to play. I noted that the calming tempo was instantly relaxing to most people and the beautiful airiness of the flute combined with the grace of the harp is so delicately exquisite, that hadn't Kat already been relaxed, she would have been asleep in the calmest possible way.

With my special lady friend totally relaxed and beginning to nod, I pulled into Mrs. Gordon's garage. It was ten o'clock and I knew Mrs. Gordon would be in bed. With the loss of motion, Kat removed herself from her trance and looked around. "We're here," I announced as I reached across and kissed her.

"Welcome to Mineral Point."

Dewey and the Decimals

Kat's eyes opened as she stretched and I outlined the need to walk the block up Chestnut hill. She was so relaxed, she didn't care. As we reached the Red Rooster, I apologized for my temporary abode. She said that as long as it was clean and filled with love, that was all that mattered, as we climbed the outside stairs. I had her in front of me and watched her fanny on each step. For being fifty, she was in great shape and filled out the jeans very nice. We reached the landing and I opened the door.

"Holy shit!" was the exclamation as Kat looked at all my albums. "I had no idea! How many albums do you have?"

"There are 533 here and I have a few hundred more out at the farm." "How do you keep track of all of them?"

"Well, I know this gorgeous librarian who gave me an idea and so all the albums use the Dewey Decimal system. The first digit is a letter that classifies genre, the second and third digits are numbers that reflect the artist; the fourth digit decade of release and fifth letter digit year. The means an F236L would be that the record is folk music sung by Bob Dylan that was released in 1962."

"How did you figure the year out?" Kat asked. The 'F' is for folk music. '23' is Dylan's number. The six is for the sixth decade and "L' is the second letter of the word Blackhorse, which is a ten-letter word with no duplicate letters."

"With the five-digit system I have the records sorted and can literally find any record you want from my collection in a matter of minutes, simply by looking at my directory and going from there."

"How do you have your directory sorted?"

"I do it two ways. The first method is by genre of music and the second by artist. If you want to listen to jazz, we simply go to that section and look at the options. If you want to listen to just Bob Dylan, you go to the artist section."

"This is incredible."

"Thanks, want to see the place?"

"Just the bathroom, right now."

I directed her, which wasn't too hard when there's only three rooms, as I put her suitcase in the bedroom. When she returned she looked wide awake as I asked, "Are you hungry?"

"Not really."

"Glass of wine?"

"That sounds good!"

With that, I got two glasses and poured some Pinot Noir. "Music?"

"Sure."

"Type?"

"Soft jazz," She replied.

I put on a Miles Davis album as we sat on the couch and I lit a candle. For 30 minutes we just leaned back and listened. It had been a long day and I looked across and Kat's eyes were closed.

"Think we should turn in!" "Uh huh!" With that I helped her up and we went into the bedroom.

Kat looked at me and smiled. "Mr. Terrill, this has been a wonderful day and I'm so glad I was able to help you find what you were looking for. Do you mind if we just snuggle for a while?"

Thank God! I thought. I was exhausted.

Madge

The Friday sun rose and we snored. Around 7:30 I finally woke up. Kat was still asleep and so I quietly got up and did what I needed to do. There was no need making breakfast as we'd just go down stairs to the Rooster and Kat could meet the cook, waitress, landlords and my friends, all wrapped up in two people named Frank and Madge.

As she awoke, Kat came out into kitchen wearing one of my undershirts. "Hope you don't mind that I slept in" as she came over and gave me a kiss.

"Not at all," was my response.

"What's our agenda?"

"First a shower, then breakfast and meeting Mrs. Gordon."

"I guess we'll need to go solo in the shower. I've seen phone booths bigger than that." Kat observed.

"We can make up for it at the pond" I replied.

With that, Kat was gone and I heard the water running and soon she came out with one towel wrapped around her torso and another her head exclaiming, "Your turn".

I went in, knowing that the mini water heater would mean a very brief or very cold shower. Sure enough, three minutes and I was shivering. What a way to wake up! Kat was still wrapped in the towel and looking at the binder with the summary of the albums in it as I walked out with a towel around my waist.

"You're shivering."

"Too small of a water heater for two people." "You should have said something."

"No problem."

With that, Kat unwrapped her towel and pulled me in. "Here, let me warm you up."

It felt good, as we stood there pressed against each other. At five- foot eight, Kat didn't need to look up too far but when she did, our eyes met and she said, "this is the happiest I've been in five years."

I looked at her and offered, "You deserve it. You've been through so much."

"How about you?" she asked.

I looked at her and said "Time does heal all wounds. I never thought I'd ever be happy again and was resolved to a life alone and now you've come along. More than the physical aspect, it's just feeling special that's turned my world around. I don't know how this is going to end or if it ever will. All I know is right now, I can't imagine being alone or with anyone else but you."

We kissed and the spell was broken. It was time for breakfast. As I was getting dressed, Kat looked out the front window and noticed the big dog on the pedestal on the building across the street. "What's the story behind the gray dog?" she asked as I was coming out of the bedroom.

"That's Pointer! He's been the town mascot for over 80 years. When Mineral Point was booming, all the Cornish merchants used some sort of statue to identify their buildings. At one time, the town was the most affluent community in Wisconsin."

"What happened?" Kat asked.

"That's what my book is going to be all about."

Kat realized I was dressed and she was still standing there in a towel and needed time to get ready. A few minutes later, she appeared in her new bib overalls with the white tee shirt - sans-a-bra, of course, and we clamored down the stairs.

As Kat opened the Rooster door, she started heading for the 'wrong' side of the island counter and away from my somewhat-reserved spot, where the folded paper sat along with the empty coffee cup, awaiting my arrival. I took her by the hand and led her to 'my spot' saying, "This is where I have breakfast, every morning. I read the paper and listen to Madge and Frank fill me in on all the Mineral Point gossip, of which I'm certain you'll be a subject the minute we walk out the door."

"Madge – Frank, this is my very special friend Katherine Johnson from Washington DC"

Pleasantries were given all around and Madge asked Kat

what she wanted for breakfast and was surprised by the fact that all she asked for was coffee and wheat toast. We ate our breakfast and listened to the day's local gossip and headed out.

"You never paid," Kat announced.

"I settle up at the end of the month when I pay the rent. It's easier that way."

"So it's an honor system?"

"I guess so, Madge just tells me what the bill is and I pay it."

Kat shook her head and smiled as we walked out the front door as she exclaimed, "Toto, we're not in Washington anymore!"

We walked down Chestnut Hill and I pointed out my future home. "It's so cute" was the comment which I guess is a woman's way of saying she liked it. As we approached the side door, I knocked three times - wrap-wrap- wrap - and opened the door slowly.

"Hank is that you?" Mrs. Gordon asked.

"Yes, mam, and I've got a special person to meet you."

"Can I show Katherine the house?"

"Sure, it's almost yours," Mrs. Gorgon shrugged.

With that, we went on the upstairs tour and I told Kat the history of the house and how it was built in 1844 by William Tregray. When we got to the big bedroom, Kat looked at me and said, "Hmmm, I'll need to come back in the winter when we can snuggle under a down quilt when it's so cold that we can see our breaths." I thought she said breasts and just smiled at the imagery.

As we came downstairs, I asked Mrs. Gordon "Are you up for lunch at Thymes?"

"Can I have a shot of brandy?" "If you want one."

"How about two?" the little, old lady snickered.

"Sure! In fact you can get all snockered up and dance on the tables if you want to."

"Then yes. Now go get the car Hank and bring it up so an old lady can get in."

With that, I was out the door knowing I'd be the topic of conversation while I was gone. Later, Kat filled me in that Mrs. Gordon considered me to be the son she lost in World War II and how she loved me as such, which made me feel grand. It was a glorious June day and the early lunch went well.

We returned to the house and I helped Mrs. Gordon back inside as she looked at me and said, "That one's a keeper, Hank Terrill. Don't let her get away."

I assured Mrs. Gordon that was my intent, as I walked out and got in the car inquiring to Kat, "Well?"

"What a sweetheart!" was the total response. "What did you think of the house?" I inquired.

"I love it, particularly the sun room on the back. Natural sunlight.

Privacy! It could make a wonderful art studio someday." "Are you ready for the mosquitos, pigs and frogs?" "Can I change?" Kat asked.

Geez, I thought, 'this woman wears more clothes in a day than I do in a week'. I pulled up in front of the Rooster and Kat said I didn't need to come in as it would only take a minute. She knew the house key was under the mat and scurried up the stairs.

Kat was gone ten minutes and when she returned was wearing some of those blue jean short shorts and a paisley rayon halter top that tied in the back where the design reminded me of huge sperm cells. I wondered if the shorts came that way and what you did with the legs you cut off.

As Kat got in the Chevy she asked. "Are you ready to get naked and have some fun in the sun?" I put on a little Led Zeppelin and we rocked to 'Good Times Bad Times' with songs like 'Babe I'm Gonna Leave You' that was originally recorded by Joan Baez for her 1962 album 'Joan Baez in Concert' then 'You Shook Me' which had a blues tone to it, even though it had both organ and harmonica overlays, thereby changing it completely from what Jeff Beck had recorded in the

1968 album 'Truth'. Finally, 'Dazed and Confused' which was written and recorded by Jake Holmes in 1967, was playing as we arrived at the farm with both of us going crazy to the music like we were teenagers.

Kat noted that during 'Dazed and Confused' she got the "Goosies" as she called them. I told her that the chills experienced by music were caused by increased levels of dopamine being released by the brain in anticipation to some part of a song. She smiled at my knowledge, as I added that one of the reasons I enjoyed so many different types of music was because of what it did to me - relax me, excite me, arouse me or even calm me down and that's why I enjoyed it so much. Kat just shook her head and smiled an envious smile as I thought about her passion for art and realized that, beneath it all, we were very much alike, it was just that hers was visual and mine was auditory, and that was a fine combination.

Skunk Hollow

We parked by the old house and I told Kat the entire Terrill story and showed her the cemetery before we began the walk to Skunk Hollow. As we reached the woods, Kat stopped. "What?" I inquired.

"I don't know. I just got this really weird feeling." "What kind of feeling?"

"I can't explain it. My whole body is simply tingling and it's almost like I've been here before."

"Do you want to turn around?"

"No, just the opposite. Hank, this place is special and I want to see it and feel it. I've never felt like this before in my life."

We stopped by a fallen tree and Kat looked at the trunk with keen interest. She looked at me as she said. "You know, looking at this trunk tells me the story of the tree's existence - how it grew and what happened around it."

Pointing at the trunk she said, "The rings that are far apart, reflect times that were good, but the wood is soft. When times were tough, the rings are closer together and yet, this is the strongest part of all. People are like that too, except we don't have to cut inside to find out. All we need to do is observe and, in a short time, we can see their tree of life - the good times when things were easy and the bad, when things were tough and it took more strength simply to survive."

In an instant, the reflection was gone and yet, it was one more instance when I realized that the woman in my life was much more observant and introspective than I ever thought. Perhaps our depths of passion for different sets of stimuli had a common thread as I too had always had a special feeling whenever I came to the forest.

We continued to what remained of the school and I explained its history and how I went to school there, as did all my ancestors. When I completed detailing the school's history, I wanted to walk to the left but Kat asked me if we could go to the right. I reluctantly said 'Sure' as we followed the deer path to where the water trickled out of the earth and the little stream began. Kat bent down, cupped her hands and drank the pure water. With that, her head tilted back and eyes closed. As her eyes opened again she looked at me and there was a different expression on her face than I'd ever seen before. "Hank, this place is simply wonderful. There's a sense of peace and innocence here that goes beyond tranquility and is almost religious. I don't know what it is, but I've never felt so – so 'calm' in my life."

Kat looked at me and then at the blanket I was carrying and smiled. Words were not needed, I knew what she was inferring as her head tilted and her chin nodded towards the tall grass. I reached for the blanket and we simply unfolded it.

Without the 'urgency' that had been a part of Chicago, this was a slow unveiling as Kat untied her top and let it fall, while slowly pulling my shirt up over my head. We kissed as she pulled me in and gently unbuckled my belt and then hers as both pairs of pants fell to our ankles. We both stepped out of the pile of modesty that had ensconced our bodies while our lips never left each other's.

I was breathing in the warmth of the summer sun as it caressed my back. For what seemed like an eternity, we explored each other's bodies, tenderly traveling across the peaks and valleys of our existence. We consummated our relationship. Gone was the intensity that had been there before, replaced by the soft, gentle expression of two people sharing each other, caring for each other, exploring the emotion called love.

As we reached our mutual crescendo, the bond between us was welded in bliss and I knew that what had been so physical before had transcended into a metaphysical sense of each other. Slowly, I took a deep breath knowing and believing we were entering a new plateau in our relationship at a pace much faster than I'd anticipated.

Words were not spoken as none were needed. What had transpired was gentle and tender and the most intimate moment we'd experienced as we lay on the blanket in total splendor - two people amongst the tall grass, simply allowing ourselves to 'return', looking up at the clouds floating by. What had started as lust was turning into passion. I could feel it, she could feel it and it was wonderful.

After an extended moment of silence, Kat spoke. "Hank, I don't know what it is or why this is happening, but I never want to leave here. I know I'm rushing things and don't want you to feel pressured or scared and I'll understand if the answer is no or not now, but I've never felt so good, so alive and so much at peace than I do right now."

With that, Kat rolled over and propped herself up on one arm and looked at me as her finger slowly made circles on my bare chest. "My entire life, I've always felt as if a part of me was missing. Here – now - I feel complete. I can't explain it, nor do I think I want to, but I've transcended from what I was, to who I am and for the first time ever, I'm what I want to be."

Kat withdrew her hand and grew pensive. "I grew up in a very structured home. There was some love, but not a lot and it was more about doing things right and being politically correct than about doing what was good and what made you happy. My father was in politics and that's why I am so adverse to it. I saw how it corrupted him and took away his integrity. Power can be narcotizing and he was addicted."

"When I was in high school, I rebelled, but the pressure was always there to toe-the-line and make certain I never embarrassed the family or jeopardize my father's reputation and career."

"Mom's family had money, lots of money, and so she was used to getting whatever she wanted, whenever she wanted it. Her parents had compensated her loss of love with material possessions and taught her that she was above the rest, which is what I heard my whole childhood - 'you're better than others, simply because we have money and dad has power.'

When you add power and money together, you can create a monster, a narcissistic maelstrom the ends up in loneliness, rejection and profound isolation. For us, it became mom's drinking and dad's infidelity and the fact that I'm an only child simply because, when I was born, there were complications and mom couldn't have any more kids - none of which was hidden from me. At night, I'd go to my room and listen to my parents argue and fight, which is the worst thing you can do to a child – make them feel as if they were a mistake."

Kat lay back down and rolled over on her back, looking up at the clouds, searching for more words. "When I went to Yale, I was finally free. I didn't know what I wanted and so I floated, being careful not to let people know who I or my father was. I fell into art because I love any mode of sincere expression visual, auditory or even physical, like this. As I started taking art classes, my friends were some of the most liberal people you could imagine

- Bohemians, communists, socialists, beatniks – the typical artsy, fartsy crowd. One day, on a lark, I applied to be a nude model for the art department and was accepted. It was my way of revolting. Mom found out and had dad's people call the University and put an end to the entire escapade."

"Did you ever pose?"

"For a class, no. Classmates, yes, several times."

Kat continued, but her tone became more direct, "When I met Ron, I thought I fell in love, but the structure became even worse. Instead of being free, I was more constrained. We got married because I was pregnant with Will and we certainly couldn't have that in our family."

"Ron and I endured but weren't happy. When Tad was born, I thought it would be better, but Ron kept moving up in rank and with it came more politics and more bullshit. Everything always had to be structured. Everything always had to be controlled and examined to determine what the consequences would be."

Once again, Kat rolled onto her stomach and raised up on her elbows looking at my face. "Ron and I became very distant and that's why the boys and I traveled as much as we did in Europe – simply to be away from a man who was rarely there and when he was, made life miserable. When Ron's plane crashed, I'd already seen a divorce lawyer, then mom got to the point she needed someone all the time and I sold my house and moved back home – back to all the crap I'd escaped from and took the job at the library for my own sanity."

Kat rolled on her side, as did I, and was looking deeply into my eyes as she continued. "I was doing my job and also doing what was needed as a daughter, nurse and caregiver."

A slight smile crossed her face as she continued, "One day this handsome guy walked into the library and said he needed to study what a politician was all about. He seemed like a nice guy and asked me out to dinner. I hadn't been out to dinner in over two years and so I went. We drank too much and yet, for the first time in a long, long time, I felt alive and with someone who wasn't so – so controlled or controlling."

"I wanted you to make love to you that night and yet, you were a gentleman for which I was at first disappointed, and then realized that you were more than a one-night stand, for which I am totally grateful. When you planned on coming to Chicago, I didn't know what was going to happen and yet, I've quickly realized you're someone I want to be with simply because we're so much alike, yet so different. Like a puzzle, the two pieces seem to be fitting together to create an image of acceptance."

Kat had let it all out. I bit my lower lip. I didn't feel the same intensity that Kat did and wasn't quite ready to bare my soul. However, I also knew that Kat completed me. She was adding the piece I was missing and was making me feel whole again, filling the void in my heart that began when Ann passed away.

For the first time in a long time, perhaps even before Ann departed, I felt alive and in love. In so doing, I also felt guilty. How could I feel this way when I was married to Ann and worshipped the ground she walked on – the mother of my children, my partner in good times and bad, happy times and sad and yet, for the very first time, I too felt complete?

We lay there and listened to the Red-wing blackbirds call each other and the hum of the bees as they went from wildflower to wildflower. This was peace! This was tranquility! This was God at his very best! As the spell broke, we arose and began walking back along the deer path from where we came.

Knee Deep

It took ten minutes for us to make it to the pond. When we arrived, Kat was in awe as it was exactly as I'd described it and she had imagined. Grandpa and dad had dug out the stream to give it depth and shape.

"How deep is it?" Kat asked. "You can ask the frogs," I replied. "Huh?"

"Sure, they'll tell you."

Kat looked at me like I was nuts and saw my silly smirk as I replied, "knee-deep, knee-deep, knee-deep!" to which Kat simply groaned. Actually the pond was eight feet deep in the middle and shaped like a perfect bowl that Mother Nature filled with clean, clear water from the spring that was warmed by the sun as it trickled along so it wasn't too cold. It was cool, but refreshing, especially on a hot summer's day and most people got used to it.

I added, "Thirty years ago, we hauled sand and created the small beach, contrary to what the DNR wanted."

Kat noticed the cattails on the other side of the pond amongst which the birds would nest and the frogs would hide. You could hear them croak, but rarely saw them. Kat looked at the area and smiled. Everything I'd said was true. There had been no hyperbole. She shrugged her shoulders and stepped into the shallow water.

I saw her flinch as I added, "You'll get used to it. It's not the Caribbean, but is refreshing."

I joined her and held her hand as we slowly made our way until the water was waist deep. I looked at her and she had a grimacing smile on her face. I knew the toughest part was yet to come - dipping our shoulders beneath the surface.

I also knew there were two ways to do it - quick and abruptly uncomfortable, or agonizingly slow and profoundly uncomfortable. I quickly ducked under the water and then pulled her in with me. For only a moment was there reticence and then our bodies adjusted and we were fine.

We stood in the water and held each other and then at the north end, 'he' came. The huge buck who'd avoided his demise for as long as anyone could remember. I told Kat to remain totally still as the buck took a drink. He spied us, at which time he simply nodded and walked away as if giving his approval of our existence in his realm, reserved for all God's creatures.

As we stood there I asked Kat what she heard. She said "Nothing".

I replied, "I know! That's why I love this place. No noise, no humanity creating havoc, just the peace and tranquility of nature and now you and me."

We stayed a while and then it was time to go. We dried ourselves off and Kat asked me what would happen if we walked naked back to the car. I noted that she would probably have mosquito bites on her butt which took to 'aura' out of the moment as we slipped into our clothes and drove back to the apartment, listening to the rest of the Zeppelin album with songs like *'Your Time Is Gonna Come'* and *'Black Mountain Side'*, which was an instrumental based on an arrangement of the traditional folk song *'Black Water Side'* and then *'Communication Breakdown'* followed by *'I Can't Quit You Baby'* and, finally, *'How Many More Times'* as I parked the car and turned off the ignition.

We sat for a moment speechless simply letting the music penetrate our minds and then Kat looked at me, reached across the seat and held my right hand. Words were not needed, her eyes said it all as she peered into my soul as I felt *"thank you"* transcend from her to me to eternity.

<u>*Arlington*</u>

Slowly we walked back up Chestnut Hill, showered and dressed for dinner. It was casual chic time with Kat attired in her white outfit and me in a white golf shirt, jeans and the blue sportscoat as we drove to Mt. Horeb.

The food at the Farm Kitchen was marvelous, as it was all organic and home grown. After dinner, we made our way back to the apartment and lit the candle on the coffee table and I put on some music and opened a bottle of wine.

"Sorry it isn't Alterego" I lamented.

"I don't think I need that brand anymore," Kat replied.

We listened to more music that Kat chose that included some Odetta, Judy Collins and Joni Mitchell. As she perused my record collection, she came to the end of the row where there were some miscellaneous albums. Pulling one out, she examined the cover of *The Sun Dance"* by Gertrude Bonnin.

Without looking up Kat pronounced with a surprised evocation, "you have the opera collaborated by Zitkala-Sa or "Red Bird" recorded in Lakota and based her Yankton Sioux heritage that was composed with William F. Hanson who was a musician and teacher at Brigham Young University."

I nodded in the affirmative and asked, "How do you know so much about Gertrude Bonnin?"

My mother was a big opera fan and assisted in getting Mrs. Bonnin buried at Arlington National cemetery when she died in 1936."

I was surprised and it must have shown on my face as Kat continued, "Red Bird was co-founder of the National Council of American Indians in 1926, which was established to lobby for Native people's right to United States citizenship and other civil rights they had long been denied."

I've read all of her books and was particularly impressed by her treatise on her personal spiritual beliefs where she countered the contemporary trend that suggested Native

Americans needed to adopt and conformed to the Christianity forced on them in schools and public life."

Kat continued, "I guess I could associate with her because much of her work is about the tensions between tradition and assimilation, and between literature and politics as reflected in her tension between wanting to follow the traditions of the Yankton Dakota while being tempted by assimilation where she told of the hardships which she and other Native Americans encountered at the missionary and manual labor schools designed to "civilize" them and assimilate Native Americans to American culture."

Kat turned to the back of the record album and read what was written, 'Perhaps my Indian nature is the moaning wind which stirs them [schoolteachers] now for their present record. But, however tempestuous this is within me, it comes out as the low voice of a curiously colored seashell, which is only for those ears that are bent with compassion to hear it.'

We put the *Sun Dance Opera* on and listened to it with eyes closed and for the first time, it had a profound effect on me. When it was done, there was complete silence as I realized the depth of passion Kat had for others less fortunate in so many ways than she.

"You said your mother was on the Arlington National Cemetery Committee?"

Kat responded by nodding her head in the affirmative as she noted, "She volunteered there for nearly twenty years. There are over 400,000 people buried at Arlington with thousands more whose families wish they were. Most were members of the armed forces who served in active duty. However, there are thousands of family members and those of particular distinction inured there and someone had to decide who was allowed and who wasn't."

"What's the difference?" I asked.

"The difference normally lies is in the type of funeral service at the cemetery where standard military graveside honors include a casket team, firing party and bugler. In addition to the standard military honors, certain deceased military veterans may also receive an escort platoon, military band, caisson and colors team, which is what we had for dad."

"Normally, the firing party is from the branch of service the deceased or their family served in. When mom was buried, you might have noticed that all five branches of military service were present because of my dad and mom's years of volunteering."

"Normally, military honors aren't rendered to civilians because mom didn't serve in the military. However, because she was on the cemetery board and then dad, the cemetery board felt that it was right, she be given the twenty-one-gun salute that you heard."

Any levity in the living room had been scoured away by the talk of death. Yet, once again, I was profoundly impressed by the depth of knowledge and sense of compassion Kat showed for others.

The silence in the room was almost deafening until Kat turned to me and pulled me in for a soft, gentle kiss as she closed her eyes and tilted her head back and whispered, "I'm at peace and peace be with you my dear, dear friend." With that we finished our wine, blew out the candle and went to bed. It had been a wonderful day, other than the two mosquito bites on my butt.

Who's Bluffing Who?

Saturday, we drove to Spring Green stopping at the eclectic *'House on The Rock'* and then Devils Lake. After the rolling topography of Mineral Point and Waldwick, Kat was amazed that Central Wisconsin had a spring- fed lake surrounded by tall "bluffs" consisting of huge granite boulders and a hiking path to the top, where you could look down and literally see the fish swimming in the lake below.

Kat took a deep breath to fill her lungs with the clean Wisconsin air and looked at me with a wry smile on her face and said, "this would be a great place to make love".

"What happens if someone comes?" I asked "Isn't that the objective?" Kat replied.

We paused for a moment to check reality only to have the temptation amplified as Kat slid the tip of her tongue across her upper lip, looked deep into my eyes and whispered, "OK!... But... I... really... want...to..." Then, she pulled me in and burrowed her tongue deep within my mouth while her hands slid down inside my pants. Slowly, she pulled back and whispered in my ear, "Wanda Duit?"

I think we would have 'thrown caution to the wind' if it hadn't been for a Boy Scout leader with ten kids hiking up the trail, which replaced passion with caution. Whew!

The air was electric and we almost couldn't handle it, but knew that patience had its virtue and so, on our way home, we stopped in Sauk City at a place called Culver's A&W and Kat became almost orgasmic with her first taste of frozen chocolate custard.

After our double dip cones, we stopped at Mazo Beach and the spot on the Wisconsin River to read the historical marker denoting the spot where Blackhawk and his nation crossed the river while attempting to escape from the white man's onslaught of tomorrow. Finally, we arrived back in Mineral Point and went to bed. We were both exhausted and needed a good night's rest.

<u>*Reticence*</u>

Sunday morning came too soon and Kat tried packing her suitcase. With all she'd purchased in Chicago, there wasn't enough room. I offered her mine. She offered to pay. I refused and so the offer was to have my once- used Sears and Roebuck suitcase move to Washington. Instead Kat suggested she just leave her 'Wisconsin' clothes with me for the next time she visited. That made sense and was an indirect way of telling me she wanted to return and my way of saying, "Yes".

As we were tiding up the living room, Kat examined Irving and looked at the outline of my intended book.

"Do you want to be my editor?" I inquired. "Sure, that would be neat," she replied.

"OK, as I write each chapter, I'll mail it to you. You can read it, correct it and send it back."

"I have a much better idea." "What's that?"

"Each time you finish a chapter, either you hand deliver it to Washington or I pick it up in Mineral Point."

A huge smile crossed my face. What a great motivator! What a wonderful way to create a schedule we both could look forward to. I nodded in the affirmative and said, "Agreed".

Kat had changed her reservation and was flying out of Madison instead of Chicago at 5:00 PM and yet I was still antsy. I didn't want her to go and yet, I was also nervous about her missing her flight. We had an early breakfast at the Rooster and Kat said goodbye to Madge and Frank, who invited her back again. We had plenty of time and walked up and down High Street.

Kat was saddened by all the empty store fronts as she marveled at their antiquity and possibilities. "This one would make a great art studio" she lamented. "And this one, too".

"I don't think any artist could make a living here."

"One no, but several could feed off each other and draw art lovers and tourists."

It was time to head for Madison and we were about to turn north on Shake Rag, Kat inquired about the abandoned hotel I'd told her about on the south side of Highway 23. I made a right and we drove down past the place. The sandstone still looked sturdy, but the windows were gone, critters had become tenants and it probably, make that, definitely needed a new roof and floors.

"It's just sitting there, empty. Has it been that way for a long time?"

"Yup."

"How sad!"

As we slowly made our way up Shake Rag towards Highway 151 Kat spotted the two small houses on the side of the street with cars out front. "What's that?" she inquired.

"The smaller cottage is called Pendarvis House. The larger two-story is called Trelawny."

"People live there?"

"No, it's a restaurant."

"They're beautiful!"

"In the 1920s and 1930s, many of the old cabins built by the Cornish miners in the 1840s and 1850s were being torn down and used to build the town swimming pool. Two residents, Robert Neal and Edgar Hellum acquired the buildings and restored them because, like our family farmhouse, they were built of locally quarried sandstone that have walls 18 to 20 inches thick and Robert and Edgar simply couldn't let them be destroyed."

"Robert and Edgar had a dream to restore all the houses on Shake Rag. However, in order to support the restoration of other buildings, Pendarvis was turned into a restaurant serving authentic Cornish meals. It's been written up dozens of times and has received wide acclaim as a five-star restaurant."

"Normally, for Friday and Saturday night, you need to make reservations six months to a year in advance. The restaurant has been so successful, it helped finance the restoration of the other buildings. Robert and Edgar are getting up there in years and word in town has it that they're thinking about closing the restaurant and retiring."

"Can we have lunch there?"

I was reticent as I knew reservations were extremely difficult to acquire, "Let me see. I've known both men my entire adult life."

We parked the car and walked to the front door. Robert saw me and a great big smile crossed his face. "Hank, how have you been?" as he extended his arm for a quick handshake.

I was a bit modest and nodded, saying, "Fine". "So sorry about Ann!"

"Thanks. It's been two years." I offered.

"My time flies!" Robert responded as if time healed all wounds.

I introduced Kat as my good friend and explained that she was in from Washington and how I'd told her about the history of Pendarvis and its world class Cornish food.

"Washington DC?"" Robert inquired.

Kat nodded in the affirmative with a brilliant smile. "A good friend of Hanks?"

Another nod. Another smile. "Interested in lunch?"

A smile and a nod from the two of us.

"Let me see what I can do," as Robert held up his hand, indicating we should wait at the front door as all the tables were full.

Robert went and whispered something to Edgar who looked up and waved as Robert returned asking, "would you mind eating out on our personal patio?"

"Not at all", Kat replied.

"We normally don't do this, but Edgar and I've decided to retire and Hank has been a good friend for so many years and we'll be closing soon."

We went through the side door as Robert led us out to the small paved patio with a table for two and a blue and white striped umbrella as he set the table and provided menus.

I thought, "What a way to end Kat's visit, eating gourmet Cornish food in a five-star restaurant that included pasty, saffron bread and home-made apple pie?"

We each had a small glass of Wollersheim wine and enjoyed the ambiance. The food was spectacular! When it was time to go, I nodded to Robert and requested the bill. Robert looked at me with a frown and walked over to the table. "Hank, you have been our good friend. You've accepted us, defended us and always made us feel welcome. This is Edgar and my way of simply saying 'thank you' for your goodness and kindness for all these years."

We rose and Kat gave Robert a hug and said, "Thank you for the food and the memory. I'll always cherish the moment."

Robert actually seemed to blush as we departed down the side of the building and back to reality.

We got into the Chevy and Kat simply said, "Wow"!

I drove a little farther up Shake Rag and Kat saw the abandoned brewery that my great, great grandfather had built in 1850, as I proudly shared its history.

"Can we pull in?

I maneuvered the car between the weeds as we walked up the creaking stairs and peaked in the windows.

"You mean no one wants this building?"

"For what?"

"It could be a great art studio. There's plenty of natural light and it's large enough for a kiln and would be a fantastic place to create pottery."

"That's a great idea Kat, but no one comes to Mineral Point. All they do is leave either to get jobs in Madison or in the back of a hearse."

"That's crazy! You have all this natural beauty. All this history and no one wants to live here?"

"Welcome to Mineral Point"

Mad-City

We entered Madison, and I took Kat on a driving tour of the campus showing her Observatory Drive, Camp Randall and Lake Mendota. She was enthralled, noting that it was the most beautiful campus she'd ever seen.

We parked the car and went to the Memorial Union and had Babcock ice cream on the patio. She loved the sailboats gliding across the water. We walked up State Street and into the Capitol rotunda. Kat thought it was more majestic than the U.S. Capitol. We went out on the upper portico and I explained the four lakes, when there are actually five and how the land was originally called Tychobera by the Native Americans and then we walked back down State Street and found the car.

I kept an eye out for the time. I didn't want to be late. We drove out to Tenney Park and watched the locks go up and down, and I explained why Lake Mendota was higher than Monona. We sat on a park bench and I looked at her adding, "I don't want you to go."

"I don't want to go."

"When will I see you again?"

"When can you come to Washington?" "I need to take care of Mrs. Gordon."

There were tears in Katherine's eyes as she asked, "Does this mean goodbye?"

Like an ice-cold dagger in my heart, she had misconstrued what I meant to say. I simply couldn't afford it. My brother was two months late on my land contract payments and my savings account was running low.

"Just the opposite. I want you here forever." "Then what?"

I was embarrassed to tell her the truth, but knew there was no other way. "My brother bought my farm on a land contract, which meant a monthly payment. Times are tough and he hasn't paid me in nearly three months. I simply can't afford it."

Kat looked at me incredulously. "Is that all?"

"Yes!"

"Hank, I have more money than you can imagine. I'll pay your way."

I shook my head 'no'. That was below a man's dignity in my mind. "I can't have you do that."

"You would rather **not** see me than accept my generosity?" Tears welled in my eyes. "It's not the way I was raised."

"Tell you what, I'll loan you the money and when he does pay you, you can pay me back."

I looked at the ground and then the lake and then at Kat. "I'd rather hitch hike or ride the rails than borrow money. I don't want to lose you, but I don't want charity either."

The air was getting chilled. "What about if I come here?"

I bit my lip. "I'm embarrassed by my apartment and the way I live." "Embarrassed? Embarrassed by what?"

"Living where I live."

"You're the richest man I've ever met. Not in material things, but in beauty, grace, sensitivity and personal generosity. Who else would take the time to make a tape of music just for me to listen to? Every day I marvel at your intellect, your passion and how you give of yourself. Every morning I thank God he brought you into my life! Every night, I say my prayers and only ask that you remain you and we stay together."

"How can you be so sure?" I asked.

"Because I can see it, I can feel it and I can appreciate all that you

are."

I took a deep breath. "And you don't mind being associated with a

dirt-poor farmer from Waldwick, Wisconsin, who lives above a diner and listens to music all night long?"

"Mind? Mind? I crave what you have. Don't you see that I'm?" There was a long pause as tears welled in Kat's eyes, "falling in love with you?"

My eyes closed, and I realized the feelings were mutual. I no longer could fathom a life without her. I looked at Kat and took her hands in mine.

"This is something I never thought I'd ever be able to say again in my entire life as I responded. "I'm falling in love with you too! Is this wrong? Am I violating my vows with Ann? I loved her, too."

Kat stared deep into my eyes and asked, "Hank, do you think if Ann were alive she would want you to be happy or sad?"

"Happy!"

Looking out at the water, Kat added. "Hank, she's gone and can't come back and so is Ron. If you truly believe she wanted you to be happy, you'd move on. Keep the memories, but don't let them ever stop you from believing in tomorrow."

I looked at Kat and reluctantly realized she was right. I understood that if it were me who had departed, I would have wanted Ann to find someone else who made her happy. Once again, I took a deep breath, and this time smiled. "You're right!" I quietly announced. "You're very, very right. I just need to accept that never is forever, and that's a long, long time."

I paused for a moment and then continued. "The second you get on that plane, I'll begin counting the minutes until I see you again. We can't rush into anything, but I also know, at the bottom of my heart, I cannot fathom living without you."

My mind wandered as I wondered if I could afford a long-distance romance? Would we really ever get to know each other or would it simply be that when we got together, it would only be *special times*. What would happen when those times were just regular times?

The air cleared, and an agreement was made. We would gradually continue and not rush into anything. It would be a huge adjustment for me in Washington or Kat in Wisconsin, and we needed to 'take time' as Kat said.

I just couldn't believe I could be so emotionally involved with someone I'd only been with three times in my life, and one of them was a funeral. How could this be? Was this a fantasy? Was this an aberration? Would either, or both of us wake up one day and realize it had been a mistake, simply because two lonely people had met each other and needed someone to make them feel special again? How could it be that Kat, with her social realm, wanted to be with someone like me? Would I be holding her back? Would I always be the one people whispered about behind my back, never fitting in, never being what she was, never really understanding that the people she knew who were so much different from the ones that made my life so important to me?

I took a long reluctant breath and looked at my Timex. It was time to go. I smiled a soft smile and regretted that in an instant she would be gone. I knew it wouldn't be forever, and that's what gave me the strength to let her go at all.

We drove out to Truax Field and parked the car, got out and checked her suitcase. I handed Kat the first chapter of 'War of My Brothers'. "Tell me what's right and tell me what's wrong, please."

They called the plane, and I took both of Kat's hands in mine and looked her in the eyes. "Mrs. Johnson, thank you!"

With tears forming in her eyes, she looked at me and said – "Mr. Terrill, thank you too!"

Kat lined up and walked out onto the tarmac. As she reached the top of the stairs, she turned and waived and threw me a kiss. It was what I needed to savor for my lonely drive back to Mineral Point, to Irving and 'War of My Brothers'.

Mrs. Gordon

July came and with it the heat. My brother came through with the past payments and promised it would never happen again. I realized Mrs. Gordon didn't have an air conditioner, so I drove to Madison and went to a place called American TV and bought one of those Fedders room air conditioners. At first, Mrs. Gordon told me to take it back. Instead, I told her I was just protecting my investment. I think she appreciated the fact that, for the first time in her life, she had air conditioning. I looked at the little old lady with a smirk on my face and announced, *"Keep your Fedders up in hot wedder"* which got a silly smirk from my dear friend.

Kat and I talked every week. She knew I was on a budget and so she called me every Sunday night at seven 'Minnie time' as we called it. I appreciated that. She sent back the first chapter with all kinds of notes on it. She said it was called redacting. I thought it incredible how my punctuation was atrocious and my spelling worse. I was just grateful Mrs. Gordon taught history and not English or she would have disowned me.

There was never a discussion of where or when Mrs. Gordon would move and, you know what, I really didn't care. We had a routine. As fall approached, I bought a leaf rake and was ready to clean the yard. As the last leaf fell, I made my way down to the house and rapped three times on the door like I always did, but there wasn't any answer. I rapped a little louder and still no answer! I looked in through the window and it appeared as if Mrs. Gordon was sleeping in her favorite chair as she normally had done. I turned the knob, and the door was, as usual, unlocked and I went into the quiet house.

"Mrs. Gordon!" I called, but there wasn't any answer. I went to her side and gently tapped on her shoulder and there wasn't any response. I realized that my dear friend had gone to be with her beloved husband, Charlie. I called the police, and they came quickly. Next to the phone was a list of numbers and I saw Sarah and John's California 760 area code and phone number. Slowly, I dialed and Sarah answered.

"Sarah, it's Hank Terrill." I didn't need to say any more. She knew her mother's time had come. "I'll take care of all the arrangements." With that, I called Gorgen Funeral Home and took care of the details. I called Kat and gave her the news. Two days later Sarah and John arrived, and I went to Madison to pick them up. I was surprised to see another person with them, one Ms. Katherine Johnson, who was on the same connecting flight from Chicago. What a wonderful gesture!

We had the funeral. It was small, but when you're 93 years old, you don't have a lot of friends. Sarah, John, Katherine and I went to Graceland Cemetery for the last rites and then drove over to Dodgeville to Thym's for lunch. I knew Mrs. Gordon was with us in her favorite restaurant.

Sarah talked about her mother and how she'd call her every Sunday night after 'Bonanza'. I was pleased when Sarah mentioned how much her mother enjoyed my company and always looked forward to my visits. Sarah said Mrs. Gordon considered me to be the son she lost in World War II and I was honored. Kat and Sarah seemed to hit it off and yet, there was a little ice between them. I never did find out why, but then it really didn't matter.

As we sat there, we agreed to a toast and ordered a shot of Korbel for each of us. I think the waitress thought it was strange to have four adults drinking shots of brandy for lunch, but we didn't care and so we ordered a second one and then, quite honestly, a third.

After the toasts, Sarah informed me that Mrs. Gordon had a will, and I was mentioned in it. She noted that I'd given a little old lady someone to talk to, someone to care about, and someone who had been her friend, who took away the loneliness that comes from being all alone.

The next day, we went to Tim Lawler's law office and her will be formally read. I was bequeathed the house and contents, except for family photos and personal items, and also received that beautiful 1958 Chevy Impala.

"Let me pay you." I offered.

Sarah shook her head 'no' saying, "The will was the will and what mom wanted."

I assured everyone it had never been my intent to be included in the will, and they knew I was telling the truth. To make sure, I outlined that we had an initial maintenance agreement, confirmed by a handshake and a brandy toast and all I'd done was live up to my end of the bargain.

Kat and I drove Sarah and John back to Madison as they left that afternoon for California with the promise to return. I knew they never would. I guess California has a way of doing that to people. They go there and never come home.

Kat and I agreed to pack up the rest of the belongings and send them to their address in some town called Escondido. I kept my word and mailed three boxes of photos and letters and never heard from them again.

Kat stayed the week and helped me sort out the rest of the things. It was sad, but sort of fun, as the lyrics to Crosby, Stills, Nash and Young's 'Our House' kept playing over and over in my head. We were becoming domesticated, and it was neat.

I quickly learned that Kat was an incredible cook. We found a small tin box filled with hand-written recipes on 6"x9" note cards. Kat's first meal was Cornish Pasty. We had to drive to Madison to get rutabagas from the Eagle Foods Store on Whitney Way, but she wanted it to be the original recipe. We both agreed that, perhaps in the future, we wouldn't need the rutabagas.

Between the love, kisses and moving 533 records, there wasn't much time for romance, but we did it, moved that is. We agreed to stay in the apartment until we had the house just the way we–make that Kat–liked it, which included taking the back bedroom upstairs and turning it into a combination study and record library, with all my albums stored up there. This made sense because I could listen while I wrote. I broke down and did the corporal thing I vowed I'd never do. I bought a record changer and installed speakers downstairs in the living room. My god! Stacked LP's! What a sacrilege!

Kat and I had a personal house-warming when the contents of the last moving box were put away and the apartment cleaned. Our special night comprised a candlelight dinner with grilled steak, baked potatoes, green beans and pineapple upside-down cake for dessert and a bottle of Pinot Noir that Kat purchased at Riley's liquors in Madison when we went to get the rutabagas.

I started a fire in the fireplace for probably the first time in twenty years, and we relaxed and listened to soft music as we watched the fire glow and toasted our love for each other.

It was time for bed as we climbed the stairs that first night and slid beneath the cool white sheets of what was my new house. I closed my eyes and thanked God for Katherine and then thought of Ann and Mrs. Gordon in heaven, comparing notes and telling tales about yours truly. Finally, I thanked God for that family with four kids who sat in my seat at the Red Rooster that started it all.

Who Am I

Why did I call this book *'War of My Brothers'*? When I was a child every Sunday, we would hook up the wagon in the summer and the sleigh in the winter and come to town and go to church. One of my most memorable bible stories was from the book of Genesis about Cain and Abel.

Cain was the first son of Adam and Eve. Abel was their second son. Cain was a farmer, and I guess that's why I always liked the story. Abel was a shepherd. When it came time to bring an offering to the Lord, Cain brought the Lord a salad and Abel brought the lord meat. The Lord was satisfied with Abel's offering, but didn't take any pleasure in Cain's. So Cain, filled with jealousy, killed his brother. 'Then the Lord said to Cain, 'Where is Abel your brother?' He said, 'I do not know. *Am I my brother's keeper?'*

I thought long and hard about what to call what I'm writing and realized that I'm my brother's keeper, simply because they were the ones who fought the battles and not me. There are no stories about specific heroes, nor about specific military escapades in my book! Instead, this is the story of the battles our town fought simply to exist. Economic battles! Social battles! Political battles! And yes, criminal battles about those who took our family and friends away, only to have them return worn and scarred by what they did, what they saw and what happened to them while they were gone. That is why the title is *'War of My Brothers'*!

For some, it's a story of those who left and never came home. Off to war! Off to seek their fortune elsewhere! Off to escape the wrath of a trusting village, town and hamlet they violated in the name of greed and personal gain. This is the story of the town I grew up in and how each person, each battle, each life twisted and turned our community, just a little to make it different from what it might have been.

Speaking of war, when you're born in 1910, you're too young to be a solider in World War I and too old for World War II and all those that have followed. In World War I, I had two brothers who took up arms you will read about and yet, there are so many other 'brothers in arms' who risked their lives so that we are free and that is what I hope to share with you.

I've chosen to segment my story into increments. Sometimes decades. In others, events so profound that they transcended years and even generations. I decided to begin in the decade before I was born, as it shaped my beginnings and the lives of those around me.

One can't write from memory when they didn't exist and so, with my dear friend Mrs. Gordon gone, I needed to refer to things told to me by others. In addition, I relied on the Mineral Point library and also from a wonderful lady at the Library of Congress in Washington, where my only goal is to explain why I am, what I am, and why I love my family, farm and country. I was born on the family farm in Waldwick, Wisconsin, in 1910. I was the second youngest of seven kids. I grew up in the sandstone house my great grandfather built a long time ago. I lived in that same house filled with love and laughter, frustration and fears until my wife died and I moved away – not far mind you – only to Mineral Point, about five miles from where this story all begins.

It seems funny to be writing things down. I don't know what's come over me, but I have a sneaking hunch. Before leaving the farm, I was walking back from the south pasture one day and had the inclination to stop at the family cemetery on the hill overlooking a place called Skunk Hollow, where our school was and the magical forest that always held my dreams. What beckoned me, I don't know, but stop I did. Chores were calling and yet, for an instant, I needed to look beyond that day and take in a deep breath of solitude.

There was a fence around the plot that was put in place way before my time, and also a rusty metal gate as well. Nothing fancy, just box fencing with wooden posts. My father used to say that they put the fence there because people were just dying to get in.

While no one ever goes to visit my ancestors anymore, the family cemetery is still sacred grounds, not meant for grazing or even walking upon without reverence. That afternoon, I opened the gate and gazed at the headstones and wondered who those people really were and whether their lives were so much different than mine. The weathered stones had seen many summers and winters as no one had been buried - no ashes-to-ashes - dust- to-dust - in the plot since way before I was born. Something about the law, I guess. These folks were all strangers to me. Oh sure, I'd heard their names and who they were. They were part of my family and my heritage and yet, like everyone else, life is for the living and there seems to be little time for the past.

Nearest the gate, I paused at each stone and looked down upon the ground, thinking perhaps a fond memory would come forward. As I came to the last row, or those buried first, I came to the second-to-the-last headstone from the corner. It was that of my great, great grandfather. I peered at his name and looked at the date of his demise. Perhaps that's what sent shivers up and down my spine. It had been exactly 100 years to the day since he passed away. I wondered, had he called me? Why in heaven's name, after all these years of taking things for granted, did I stop today? I peered down and wondered if he was trying to tell me something. So much had changed, and yet so much had remained the same.

I made a vow that I'd write what I could so that the people of my life wouldn't be strangers to those who followed in my footsteps. Where do I begin? How do I begin? What can I say that hasn't already been said?

When you're nearly sixty years old, the who's and what's of those first years of your life are buried deep within so many other memories. Like coats of varnish, time has covered them to the point they rarely show through and yet they are there.

Family

I guess I'll begin at the beginning and hope it gives you some idea about the Terrill farm and the Terrill family and the Terrill history before I'm too old or too senile to talk about it. I hope what I type is clear enough. When you've been farming all your life, your hands get gnarled like the roots of an old oak tree. I'll do my best. My great, great grandfather was George Terrill who emigrated from Cornwall, England where he had been a tin miner. Story has it, his first wife died on the ship coming over and he married Elizabeth, my great, great grandmother, his best friend, Henry's, widowed wife, who was making the journey with them. We've heard tales that there was a rift between George and his brother and that somewhere, we have relatives who spell our family name the old-fashioned way–"Tyrill". None of us ever took the time or had the inclination to try to look them up.

George Terrill came to America with the same dreams as all the other Cornish miners. Once in America, he journeyed to Southwestern, Wisconsin. His intent was to dig within the earth and reap its bounty. Along the way, great, great Grandfather Terrill realized he didn't need to dig so deep, nor be limited to a few narrow spots or the price of ore established in New York City. Where he once plucked the ore, he could plant crops and harvest the bounty year after year, not below ground, but on the surface and from this, he made a life and living that we continue today.

My great grandfather was Henry Terrill. He used to say there was land owned by our family in Virginia. Who knows? It's been so long, we don't know where the land is or whatever happened to it. Sometimes, it's better to let sleeping dogs lie. I was told that great grandpa Henry married a former slave who taught school at Skunk Hollow, the school his father built to make certain all his children had an education.

Henry and his wife moved to Mineral Point and did quite well for themselves. However, when great grandfather's brother, Mathew, died, Henry came back to the farm and realized he didn't want to be anywhere else. I'm named Henry, after that great grandfather who passed away at the age of 80, twelve years before I came into this world.

My grandfather was Thomas Terrill, who was named after a great uncle who died in the Civil War. They say my great uncle's death broke my great, great grandmother Elizabeth's heart, and she died from that - wanting nothing more than to be with her son.

My father was George Terrill the Second. He was named after the man upon whose grave I pondered. My dad was a good man - a hard-working man - a man who only wanted to put bread on the table, have a good laugh every now and then and a pint of beer in town on Saturday night.

Dad believed in four things. He believed in God. He believed in my mother and he believed in his kids and our education. George and Mildred Terrill bore seven children – James (whom we called Jack), William, Irene, Anna, Henry (me), Susan and then Thomas. Jack was the oldest born in 1896. William came a year later. Folks said it was a cold winter and we all still chuckle. Irene was born in 1907, Anna in 1908, me in 1910, Susan in 1911 and Tom in 1915. Behind our parents back, we called Tom, "Ooops"!

Seven Terrill children! Seven of us who shared two bedrooms in the sandstone house! Jack, Will and I, three-to-a-bed. Irene, Anna and Susan in another. Tom with mom and dad. I was born in the farm house my great, great grandfather built. He lived there, great grandfather lived there, grandfather lived there, my dad lived there and my wife Ann and I lived there, as well. The two-foot thick sandstone walls kept much of the heat out in summer and cold in winter. The walls weren't insulated and they had horsehair mixed with lathe for the plaster on the interior walls that had been put there so long ago, no one really knows when it happened.

The house had no closets, only wardrobes, where we hung our clothes which consisted of your work clothes and your Sunday best. Being the second youngest boy, the clothes I wore weren't store-bought, they came from my brothers, carefully stored in the cellar in a cardboard box that had moth balls in it until I outgrew the hand-me-downs that came before and then were put away for my brother, Tom.

The bedrooms were small and only meant for sleeping. The parlor was for company and the kitchen is where we gathered. There is a fireplace in the front room and someone added space heaters in the parlor and kitchen just to take away the chill, but never to keep you warm, that's what coats and sweaters were for. The bedrooms had no heat. In winter, we all slept under goose down comforters. On cold January nights, you could see your breath, but we didn't care. There was never any lollygagging when you went to bed.

The stairs to the house and those to the upstairs were cut from the oak trees on our land. The years had softened their edges, while the nicks and cracks of years of use had given each board its own personality. As one climbed the stairs in winter, each one would give out a small squeak and, even though you were in bed, you could tell who was coming and which stair they were on, simply by the noise each stair made. When it was mom or dad, and we'd been silly, we knew it was time to pretend we were sleeping and that's exactly what we did.

Below the house was the cellar. It was constructed of rocks that were mortared together. Because it was always cool in the basement – never hot and never cold, it was called our root cellar, where we stored vegetables in Ball Mason Jars that mom had prepared that sat on hanging shelves to keep the vermin away. The family worked the farm and got together each night to thank God for his blessings.

As soon as I was old enough and strong enough to carry a pail, my job was to bring water in from the well and go 'fetch the cattle' when it was milking time. We always had a farm dog who slept in the barn who knew what their job was – help bring in the cows.

As soon as Charlie, who was my favorite, saw me, he would get all excited and head for the pasture gate. Chasing cattle was the one way he had fun and he knew when all the cows were in the barn, it was either breakfast or supper time. Charlie would sleep in the barn under the hay. He was our watchdog, too, and would begin growling and barking when a racoon, coyote came moseying around looking for eggs or small chickens they would eat for their dinner.

We didn't have too much time to play, but still had fun. Dad swung a rope on a limb of the old oak tree next to the house and tied an old tire to it so that we had a swing. It was fun to twist the rope and then let it spin around with you inside until you were so dizzy you saw the world go whizzing by. If you didn't wait, you would step out of the swing and fall on the ground.

Summertime meant going down to the stream where grandpa and dad had dug out an area we called the pond. It wasn't very big, but it was cool and refreshing. Because it was spring-fed, it was always cold and so you would jump in and jump out. We always had fun lollygagging by the stream, trying to catch the minnows or tadpoles that swam by. In the Fall, we would rake the leaves into a big pile and jump into them. In the winter we would build snowmen and take some of the coal from the kitchen stove to make eyes, a mouth and buttons. We had an old top hat mom bought at a second- hand store that we put on the snow man's head with sticks for arms and he would serve as the formal guard of our house, although, the door was never locked.

The barn was supposed to be all business, but the hayloft made for fun and we would play hide-and-go-seek or red-rover in there. In Spring and Fall, every Saturday night was bath time. Mom would get out an old wash tub and put it outside the kitchen door by the pump and fill it with warm water she heated on the stove.

When we were young, she'd soap us up and take a sprinkling can and douse us with well water to get all the soap off. In the Winter, we would stand in the kitchen and mom would use a warm, wet towel to wash us and then scrub our hair over an old porcelain tub and rinse it off as well.

My sister, Susan, and I and then Tom took baths together. We did think anything of it as we had done it our entire lives. We only had an outhouse until the 1940's when the house finally got indoor plumbing and we were able to afford a septic tank set in the field behind the house. When your house was already nearly 100 years old, it wasn't designed for an indoor bathroom and so we had to take mom's pantry and turn it into what they call a 'half-bath' today with a toilet and sink. With that, we added a shower stall in the barn with a heat lamp above and that's what I used to take a shower until I moved into town.

I always looked up at my older brothers. They were my heroes. I looked up at my dad too - weathered and beaten by working too long and too hard for too little. In winter, there was the goose down comforter I mentioned to keep us warm. In summer when there was a cool breeze that came up from the valley, that would make the heat tolerable.

Every morning, rain or shine, my job was to fill the wood pile in the kitchen and bring in the water. In Winter, I'd to bring coal in for the space heater, when we could afford coal that is. I also helped pick berries in the Spring, apples in the Fall and cut asparagus when it was time, as well. I quickly learned not to cut it too short because that would kill the plant or leave it too long which meant you wasted someone's dinner. In the Summer, even when you're six years old, you learned how to pull a rake and weed a garden.

Before Susan, Tom and I were old enough to attend, we would watch our brothers and older sisters walk the mile to Skunk

Hollow School and yearn for the day when we could join them. While they were gone, we'd 'help' mom with her chores and try to stay out of her way. It's tough being five years old on a farm.

This is my story and yet, if you don't mind, I want to share a little bit about each of my sisters and brothers so that you have an understanding of who we are and have a little better understanding of me. You see, when you live on a farm, you're all alone a great deal of the time and so you only have your family to talk to, rely on and share good times and bad, happy times and sad.

As I noted, my father believed in education. He always thought that the only difference in most people was how well they were educated. He would say that education allowed you to become 'who' you are instead of 'what' you were - something I've abided by my entire life. All seven of us went to Skunk Hollow elementary school, which sat on the edge of our land in a forest that dad said God put there for eternity. It was a mile from our house to Skunk Hollow and we walked the path everyday as did all the kids who lived on the farms nearby.

There was never a road to Skunk Hollow. As was the custom, the oldest boys at school had the honor of going for water at the spring each morning. This was the reward for perfect attendance or doing well in your classes. Skunk Hollow was used as a school until a few years ago when someone in Madison decided that one room school houses shouldn't be allowed. Instead of teaching compassion or helping those younger or less able, we were to be isolated, segregated and placed in grades whether we needed to be or not.

My three brothers, three sisters and I all attended classes every single day, come rain or shine. We walked the mile to the school house where we learned reading, writing, arithmetic and geography. Mom and dad taught us about animal husbandry, farming and the like. When we were through the eighth grade, we would travel every day into Mineral Point to attend high school. While a lot of farm kids stopped in the eighth grade and others, when they had their high school diploma, it was dad's wishes that we all go to college, even my sisters.

My two oldest sisters, Irene and Anna, graduated from Mineral Point High School, went to Dubuque and studied to be nurses. My two older brothers and I all went to Madison to attend the University of Wisconsin. My little sister, Susan wasn't into school much, but there are reasons and she went to Madison Beauty College and learned to be a beautician while Tom didn't go to college at all because of the depression, but I'll talk about that a little later.

My older brothers were my heroes. Jack could handle our two plow horses Danny and Blue by the time he was 12. William, or Will, as we called him, was our athlete and also a musician. He could hit a baseball further than anyone in Mineral Point and played on the basketball team, where he was the captain. I loved to go and watch my big brothers and dreamt of being just like them.

When times were good, my parents bought a piano. It was used and some of the ivory keys were missing their tops, but it didn't matter. Even though some of us weren't interested and didn't want to practice, our mother required that we all learn to play. Will was always the best piano player and the one who loved it the most. It was his love of music that set the tone for Will's life.

Before the war and even when Will was in Madison at the university, he would come home and, along with my sisters and perform in a musical trio in and around Mineral Point. Will had a real talent and learned to play the trumpet, while Irene played the violin and Anna sang. Some of my favorite memories are from those times when we would all gather round and listen to Will play the piano.

When I was four, Jack left for college. It was a big deal with him going all the way to Madison and college and such. I remember dad having to sell two cows to pay his tuition. The next year Will joined Jack and they lived in Madison in a dormitory. They had to work to pay for incidentals and I know it was tough on the two of them and on my parents, especially when the U.S. Government instituted the Federal Income Tax with the 16th Amendment to the Constitution.

I remember Mrs. Gordon's section on the Civil War where she told us that it prompted the first American income tax in 1861. At first, it was a flat 3% tax on all incomes over $800 which is the same as $3,300.00 today. Congress repealed the income tax in 1872, but the concept didn't disappear.

After the Civil War, the growing industrial and financial markets of the Eastern United States generally prospered along with areas like Mineral Point, which saw the value of lead and zinc increase dramatically. However, the farmers in other areas suffered from low prices for their farm products, and were forced to pay high prices for manufactured goods.

To level the playing field, these farmers formed such political organizations as the Grange, Greenback Party, National Farmers' Alliance, and People's or Populist Party that advocated many reforms including a graduated income tax. In 1894, as part of a high tariff bill, Congress enacted a 2% tax on income over $4,000. The tax was almost immediately struck down by a five-to-four decision of the Supreme Court, even though the Court had upheld the constitutionality of the Civil War tax as recently as 1881.

Although farm organizations denounced the Court's decision as a prime example of the alliance of government and business against the farmer, a general return of agricultural prosperity around the turn of the century softened the farmer's demand for reform. In 1909, progressives in Congress again attached a provision for an income tax to a tariff bill. Conservatives, hoping to kill the idea for good, proposed a constitutional amendment enacting the tax, believing the amendment would never receive ratification by three-fourths of the states.

Much to their surprise, in 1913, the 16th Amendment was ratified by virtually every State, simply because no one thought it was going to affect them due to generous exemptions and deductions and the rate was only one percent of their net income after all the deductions.

I remember my dad sitting at the kitchen table shaking his head and even saying the word 'damn' which was forbidden in our house by my mother. Dad already knew that, once again, the little guy was going to get screwed and it didn't take sore bunions to predict that outcome.

You see, while politicians had promised little effect on the 'middle class' it got tricky simply because the tax was based on net income after allowable deductions. Here the rich folks with savvy accountants figured out how to have so many deductions and make it so complicated they had little or no income at all, while those too poor to make ends meet also escaped the demands of the federal government. This left the rest of us in the middle class to foot the bill for everyone else. In looking back, the government would need to raise money somehow when 1914 produced numerous stories about troubles in Europe.

When you're four years old, anything further away than Dodgeville seemed like the other side of the world. What can I say about all that happened, other than hindsight is always 20/20. By the summer of 1916, with Jack and Will helping at home and getting ready to go back to school, my little sister, Susan, had just turned five and loved to play with the corn cob doll house that Pa made for her. Both of us, knew the wrath of the razor strap for sassing or not doing our chores, but Susan would just laugh it off, even at her age. She was one tough cookie. It was fun watching mom trying to give her a spanking as Susan was faster than dad and one night, when she tried skipping out on doing the dishes and sassed him, out came the strap.

Susan took off and hid behind the parlor doors as dad's temper grew until he looked at mom and she at him and they both burst out laughing. I never knew what was so funny, but I do know Susan thought she was going to get it. It was the last time Pa ever took out the strap to Susan. That summer, she woke up and was having a hard time walking.

I remember mom writing things down that included abnormal reflexes, back stiffness and difficulty lifting her legs when lying flat on her back, along with a stiff neck that she had trouble bending.

Mom was worried about what was going on and took her into Mineral Point to see Doctor Clemens. Susan had polio. Her left leg wasn't working and she was in pain. Mom brought Susan home and all the treatments of hot baths began. Susan's leg was wrapped in a tight cloth that had some kind of ointment on it as she lay on the porch while the rest of the world passed her by. She was only five years old and was a cripple.

Once you contracted the disease, there was no cure. Susan was lucky! Many victims were often isolated in hospitals, away from their families. The only treatment to help Susan was intensive physical therapy including hot baths, scalding hot rocks and painful pulling and pushing of arms and legs that mom did three times each day until mom was exhausted and Susan's tears were dry simply because there were no more to shed.

The love of a mother cannot be explained. Every day, mom would dress the ravaged leg and provide the tenderness and loving care that simply said 'It's all right'. It put confidence in my little sister, giving her the willpower and ambition to simply get better.

We were lucky! Because she was a farm girl, Susan got to stay home, but was forbidden to go into town. Polio was contagious and no one knew where it came from. I really don't know which was worse for Susan, the polio or not being able to be with her friends - an outcast, isolated, quarantined from reality!

A few days after Susan came home, the sheriff came to visit and there was quite a ruckus. Doc Clemens had reported Susan's condition to the authorities and back then, they thought polio was spread by cows. That afternoon a trench was dug and 29 dairy cows were led one-by-one into the trench where they were shot. I remember looking at their eyes and seeing the fear of death in them.

As the pile grew, the resistance got worse as the cows knew their time had come and wanted no part of dying. When the last one was still, dad, Jack and Will began the slow process of throwing dirt upon them. For the first time in 80 years there were no dairy cows on the Terrill farm. I saw the sadness in mom's eyes and the fear in dad's heart. How could the Terrill farm continue on? I don't think Susan ever got over her feeling of guilt. I know she wished it was her in that grave instead of those cows.

Dad gathered us together and said that God would provide, then he hugged his youngest daughter and told her it wasn't her fault and he loved her. When all the cows were buried, big brother Jack asked me to go with him to the forest by Skunk Hollow School. I knew he wanted to share something important. These were our woods. This is where Jack and I went to share our brotherly secrets. There was peace and tranquility and a bond so strong no one could ever break it. Brothers, linked by love for each other! Gone was the difference in ages and experience simply replaced by brotherly love.

I knew it was important because we walked in a rush. Jack, with giant strides and me with smaller steps, walked passed the ancient apple trees and the small schoolhouse and continued through to woods to the point where the water trickled from beneath the sandstone rocks. This was purity! This was innocence! This was where all life began on the Terrill farm!

Jack had always been the quiet one - the one who thought long and hard before opening his mouth. That day, as if it were yesterday, he knelt down and scooped the fresh, clean water in his hands and looked at me. *"This is what's right"* he said. *"Purity and honesty and integrity."* I looked at him with innocent and naïve intent, having no idea what he was talking about until he told me that he and Will were planning on enlisting in the army and, in the fall, going off to war. When you're little, you believed it would be exciting, uniforms and all, seeing what there was beyond Waldwick. You also thought every one you loved would be there forever.

Death was not an element of a kid's life, even on a farm and so I was made to promise to say nary a word and kept that promise. Jack's and my brotherly bond was much greater than the thrill of filling someone's mind with another's secrets. The summer of 1916 was long and hot and because there was no money and Susan having polio, we never went to town. Susan was lucky! She escaped any further ravages with only one leg that wasn't as strong as the other. She was required to stay at home for an entire year. I guess it was her penalty for being sick.

Susan's left leg was withered and they cut the cord in the back so that her foot touched the ground, but she could walk and walk she did. At first, the process was a few steps and with each day she would take a few more. Susan's first goal became the barn and then the pasture behind the barn that had an apple tree in it. She wanted to be able to walk out to that tree in October and pick her own apples. By God, she did it, as we all cheered and mom took the apples Susan picked and baked an apple pie. We couldn't afford it, but dad went to town anyway and brought home ice cream and we had apple pie ala mode to celebrate. It was the best desert I ever tasted in my life.

There were so many memories from back then. I remember mom making ice cold lemonade in a big ceramic jug. Mom would make it and my job was to take it, along with sandwiches, out to the hay makers. Farming was good then and there was even enough money to build a new barn that still stands. Pa was really proud of that barn and Billie and Blue, our horses, finally had an indoor stall to call their own, even though they had cows, cats and Charlie as roommates.

I remember those days as if they were yesterday and not so long ago. I can still hear Billie's hooves going clippity-clop as we went to town every Sunday to go to church and thank God for all that we had, especially our health and each other. After her year away from school, Susan began walking the mile with me to Skunk Hollow and never missed another day, never made an excuse to get out of doing chores and never ever forgot to smile. By the second year, other than a slight limp, you would have never known that she had been ill.

That fall Jack and Will went back to Madison. They would come home on the weekend to help dad with the chores. The new barn that had once been filled with milk cows seemed so desolate and yet, if you've never been a farmer, you don't know anything about the brotherhood that links farmer- to-farmer, man-to-man, family-to-family.

Farmers stick together because we're all kindred spirits! Empty barns meant for cows soon became filled with 'loaners' from neighbors. Heifers would show up in the middle of the night in the back pasture. Proud people don't want charity, yet are always gracious when it meant the difference between earning a living and losing the farm.

Even with times turning bad, my parents still made a point of making a few moments special such as going into town and 'window shopping' as mom called it. On Saturday night we'd have ice cream or go up to the hollows after dinner to visit the neighbors and see the kids we went to school with, but hadn't seen in months.

Susan and I loved to go to Darrow's Old Spring House and would be disappointed if we didn't get one of their delicious cinnamon rolls as a treat. Life was good, but there were storm clouds on the horizon. We all heard about the Zimmerman Telegram where the Mexican Telegraph Company in Galveston, Texas retransmitted a telegram to the German envoy to Mexico saying. *"that if Mexico would enter the war on behalf of the Germans, Texas, New Mexico and Arizona would be given back to Mexico."* Needless to say, there were a lot of really upset Americans.

I remember sitting on the front porch one weekend that Fall when Jack and Will came home from school and told mom and dad that they were going to enlist. The government was talking about a national draft and it was my brothers' way of showing the world they were willing to fight for our freedom. They also knew there wasn't enough money for college for the two of them and it was one way for them to have some reason to take the burden off my parent's plate.

Neither of my parents were happy and yet they knew it solved two purposes - how to afford college and how to serve our country. In January of 1917, the first UW men left for France to serve in the American Field Ambulance Corps. That spring, the University authorized intensive military training to prepare students for officer's commissions.

Every single department offered classes geared towards serving in the war effort. With their farming background, Jack and Will were assigned to the county farm as home agents for training until it was learned that both of them were expert marksmen and they were transferred into the regular infantry, designated for battle. Once Will was transferred and they found out he could play a bugle, he was reassigned as a bugler, but more about that a little later.

My parents were reluctant and yet supported my brothers and when it was time for them to be deployed, the entire family went to Madison to honor my brothers. I was young and I remember it as if it were yesterday. On May 12, 1917, the student cadets marched up State Street from Bascom Hill towards the new capitol building. Camp Randall had been used as training grounds for the Civil War and while some of the grounds had been turned into the football field, it was still where Jack and Will trained.

At graduation in June of 1917, 1105 students received diplomas from the University of Wisconsin. An additional 252 graduates were marked 'absent - in war service' including James and William Terrill. They were still in Madison, but classrooms had given way to boot camp - books-to-rifles - casual days of sailing on Lake Mendota to training in hand-to-hand combat against an enemy no one knew.

Everyone in Madison turned out for the parade. State Street was lined six deep from end to end with a mile-long procession of people who came to honor those going off to war. As the formation made its way, the cheers began with the band playing and people waving as they all marched by.

I didn't really understand where they were going or the things they would do, but I was so proud of my brothers who were going to fight for us.

We stood near the Capitol-end of State Street and waved at the passing convoy of student cadets, hoping to see my brothers as they marched off to where ships would take them to what was then known as the Great War. I saw Jack and waived my American flag with 46 stars on it. Stars for Arizona and New Mexico had been added in 1912, but our family couldn't afford a new flag and I don't believe anyone realized except me.

I think Jack saw me as there was a small smile upon his face, but his eyes were glued to the man in front of him as they ceremoniously marched to what would be some of their oblivion. When the parade had passed, we all got back in the wagon and headed home to Waldwick. Nary a word was spoken! Reality was settling in.

Jack and Will were given three days furlough before they we going to ship out and came home in their dark blue uniforms. Mineral Point wanted to have a parade just for them, as they were already heroes in a town filled with heroes, but my brothers said 'no'. They'd come home to simply say goodbye.

Will had proposed six months earlier to Sarah Fitzsimmons and during the furlough they were married in the Methodist church that my great, great grandfather helped build. I remember Will in his army uniform, all prim and proper, with Jack acting as his best man and Sarah in her white wedding gown. There was a small dinner at the Masonic Temple and then they had their wedding night.

The next morning Jack and Will went back to Madison. We all said goodbye at the bus station. Will and Sarah had a lingering kiss and then the door closed on the bus and we waved goodbye. That summer Susan and I were like two peas in a pod. We would do our chores and then have time for fun. Susan's job was feeding the chickens. She didn't like it much, as they were so aggressive and always pecking at her legs and feet.

We had a rooster named Willie who was really intimidating. He would go after Susan and make her run. One day, Susan had enough and she grabbed Willie by the neck and stuck his head under water in the horse trough to teach him a lesson. The problem was, she tried to teach him too good and when she brought him up, he wasn't breathing. If it had been one of the chickens, it would have meant we were having chicken dinner that night, but not dad's prize rooster.

The look on Susan's face was one of pure panic as I rushed over and grabbed Willie and began pressing on his chest. At first, there was no response and then green, slimy water came oozing out of Willie's mouth and his eyes opened. He looked at me and began to shake. I know that if he could have talked he would have said. "What the hell happened?" Instead, Willie stood up on wobbly legs until he got his bearings and took off for the hen house. I'd saved the rooster's life and Susan's hide, but from then on, that rooster never bothered Susan again.

Speaking of chicken, at the end of summer, it was time for the Mineral Point Fair and mom would make fried chicken with all the fixings for us to take. She was a wonderful cook who would bake pies with apples or berries from our garden, her own biscuits and bread covered in jams and jellies she canned herself.

We loved going to the fair and trying to convince Ma and Pa that we just had to have one of the toy balloons, whips or green celluloid glasses in order for our lives to be complete. Even when there wasn't much money, there was always a little for something for which I've always been grateful. Back then, I didn't realize how bad things really were and how mom and dad went without so that we could have a little something that made the day, the event or the circumstance special.

The War to End All Wars

When you're seven years old and living on a farm, you hear little about what's happening in the world. However, when Archduke Franz Ferdinand, heir to the Austrian throne, was assassinated, everyone knew there was hell to pay. While the death of anyone is tragic, one would never have believed that one assassination could set in motion a series of events that escalated into a full-scale war in just two months that would cost millions of lives and last four years until the final Armistice with Germany in November 1918.

What can one say about a world war that began in a land so far away in countries you had never heard of, that lasted from the time you were seven until the age of eleven? What can one think of a war that saw more than 70 million soldiers become involved, in which nine million died and 21 million more were wounded, along with seven million civilians who never saw another day?

How can a child imagine sixteen million people dead in a state where only two million people lived? How can a child comprehend mayhem and oblivion? Had the war been in America, one-in-six people would have perished. Men, women, children, soldiers! *My Brother's War*, as I've always called it, was one of the deadliest conflicts in history. It affected, infected, corrected and directed all that had been and all that there was to be.

In the beginning, our country, the United State of America, remained neutral but was certainly a very, very long way from being united. President Wilson had been elected because he promised neutrality. As I grew older, I learned that political promises mean nothing.

Many people didn't agree with the government's decision on neutrality, others wanted to enter the war. In the beginning dad said it was all just talk that focused on the differences between the different immigrants.

When you're young, you only believe your dad! When you live on a farm in Waldwick, Wisconsin, your concept of the world is much smaller than that of many. However, I could readily see that the differences seemed more defined as sides were taken and folks really didn't like each other that much.

The threat of war greatly increased the need for zinc, and the Mineral Point mining industry was more than ready to take advantage of rising prices and increased demand. For three years, the miners couldn't mine enough, process enough or sell enough to keep up with what was needed as 5,000 workers pushed the zinc from the hills surrounding town to finished product ready for war, as the money flowed. In my seventh year of existence or 1917, zinc production hit its peak and then began a decline that would literally see the bottom fall out three years later.

All was not good, even in boom times. The Irish, Italians and Norwegians all congregated in towns of their own as did the Cornish and Welsh. In 1917, one-in-four people in Wisconsin were German-Americans! They had either come from Germany or had relatives there and many still spoke German! They were Americans like the rest of us, who all had deep ties to their past and, yet, their homeland, families and friends were about to begin one of the darkest, most vicious wars mankind had ever seen. There were a lot of arguments about the war at home and I remember listening to my dad and other farmers talking about whether America should fight or let it ride.

In any argument, there is always something that tips the scale one way or the other and, for many it was the sinking of the Lusitania. When it happened, Germany and Britain were at war and America was still neutral. It was not like the Germans surprised anybody about what they were going to do.

Before the Lusitania left New York City, Germany declared the seas around the United Kingdom, a war zone. They said that any ship carrying war materials was a target for destruction. America was neutral and yet people knew that the Lusitania carried more than people. Things were so obvious that the German embassy placed newspaper advertisements warning people of the dangers of sailing on that great ship. They believed that humans were being used as shields to protect the most valuable cargo - munitions.

Oh, the ravages of war where lives are moved like pawns upon a chess board allowing sacrifices to be made, all in the name of victory. People either just didn't listen or didn't believe it was going to happen to them. There had been war rules about attacking passenger ships and passengers felt that the rules would protect them and save their lives. Little did they know that in the holds below was stored a lethal dose of innocence. The ship departed from New York City on May 01, 1915 and made it across the Atlantic until, on the afternoon of May seventh, just six days later, and one day from port, a German U-boat torpedoed the Lusitania off the southern coast of Ireland and 1,198 passengers including 128 American's died. Now war was one thing, but sinking a ship filled with women and children was another. At the same time, putting women and children on a ship filled with munitions was yet another.

No one changed sides because right was still right and wrong was still wrong as the ship sank quickly when the hidden munitions below exploded ripping an enormous hole in the bow of the ship and the hearts of many. The spoils of war were strewn upon the white caps of the Atlantic where neither side was lily white, nor neither side totally wrong and the only consequence were the 1198 people swallowed by the sea when the ship went down. And so it began! And so it began - the subtle shift that led to war.

At first there were those who'd seen enough of death and destruction and sincerely believed that the American dream didn't include yet another war. Reality raped innocence, pummeling it, shattering it, destroying it. The Germans took the shackles off its submarine corps allowing them to hunt for anything, everything, unrestricted in warfare. America stood at the precipice. Those who had enough! Those who had families and friends in Germany! Those who couldn't tolerate yet another war realized that, once again, death was at our doorstep and no American ship was safe. And so it was, America declared war on Germany on April 06, 1917.

The country was at war - yet again! Sixty days! Just sixty days and what had been peace was shattered when, on June 5, 1917 American men were called to register for the draft under the Selective Service Act. I was but seven and yet I knew that is was a sad day when boys would leave and return as men some with wounds, some with scars, some with memories of things no man should ever see. They were the lucky ones, as some would never make it back, instead buried deep in the soil of a foreign land to be remembered, yet still forgotten - nothing more than a little white marker, side-by-side, with another soldier who had died - adjacent, complacent, forever marked of what was once a life and would be nothing more than a memory.

As had been the case with the Civil War, Wisconsin men and women were ready to support their country and their freedom. When the State proclaimed "Duty Day" over 122,000 men and women from Wisconsin signed up and served, including my two brothers Thomas and Will who volunteered to serve their country. Fight? Those of Wisconsin did! The Wisconsin National Guardsmen became part of the 32nd 'Red Arrow' Division. Wisconsin men and women served in all branches throughout the world - posturing the belief that we lived in the land of the free and the home of the brave. As the old negro spiritual rang out...'Nobody knows the trouble I've seen'...This was to be a war unlike any other before it. Who would know brutality such as this? How could anyone comprehend the consequence when warriors used modern weaponry against antiquated tactics that resulted in unprecedented levels of carnage and destruction almost beyond comprehension?

I remember the atomic bomb blasts in Japan and their devastation and, yet, while they were horrendous, they were instantaneous. The *War of My Brothers* was one by one, individual by individual, heartbeat by heartbeat as soul after soul after soul was extinguished not by one single blast, but the never-ending incest of inhumanity! How could this possibly happen? It seems that Germany's Schlieffen Plan detailed that if Germany went to war with both France and Russia, Germany had to eliminate one opponent quickly before attacking the other. The plan relied on a strict timetable. France considered Germany to be a threat and defended its northern border to ensure their safety. This meant that any German attack would have to come through Belgium or the Netherlands.

France developed their own invasion strategy called Plan XVII into Germany's industrial Ruhr Valley where they believed that it would cripple Germany's ability to wage war. Russia had their strategy called Plan XIX. The Russian plan called for the mobilization of its armies against both Austria-Hungary and Germany. All three plans created an atmosphere where generals and planning staffs were anxious to take the initiative and seize decisive victories using these elaborate mobilization plans with precise timetables.

Once the mobilization orders were issued, it was understood by both generals and statesmen alike that there was little or no possibility of turning back or a key advantage would be sacrificed. At the beginning of the war, men rode horses into battle. By the end of the war, the horses had been shot or eaten and men rode in tanks. Instead of open battles, trench warfare took place, where armies would be a few hundred yards from each other, simply trying to snipe the other one by one until death did you part.

While there had been previous wars, none had seen the likes of machine guns, tanks, airplanes and chemical weapons from which men were either maimed or died. Four years or carnage! Four years to advance man's brutality towards man!

My God, where was He while all hell took place? While the *War of My Brothers* was fought by most of the countries of Europe, the actual fighting was on many different fronts.

The Western Front was where most of the fighting between Germany and the Allies happened. There, most of the fighting was trench warfare and it was where Jack and Will went to battle. The Eastern Front was fought in Central and Eastern Europe and was one of the main places where the war took place. Fighting on the Eastern Front was not trench warfare, like it was on the Western Front, but depended on having front lines of soldiers ready to fight the enemy who were simply mowed down by machine guns, burned to death or gassed.

When our country declared war on Germany, they simply took the materials left from the Spanish-American war and put them to use. American troops entered the war in the Spring of 1918 as the U.S. mobilized over four million military personnel. As American troops shipped overseas, a group of Wisconsin men suffered a tragedy. On February 5, 1918, the troop ship Tuscania, carrying over 2,000 U.S. soldiers, was sunk by a German U- boat off the northern coast of Ireland, becoming the first U.S. troop ship to be sunk during the war.

The Tuscania carried several components of the 32nd Division, and thus Wisconsin men were found among the more than 200 dead. Fortunately, none were from our area. Jack was assigned to infantry and the 32nd Division, comprised of the Wisconsin and Michigan National Guards. The 32nd was formed on July 18, 1917 and trained at Camp MacArthur, Texas. Jack arrived in France in February 1918 and served at the front from May through the end of the war. Their first duty station, Alsace, put them on German land, making them the first American troops to touch German soil.

The 32nd Division served in three major offensives—the Aisne- Marne, the Oise-Aisne, and the Meuse-Argonne, where Jack was killed in action. The French bestowed anom de guerre on the division—Les Terribles. The men of the division adopted a barred red arrow as their insignia, signifying that they pierced every enemy line they faced. Proudly, the men and women of the Wisconsin National Guard continue to proudly wear the Red Arrow today.

Will was assigned as a bugler to the 42nd Division, made up of units from 26 different states, including a concentration of Wisconsin troops. Its 150th Machine Gun Battalion was largely made up of men detached from the Wisconsin National Guard. Activated in August 1917, the Rainbow Division saw action in the Champagne-Marne, Aisne-Marne, and Meuse-Argonne Offensives, as well as the Battle of Saint-Mihiel.

The war took its toll at home as well as in Europe. During 1917 and 1918, German culture became suspect. Some Wisconsin towns refused to teach German in their schools and German books were burned on Wisconsin streets. Indeed, anyone with a German name was a target for harassment where a widely publicized notice from the American Defense Society stated that any German American, 'unless known by years of association to be absolutely loyal, should be treated as a potential spy.'

Folks in town and those on the farms, banded together to help out with the war. Women and girls joined Red Cross groups to knit, sew and make hospital supplies while the newspapers all pleaded for more knitters. Many a night mom and my sisters would sit by the fireplace and knit until their fingers were numb. The sacrifices didn't stop there. We were in a war and needed to support our sons and brothers as we sent every book and magazine we had to the camps where the men were deployed.

Mom's recipes also changed as she conserved wheat and we ate what was called liberty bread, which mom made using baking powder and cornmeal. It didn't taste very good but it was another way we could support the troops by sending flour overseas to feed our soldiers.

My mother worked with the State Council of Defense as well as a County Council of Defense. These organizations helped to educate citizens on the war and the sacrifices that were demanded of them, such as meatless and wheat-less days. When you're a farmer and are supporting your farm and family that way, going without the food you've grown, that you rely on to pay the bills, shows the level of commitment you had for victory and peace.

I sat at home, young and innocent, wondering, wondering, wondering what it was like to wear a uniform and be a hero. My mother shook her head and hoped and prayed that I'd never need to follow in my brothers' footsteps. To bring me back to reality, mom decided to tell me in detail what it was like to be wounded. Mom knew a lot about medicine. It's necessary when you live on a farm. In addition, she volunteered in Mineral Point to help those who returned battered and torn, broken in mind, body and spirit, praying each and every day that those on the train didn't include her sons. A mother's love never ceases.

I wanted to support my brothers and so mom added a few rows to her garden and told me that all the food I could grow, would be donated to the cause. I was honored and proud of the beans, squash, tomatoes and corn that I was able to grow.

Life wasn't all work! Mom and dad would hook up old Billie and we would go into town to attend patriotic rallies, box socials, picnics and parties to raise Red Cross funds. At the same time, everyone in town bought liberty bonds to help fund the war.

As members of the Women's Nurse Corps came home, they filled my mother with what it was like and she brought the truth home and shared it with me. There were stories told and examples given that took away the romance of war! While she was attempting to eliminate my verve, I hope and pray it was done to ease her soul and remove her remorse. Sadly, she shared how the nurses recounted that they had seen hell with their own eyes.

The intense battle with the new type of weapons and an old style of warfare resulted in some of the worst wounds nurses could hardly imagine. Artillery and gas caused horrendous damage to not only the bodies of soldiers, but their minds, as well, and the wreak of remorse overcame the stench of rotting flesh that burrowed deep within the arms and legs of those who had marched away in valor only to be carried home battered, broken, beleaguered by what had been.

One day I asked my mother again about the soldiers who were wounded and she told me that when a soldier was injured, he was given first aid and removed from the front line, away from the intrusions of hate.

Mom noted that the soldier was sent to the battalion aid post, where they were given anti-tetanus shots and a diagnosis tag, and then sent to the closest ambulance dressing station. At the dressing station, more first aid and shots were given to those who didn't receive it the first time, and then, if their wounds were serious enough, the soldiers were transported to the evacuation hospitals.

Mom looked into my eyes and said that wounds were classified based on probability of survival and yet there was a fine line. If the wound was too great or too small, little attention was given. It was those in the middle who might have a chance who came first! I shuddered in acceptance. War was about death and not about uniforms and parades!

At the evacuation hospital, mom added, the goal was to cycle patients through within 24 hours. If the case was not severe, such as broken bones or flesh wounds, the cases were only given minimal treatment and sent to what was called the Shock Ward, which was a tent kept where the temperature was kept at 90 degrees. Here, the nurses kept patients under warm blankets and gave them hot liquids, while administering shots to fight infection as they changed their dressings.

Mom continued, noting that severe cases that required surgery, if there was a chance for survival, were operated on at the evacuation hospital and given priority. If it was deemed that there was no chance the soldier would live, they were given morphine to control their pain and stop their moaning and crying until they died. Then they were taken to the cemetery and buried next to another soldier who had met the same fate. Some days there were few, other days there would be so many that the grave diggers simply couldn't keep up.

If the soldier's religion was known, they would be buried beside those who with whom they had prayed to God for survival. It not, then it was side by side until the row was filled and the grave diggers began again - another day - another row - another grave.

Mom said it was normal that 25% of the casualties were serious enough to require surgery. Following surgery, if the soldier was still alive, they would remain in the evacuation hospital until they were stable enough to be transported to a base hospital which was even further from the front. At base hospitals, the care level, and time that someone stayed, increased until the soldier either went back to war or went home.

Mom said that base hospitals were the backbone of the medical core, located several miles behind the front so that they were out of the way of artillery. When the soldier was to the point that it was believed he could tolerate travel, he would head for home - battered, broken and scarred, a mere shadow of what had been. Physically he was altered. Mentally, he would never be the same. The haunts of death would be with him forever. The moans of wounded comrades would puncture his ears and whisper to him in the night, awakening him, reminding him, ensuring him that he had truly been to hell.

Sadly, at that time, the war was not going well and my brothers were split up. They were both in the infantry, but the army wouldn't allow brothers to fight side by side. I guess they thought it was too big of a risk. How quiet the streets of freedom when the soldiers marched away. How lonely the valor that one expresses when solitude comes your way. How sad, the faces of mothers and brothers who see their sons depart. War is not about victory, but sadness in one's heart.

After the boys left, mom or dad would go into town each week and check to see if there was any news or letters. The saddest look on my dad's face would be when he would come home and shake his head no - nothing had come. Letters arrived from New Jersey and mom hoped that my brothers would be OK. Regardless, mom was a nervous wreck and each week she or dad would go into town to the post office to get the mail. Both would read the letters my brothers sent until I thought they would wear the ink out.

I was eight years old and it was a warm July day in 1918 when two men in uniform rode up on horseback. Mom let out a yelp that only a mother can make. She knew that one of her boys was gone. I stood outside and watched the two men approach the front door. Mom put her apron to her face as they read the letter from the President of the United States saying that their son James Terrill had died fighting for his country and presenting mom with a medal. One medal - one life!

Mom sat down on the stoop and cried. I ran out into the field and got dad. He could tell by the expression on my face that something was terribly wrong as he went running to the house. Mom's head was propped against the door jamb with the letter still in her hand. Dad grasped the letter from the President telling one set of parents that their son died in action in France and wouldn't be coming home. He was buried with honors in a field called Verdun.

That night the house stood as quiet as it had ever been. I knew better than to say a word and so Susan and I did our chores, lit our lanterns, went to our rooms and said our prayers. The next morning the neighbors began arriving with food and condolences.

Word spread throughout Waldwick and Mineral Point that one of their own was not coming home. Chores were forgotten, tasks deferred, smiles sequestered all in the name of James Terrill. For those who had their own boys at war, I can only imagine that they got down on their knees and prayed to God that it would only be the Terrill boy and not theirs who would give his life for their country. Twenty-three times, the horsemen made their call. Twenty-three times Mineral Point's church bells rang and tears trickled down cheeks as mothers and fathers held each other and said goodbye. Besides Jack, others from Wisconsin who went to war never came home.

Of the 110,000 soldiers who died, 1,800 were from Wisconsin and 90 were from Dodge County. Of the 204,000 wounded, nearly 300 came from Dodge County, including my brother, Will. The 'Great War' was so much more than men and machine and Newton was oh so right. - *for every action, there is an equal and opposite reaction.*

From a few years of incredibly intense hatred that spewed forth like a volcanic diatribe, the global social, emotional and financial consequences were such that I, a simple farm boy from Waldwick Wisconsin, could hardly imagine they were sowing seeds for the great depression, a rise of Fascism and the Second World War, all of which I lived through.

Sadness can be such a lonely place. Yet in Waldwick and Mineral Point people came together to hold each other up and provide strength so that they could go on. In late summer, as the war was nearing its end, Will's, wife Sarah, came to the house. She had received word that Will was on his way home. The letter said that he had been wounded. That's all it said.

Mom, dad and Sarah took the wagon and drove to Madison. Our Aunt Ruth came to stay with Susan, Tom and me and the neighbors came and milked the cows. Two days later, I saw the buggy as it headed up the drive. Dad was driving with Will sitting next to him and mom and Sarah in the back. I thought everything was fine until they got to the house and dad pulled the horses to a stop. Dad got down and went around and helped Will off the buggy. Sarah came and grabbed his arm and led him into the house with Will using his other hand to make certain there was nothing in front of him.

Will's physical wounds were his eyes. He had been blinded by poison gas and couldn't see. I'd never seen a blind man before and stood and watched as Will settled in with awkward smiles upon his face. His eyes were closed and his shoulders stooped. In twenty-four months he had aged fifty years. Death of others had also wounded Will inside and that was the most painful part of all.

My brother, who had been so full of life, came home a broken man, filled with the guilt, shame, anger and isolation of killing men he didn't know and watching those he did close their eyes one last time, taking with them every single bit of passion they had and shredding it into emotional strips to form scars that would last forever. Will called my name and I approached him.

Will stuck out what had been a powerful hand capable of lifting huge bales of hay and I put mine in his. Instead of muscles and callouses his hands were as soft as butter. Will reached up and felt my shoulders and tried to reach the top of my head but I was too tall for him to reach sitting down. His head cocked to one side and he leaned in and whispered to me, *"Don't ever go to war!"*

That night Will and Sarah slept in our old room as man and wife. I'm certain there were tears of both joy and sorrow. I'm certain that they knew not what lie ahead. I'm certain that Will offered to annul the marriage and I'm certain that Sarah said no. Farming is not for a blind man and so Sarah and Will found a tiny house in Mineral Point with a large front porch where Will could sit and listen to the world go by. The government gave him a small pension and Sarah got a job at Burgess Battery. They saved their money and were the first people in Mineral Point to own a wireless radio. It allowed Will to while away the hours simply waiting to die. They would come to church with us each Sunday, Will with his red-tipped, white cane and we would go and visit them whenever possible filling him in on the baseball and basketball teams.

Will and Sarah had three children, Will Junior, Annabelle and Mary, who understood and accepted their father was blind. But then, when it's all you know, what else can you do? Will died at age forty-five. Some say he died of a broken heart. Others say he just went to be with his brother. I believe he lived a full life filled with the joy of having a wife and children who loved him, accepted him and never let being blind come between him and this thing called life.

Sarah still lives in the little house and her kids and grandkids keep her life filled with smiles and memories. None of us know what tomorrow will bring. All we can do is talk of life and accept the challenges it provides. At eleven AM, on the eleventh day of the eleventh month of 1918 the Great War came to an end. Armistice Day was affirmed by the peace treaty signed between the Allies and Germany at Compiegne, France for the cessation of hostilities on the Western Front.

Word spread fast, punctuated by the sound of the Milwaukee Road train's whistle as it steamed into town with its whistle going full blast. Word had already been sent by telegraph before the train arrived, yet that whistle seemed to make it final as shortly thereafter, the bells on our Methodist Church rang out that the local sons and brothers were finally out of harm's way and would soon be home.

As word spread, everyone stopped doing what they were doing and crowded into the streets. Food was left uneaten, haircuts only half done, conversations abruptly stopped as the joy of peace transcended the hearts and souls of those who had waited for the war to end. We could hear the church bells ringing and factory whistles blowing all the way to Waldwick and we knew what had happened. We begged dad to take us into town and he obliged as we listened to the Mineral Point band play and watched a huge bonfire burn in Jerusalem Park.

Times had been good for our little town because of the war, which had sparked a two-pronged economic boom. First, the demand for zinc exploded. Second, the demand for agricultural products rose to unheard of levels as war-ravaged countries in Europe could no longer produce their own needed supplies. This demand for food created a shortage that drove up prices for farm commodities.

In Iowa County, the season-average price per bushel of corn rose from fifty-nine cents in 1914 to $1.30 in 1919, while the average price of hogs increased from $7.40 to $16.70 and milk from $1.50 to $2.95 per hundred weight. To meet the demand, the U.S. government encouraged farmers to produce more. In 1916, Congress passed the Federal Farm Loan Act, creating twelve federal land banks to provide long-term loans for farm expansion. Believing that the boom would continue, many farmers took advantage of this and other loan opportunities to invest in land, tractors, and other new labor-saving equipment at interest rates ranging from 5% to 7%. By 1920, 52.4% of all farmers carried mortgage debt. We didn't.

After the U.S. entered the war in 1917 and continuing into the post- war years, 40 million acres of uncultivated land in the U.S. went under the plow, including 30 million acres in the wheat and corn producing states of the Midwest. The demand for land inflated the price of farm real estate, regardless of quality. The average price of farm land more than doubled between 1910 and 1920, from $46 to $109 per acre.

After the end of the war, relief efforts kept the demand for U.S. agricultural products high. Gross exports of all grains in 1918–1919 totaled one-half billion bushels. During that period, the U.S. shipped more than 2.9 billion pounds of pork, 1.1 billion pounds of beef, and nearly 8.8 million pounds of dairy products to allied countries, various relief programs, and American Expeditionary Forces overseas.

Another export consisted of those who were born and raised in our town and had survived war's wrath. The war had changed them just as much as our town had changed with them. Sadly, their hopes and dreams no longer included Mineral Point, as they sought their future elsewhere where there were more jobs, more opportunities and a different way of life from whence they came. Times were good as farmers continued to produce more, expecting demand and prices to remain stable. However, as Europe began to recover, the U.S. farm economy began its long downward trend.

The Spanish Flu

How can I explain the loneliness of isolation? When one lives on a farm, it's just you, your family and God. Social graces aren't really learned, and talking to yourself only becomes a challenge when you end up in an argument. When you wanted anything 'social' you went 'to town'. However, when you're a freshman in high school, you went every weekday, until going to town wasn't special anymore.

In late 1918, the Spanish Flu roared into Mineral Point like it did in all of America and everything changed! The stores were empty, the lights were out, bars and restaurants stood silent, devoid of the rhythm of laughter. Schools, churches, movie theaters were all dark. No music played, no church bells rang. The only thing moving thing on the streets of Mineral Point was the wind. Sadly, there was no one around to feel its chill. If you were brave enough, foolish enough, or dumb enough to go into town, you were struck by the eerie solitude caused by the lack of traffic on foot, hoof or even the periodic automobile, all rushing to simply get away.

If you attempted to support one of the local businesses that was brave enough, foolish enough or broke enough to remain open, you had to marvel at how the transaction felt almost illicit - almost like some back-alley deal conducted through a little used side door. You stood alone, looking at others, watching them breathe, hoping and praying they didn't sneeze and send fear roaring your way, as they stared back, idly watching, awaiting their turn, as nothing moved, except the wind. This is how it was from February 1918 to late summer 1919.

The Spanish Flu was infecting one-third of the world – enveloping, eroding, destroying civilization, if that's what you called the ravaged remains of a brutal war. Each wave of the four successive tsunamis murdered more, where those who thought they'd escaped God's wrath faced its peril until somewhere between seventeen and fifty million and even as high as one- hundred million people lie motionless, eyes blankly staring at heaven - destroyed by an enemy they couldn't see nor feel, until it was simply too late.

Some say it started in Kansas or New York City in December 1917. Others say it began at Camp Greene, North Carolina, and came home with returning soldiers who were just happy to be back from the Great War. No one really knew! In September 1918, the epidemic reached Wisconsin and Mineral Point. By December, influenza had sickened almost 103,000 Wisconsin residents with 8,459 residents eventually dying, resulting in more deaths than all those killed in World War I, the Korean War and the hated Vietnam War so far. Critics bellowed, "People should have been informed and prepared!" Hindsight is always 20/20.

Sadly, to maintain morale regarding World War I, government censors withheld information to minimize the fear of the flu invasion. The first Amendment was curtailed 'for the good of the nation'. Newspapers were allowed to report on the epidemic's effects in Spain, giving rise to the name 'Spanish' flu. It really wasn't from there and the belief that the end was 'just around the corner' and 'this will magically disappear' were profoundly false.

The pandemic stopped, but then it didn't. For some it meant caution. For others, simply an inconvenience, as they sincerely believed the Spanish flu would never affect them. Some cities hunkered down. Other cities kept going as if it was just another autumn with falling leaves and death hiding behind the next cough. September, 1918 was a brutal month that truly marked the beginning of the end for thousands of people. Philadelphia held their Liberty Bond Parade to promote the government bonds that were being issued to pay for the World War. Attended by over 200,000 people and featuring John Philip Sousa, folks were standing side by side cheering on the bands and saluting each time the Stars and Stripes marched by, all-a-flutter with its 48 stars making everyone so proud, with no one realizing the consequence! The parade passed and the silence of death marched on.

Within seventy-two hours of the last step of the last band, deaths spiked as those packed so close together huddled in the incubator of misery. Pennsylvania learned its lesson and on October 3rd, the State ordered all theaters and saloons closed, while adding schools and churches to the list.

Sadly, it was too late! In just one week, 4,500 people died in Philadelphia alone. The march of death continued on as massive crowds gathered to celebrate the end of the 'War to End All Wars' with the signing of the Armistice on Nov. 11, 2018. There was no warning! There were no restrictions! There was nothing, simply because the government felt 'the absolute imperative was to sustain morale.'

Newspapers beat the drum to create the cadence of the death march as they enthusiastically participated to the point that 'no bad news was allowed' perpetuating the spirit that lingered after the tragic human war to 'allow the nation to heal', when in fact, it did just the opposite. While a few newspapers reported the peril, others like The New York Sun, wrote of families welcoming returning military personnel they didn't even know into their homes for dinner. What was becoming a medical tragedy was evolving into a political football as potential 1920 candidates for the presidency jockeyed for position. Public health be damned! All that mattered was the power, prestige and perks that came with governing others.

Competing newspapers took sides depending on their editorial board and who they were backing in the next election. They slanted their stories to appeal to those who believed the pandemic was real and those who didn't – filtering truth and skewing it to fit what they felt would appeal to those who read their daily news – enticing them, seducing them, moving them to-and-fro, simply to have them fit the editorial perspectives they clamored for, thereby allowing the newspaper to generate more advertising revenue.

Because of the 'Great War', people had already lived through rationing and watching loved ones be maimed or die. With the flu, they began to see others expire in front of their eyes as every day became the ultimate hardship with people reeling from their total immersion in sadness. Like so many other calamities, some folks believed the illness was reserved for others and certainly not them. Their lack of concern wasn't really surprising.

Many people sincerely believed what was happening was simply the 'flu.' They were familiar with its symptoms, but not aware that some exotic plague they were about to encounter, had different symptoms and circumstances. Sadly, the nation had no organized response from the federal government. There were no standards! There were no ultimatums!

Somehow, somewhere, someone believed that political boundaries could stop the disease and it should be left up to the communities to decide how to fight the insipient aggressor. Decisions were left to the states and local governments who feebly attempted to enact rules and regulations that differed from states to towns to counties to cities and even wards within each city.

Rules and regulations were established and controlled not by medical experts, but by politicians who thought they knew more than those who really knew. There was no consideration for supplies or even consistent planning and resource allocation. Like a farmer trying to plow at night, many had no idea where they were going or what they were doing as sons and daughters, fathers and mothers, grandfathers and grandmothers became morbid statistics in the dark field of death.

While some cities required folks to wear masks, others only shut down theaters and saloons, simply mentioning the importance of getting fresh air and exercise. This seemed to work until opposition by retailers, theater owners, unions, mass transportation companies and other economically stressed businesses forced politicians to rescind safety in the name of commerce and ensure re-election of the politically aligned, when the time came.

Deep down, Mineral Point was once-again on the verge of becoming a vibrant city bustling with life, still rebuilding from the roller-coaster decades of financial upheaval. Many felt the town couldn't survive another financial debacle. Sadly, the desired tranquility was a façade as fear slowly crept from house-to-house as friends became strangers and associates became threats. Families went into self-isolation, packing themselves away until further notice – sealing their lives within the confines of just each other – hiding behind closed curtains, where they would hopefully safely await the latest news, all the time wondering how long their isolation could last. Each day meant measuring their stockpile of singularity while gauging their eventual exposure when supplies were gone and they, too, would need to be exposed – naked to the ravages, both real and imagined, that swirled around their town and their imaginations.

Rancor erupted! Disbelievers prevailed simply because they knew of no one who had been affected, thereby concluding the pandemic had magically missed Mineral Point and they were safe or believing the media had simply sensationalized everything to sell more newspapers. Some folks even believed the rumor that the Spanish flu was only hard on people of color and those who were marginalized - too poor to pay to fight back, along with the elderly 'who were near their end anyway.'

Sadly and with profound disregard, Mineral Point celebrated the end of the Great War. People were anxious to forget the epidemic they didn't quite understand. A walk down High Street on a Saturday, found the sidewalk cluttered with people abiding intermeshed with others refusing to wear masks or keeping safe distances from each other. Tempers flared as the disbelievers protested the intrusion arguing that masks took away the freedoms of the Constitution and the democracy our boys had fought for in the Great War. Others simply refused the obligation, calling the masks feminine or silly and 'not for real men'.

Life went on all over America as dark clouds of death accumulated on the horizon. People looked up, but the threats didn't stop them from celebrating the holidays. 'Best Thanksgiving in History of City,' proclaimed a headline in the New York Sun. Philadelphia, despite a day long chilly drizzle, was the venue for Thanksgiving parades, sporting events, and 'flag raisings.' Sadly, it didn't stop at the local level. Mask-less, President Woodrow

Wilson, in his annual Thanksgiving proclamation, didn't even mention the flu, which he later contracted himself. In other cities Thanksgiving rituals brought a welcome sense of normalcy. Many Americans returned to religious services, performed charity work and went through with planned football games, parties and performances.

Newspapers wrote, 'The chimes of church bells will once more be heard throughout the city, beckoning one and all to attend their chosen place of worship, where a double celebration will be held, first over the suppression of autocracy and second, over the eradication of a frightful plague. People are urging others to be considerate of one another and care for one another. There are messages of putting the smallness of the individual into perspective, replacing it with the vastness of humanity.'

Like sheep to slaughter, folks went back to their daily lives. Not knowing! Not realizing! Not understanding that death swirled at their doorstep. In Wisconsin, health officials concentrated on preventing the flu's spread through public information campaigns. It was only when reality struck that local authorities printed posters and the State Board of Health issued quarterly bulletins on the progress of the disease, as well as information on how to prevent its spread, where the only booming business was that of engraving headstones.

As time progressed and the intensity of the calamity raised its ugly head, the leaders in Mineral Point began to accept reality as they ordained various local quarantines while mourning departed loved ones, finally implementing curfews as the entire town locked down for weeks at a time. Life stood still, temporarily closing the schools, library, theater, dance hall, churches, ice cream parlor and soda shop. 'Stay home and stay safe,' was the warning, while going to town became off limits and the security of isolation afforded by living on the farm somewhat gave us a sense of security.

While the risks were less, life was still a sacrifice for dairy farmers. There was no way to sell milk that dad simply poured in the fields to make way for the next day's disappointment. Ma and Pa concurred with what transpired. They'd seen enough death and wanted none of it.

Even though people knew that most of the time regular flu killed the very young and very old, the Spanish flu was reported as different, murdering those in-between and they didn't want to take any chances. All one needed was to take a walk-through City Cemetery and read the markers and they could see the ravages of the past where the names of so many are etched in yesterday with the word 'flu' engraved upon their headstone. The viral storm raged on.

The December 6th, Daily News in St. Paul, Minnesota announced that more than 40 Minneapolis schools were closed with the headline 'SANTA CLAUS IS DOWN WITH THE FLU,' as Minnesota health officials asked 'moving picture show' managers to exclude children, while they closed Sunday schools and ordered department stores to dispense with 'Santa Claus programs.' In Mineral Point, there was a brief two-week respite in early December and relieved residents hoped the storm had passed.

Tragically, the pandemic didn't go away, roaring back with a vengeance by mid-December. No Merry Christmas! No church! No bells! No joy! Grave diggers were told to 'Dig those graves before the ground freezes and we have to store remains of loved ones on ice until spring arrives!'

Immediate death and closure is tragic enough. Waiting for the Spring thaw to close the emotional book had to be profoundly heartbreaking! Unhappy New Year arrived! In the first six months of 1919, influenza deaths matched the annual totals of 1915, 1916, and 1917. Finally, the vicious maelstrom began to subside.

Why had this happened? Perhaps the outbreak had been caused by malnourishment, overcrowded hospitals or even poor hygiene, all magnified by the end of the Great War and the return of bedraggled soldiers – alive, but dead – surviving, but carrying a deadly superinfection that killed most victims, in a slow, agonizing march that took the last gasps of life and squeezed until they were no more. By late summer, the Spanish Flu was beginning to subside in Southwestern Wisconsin as people opened doors and windows and life slowly began to trickle back towards normalcy.

The post-mortem by medical experts said the pandemic wouldn't have lasted as long or been as deadly had people only kept to themselves, wore masks and kept their distance. Perhaps next time! Death is always reserved for someone else and not for the living! In the end, the wrath of God killed 675,000 Americans. Even I knew death's meaning – an absolute hole that can never be filled – except with tears and memories.

Out in the country, you were away from the infected and the only risk was when you went to town and so we simply didn't go. Farming continued, but there were very dark clouds on the horizon. With heavy debts to pay and improved farming practices and equipment that made farming easier to work more land, farmers found it hard to reduce production. The resulting surpluses caused farm prices to plummet. From 1919 to 1920, corn tumbled from $1.30 per bushel to forty-seven cents, a drop of more than 63 percent while the price of hogs dropped to $12.90 per hundred weight and like all our neighbors, we were hurting.

The Roaring Twenties

The 1920s was a decade of change, when many Americans began owning cars, radios, and telephones, but not the Terrill family early on. Prosperity was on the rise in cities and towns, but not on the farms and social change was in the air where fellow farmers were leaving their farms in order to receive a regular paycheck in the factories.

Unions were on the rise. Women shortened, or 'bobbed' their hair, flappers danced and wore short fancy dresses, and men shaved off their beards, except dad of course and me. Dad because he was stubborn and me because I've never been able to grow one that didn't have bare spots all over my face.

In 1920, I turned ten years old. Late that year, the mining industry was struck by one of the steepest depressions of all time. Ore that sold for

$135 per ton in 1918 was bringing less than $30 per ton by 1921. Those who had speculated were wiped out. Those who had been careful and frugal accepted the fact that Mineral Point had ten glorious years of incredible prosperity that allowed the town to stabilize and grow.

During the 'Zinc Years' all the streets had been paved with asphalt, the city library opened, a new municipal building was constructed, the waterworks was enlarged, a system of garbage collection was created, all night electric street lights were installed and Mineral Point residents got free mail delivery right to their house. When times were tough, there was no need to stop building simply because the improvements that had begun were already been paid for. Chalk one up to those politicians. They got one right! With the end of the war, our focus turned to peacetime pursuits.

Gone were the knitting needles and social functions to raise funds for war bonds as tranquility seeped its way back into everyday life. While the demands of war had allowed for abnormal growth and prosperity during the times of strife, no one seemed to mind that the rewards weren't as profound, simply because the fear of war had been relinquished. No more knocks on the doors by uniformed soldiers! No more mothers with aprons to their faces hoping, wishing, praying the letter they were handed wasn't true. There's more to life than prosperity and nothing more valuable than feeling safe and secure.

By 1921, both farming and mining had 'settled in' to normal peacetime activities. The area mining industry continued, albeit at a less frenetic pace, while farm prices temporarily improved.

As the years rolled by, changes took place on our farm. First, my two older sisters graduated from high school and because of the war and farming being good, mom and dad were able to afford to send both of them to nursing school in Dubuque, Iowa.

Had farming remained the same. Had prices remained high. Had, oh hell, why even think about it? Like everything else in life, the only thing that is constant beside death and taxes is change and Mineral Point's roller- coaster economy that had been scooting along on the peaks of prosperity was about to hit one of the deepest slopes in its 100-year existence.

My sister, Irene, finished her education and stayed in Dubuque. She married a man who was going to be a priest until he met her. I've seen them many times and really have never met finer people. There's never an argument or a hard word towards anyone or each other.

Irene remained a nurse until her own children came along, and then she stayed home to raise them. Their son must have gotten the same genes as my brother, Will, as he was an outstanding baseball player and is full of the same mischief as my brother, Jack. He joined the Marines and was a drill instructor. Word was he set some kind of record for the most sit-ups ever done by a Marine.

Irene and her husband also have a daughter who became a nurse and married a teacher, and they moved to Cedar Rapids, Iowa. Another set of really good people. The apple didn't fall far from the tree, my mom would say. I love it when they all come to visit, as they remind me of mom and dad. So full of dignity, honesty and compassion. Such a wonderful family!

My sister, Anna also became a nurse, but then you know that! She always had the wanderlust and went to Alaska and California, where she met a man who went to work for the government in Washington DC. Anna had no children.

In 1949 she and her husband were is a horrific car accident that should have killed them both. Word has it there was a bee in the car and her husband tried to swat it. Anna spent months in the hospital and had over a dozen surgeries to try to reconstruct her face. It ended up all scarred, and she was always embarrassed by the way she looked. She was always beautiful to me. Kind of heart and quick of wit. She and her husband would come home and I know she was reluctant at first, but like Will, life had thrown her a curve and she never let it get her down.

At Christmas and Easter they would call long distance from Washington DC and each of their nieces and nephews would have time to talk to them, but were told to keep it brief, because it cost money to talk long distance on the telephone.

My little sister, Susan, never got any more polio than that in her leg. She lost a year in school and yet she pushed on. She lives to laugh and I sit in awe of her spunk. Although she walks with a slight limp, she became a beauty operator and lives in Madison with her three children. Her husband died young, and yet you never see her without a smile on her face or a song in her heart. Tommy was five in 1920 and just beginning school in Skunk Hollow.

1920 saw the last American troops return from Europe to families, friends, and jobs. Most of the soldiers had never been far from home before the war and their experiences changed their perspective of life and they wanted some finer things for their families that they saw in Europe.

In August, the Nineteenth Amendment was passed, giving women the right to vote. I remember how excited mom was because she believed she finally had a say in the way our country should be run and planned on voting for better roads and better education for us kids.

Music styles were also changing.

In 1922 Louis Armstrong started improvising and adding personal musical variations with his trumpet playing in a style known as jazz, and I became hooked on music. At age twelve, I worked my butt off to save enough money to buy a used Victor talking machine, where you'd turn the crank that spun the records at 78 RPM's and play the tunes that I simply loved. Mom and dad weren't too happy and made me play my music in the barn, but it made no matter except it made the cows skittish unless I played something slow, which rarely happened.

In 1924, Congress passed a law that made all American Indians citizens of the United States. The Fourteenth Amendment had already given colored people citizenship in 1866. It never ceases to amaze me that it was their land, and it took 150 years to recognize them as citizens and not captives of our society and culture.

In 1925 the flappers found a new dance craze, called the Charleston. I was fifteen and could do quite the dance, starting with a simple twisting of my feet to the rhythm in a lazy sort of way that quickly became a fast-kicking step where I was kicking my feet both forward and backward and then reversing my hands between my knees. It was fun and the girls loved it and that's how I got up enough courage to ask what became my wife to go out on our first date to the World Theater on High Street.

Mineral Point's economy was being elevated by the updraft of the 'roaring twenties' measured by new businesses and new buildings, such as the Wisconsin Power and Light building in 1924, the post office and high school in 1925 and two new industries that focused on farming called the Mineral Point Canning Company and the Sanitary Creamery.

In 1927 *'The Jazz Singer'* became the first successful "talking picture." Before that time, motion pictures had been silent. We went to Madison to see it at the Capitol Theater and couldn't believe our eyes. There was a man on the big screen named Al Jolson and boy could he sing.

In 1928 Mickey Mouse first appeared in the cartoon *'Steamboat Willie'*. Little did Mickey realize that in 1955 an entire amusement park in California called Disneyland would open with another being built right now in central Florida of all places called Disneyworld. I don't know who thought of that place with mosquitos, snakes and alligators, along with humidity that makes Waldwick's worst summer day seem filled with a soft summer breeze.

Aviation represented another area in which things were changing the world. In 1927, Charles Lindbergh flew solo from New York to Paris, and in 1928, Amelia Earhart became the first woman to fly across the Atlantic Ocean. They had my imagination and dreams of flying with them as I always wanted to see the world.

The Left Hook and Right Cross.

While many people thought progress had passed us by on the farm because we still were using horses to plow and had no electricity or indoor plumbing, the thrill of wealth never became an addiction and so the pain of failure also never inflicted its wrath in my father's soul.

Tractors, electricity and toilets were all considered luxuries, and it was something we just couldn't afford, even though times were good and farm revenue was the best it had ever been. I reached full physical maturity and was doing the work of most men. Like my brothers, I enjoyed exercise and began the regimen of 100 push-ups, 100 sit-ups and 50 pull-ups each day, something I'm proud to say, I continue to this day.

Because farming is a seasonal event where you're the busiest in Spring and Fall, any chance of playing football just didn't exist. I was needed on the farm. During the winter, when things slowed down, I took part in wrestling. Never any good at basketball, I took my size and strength and used it to compete. At first, I was in the 125 to 132-pound class, then as I filled out, the 150-160-pound class.

As the Mineral Point wrestling squad competed, our fame grew and so did our heads, I'm embarrassed to say. We were tough, but not that tough and yet, we kept winning. As we reached our championship series, I hoped mom and dad could take time to come and watch me wrestle. As I looked around the gymnasium, I saw the two of them sitting in the bleachers anxiously waiting for my match. I was so proud they came to see me, I almost pee'd my pants. Unfortunately, I was wresting Johnny Dodge who went on to win State in our weight class who pinned me with a quick double leg takedown.

I put up a good fight, but he was faster, stronger and two years older than me. As the match ended and the entire team tucked their tails between our legs, mom and dad came down to get me.

My head was bowed as I was embarrassed. Pa said, "First, you didn't use your legs properly and so he had a leverage advantage on you. Second, when he was about to pin you, I think you could have spun around and kicked his legs out from beneath him or used a half-Nelson, arm bar or cradle on him. Other than that, for your first year, against that kid, you did pretty good."

I sat shocked. Dad had actually watched the match and realized my errors. I never knew he'd wrestled when he was in high school, as he never brought it up. He promised to work with me and was always one to keep his promises. Sure enough, we built a ring in the barn and began training. I vowed, no one was ever going to beat me again.

After a few months of training, dad showed up with a pair of boxing gloves. "If you're going to learn to wrestle, you're going to need to learn how to box." I was shocked, never seeing any correlation between the two sports, until I put on a set of gloves. As he taught me, I began to see how the motion and stamina of one would help the other in terms of balance and reaction time.

As the weeks went by, dad began teaching me all about jabs, hooks and upper cuts and the importance of footwork and how each punch was directly related to how and where my feet were placed for maximum efficiency and force. He also shared with me the secret of wrist twisting to create maximum power.

After a few weeks, we went to town and dad bought some rope. I thought he needed it for the farm. It was for me to use to increase my overall speed, endurance and dexterity. It was then that I realized dad was working with me on my agility and speed to help me be a better wrestler.

One day, a leather punching bag was set up and I began pounding on it. A few weeks later, he bought what we called a speed ball, which was an inflated leather ball on a hook. By summer's end, I was proficient enough on my punches and footwork that I felt ready to compete in boxing. Mom and dad told me they didn't want me doing that. It had all been to overcome the shortcomings dad had seen in one wrestling match.

The winter of 1921, I was in the 160-pound class. I was faster and more proficient and had learned about leverage. As the matches came, so did my victories and with it, my reputation. No matter where or when there was a match, two people were always there in the gym watching me, cheering for me, supporting me – mom and dad. Afterward, dad would talk me through the match outlining the opportunities I took advantage of and the mistakes I made – not to criticize me, but to make me aware of areas I could improve. There's a big difference between the two and I appreciated the help I was getting.

I went to State and got beat in the finals, but never forgot the time and attention my dad gave me and the pride that showed whenever he saw me in my Mineral Point jacket with the "MP" letter with the gold wrestling pins on it. In the end, dad had given me a lesson of life that I've always tried to live by, "Never think you'll be the best, but always try to do your best."

Jumping Rope

One day, Susan was out in the barn and saw the rope hanging on a hook and began slowly jumping. Even with a gimpy leg, she was brave enough, determined enough, and stubborn enough to never give up. At first, she would jump until tears came in her eyes as she counted each repetition and remembered each failure. As she increased from five to ten to twenty to fifty, Susan's confidence grew and with it, her dexterity as her "limp" began to slowly disappear. Susan was beating polio at its own game. As Fall came, Susan got to fifty repetitions without an error. As December approached, she asked mom and dad to buy what was called a stop watch for Christmas that would measure how long it took for her fifty repetitions to take place. I don't know where the money came from, but Santa brought Susan her that stop watch.

After our Christmas dinner, Susan made her way out to the barn with her Christmas gift. Pressing the little button on the watch and seeing the hands spin, her goal became taking less time to complete the fifty repetitions. Some days were faster and there would be a broad smile on her face. Other days, the timing would be slower, followed by one simple word, "Again." And she would do another fifty and then do it again and again and again.

While I was a wrestler, Susan was the real fighter. After a year at home, separated from family friends and considered a polio outcast, Susan was held back a year at school, which she never forgot. Susan pushed and pushed and pushed and, by high school, she wasn't handicapped, she was an athlete, accomplishing something no woman in Wisconsin had ever done before–winning a high school athletic letter as a cheerleader.

My little sister! My little sister, who was isolated for a year and lived the nightmare of watching the family farm in jeopardy because of her malady. My little sister who had polio and couldn't walk straight. My little sister who sat alone with during the Spanish flu with no friends, no electricity and no indoor plumbing, wondering if that was what hell was really like, walked across the graduation stage at Mineral Point High School, head held high with teachers and fellow students alike, standing and cheering for the little girl, stronger, tougher, braver than them all.

Mr. Big

My entire life, I knew farming was all I ever wanted to do. While some folks in Mineral Point were enjoying relative prosperity, depression for the American farmer quietly began right after World War I as the never-ending cycle of debt stemming from falling farm prices and the need to purchase machinery kept quietly eating away at every nickel they could make.

We weren't alone! The town of Mineral Point wasn't spared, as the gradual evolution from mining to farming resulted in farming playing an ever- increasing role in the wellbeing of the community simply because, for the very first time in 100 years, there was no additional source to give the town the boost it had seen so many times before.

As surpluses mounted, the federal government promoted lowering production, creating programs designed to help stabilize prices. The government's goal was to achieve parity – to bring prices back to prewar levels and equalize the prices farmers received with the prices they paid for goods. The passage of the Capper-Volstead Act on February 18, 1922 legalized the sale of farm commodities through farmer owned cooperatives, cutting out the middlemen who often underpaid farmers for their products.

Congress also passed the Agricultural Appropriations Act later that year, creating the U.S. Bureau of Agricultural Economics for economic research and with it, the government got more involved in agriculture. Foreign trade restrictions, such as the 1922 Fordney–McCumber Tariff, imposed high taxes on imports in an attempt to protect U.S. farms and industry.

International trading partners reacted by increasing import fees on American goods to the point that U.S. export of farm products declined, surpluses grew and prices continued to drop. With no electricity, we had to milk cows by hand and this meant dad and I doing all the work, as we couldn't afford to hire milkers.

With high school over, the thought of my going to college went out the window. My parents couldn't afford the tuition and needed me to help around the farm. With falling prices, dad realized we needed to produce more from the same land and couldn't rely on hands and horses to do the work. We needed to purchase a tractor, along with a plow and harrow to break up the soil and smooth out the surface. We did our homework, as this was to be the biggest gamble of dad's life.

We knew that there was no need looking at huge steam tractors that weighed between 20,000 and 30,000 pounds and were very expensive. We started looking at Hart-Parr, International Harvester, Case, and Rumely and were inclined to buy the Harvester when a rumor spread that Henry Ford was introducing the Fordson model that reduced the weight to 2000-6000 pounds and cost under $1000. We thought we had the answer and started saving our pennies when Ford initiated a price war that cut the price from $625 to $395.

Reports surfaced that the Fordson was excellent for plowing and harrowing and quite capable of driving mowers and reapers but wasn't very good for cultivating corn and cotton. I looked at dad and he at me and there was a nod and we both knew it was time to buy.

For the first time in his life, dad went to the bank to borrow money. Sadly, he was turned down. It wasn't because of bad credit. It was because so many farmers were struggling to repay loans for land that had lost its value. If depressed land and commodity prices weren't bad enough, increases in property taxes, freight rates, and labor costs added to the family's financial hardship as Iowa County farmers began to default on their loans.

Those around us weren't alone. Six percent of all farmers in the U.S. either lost their farms or filed for bankruptcy. We needed that tractor and $395 was a great price. Dad was forlorn when the Ford dealer told him he too was sorry, but couldn't extend credit.

We went home and mom saw the dismay. Instead of giving up, mom went into town to visit the Ford dealer and offered to work for him doing his books as he needed someone to handle his finances. The Ford dealer knew he had us over a barrel and while the average wage for a common laborer in Mineral Point was forty-cents per hour, he offered mom twenty-five cents an hour for the grand total of ten dollars per week. However, instead of paying her wages, he would extend credit on the tractor and harrow for a total of 500.00 and use mom's weekly wage to pay it off. It meant mom would work for nearly a year, but we would have the tractor we so desperately needed.

The Ford dealer was a heavy-set, make that fat man, who wore a white shirt that was one size too small that had the buttons bulging and was always hanging out of his pants. His neck tie was always loose and even in the winter, he would sweat profusely. Never did we see him without a half- chewed cigar hanging out of his mouth and his suspenders had never been cleaned. Dad didn't trust him and yet, he had us over a barrel.

At first, all mom did was keep the books. Soon Mr. Big, as we began calling him, realized that mom had more skills than just book keeping and made her office manager with a raise to thirty-five cents an hour. Mom had it all figured out that she needed to work for eight months to pay for the tractor.

Mr. Big always went out for lunch one day and a fellow farmer walked in while he was gone and wanted to know about the Fordson. Mom took it upon herself to show him all the details and when Mr. Big returned, mom was writing up the contract. It was her last day as office manager and her first day selling tractors. No one in Mineral Point would have ever believed that a woman could be a salesperson, especially selling tractors. Mr. Big continued to pay mom thirty-five cents an hour and ten dollars on each tractor she sold. The one-year timetable quickly eroded and in six and one-half months the tractor would be fully paid for.

Even when the note was marked 'paid in full', Mom kept working for Mr. Big. One Thursday, Mr. Big went to lunch, had a couple too many drinks and came back and got fresh with mom. She high tailed it out of the showroom and when she got home early, all in a tizzy and flustered, dad took after Mr. Ford with a bull whip and shot gun and scared the ever loving be-Jesus out of him. I wasn't there, but heard tell that Mr. Ford was crying and begging for mercy when the police showed up to calm things down.

Needless to say, we didn't buy any Ford parts in Mineral Point and had to go all the way to Barneveld for service and mom didn't go back to work for him.

Mr. Big had always acted like he was too big for his britches, both literally and figuratively, until one day in 1928 when Ford Motor Company pulled the plug on everything. You see, production of tractors was always a sidelight to Henry Ford's business of manufacturing automobiles and the Fordson production lines were needed to make the Model-A. In a matter of days, Ford Motor Company left the tractor business and our Mr. Big had nothing to sell. At first, he looked for another brand, but no one would take him as the Ford Motor Company price war had destroyed so many dealers and so many other brands that any association with Ford, especially when you thought you were high and mighty, meant no one wanted to do business with you.

One night, Mr. Big slipped out of town with the bill and tax collectors on his tail. Word has it, he went to Colorado and when the crash of 1929 struck, he lost everything he'd stolen from so many people in Mineral Point and simply disappeared, half-chewed cigar and all.

As I noted, farming never was as lucrative after World War I. First, the changes in technology with tractors instead of horses, secondly, electricity and other devices created a glut of supply and limited demand. When you're a dairy farmer, any way to speed up the milking process meant all the difference in the world. To that end, the surge milker was invented in 1922 by Herbert McCornack. It sat on the ground under the cow and was always exposed to the cow kicking it.

A later model hung below the cow by a strap that went around its body where the advantage was that the tubing from the teat to the bucket was only about 4 inches long. This lessened the risk of contamination within the tube and when the cow was finished milking, the tubes automatically fell off. Also, hanging there eliminated the risk of having the cow kick the bucket. The machines increased productivity which allowed for more cows in the same milking time, which meant more milk.

There was only one problem – you needed electricity to run the milker. Even though Wisconsin Power and Light expanded beyond Mineral Point and the lines ran near our house, we didn't have any electricity. Our herd was small and there were two of us and we continued to do it by hand. Speaking of productivity, besides the temperance movement, a number of other forces joined together to force Prohibition on America. The woman suffragists, were all for it because of the negative effect alcohol had on the family. Industrialists wanted prohibition because they were keen on increasing the efficiency of their workers who wouldn't have hang-overs or be drinking on the job. In January of 1920, the Volstead Act went into effect with a total of 1,520 Federal Prohibition agents given its enforcement for the entire nation. Good luck!

For the first time in American history common, law-abiding citizens became criminals simply for doing what they'd been doing their entire lives and, for the first time since the Civil War, belief in the government that had been so strong during the World War I took a turn for the worse. Called Prohibition, the Volstad Act didn't making drinking alcohol illegal, it made the manufacture, importation, sale, and transport of alcohol, defined as one with greater than 0.5% alcohol, illegal in the United

States. However, like most laws there were this's and that's which ended up making the entire limitation a farce.

Section 29 of the Volstead Act allowed wine and cider to be made from fruit at home, but not beer. The Act didn't prohibit consumption of alcohol and those with money stockpiled wines and liquors for their personal use before the law went into effect. It also allowed for the sale of sacramental wine to priests, ministers and rabbis for Sabbath and holiday use, along with consumption at home, thereby allowing for abuses in the system, with imposters and unauthorized agents using loopholes to purchase wine.

Since alcohol was legal in neighboring countries, distilleries and breweries in Canada, Mexico, and the Caribbean flourished as their products were either consumed by visiting Americans or smuggled into the United States illegally. The Detroit River, which forms part of the U.S. border with Canada, was notoriously difficult to control, especially from Windsor, Canada.

When the U.S. government complained to the British that American law was being undermined by officials in Nassau, Bahamas, the head of the British Colonial Office refused to intervene. There was even a rumor that the father of one of our Presidents made a huge fortune 'importing' brandy from Canada during Prohibition. The net result of this misguided law, that virtually everyone ignored, was the rise in crime with organized gangs like Al Capone's that continues to run rampant through every major city, compounded with the loss of absolute belief in the laws of the land.

The Volstead Act specifically allowed individual farmers to make certain wines 'on the premise that it was a nonintoxicating fruit juice for home consumption' and many of us did just that, making 'fruit juice' out of apples, grapes, dandelions and rhubarb, while others used malt, hops and their wives yeast to create their own beer. The county sheriff knew about it, but he had other things to worry about. As long as it was for 'personal consumption' farmers were, for the most part, left alone, including us.

Dr. Banks

I graduated from Mineral Point high school in June 1928. I really wasn't interested in going to college, but mom and dad said there was no discussion, I was going. Both my brothers had started and never finished because of World War I. My older sisters went to school and were nurses, and my parents were determined that their two other sons would be college graduates.

Because of mom's experience at the Fordson dealer, she had a reputation of being good with numbers and was offered a job at the Iowa County Bank and used the income for my tuition. I was on my own regarding room and board. The first year went well, and I did fine. I enjoyed my classes and worked as a busboy in one of the 'hoity-toity' dorms that catered to the rich East Coast kids whose parents had money.

I guess when you're poor, you can tolerate almost anything, including the taunts. You can be called so many names, so many times like hick and plowboy until you get used to it. The job was too important to screw up, simply because these clowns needed someone to look down on.

I worked with a colored fella by the name of Clarence Banks, who was in pre-med. Clarence was following in the footsteps of William Smith Noland, who was the first known colored person to graduate with a B.A. from the University of Wisconsin in 1875. Clarence kept to himself and listened to all the names he was called, of which 'boy' was the one that I saw get him most riled up.

Clarence, not once sassed back or let the rich, white boys know they were getting under his skin. He quietly seethed at their indiscretions. Part of our deal at the dorm was we got our meals included. We'd sit in the kitchen with the cooks and eat our food. It wasn't great, but better than nothing.

As Clarence and I worked side by side, I learned that Clarence's dad worked on the railroad as a porter and that it was a terrible job. All the time it was "Yes sir, no sir!" "Yes mam, no mam," while he was thinking "Shove it up your ass mam!" Clarence said that at first, his dad had nowhere to sleep and would 'catch forty winks' crouched down between rail cars. While working conditions were terrible the money was half-decent.

Under the leadership of A. Philip Randolph, over 10,000 porters formed the first all-colored union, the Brotherhood of Sleeping Car Porters, in 1925 that expanded to include parlor and dining cars.

Clarence said that his dad worked hard so that his kids could go to college. He noted that, being from Milwaukee, he always wanted to go to school in Madison, while his brothers went to 'all-colored' colleges in the south.

After a few days, I forgot we weren't the same color. It made no difference to me. Clarence was not only a good guy, but hard working and very intelligent. As we took a break, there would be times when he'd tutor me in math, which was my weakest subject.

As we cleared the tables, there was one fella who got under both of our skins. His name was Hatfield, from New York City. Hatfield would do anything and everything to insult us and belittle who we were. One day, he called Clarence, "Jim", and it caught Clarence off guard.

"Heh, Jim," Hatfield said. "You think you're going to be a fancy doctor. I can see it now – Doctor Jim Crow taking care of them colored folks, but never getting to vote. Heh Jim, do you think you're good enough to take care of white folks, too?"

Clarence had enough and put the dirty plates down. I could tell there was going to be trouble. Now a colored boy getting in a fight would mean he'd lose his job and perhaps go to jail, even in Madison. For me, well, it might mean unemployment, but satisfaction.

I stepped between Clarence and Hatfield and told Hatfield that he needed to keep his mouth shut. Hatfield told me to "get back in the kitchen **boy**, you're nothing more than a white nigger."

I paused and reflected on college. I thought about my mother working to pay my tuition and then I thought about Clarence's dad riding the rails – "Yes mam, no mam," and it was enough. I looked down at the ground and then at Hatfield. I was going to pop him right then and there when I felt Clarence's hand on my arm. "Tis enough, Hank. Tis enough!"

"Not this time Clarence. I'm sick and tired of being insulted by this piece of shit."

With that Hatfield stood up and I realized he was a good four inches taller and thirty pounds heavier than me. "Not here! Not now!" I exclaimed. "Chicken shit, why don't you go back to the kitchen and clean those

dirty dishes before I kick your nigger-loving ass – BOY!"

"Not this time! Not anymore! You want a piece of me and you think you're man enough to do it, now's your chance," I replied.

With that, Hatfield took a swing and missed. I looked at him and laughed. "Come on, smart ass. You want to fight, bring it on!"

Hatfield took another swing and I ducked.

"You can insult us all you want, but you're not man enough to fight!" I announced.

Hatfield's temper caught the best of him and he came in close with another swing. I hit him with the left hook and then the right cross that dad taught me and watched the son of a bitch's knees buckle as he lunged at me. Like a fool, he came again. This time, instead of boxing, I put him in a head lock, spun him around, used my hip for leverage I learned from wrestling and tossed him on the floor as I decreed, "Get up, you son of a bitch and the next punch will splatter that big fucking nose of yours all over your face."

I looked at his cronies and could tell that they were intimidated as I announced to them, "if any of you EVER insult my friend again, I'll take each and every one of you on and won't be as easy as I've been on this pathetic pussy."

Hatfield reached for my foot and I saw it coming. I jammed my boot down on his wrist and watched him writhe in pain just as the dorm's resident assistant came running through the door. "What in hell is going on here?" the RA commanded.

"Go ahead, Hatfield, tell him what you've been saying. Better yet, tell him about the three times you took a swing at me and I had to defend myself."

The RA looked at the assemblage and inquired if it was true. It was then that I learned most of his dorm mates couldn't stand Hatfield and all nodded in the affirmative. "Terrill, to my office now!" was the command. With that I departed as the room was a-buzz in muted excitement, wondering of how I took a guy larger than me who had pushed his way around and simply beat the crap out of him.

We made it to the RA's office and he looked at me asking "You OK?" "Sure, he never got to me."

"Bout time someone put him in his place. I suppose I should reprimand you or something, but for what? For defending Clarence? For fighting back? You did what any good man should do, you stood up to a bully and he took the first swing."

I looked down at the ground and then at the RA. "I shouldn't have lost my temper and I'm sorry for that."

"No apologies needed. Did he really swing three times?"

"Yes, sir".

"Did he ever hit you?" "No, sir!"

The RA chuckled. "I don't know what's going to happen tomorrow, but right now all I can say is I'm sorry I missed it. I'll tell you this, Hatfield is coming in next and given two options. Option one is that he either stops insulting people or he's out of here and option two is that the next time he insults you or

Clarence, you have my permission to kick the ever-loving shit out of him and I'll stand there and applaud. Now get back out there and eat your dinner."

The conversation was over and my fears were gone as the RA and I both stood and he smiled and shook my hand. "Remind me never to get you pissed at me."

"Sir, you don't have to worry about that. I don't think you're that type of person."

"Thank you, Henry. Enjoy your supper."

I walked back through the dining room with all eyes on me. As Hatfield was about to speak, the RA called, "Hatfield, in my office NOW!"

Clarence had all the dishes cleared and they were in the washing machine when I entered to a soft round of applause from the kitchen staff. They appreciated the fact that someone finally stood up for them.

Clarence looked at me and said, "Thank you." " You're welcome, Doctor Banks, Now let's eat!"

Doctor Banks and I remain friends today. He volunteered for the Army Medical Corps during World War II and saved the lives of dozens of men, both colored and white, who didn't seem to mind that a negro, was keeping them alive, until after the war that is, when they wouldn't let the doctor and his family live next door.

Never is Forever, and That's a Long, Long Time

I'll never forget Tuesday, October 29, 1929. I was a sophomore at the UW when Black Tuesday hit Wall Street as investors traded some sixteen- million shares on the New York Stock Exchange in a single day. Billions of dollars were lost, wiping out thousands of investors.

One of my classes was Macro Economics, or how the global economy worked. We all knew that during the 1920s, the U.S. stock market had undergone rapid expansion, with everyone but farmers speculating on anything and everything in their quest to get rich quick, with most sincerely believing it would never end. Right before classes were to begin that fall, the stock market hit its peak. Unbeknownst to the suckers and losers who bet everything on tomorrow, production had already declined and unemployment had begun to rise, leaving stocks in great excess of their real value.

People were betting everything. Even though wages were low, there was a tremendous proliferation of debt. Farmers were still hurting, and there was an excess of large bank loans that couldn't be liquidated. Those watching the market realized that stock prices began to decline in September and early October 1929, and on October 18th the fall began. Panic set in, and on Black Thursday, October 24th, a record of nearly thirteen million shares were traded.

Investment companies and leading bankers attempted to stabilize the market by buying up great blocks of stock, which produced a moderate rally. However, on Monday the storm broke anew and the market went into free fall. Black Monday was followed by Black Tuesday in which stock prices collapsed completely and nearly 16.5 million shares were traded on the New York Stock Exchange in a single day.

Billions of dollars were lost, wiping out thousands of investors. The stock ticker tapes ran hours behind because the machinery couldn't handle the tremendous volume of trading as people bailed, trying to save what they could. Almost like drowning, they grasped for whatever they could hoping they wouldn't be taken under. Some thought it was temporary and that an 'adjustment would be forthwith'. It never happened! Prices continued to drop as the United States slumped into the Great Depression and three years later, stocks were worth only about 20% of their 1929 value.

Mineral Point was not spared, nor was our family. We didn't have a dime in the stock market but low food prices resulted in less income which resulted in the loss of things we had become accustomed to.

First to go was the electricity. Not because we didn't need it, but because we couldn't afford it and we went back to milking by hand. Next to go was the Fordson tractor. We had it, but at eleven cents a gallon for fuel, we couldn't afford to operate it. Finally, the last thing to go was our dignity, except that mom and dad paid all their bills, albeit sometimes late, but everyone got paid. I wanted to quit school and come help on the farm, but mom and dad did what they could to keep me enrolled as I scrounged for anyway to make money.

My altercation with Hatfield resulted in quite a reputation. I learned I could earn five dollars for simply getting in the ring and boxing three rounds against someone else too hungry to care, too anxious to worry and to confident to believe that it would them lying in the middle of that canvas ring, blood oozing from their nose, to the raucous cheers of those who paid a dime simply to see two men fight.

Twenty times, I climbed between the ropes. Eighteen times I walked away, battered and bruised, but not broken, carefully stuffing my five-dollar bill in my trousers to give me another week where I could eat, another week where I could learn, another week when I was still alive.

Hatfield's father had been one of the biggest speculators and bet everything on the stock market and with it the high lifestyle that Hatfield attested as his birthright. When the market crashed, Hatfield's father went to the roof of the stock exchange for solace and looked to heaven for forgiveness and took that one last step to eternity. The following morning, the RA called Hatfield to his room and informed him of his father's demise. At first, there was denial, then disbelief. As reality set in, the boy who thought he knew it all, had it all and believed it would never end, quietly packed his case and slipped out the back door of the dormitory. Some say he went back to New York. Others say he went West. Still others believed that he tried riding the rails, was robbed and dumped from a moving train never to be seen or heard from again.

At home, Susan gave up on the idea of becoming a nurse and went to beauty school simply because she could complete the classes in six weeks and then try to find work instead of two years of nursing school. She moved to Madison and we would get together the one year we both were there. Lead had petered out decades before as the surface veins were mined and those that ran deep were too thin to make them valuable.

In 1928, the zinc works was going gangbusters with high market prices and over 200 men producing oxide every day. In 1929, Mineral Point watched the last gasps of mining in Wisconsin as less than half the ore processed two years prior went through the smelter.

One year later the Mineral Point Zinc Company locked its doors for good and 150 men and their families found themselves without work, without food and with hope for a better tomorrow. Worse than any previous downturn, the Great Depression wiped away not only a way of life, but a lifeline for the community to cling to until the next surge in demand in either food or ore would salvage those hopes and dreams one more time.

With doors of opportunity closed, the eerie sound of nothing rattled the windows of the once bustling town as the noise of the ore laden trains, wagons and trucks of the oxide factory, acid plant and mining machinery were silenced and then forever gone. The mining industry upon which MINERAL Point had been established, forever changed, never to fully recover. Gone was a century of mining history as the minerals formed for millions of years were scraped away in less than one hundred, leaving behind empty holes and empty dreams filled with the sweat and tears of those whose dreams were forever lost.

As the hills gave out their last gasp and the industry upon which the community, the county and the state evaporated, all that was left were struggling farmers too poor to quickly recover, too proud to walk away and too stubborn to simply move on. Our town became a farm town whose peaks and valleys became dependent on the wind and rain, sun and snow and sadly, the government.

I'd hitchhike home from school to see a town that reminded me of an old man - slow in tempo, now old and shabby and out-of-date, frayed out upon the ridges, simply begging for more. As I looked out upon the dotted hills, I'd watch the wind blow the wild flowers and long grasses that covered the eastern slopes growing high besides abandoned ore dumps, leaning across dark pits in the hillsides that once teamed with men who only had a dream that created the nickname for our State – Badgers.

The 1920's represented an era of change and growth. The decade was one of learning and exploration. America had become a world power and was no longer considered just another former British colony. American culture, such as books, movies, and Broadway theater, was being exported to the rest of the world. World War I had left Europe on the decline and America on the rise. The decade of the 1920s helped establish America's position in respect to the rest of the world, through its industry, inventions, and creativity in all areas including farming.

The American Nightmare

While in high school we learned about the American Dream" stated as the belief that each American had the freedom to pursue a better life motivated by "rags to riches" stories. This premise held true until the Great Depression, and then things began to change.

Alexis De Tocqueville came to the United States during the 1830s primarily to answer the question, "Why are the Americans doing so well with democracy when other countries weren't and then, what happens to the American dream when one of the pillars crumbles?

De Tocqueville identified several factors that influenced America's success — abundant and fertile land, countless opportunities for people to acquire land and make a living, lack of a feudal aristocracy that blocked the ambitious, and the independent spirit encouraged by frontier living.

The American political culture that De Tocqueville described had changed in the one-hundred years since he first observed it. However, in many ways, it had remained remarkably the same. The American view was characterized by several familiar elements. The first is liberty. Most Americans believe in the right to be free, as long as another's rights weren't abused, which was exemplified by the Civil War. The second is equality. This translates into "equality of opportunity," not absolute equality, which has been a dark part of the American legacy in terms of Native Americans and people of color. Third is democracy. In America, elected officials are accountable to the people, and citizens have the responsibility to choose their officials thoughtfully and wisely and do so through their right to vote for whom they think will best lead the people. Fourth is what De Tocqueville called 'The Rule of Law'. The U.S. government is based on a body of law applied equally and fairly, not on the whims of a ruler.

Despite some current negative attitudes toward the government, the fifth point is nationalism. Most Americans are proud of its past and tend to de-emphasize problems, such as intolerance, military or social setbacks, including the belief that we're stronger and more virtuous than other nations.

The sixth point is individualism. We believe that individual's rights are valued above those of the government to where individual initiative and responsibility are strongly encouraged. Finally, there is capitalism. It is the heart of the American Dream, based on beliefs in the right to own private property and to compete freely in open markets with as little government involvement as possible.

The Great Depression challenged the American Dream and changed the lives of people who lived during this time and changed America as well, particularly for the fifth and sixth points of De Tocqueville's hypothesis. Nowhere is that easier to see than in agriculture, where government programs that helped people live through the 1930s changed the future of agriculture and the agrarian society and the American Dream forever.

The 'Dirty 30s was a terrible time, where weather touched every part of life with dust, insects, summer heat and winter cold like no one had ever imagined. Iowa County farm families didn't have heat, light or indoor bathrooms like people who lived in town and that only made things worse than it was. Many farm families raised most of their own food – eggs, chickens, milk, beef from their own cattle and vegetables from their gardens. Those of us who grew up during these times realized that we weren't alone in terms of the struggles we faced as no one had any money.

Neighbors helped each other through hard times, sickness, and accidents. Farm families got together at school programs, church dinners, or dances. Children and adults found ways to have fun for free – playing board games, listening to the radio or going to free outdoor movies in town. When the weather destroyed the crops, farmers were left with no money to buy groceries or make farm payments. Some people lost hope and moved away. Many took government jobs building roads and bridges, waiting for electricity to make farm life easier and safer.

After the stock market crash, Americans cut back their spending on clothes, household items and cars. Instead of seasonal changes of wardrobe, even the rich folks bought clothes that could be worn for years. Old cars were patched up and kept running. From clothing and automobiles to architecture and interior design, the aim was to 'use it up, wear it out, make it do, or go without.' Many people including those in Mineral Point, had to acclimate to unemployment or low pay. Farmers left their land and searched for work in the cities.

In the early 1930's charities in the cities had to help the starving and homeless, many of them were arriving from rural areas, until the charities themselves ran out of money. A lot happened in Mineral Point during the 1930's that only cemented the community as a farm town and not the financial center it wanted to be. In the end, the changes curtailed aspirations, but allowed the community to actually survive.

I received my UW degree in 1932 and headed home to help on the farm. The depression was as grim as one could imagine. It affected our family and those of our neighbors plus our town and state, just like everywhere else. While there had been peaks and valleys before in Mineral Point, the combination of agriculture and mining had always been such to keep the town going. The Great Depression saw depressed farm prices and a huge drop in the demand for ore. Just like in the ring – the economic left hook followed by a right cross that floored everyone in town. For me, there were no jobs, no opportunity and certainly no belief that things were going to get any better.

There's an old saying, when you're in a hole, stop digging! America, in 1932 was certainly in a deep hole. A year later, nearly half of America's banks had failed, and unemployment was approaching 30%. Still Ann and I decided to get married.

Back in high school there was a saying about girls who got pregnant – they were 'in trouble' and those who didn't get pregnant were 'good girls'. The only difference between good girls and those 'in trouble' was how careful they were. It's not what they did that made the difference or even how often. It was just either luck or planning. We had a very small wedding consisting of Ann's parents and mine and my sister Susan.

Our "honeymoon" meant a night in the hayloft because that's all we could afford. We lived with my parents and I farmed as Ann looked for a job.

Eight months later our son Scott arrived. Surprise! I think mom knew and dad didn't care as long as I made Ann an 'honest woman'.

Our only salvation was having a radio. Dad bought a Crosley in 1927 when he sold a couple of cows. Radio allowed America and the Terrill family to forget! In terms of music, new forms and styles developed from the 1920's jazz and Charleston. What was called 'Swing' emerged using a strong rhythm section consisting of double bass and drums as the anchor for a lead section with trumpets, trombones, saxophones, clarinets, and sometimes violins and guitars behind it. If you lived on a farm and had electricity you could listen to music every single day on Madison's WIBA radio station.

At night, we'd all gather around the Crosley and dad would turn the dial to Chicago stations WGN, WMAQ or WLS and we'd laugh at 'Fibber McGee and Molly' or 'Amos 'n' Andy'. Mom and Ann also enjoyed what were called soap operas like 'Vic and Sady' and "The Guiding Light' to which dad would simply roll his eyes. Dad really enjoyed 'The National Barn Dance with Gene Autry'.

After mom and dad would go to bed, Ann and I would lie on the parlor floor, watching the flickering flames of the fireplace. In the night's silence, we would imagine that we were at the Empire Room or the Edgewater Hotel in Chicago as we listened to the sounds of Count Basie, Cab Calloway, Jimmy and Tommy Dorsey, Duke Ellington, Benny Goodman, Fletcher Henderson, Earl Hines, Glenn Miller, Artie Shaw, Harry James, and Louis Armstrong.

I don't know if it was my love of Ann or being able to escape from reality, if only for a little while, that planted my passion for music so deep within my soul. All I know is that I don't think a day goes by when I don't sit and listen to something that brings back memories of a time so terrible that was also wonderful, and a time so dark it was filled with the light of simple joys comprising nothing more than love and laughter that meant more than any bauble I've ever owned.

We all thought things would start getting better after the Presidential election of 1932. Where I got to vote for the first time. When you live on a farm, you normally want less government and that always meant being a Republican. However, the mess we were in had many of us swinging the other way and President Hoover was defeated in a landslide by FDR as he was known, and became President Franklin D. Roosevelt, who had been the Governor of New York .

We all hoped that a new leader would immediately stop the carnage. However, time and action was needed, and the problems were a lot more complex than anyone thought. When the market crashed, we were taught in school that, if nothing else occurred, this one event would probably have caused only a recession, but that's not what transpired. What really created the Depression was the collapse of the banking system that quietly started in 1930 and didn't end until 1939.

Many people thought the beginning of the Great Depression was when the stock market crashed. Taking economics in college really helped me understand that the central challenge of any economy is being able to naturally balance the demand for goods with their supply and do so at a price that is acceptable to both the buyer and seller which is called the Equilibrium Price.

I learned that the farther prices are from their equilibrium in either direction– higher or lower - the faster prices will change and the more imbalanced and, therefore, weaker the economy will be. Bringing an economy that's either in a recession or depression back to health is righting the imbalances between supply and demand that created the problem in the first place.

During the initial months of FDR's administration, the general belief was that the troubles were caused by "cut-throat competition" between businessmen which caused businesses to fail. As a result, the Roosevelt administration first attempted to deal with the crisis by minimizing competition through the National Industrial Recovery Act of 1933, which created the National Recovery Administration or NRA. This administration was empowered with the goal of bringing government, industrial corporations and labor unions together to get rid of "cut-throat competition". The three sides were supposed to do this by writing codes of fair competition, setting minimum wages and maximum weekly hours for workers along with setting minimum prices at which products could be sold. FDR's New Deal began in 1933 with a goal to bring about immediate economic relief as well as reforms in industry, agriculture, finance, waterpower, labor, and housing, while vastly increasing the scope of the federal government's activities. For the first time in American history, politicians generally embraced the concept of a government regulated economyaimed at achieving a balance between conflicting economic interests.

The New Deal, with its core idea of the government's intervention in the economy, politics, and social life, included programs that funded and promoted various cultural projects, many of them focusing on the documentation of the experience of ordinary Americans during the depression. There were several acts created to micro-manage struggling segments of American society, as well.

In March 1933, President Roosevelt signed an amendment called the Cullen–Harrison Act, allowing the manufacture and sale of 3.2% beer and light wines. Upon signing the Cullen–Harrison Act, Roosevelt remarked, "I think this would be a good time for a beer," and the Eighteenth Amendment was repealed on December 5, 1933, with ratification of the Twenty-first Amendment to the U.S. Constitution. That night, dad and I went into town and picked up my brother, Will, white cane and all, and went to the tavern and had a beer together. It was a splendid night and trust me, most folks had more than one, including us, thanking God the horses knew the way home.

Before prohibition, women who drank publicly in saloons or taverns were seen as immoral. As saloons died out, public drinking lost much of its macho connotation and there was an increased social acceptance of women drinking in the semi-public environment of the speakeasies which got their name because of the practice of speaking quietly about such a place in public, or inside so as not to alert the police or a neighbor.

Repeal of the Volstead act wasn't really done out of conscience. It was done because the country was in the depths of the Great Depression and state governments needed money. Prior to Prohibition, approximately 14% of federal, state, and local tax revenues were derived from the sale of alcohol. When the Great Depression hit and tax revenues plunged, the governments needed the funds and the millions that could be made by taxing beer.

The other consequences included the development of organized crime on a national level along with loss of totally blind allegiance to the laws of United States of America by the average person! Gone was the belief that, to be a good American, you had to follow all the rules. Men and women simply shrugged their shoulders and did what they thought was right, which was have a drink when they wanted one.

The government passed the Farm Credit Act of 1933 to help farmers refinance mortgages over a longer time at below market interest rates and do so at regional and national banks. Then the government created the Emergency Farm Mortgage Act that loaned funds to farmers in danger of losing their properties by refinancing 20% of their mortgages. Fortunately for us, we had no mortgage and didn't need the government's help or intervention, but those who did became more dependent on the government for their survival.

President Roosevelt's Executive Order also placed all existing agricultural credit organizations under the supervision of one new agency called the Farm Credit Administration. This was independent until 1939, when it became part of the U.S. Department of Agriculture. It then became independent again under the Farm Credit Act of 1953, which created a Federal Farm Credit Board with 13 members consisting of one member from each of the twelve agricultural districts, and one appointed by the Secretary of Agriculture, to develop policy for the Farm Credit Administration.

The act was a disaster! In 1935, the Supreme Court unanimously declared the NIRA Act unconstitutional and during its two-year existence the government regulations reduced the amount of wealth that the economy produced which is probably one reason why the depression lasted beyond 1935.

That same year, the government created The Works Progress Administration or WPA, which was part of FDR's Second New Deal program. The WPA employed over eight million job seekers having them carry out public works projects such as roads, bridges, schools, courthouses, hospitals, sidewalks, waterworks and post offices.

There were three that I remember. The first is the bridge over the Yahara River on East Washington Avenue in Madison that is marked with the initials CGL in the cornerstone who was the person who designed it.

The second is Washington Elementary and Orthopedic School, near my room on Francis Street in Madison. It's a very distinct building designed in what was called the Art Moderne style by an architect named John Flad. The building opened in 1939 and is constructed of orange brick and has curved corners and horizontal design elements that produce the streamlined effect. According to the Capitol Times, "the building is significant for embodying progressive educational ideals and included a gymnasium, library and science, art and music rooms".

The orthopedic wing of the school served physically handicapped children and provided physical therapy treatment rooms, replacing three older, smaller schools in the area and specialized in serving children with disabilities, especially children who had been stricken with polio.

The land was cleared next to the Northwestern railroad tracks and all the labor consisted of WPA employees, including carpenters, electricians, heating people, painters and plasterers where the goal was not to see how fast they could build the school, but how long they could be gainfully employed. In the end, these craftsmen created a masterpiece where the interior walls are all enhanced by small vertical tiles that were hand laid below the plaster above. The walls in the lunch room included murals of hand painted nursery rhymes, created by local artists.

Word tell, the library has a cork floor to reduce noise and the windows in the auditorium consist of tall, slender glass panels protected by hand-turned sixteen-foot-tall wrought iron grates. If you look closely, you'll also see that each grate represents a different famous children's play.

The WPA also built some things that were probably not the most urgent of needs for an economy in depression, including swimming pools, parks, playgrounds, zoos, fairgrounds, and botanical gardens. This included the public swimming pool in Mineral Point that opened in 1936. As one of the 805 swimming pools built nationwide by the WPA, the pool's bathhouse, pump house and walls are constructed of stones from nearby cottages and so some of the heritage of our ancestors lives on.

To save on operating costs, the Mineral Point pool was designed as a freshwater system with the water sourced from a nearby spring so that, even on the warmest summer day, you didn't dawdle in the 'cement pond' as the kids call it. Brrr!

Beside the WPA, the government attempted to control agriculture, as well. With farm prices falling, the government passed the Agricultural Marketing Act of 1929 that established the Federal Farm Board from what was once called the Federal Farm Loan Board. The board was an off-shoot of the Federal Farm Loan Act that started a revolving fund of half a billion dollars. And you thought farming was uncomplicated!

The original act was sponsored by Herbert Hoover to stop the downward spiral of crop prices by seeking to buy, sell and store agricultural surpluses or generously lend money to farm organizations. Money was lent out to the farmers in order to buy seed and food for livestock, which was considered especially important, since there had been a drought in the South.

The Federal Farm Board's purchase of surplus crops couldn't keep up with the supply simply because the politicians forgot to put limits on individual production and therefore on what could be claimed. Smart farmers realized they could sell the government their surplus and simply reimplemented the use of fertilizers and other techniques to increase their yields. This increased the surpluses that resulted in the government buying more crops and totally depleting the funds appropriated. In the end, not only was there more product for sale at lower prices, but the fund ran out of money and losses to the farmers kept increasing.

The government then developed the Agricultural Adjustment Act (AAA) designed to boost agricultural prices by reducing surpluses. With this plan, the government bought livestock and paid farmers subsidies not to plant on part of their land. The money for these subsidies was generated through a special tax on companies which processed farm products. To monitor the program, the act created another new federal agency called the Agricultural Adjustment Administration as part of the U.S. Department of Agriculture, that continues to oversee the distribution of subsidies today.

In 1935, the Supreme Court declared that the Agricultural Adjustment Act (AAA) unconstitutional. Politicians then looked at the drought and conservation issues facing a section of the Great Plains that included southeastern Colorado, southwestern Kansas, the panhandles of Texas and Oklahoma along with northeastern New Mexico and created the Soil Conservation Act for the entire country, bringing within the policy and purposes for all farmers, the improvements and preservation of national soil resources to everyone.

The politicians put a spin on what they were doing by telling those they governed that with express purpose of the bill was to *"encourage the use of soil resources in such a manner as to preserve and improve fertility, promote economic use, and diminish the exploitation and unprofitable use of the national soil resources"* which FDR signed into law in 1936 applicable to all farmers, including those of Iowa County, Wisconsin.

The act was meant to help resolve some of the problems with the previous Act, most notably its failure to protect sharecroppers and tenant farmers, none of which existed in Iowa County. With the new law, landlords were now required to share the payments they received from the government for cutting back production with those who worked on their land.

The act attempted to correct an earlier government policy that had encouraged farmers to use their land without concern to the repercussions. The act was justified because it was supposed to both educate farmers on how to use their lands without damaging them, and limit the Dust Bowl by planting trees and native grass. In other words, the government decreed that all farmers were too stupid to realize that the asset they relied on for their livelihood needed to be protected.

Once again, lawyers who became politicians and were elected to the U.S. Government, took it upon themselves to remove free market conditions and establish programs run by bureaucrats that controlled supply and demand making all farmers dependent on the concepts and intents of lawyers and bookkeepers in Washington for their wellbeing.

As a result of their brilliance, agricultural production decreased and food costs increased for the general population of which 30% were without jobs and the AAA mandated reduced agricultural output which probably increased the duration of the Great Depression.

Needless to say, the 1920s and 1930s were tough times for everyone. The government did what it thought was best and yet, some policies and procedures put in place still remain and have caused the demise of many farmers, while the profits from farming became reliant on government control and subsidies that need to be factored into the farming equation today.

Most folks don't become or remain farmers to work for someone else. Yet, we all ended up working for the government and are almost welfare recipients dependent on the whims of politicians who adjust, control and limit our lives in virtually every way through legislation that all began when times were bad and someone, somewhere thought they had a better idea than allowing us to control our own destiny. Still, some things were needed simply to keep pace with technology and one of them was electricity and so the government passed the Rural

Electrification Act of 1936 that provided federal loans for the installation of electrical distribution systems to serve isolated rural areas of the United States. The funding was channeled through cooperative electric power companies, hundreds of which still exist today, which was great if you had the money and could afford electricity.

In Mineral Point, the Farmer's Savings Bank opened in 1935 and the Iowa County Democrat newspaper merged with the Mineral Point Tribune that had been around almost as long as the town, to form the Democrat Tribune.

The Mineral Springs Brewing Company opened in 1902 in the building my great, great grandfather built in 1852 after being owned by Maurice Minor from 1886 to 1898 and Ballo Brewing from 1898 to 1902. The company changed hands but kept the same name in 1920 and kept going throughout Prohibition by producing "near-beer" which was very low alcohol and bottling sodas or other beverages. The company changed hands again but still kept the name in 1936 until 1961 when it sadly closed for good, much to the chagrin of the locals who believed that no matter how bad times were, no upstanding Cornish farmer would ever go without a pint now and then.

Farming became the engine that drove the town, and the May Byrne Martin Company actually opened to manufacture the "Once Over" tractor seeder you installed on the front of your tractor so that you could plant and harrow at the same time. The Golliner Machine and Boiler Company kept manufacturing boilers, tanks and smokestacks, while the full the Purity Dairy, Sanitary Creamery, Mineral Point Cheese and First Swiss Cheese Companies along with the Mineral Point Co-Operative Packers survived by processing the milk and crops the Terrill family and other farmers produced every day. Reality had it that if you weren't farming or serving farmers, you could no longer make it in Mineral Point.

1937 was a tough year for the Terrill family. Dad had been a smoker as long as I could remember. At first it was Camels, then Chesterfields and Lucky Strikes. When we ran out of money, he began smoking a pipe and buying Prince Albert in a can, which we used to joke about behind his back. Dad always had a raspy voice and so, when it got a little rougher, we thought nothing of it. Sadly, Dad also began losing weight and his complexion was changing to a pale gray. Mom knew something was wrong, but stubborn dad wouldn't go to the doctor and I guess it wouldn't have mattered, anyway. He had lung cancer that quickly spread throughout his body and in six months; he was gone. We couldn't afford a coffin for a formal funeral and so I made his out of oak from the land and we buried him in Graceland Cemetery. He was one tough son-of-a-gun who made me vow right before he died that I'd take care of mom and never start smoking. I've kept both of my promises.

Twenty-seven months later, it was mom's turn, as she joined dad and all our ancestors first at Graceland and then in heaven. I think she died of a broken heart as she was never the same after dad was gone. On Thursday, August 3, 1939 Ann and I went to bed in our house with only Scott and Jane in the house and it was the first time in our marriage we were actually alone. I'd have given anything to keep sharing the house, but God had other plans. Rest in Peace Mom! I'll always love you!

My brother Tom and I were the only kids still on the farm and the only ones interested in doing it. Jack was dead, Will was blind, and our sisters were gone. We thought we'd just be able to keep on farming. No distribution of assets had taken place prior to our parents' deaths, and we faced some tough choices. All of us kids agreed the farm should remain at it was. Everyone knew that cash was in short supply and so it was necessary to devise a plan by which all the demands could be met as equitably as possible.

With the economy in shambles and land values so low and so many foreclosures of other farmers who had financed their inheritance compounded by the government requiring inheritance taxes, we agreed to own the farm "in common" and therefore no immediate transfer of ownership. This meant no mortgage and no one time inheritance taxes. We had the value of the entire property determined by a third party and went from there. As we went through probate, we signed a document agreeing to the common ownership with an established value on the land, buildings and equipment. We also agreed to a land contract to be paid over twenty-years where each member received one-sixth payment of one-twentieth of that estimated value each year, to which each of us then had to pay income taxes on our inheritance. It was tough, but we did it and no one got cheated or felt they weren't getting their fair share, which made all of us proud.

From that agreement, Tom and I came to a second agreement where we split the land with me keeping the house and barns and a smaller amount of acreage, while Tom took more land so that the split was equal in value. Tom then bought the farm south of us and the buildings on it so that he and Sue had a home as well. We then agreed to share planting and harvesting equipment instead of duplicating the investment.

In the end, having your brother as your neighbor made all the sense in the world, especially when both of us got what we wanted. Six years into it, land to the west of "my side" became available, and I bought the acreage so that both farms were about 350 acres apiece and big enough to support our growing dairy herds.

This entire experience made me glad I'd gone to college and had some idea on what to do as I felt I'd gone from farmer to agri-businessman and realized that there was no future in farming, but a tremendous opportunity in agri-business.

As the government added more spices to try and enhance the Depression Stew, there was only one way to get the economy going again, and that was about to happen in a very brutal way that would touch the lives of every American. While the Great Depression now serves as nothing more than a point in history, it continues to define our society and economic structure. To have and then lose is much more profound than to never have had at all. The great depression ripped away the pretense of wealth, stripped away the concept of security and obliterated a sense of well-being. In its place, it left a country suspect, fearful and insecure. For nearly a decade the issue was not economic growth, but a sense of sustaining one's life against what must have seemed to be incredible odds.

Pennies From Heaven

With the move to the house complete, it was time to retrieve all the items that hadn't been in the apartment and were still stored out at the farm. Included were over 200 albums that needed to be categorized and a bunch of stuff that should have been taken directly to the dump.

One thing, though, was a metal file box I'd completely forgotten about that was full of all kinds of old papers. I was going to toss the bunch and thought better, which was a wise decision. Instead, I took the box back to the house and sat at the kitchen table. To my left on the floor was an empty grocery bag from Painter and Tonkin. On my right was a matching bag. The idea was, if it was junk, it went to my left. If it was something I should keep, it went to my right.

As I was reading each piece of paper, the routine became quite easy: left, left, left, left, left as old agreements, articles and who knows what, became destined for the fireplace. It was then I realized that no matter how much you pushed the paper, it would still be stationary. Now and then, there would be something I thought I should keep and so I'd reach down and put it in the right bag. As the height of the pile diminished, I was about to pick it all up and go left when I came across an insurance document that had been taken out twenty years prior marked 'paid in full'. Across the top it stated in bold letters ADD and then Hartford Insurance.

As I perused the information, I quickly learned that it was one of those Accidental Death and Dismemberment Policies I'd purchased in case something happened to me while I was farming. While my name was on it, the fine print also said that it covered our children up to age twenty-one and spouses, as well. I paused and wondered if it was legit. The document was signed by Mr. John Thornton, who had been our insurance agent, and had a serial number on it.

The further I read, the more I saw that there wasn't any expiration date, and the amount was $20,000. I almost gasped, not wanting to get too excited, but also eager to know if it was legit. I'd been a Hartford customer for years and so I called Johnny Williams, our new agent, who took over for Mr. Thornton when he retired.

"Johnny, it's Hank Terrill."

"Hi Hank, need to upgrade your home owner's policy on the new house? We have a great new integrated policy that can save you money on your car insurance, too."

"Not right now, Johnny. I was going through a bunch of papers and found an ADD policy from twenty years ago."

"Twenty years ago?"

"Yah, when John was our agent."

"Just a minute Hank, let me get your file."

Johnny was gone for more than a minute and returned saying, "Sorry for the delay Hank, your old files were down in the cellar and I had to dig them out."

There was a long pause as Johnny was reading the policy and saying, "Uh huh, uh huh, uh huh," as he followed along. "Hank, this policy looks as if it's still in effect. Hartford stopped offering these before I became an agent and so I didn't even know they existed. You don't happen to have a copy of the policy and Ann's accident report do you?"

"Yes," I said.

"Can I stop by and pick them up?"

"How about me going to the library and making one of those photocopies for you and dropping them off?"

"That would be swell."

The last thing I wanted was Johnny sitting down trying to sell me more insurance. I did as I was told and dropped off the copies during what I knew would be his lunch hour. That afternoon I called to make certain Johnny had the copies and he said he did, indicating that it would take a couple of days to find out from Connecticut.

Two days later, Johnny called and said, "Good news Hank, the policy is good and with interest, you'll be receiving a check for $23,465.00."

Holy shit!

Johnny, being a good salesman, tried talking me into creating an annuity with the funds. Me, being a stubborn farmer, politely told him, "NO".

Sure enough, a week later I received the check. I was shocked. Had I taken the paper pile and 'gone left', this would have never happened. I put

$20,000 in the bank and took the $3,465.00 and decided it was 'found money' and I needed to buy some new clothes I wasn't ever going to be the topic of conversation again when I was with Kat.

My sister-in-law, Sue, had taken a job at Land's End in Dodgeville. The pay wasn't that great, but it included group health insurance, which helped out on the farm. I'd never purchased anything at Land's End, especially from her, as I thought it might be improper and never wore their type of clothes. I called Sue at work and asked for a favor. I told her I wanted to upgrade my wardrobe from dirt-farmer to whatever. Sue laughed and said, "No problem."

I asked her what she would recommend. She asked me what my budget was. I told her my limit was making me look good. She'd met Katherine and knew what it was for. Sue recommended that I go to the Land's End outlet and see what I liked. It was just north of Dodgeville and fifteen minutes away. I went over and was shocked. The place was packed with merchandise and people.

As I looked though the men's department, I quickly saw the fashion trends for men, golf shirts, button down dress shirts, turtleneck sweaters, and pants and then pants and more pants. Instead of buying, I picked up one of their catalogues and brought it home.

Sitting at the kitchen table, I first dog-eared the categories and then went back and circled the items I liked. My biggest question was, which colors? I called again and asked for Sue and told her to assume that I had no wardrobe, what should I buy?

There was a pause and then Sue replied, "First, stay away from what we call 'trend clothing'. Stick with the basics. Second, there are four primary colors for pants - black, navy blue, charcoal gray and tan. If you want to go wild and crazy, throw in a pair of cream-colored pants as well."

"Ok, I'll take one of each."

"Huh?"

"One of each size 34"x32".

"Pleated or flat front?"

"What's the difference?"

"Hank, you're in good shape, you want the flat-front pants. Pleated pants are designed to hide some belly fat."

"OK, flat"

"Cuffed or plain?"

"I don't know."

"Plain will make you look taller"

"Plain." I had no idea buying pants could be so complicated.

"Now you need some shirts."

"Yup"

"Golf or dress?"

"I don't golf."

"Still, you want golf shirts that are also called polo shirts, that you can wear to contrast the pants."

"What color?"

"The most popular colors are white and black followed by red and blue."

"Ok, give me one of each. Make that two white and one each of the other colors."

"Are you sure?

"Yup!"

"Size?"

"Large."

"In dress shirts, are you going to be wearing a tie or open collar?"

"I think both."

"Then you'll need what's called a spread collar, when you're wearing a tie and button-down when you wear it open."

"I've got the spread collar already."

"How about color?"

"White?"

"How about adding a light blue button down, as well?"

"OK."

"Hank, this is getting expensive."

"It's OK. I need to get out of the forties and into today."

"Size?"

"17x34" and throw in one of those spread color white ones, too."

"How about sweaters?"

"It's summer!"

"I know. However, now is when they're the lowest price."

"OK."

"I recommend navy blue and black cashmere turtlenecks."

"Cashmere?"

"Light weight, yet warm and they never go out of style."

"OK."

"Size – Large?"

"How about belts?"

"Huh?"

"You need both black and brown dress belts."

"OK, put them in there too. Are you sure you're not selling insurance on the side?"

"How about shoes?"

"I've got one pair of fancy, lace-up ones."

"You don't wear those with upscale casual. You need some loafers and we have some calf-skin models with tassels that are gorgeous."

"OK."

"Black and brown?"

"Sure, why not?"

"Size?"

"11D."

"How about a navy-blue blazer?"

"Got one."

"Single breasted or double breasted?"

"Huh?"

"One row of buttons or two?"

"Just a minute, what page are they on in the catalogue?"

"73."

I looked and was smitten, adding, "44-long, double-breasted."

"I'd recommend adding both light tan and black single-breasted blazers. Stay away from the other colors and patterns, they're too fashion- oriented, which means they're in style today, but will look old tomorrow."

"OK, toss the tan and black ones on the pile too."

"Let's see pants, casual shirts, dress shirts, belts, shoes, sportscoats and sweaters. You're going to be the best dressed man in Mineral Point."

There was a pause as Sue was adding everything up. I heard her talking to herself $1,320.00 less 20% sales discount equals $1,056, plus four percent sales tax is $1,100. "Hank the bill is $1,100," Sue said incredulously.

"OK."

I think Sue was shocked as she inquired. "How do you want to pay for this?"

"I can drive over with cash."

"How about a credit card?"

"I don't have one."

"If you open a Master Card Credit Card, I can knock another 10% off."

"Then what?"

"You'll get the bill next month and, if you pay it in full, it costs you nothing."

"Do you get credit?"

"Yes!"

"OK, let's do it."

"Your bill is $990.00. Hank, you really got a deal!"

"How do I get the clothes?"

"They'll ship tomorrow as everything is in stock."

"Can I pick them up instead?"

"Sure. They'll be under your name at the outlet after 10:00 o'clock."

"Thanks, Sue!"

"No, thank you, Hank."

I never thought you could spend money so fast over the telephone. The next morning at 10:00 I was there and sure enough, so were all my clothes. I took them home and tried everything on. I smiled as the old farmer had a new look.

I decided I needed another suit and drove to Madison and went to a store on the Square called 'Ed Schmitz and Sons, the Hub'. I could have gone to the new West Towne Mall, but wanted something more traditional. The Hub must have had a thousand suits on display. I looked over the assortment and told the salesman I already had my navy-blue pinstripe suit and red tie and wanted to add to my options.

He said a good assortment should include black, blue and charcoal gray single-breasted models. They were $400 each including alterations. I didn't care and took all three. The tailor measured me and I picked out two neckties to go with each suit which is when I wished Kat was there.

The salesman asked about socks and sold me a pair of over-the-calf and four pairs of regular socks. He tried selling me some Sans-A-Belt pants, that you could wear without a belt, but enough was enough as my bill was already $1,636.

I added the total to my Land's End purchases and realized I'd spent a total of $2626. I was still under budget and so I added two pair of jeans and two black cotton tee-shirts both of which had some sort of elastic cloth called Lycra Spandex in them so that they kept their shape which the salesman said would look good because I was in such good condition. It was another $335.00, making my total $2,971.

I was under budget and happy as a pig in shit. I went home and the next morning I walked up Chestnut Hill to have breakfast with Frank and Madge wearing my new jeans and black tee-shirt. Madge was shocked!

"Hank Terrill, you're becoming a hunk! Katherine had better watch out. Every eligible woman and even some who aren't, in Mineral Point will be chasing you."

I smiled as Madge as she added. "There's just one thing"

"What's that?"

"Your hair."

"What's wrong with my hair?"

"It's early farmer."

"This is the way Tony's been cutting it for years."

"I know and it shows."

"So what do I do?"

"Let me call Sally and see when she can see you."

With that Madge made the call and fifteen minutes later, I was in a lady's beauty parlor, embarrassed as hell. An hour later, I walked back into the Rooster and smiled. Madge almost dropped the tray of food she was carrying.

"Is that you, Hank Terrill?"

I smiled more.

"My God. What a difference! That lady friend of yours is in for a real treat. When's she coming to town?"

"She's not, I'm going there."

"You're going to be the best-looking man in Washington."

"Thanks, Madge," I said with a shy grin.

As I was leaving the Rooster, I saw a poster noting that Earl Clauer was having an auction of the Ramsey Estate that afternoon and I still needed a few things for the house. The auction started at two and the preview was just about to begin. Instead of walking down Chestnut Hill and home, I walked up High Street and crossed Doty and saw the crowd. Most of the items weren't what I needed and I was about to leave when I spied a three- piece set of Hartman Leather luggage. It sure looked a lot nicer than the stuff I bought from Sears Roebuck.

Earl worked his magic on everything I wasn't interested in and finally got to the luggage. He told the story about how Mr. Ramsey had purchased it to take Mrs. Ramsey on a 50th anniversary cruise and they never made it and so the luggage had never been used.

"Who'll start the bidding at $1,000?"

No one said a word as Earl looked shocked in his best vaudevillian way.

"Ladies and gentlemen, how about $500.00?" There was total silence.

"$300.00?" I raised my hand.

"I've got three-hundred, who'll give me $350.00?"

Silence!

"This is a $1,000 set of luggage!"

"Who'll bid $340?"

I knew everyone there and everyone knew what had happened to Ann. I don't know if that's what did it or not, but no one spoke. "Three hundred dollars once, three hundred dollars twice, three hundred dollars sold to Hank Terrill." I smiled and walked up and paid Earl's assistant and walked home with my new luggage. I'd blown my wad! The extra interest was spent on new clothes and luggage and I was happy. That Sunday when Kat called, I didn't mention any of my purchases. They were intended to be a surprise.

<u>*Surprise*</u>

We'd agreed that I'd return to Washington, and Monday was a travel day as I made my way to Truax and parked my car. Imagine a dollar a day to park your car!

I looked at the anti-war demonstrators who were there to "welcome home" the soldiers with profanity, vulgarity and spit and shook my head remembering when we came to Madison when I was a little boy to watch my brothers march off to war, wondering how in hell, they could do what they were doing and why.

I'd decided to "dress up" and was wearing the cream-colored pants with the white, open-collared button-down dress shirt. Madge told me to keep the top two buttons open, and I did. I then added my navy-blue, double-breasted blazer and tan tasseled loafers, while carrying my new Hartman large leather suitcase and overnight bag that had the first two chapters of *'War of My Brothers'* in it.

I must have made the right impression as both the ticket and gate agents called me sir and when we boarded the plane, I was invited up to first class where the stewardess offered to hang my coat so that it wouldn't be wrinkled and then winked at me. I was shocked. No one had winked at me since one of our cows had a fly in its eye.

After take-off, it was all "Yes sir, no sir," complimentary cocktails and warm cashews. The plane stopped in Milwaukee and then it was only a 75- minute flight to Washington. Everyone must have thought I was someone as they waited for me to get my sports coat before we disembarked.

Washington National had one of those new Jetways, and so we walked right into the terminal. I told Kat I'd meet her by the baggage claim and took the escalator down to the claim area. Kat was waiting at the bottom of the escalator and looked at me and looked again as her mouth dropped open.

"Hank?"

I nodded yes and smiled.

 "Hank?"

I nodded again.

"You, you look incredible!"

I smiled and inquired, "Too much?"

"Are you kidding? You're a hunk!"

My smile grew wider as she threw her arms around my neck and gave me a huge kiss. I had my leather carry-on, and she thought that was it, especially after Chicago, when I showed up with only the clothes on my back. "I've got another bag I had to check," as we waited until it came. I grabbed the second leather bag.

"Hartman leather luggage? Did you find a gold mine?" Kat asked.

"Sort of" I responded. "I'll fill you in later. I just wanted it to be a surprise."

Kat stopped and looked at me and shook her head in disbelief, adding "My God, what a difference."

"You like?" I inquired.

"Nope! I love!"

We walked outside and a black Cadillac limousine was waiting. "You didn't need to rent a limo for me."

"I didn't, this has been the family car for the past few years."

With that Charles, the chauffer, came round and held open the door as Kat entered and slid across the seat. Charles took my bags and opened the trunk as I slipped in next to Kat and we discreetly shared another kiss. Kat looked at me and shook her head. "I just can't get over it."

"I want you to be proud to be with me," I replied in all earnest.

"I was proud before. Now I'm afraid."

"Afraid of what?"

"Every other woman out there."

The Mansion

The electric gate opened, and we passed what looked like a small house about the size of mine and I thought we were there. As I reached for the car door, Kat shook her head and waved her hand. "No, this is where Charles and Annie live. Our house is just beyond the bend."

Slowly, we made the curve in the driveway and before me stood a stately white Georgian mansion with eight pillars across the front.

"Holy shit!" I exclaimed.

"Too much?" Kat inquired.

"Not if it's filled with love."

"It will be tonight," Kat replied.

Charles made the circular drive and stopped. I got out and helped Kat as well. I went for my bags and caught the eyes of Charles and knew that was his job. Just then, the door opened and a large colored lady was standing in the doorway with a huge smile on her face.

"That's Annie," Kat whispered. "She's been with the family for nearly 40 years. Annie raised me and was my genuine mother when times were tough."

We went to the front door. I stuck out my hand and Annie looked at me, cocked her head and then stuck out hers. "It's so nice to meet you, Annie," I announced as I gently shook her hand.

"Could I have your last name, please?" "Harris"

"Do you mind if I call you Mrs. Harris?"

Annie was taken aback as she looked at Kat, who nodded in the affirmative.

"I'd be honored, Mr. Terrill." "Thank you, Mrs. Harris."

At that Charles brought my two bags, and I thanked him with 'Mr. Harris' as well, but could see that he wasn't amenable to that. "Charles, please put Mr. Terrill's bags in the master suite."

"Yes, Ms. Katherine," as Charles headed for the circular stairway.

I looked at the man carrying my bag and realized it was the first time anyone had ever done that for me in my life as I simply called, "Thank you, Charles."

We entered the house, and it was like something out of a movie. There was a two-story foyer with matching circular stairways to the second floor on each side. In the middle was a round glass table with fresh flowers on it. To the right was parlor with a fireplace and sliding pocket doors. To the left was the formal dining room. Behind the parlor was a study and across the back was a huge sunroom and kitchen.

"Do you need to freshen up?" Kat asked.

"I might want to change, if you don't mind." "Up the stairs and the first door on the right."

I excused myself and found the master suite which was bigger than the entire first floor of my house. It had one of those California king-size beds, a couch and table and then a bathroom with a Jacuzzi and huge walk-in shower with enough drawers under the counter for all my clothes–not just the ones I brought–but ALL my clothes and then some.

Between the bedroom and bathroom was a walk-in closet that was big enough to be a dance hall. I knew Kat had money, but this was ridiculous. I quickly changed into jeans and a black tee-shirt, took off my socks and put my shoes back on and headed downstairs.

"What a beautiful house," I exclaimed.

Kat looked at me and shook her head and replied, "What a beautiful man," as we headed for the sunroom as she whispered,

"You didn't un-pack, did you?" "No, I just changed clothes, why?"

"You'll be staying in my room, won't you?"

"I hope so."

"Tonight, we're having dinner at the club. I don't want to, but they're honoring my parents as they were the last of the founding families."

"I'm honored."

"Did you bring the blue suit?"

"No!" I replied.

Before I could expand, Kat responded, "Darn, I guess we can go casual.

"We won't need to, I have a couple of new suits I brought, just in case."

"Really?"

"Yes, do you prefer black or charcoal gray?"

"You really brought two suits and the sportscoat? You've become quite the clothes horse."

"When you're with a classy lady, you need to dress like a classy man," I replied.

"Care for a drink?" Kat asked. I shook my head in a negative manner.

"Unless its lemonade or water, I'm fine. I don't want to cloud my head when I've been looking forward to seeing you since the minute you waved goodbye."

Kat's lower lip pursed as her head tilted down and she whispered, That's one of the most romantic things anyone has ever said to me."

I looked at her and smiled, adding. "It wasn't intended that way. It's just how I truly feel. Every week, I count the days until Sunday when I hear your voice. When the phone rings, my heart skips a beat and the music of your hello fills me with joy as the profound warmth of feeling wanted, needed and loved radiates throughout my body."

"My God, you are making me so – so happy that you're here."

We spent the rest of the afternoon getting caught up and having Kat review the two chapters of "War of My Brothers". She made some changes, corrected some spelling errors and put commas where they were supposed to be.

We sat side by side and shoulder to shoulder and I was filled with bliss. At five, Mrs. Harris brought a cart into the sunroom that had a myriad of different types of alcohol on it. My eyes widened at the selection as Kat whispered, "leftovers from my mother."

After a drink, it was time to get ready. My bags had already been moved to Kat's room with my clothes hung up in the empty closet. I quickly realized that the guest room and Kat's suite were identical and therefore easy to navigate. I took my shower and came out with a towel around my waist.

Before Kat went in, I asked her if she preferred the black suit or the gray. Kat preferred the gray, saying it would match her dress. I put on the white shirt and gray suit and asked her which tie. She liked the maroon and gray striped tie the best, as I slipped into over-the-calf socks, which I quickly learned to hate, and my new formal black shoes that I laced up.

I went downstairs and Charles inquired as to whether I'd care for a drink as I waited for Ms. Katherine. I replied, "Yes please," and then, "Thank you," when he provided a glass of Kentucky bourbon with seven-up, just the way I liked it.

There was an awkward silence and I didn't know if I was supposed to continue the conversation or not and so I kept my mouth shut as Charles simply stood there.

Kat came cascading down the stairs in a different low-cut gray and silver evening gown with the same diamond necklace and earrings she'd worn in Chicago. I stood at the bottom and smiled. As she reached the last step, my voice went down about an octave as I whispered, "You look gorgeous."

Kat smiled and nodded and then asked if I'd do her a favor. I nodded in the affirmative. With that she held out her hand and offered her dad's Rolex watch to me.

"This was my dad's, and I'd be honored if you would wear it tonight."

From Timex to Rolex? That wasn't a favor, it was a thrill as I examined the incredible detail and realized I was being honored as I asked Charles to take our picture by the staircase and offered my Kodak. Charles abided and soon it was time to go.

The Club

We arrived at the club to see a bevy of Lincolns, Cadillacs, Mercedes and even a Rolls Royce or two, along with a Ferrari. The attendants opened both back doors and Kat and I climbed out. The doors closed and Charles and the limo were gone.

We entered the ballroom to applause and were guided to the corner so that the others could form a receiving line. I had no idea what to do and stood there as the guests introduced themselves and Kat shared I was her special guest who'd flown in from Wisconsin for the evening with no mention of cattails, pigs or mosquitoes.

After the formal reception, a waiter appeared and rang a small bell, indicating it was time for dinner. We entered the dining room and were escorted to the head table and sat immediately to the right of the podium. For the next fifteen minutes, all the elected officers of the Country Club arose and gave speeches about Katherine's parents and their generosity and kindness. It was then that I learned they had donated several million dollars towards the construction of the clubhouse.

After the speeches, Kat arose and took center stage. "thank you for coming and for your kindness and generosity and for recognizing my mother and father. This club was the center of their lives and there are countless memories they shared with me about how wonderful you all have been."

There was a round of applause and then, before the food was served, the president took the microphone again and said, "Katherine, we have a very special memento we would like to share with you." With that, an oil painting of her mother and father was unveiled to a hearty round of applause from all, to which the president added, "This portrait will hang in our lobby as a reminder of the warmth and generosity of the Stimson family. Thank you. Thank you, very much." To which there was another round of polite applause, and then dinner was served.

By ten o'clock, the evening was over. Numerous people had visited our table, congratulated Katherine, and thanked her for the family's generosity. I simply sat there, smiled and nodded and could easily have been one of the waiters and they would have cared less.

Discretely, Kat opened her purse and pushed a button on her pager. We stood and said thank you to the people at the head table and exited. As the front doors opened, Charles was already there, waiting with the limo.

The valets opened the doors, and we climbed in, to which Kat said, "Whew, what a bunch of bullshit. My parents hated half the people in the room, and those people despised mom and dad. If the money hadn't been there, this would never have happened. Welcome to Washington!"

We headed back to the mansion and climbed out of our clothes and into bed. Kat turned on TV just in time to watch the eleven o'clock news about the demonstrations and rioting in so many cities we couldn't keep track. As we were watching, I looked over and saw closed eyes and took the remote from Kat's hand and shut off the TV. She had fallen asleep and I'd soon follow whispering, "Goodnight, princess," to the one I was falling in love with.

The Studio

Morning came quickly, and I did my sit-ups and push-ups as Kat took her shower. She came out to see me on the floor doing the last of the push- ups and giggled, "So that's where you get all that stamina."

I stopped and laughed and realized it was my time in the shower. I missed having her there, but also realized we needed to save that for special moments. As I finished, I went to the closet and took out the tan pants and black golf shirt to Kat's approval.

"Annie wants to know what you want for breakfast," Kat inquired. I shook my head and said scrambled eggs and wondered if there would be a bar stool like the Rooster.

To my surprise, when we came downstairs, not only were the scrambled eggs under one of those silver warming domes, but bacon and cooked ham as well. We went into the sunroom to eat and sure enough, there was a folded paper sitting on the table where I was directed to sit. It was the Washington Post and not the Wisconsin State Journal, but the thought was certainly enough to make me smile.

As I looked across the backyard, I noticed a small building about 200 feet away. "What's that, I asked?" "My studio," Kat replied.

"Studio?"

"We had a pool and tennis court no one used, and so we had them filled in and planted grass. Instead of tearing down what had been the changing room, I had it remodeled, added a couple of skylights and turned into my studio where I get to putter with my drawings and pottery.

"Can I see it?"

"A little later"

After breakfast, we made our way to Kat's studio. It was the size of a three-car garage with windows all around. As we entered, there was a foyer. To the left was her drawing room, full of dozens of sketches. Some were in charcoal and others in fine pencil drawings. The subjects ranged from landscapes and individual drawings of inanimate objects to faces and full bodies, including several naked people. I was taken aback by the detail and symmetry, and they reminded me of the classical music I listened to.

Next to the sketches and stacked on the floor were about a dozen water colors of everything, from flowers to landscapes to even some modern art. Finally, hanging on the wall were a series of oil paintings of every subject I'd seen in her sketches.

I was speechless and yet inquired, "You drew these?" The nod was simply 'yes' as a proud smile made its way across Kat's face.

"Kat, some of these belong in a museum; they're gorgeous."

"Thank you."

"Where do you get your ideas?"

"Some are just my imagination. Others I take photographs and then draw from them. Still others are inanimate models. Finally, some are actually models who pose for me" pointing to the small elevated platform.

We left the drawing room and went through the foyer to the other side. While the drawing room was pristine, the other room showed signs of work as it was her ceramic and sculpting room. Kat had taken the former shower and installed a kiln so that she could do ceramics and bake them right there. The walls were ensconced in shelves with all types of ceramic bowls, pots, cups and vases that she had shaped on her potter's wheel, painted and finished. In the corner stood a small collection of unfinished sculptures.

Nodding at them, Kat noted "I'm still learning."

After a pause, Kat asked me, "Did you know that Michelangelo once said 'The sculpture is already complete within the marble block, before I start my work. It is already there, I just have to chisel away the superfluous material.' I'm still trying to figure out how to get that finished product out of the block of wood or stone," as she shook her head in frustration.

"Lately, I've been working with wood, trying to create cups and bowls from a single piece. It's tough, but I'm improving."

I just shook my head at the talent and patience I saw unfolding before me and thought of Harry Knorr back in Mineral Point and his burl wood bowls.

We went back into the drawing room and Kat had a smile on her face. "I have a gift for you."

With that, she picked up a cardboard tube and told me to unroll its contents. We attached one end to her easel and I unrolled the pencil drawing of my new house.

"Do you like it?" "How did you do this?" I incredulously asked. "From memory."

"This is incredible! I love it," as I wiped a tear from my right eye.

I looked at Kat, smiled and pulled her in to give her a deep kiss of appreciation. "It's one of the nicest presents I've ever received."

"Where are you going to put it?"

"How about out in the garage?" for which I received a swift punch to the stomach.

"Actually, above the fireplace."

"Let me show you one I'm working on."

With that Kat pulled the cover off a small pencil self portrait of her laying naked on a couch. I stood looking at the sketch and the tantalizing smile on her face that was tastefully done. This wasn't erogenous, it was conveying a sense of purity and innocence and my heart pounded with joy instead of some form of physical endeavor.

How could I ever leave her? Kat had burrowed her way into my heart and my only regret was that it wasn't forever, right then and there.

"How did you do this?" I asked, pointing at the drawing.

"Simple, I took some self-photos of myself with my Leica and then drew from that."

"Where did you get the pictures developed?" I asked wondering if she was embarrassed when she picked them up.

"You just take them into Insty Prints. They don't care."

I looked at the drawing again and was amazed at the detail, realizing how attuned Kat was to the small things most people would never notice, nor ever see. It was then, my respect for her increased even more – beautiful, intelligent, sensitive, articulate and talented, very, very talented and so, so observant. What more could a man ask for?

"I wanted to have it done when you got here, but ran out of time." Kat added.

"This one's for me, too?" Kay nodded. I thought for a moment and realized it was going to be on display in conservative Mineral Point. "How about you bring it the next time you visit and we can hang it in our bedroom? That was the first time I said the word 'our' in our conversation. It might have been one of those Freudian slips, and yet I knew I meant it.

There was a pause and then Kat asked, "Before you leave, can I draw you?"

"Like that?" I said, nodding at the sketch.

"No silly. I want you standing completely naked on the pedestal so that I can admire your entire body. It will only take a few hours."

I was mortified until I saw that evil grin cross her face and realized she was kidding. In the end, Kat confessed that all she wanted was a portrait as she would leave the rest to her imagination. We spent the rest of the week going places I hadn't been and seeing things left to see. I sat and let her do her thing with the understanding that it was for her. I admitted, I never liked pictures of myself and thought a portrait would be even worse. Kat disagreed.

Even though it was a lovely week, it was still a little weird. I guess it would take a time for me to get used to the servants, and the fact that you're never really alone and therefore always need to be on guard. I didn't say anything to Kat, but I think she could sense it. I wondered what Charles and Mrs. Harris were saying behind our backs. I probably shouldn't have cared, but I did and that was the only thing in the entire week I regretted.

Our goodbye was painful. I didn't want to leave and Kat didn't want me to go Yet, I needed to get home and back to my reality. Kat needed to get back to work and her life without Hank. Kat made me promise I'd call her when I got to the house. I told her I'd call person-to-person and ask for myself and when she said, 'no', she would know that I made home and there wouldn't be any long-distance charges. I made her promise she would miss me. She made me promise that I'd miss her. We both kept our promises.

The Seven Elements of Forever

They say there are seven steps to a successful long-term relationship – attraction, association, communication, understanding, trust, compromise and forgiveness. Kat and my attraction to each other had moved beyond the purely physical, raucously amorous stage to one of acceptance and gentle sharing and it was nice.

While living nearly a thousand miles apart, our times together were allowing us to share moments and create memories that both of us honored. Our Sunday night telephone calls had started off as brief 'hellos' but were becoming verbal marathons that touched on a myriad of subjects including politics, religion, finance, love, hate, desperation and frustration. The depth of each conversation was such that I believe we both were beginning to understand who the other one was as we, or at least I, learned more about myself.

Trust is always a difficult challenge as it's an emotional state and not just an expectation of behavior which can only come when one sincerely believes that the acts of another are for the good of both. In the perilous beginnings of any relationship when the roots aren't deep enough to make it easy to simply walk away without emotional consequence, trust is the most difficult to achieve.

Past events, past relationships, past circumstances all have a way of diluting trust and making it difficult to ascertain. Kat and I were beginning to implicitly trust each other as the roots grew even deeper. When a relationship, any relationship endures for a period of time there will be events and circumstance that one party doesn't agree with and this is where the combination of the other six come into play. We must learn to forgive and accept that no one is perfect and when we look in the mirror realize that we, too, are not perfect.

When one member does something the other cannot comprehend, then all seven ingredients must combine to sustain the feelings and emotions that were euphorically there before it happened. While I was totally enamored by my new very special friend, I was also concerned because of the dichotomy.

I live in a 100-year-old tiny brick house in Wisconsin. Kat lives in a mansion in Washington DC. I'm a dirt farmer, who barely made it through college. Kat went to Yale and is an artist. I had to take some of my wife's life insurance money to buy decent clothes. She wears diamonds as if they were rhinestones. The pieces shouldn't fit together and yet they do.

Who's supposed to change, Kat, me, or perhaps both? Even with so many 'differences' we were being drawn to each other like two particles in space attracted that cannot be pulled asunder. I finished another chapter in my Mineral Point epistle and the date was set for Kat to come and see me. What an incredible creative incentive! We'd grown comfortable with each other and the somewhat obscene passion had almost dissipated as the urgency of gratifying copulation gave way to slow, gentle episodes of physical interaction that started with kisses and massages and ended up, well you know, which was fine with me.

I knew that we had evolved into the next phase of our relationship that made me more comfortable than the erotically physical one in which we had begun. Instead of my libido careening out of control, the warmth in my heart grew with each passing day. Was this love? It had been so long, since that 'ping' had been there I didn't know.

I drove to Madison to pick Kat up. The plane landed and there she was. Smiles abounded! Urge's overcame propriety. She held my hand as we made our way back to Mineral Point. My God, it was good to see her, feel her, share her!

When we arrived at the house, Kat immediately noted that her house sketch was above the fireplace as I'd promised and that put a smile on her face. With that, she opened her garment bag and took out a carboard tube.

"As promised sir, something for above **'our'** bed".

She'd completed the sketch of her in repose. I looked at it and then at her and smiled. She was sharing more of her with me and it warmed my heart. It was to be a week of nothing. Like an old pair of jeans, we'd become a couple, comfortable with each other and quite honestly in love.

Not much had changed at the house or Mineral Point, for that matter, since her last visit. A little new paint here and there on the kitchen walls to replace some old wallpaper. Perhaps, there were a few more gray hairs on my head. I was thankful the hairs were there instead of having departed like so many of my peers.

The first morning, we lay in bed and 'snoozed' as she called it. This was our quiet time when all we did was hold each other and enjoy the simplicity of our existence. Kat rolled over on her stomach and looked into my eyes. "Have I shown you Mr. Terrill that I'm madly in love with you?"

I smiled a contented smile and nodded in the affirmative as I breathed a deep, contented sigh. Then for the first time, I responded. "Katherine, my sweet Katherine, you've brought the sun back into my life and taken away the darkness. You've shown me love that I thought would never be there again." I smiled and looked into her eyes and said "I love you too, more than the moon or the stars, more than the sun and the sky, you complete me and I'm the happiest I've ever been in my entire life."

Tears slowly slid down Kat's cheeks as her lips met mine. The sweet, salty taste of her expression was like nectar to me as I knew that she understood what I meant and we would always be together. As we lay there, ensconced in each other, I thought of Ann and how we had slowly simply adjusted to each other and began taking each other for granted. There was nothing wrong, it just happened and I vowed, this wouldn't be the case again.

Once again, Kat propped herself up on her elbows as my hands slid up and down her side and her asking "Can we go to the forest today?"

"Of course,"

I replied, knowing that the feelings she had the previous time had been so profound. It was fall and we went to the farm and walked into the forest. Kat breathed the deep cool autumn air and closed her eyes. A soft smile crossed her face that was unlike any I'd seen in Washington. She looked at me and mentioned, "This fulfills me unlike anything I've ever experienced before in my life, except you."

I was humbled.

"Hank, promise me that this will always remain like it is right now."

I reiterated that I had an agreement with my brother and assured her it was forever, to which she squeezed my hand and smiled as we walked along, looking at the red and gold leaves that were beginning to tell us winter was on its way.

"Do you want to go skinny dipping?" I asked in jest, knowing that fifty-degree weather wasn't conducive to jumping into water that was probably ten degrees colder.

Kat looked at me and grinned asking, "Wouldn't that cause the medical condition called 'nippless erectus'?"

I chuckled and noted, "And two little friends of mine would certainly be heading for cover".

Needless to say, the skinny dipping was deferred as we walked back to the car and headed for home. As we neared Mineral Point, Kat asked if we could turn right and drive up Shake Rag, which I wanted to avoid. At her insistence, I turned off Highway 23 and a tinge of guilt permeated my body.

"There something, I need to tell you," I offered. "What?"

"Pendarvis is closed."

"I know," Kat responded.

"Roger said that he and Edgar were retiring when we had lunch there."

"There's more"

"What?

"Some corporation bought the brewery."

"What? When?" Kat asked in an anxious way.

"A couple weeks ago." Kat's shoulders sagged as if in profound dismay.

"There's more bad news," I added.

 "What?"

"Someone else bought the old hotel."

"Incredible," was all Kat could say.

"It's absurd! Both buildings sat empty for years and then, in two weeks, both of them sold and to different people. For what? They're both disasters."

I was agitated and perplexed.

"They both could be torn down. Then what? Another part of our history destroyed?"

"That's not going to happen." Kat replied. "How can you be so sure?"

"Because I bought them."

"What?" I inquired incredulously as my suspicions came true.

Kat had gone beyond me and without any discourse, made a major decision that could affect the rest of our lives. The woman who I was beginning to believe would be with me the rest my life had purchased my great, great grandfather's brewery and the old, dilapidated hotel. I asked her why.

Kat looked at me and said, "The prices were right and I see an incredible opportunity, Hank, to help turn this town around."

"But what if they're unstable?"

"I had an engineering firm examine them before I made the offer.

The exterior walls and foundations are fine. They need

everything else."

I must have had a strange look on my face wondering why she was going around me as Kate added.

"I love it here. I love the tranquility and above all else, the innocence. The last time I was here, I mentioned I thought this could become an artist's colony. Hank, I paid pennies on the dollar for the two buildings. Even if I do nothing, the cost was minimal!"

Kat looked at me and outlined her rationale. I'd introduced her to Roger and Edgar and she knew that Pendarvis was closing. Her idea was to take their recipes and remodel the old hotel into two apartments on the north end that could either be used as hotel suites, or rent them or sell them as condos, while adding art showrooms in some of the other former rooms near the restaurant located on the south end.

Kat knew the building was too big to be used as a restaurant, too big to be used as a hotel, too big for art studios and too small to be converted into condos, but slicing the building in sections, made all the sense in the world.

"If you look at Wisconsin, there is only one true artist colony and that's way up in Door County. Why not Mineral Point? It's closer to Milwaukee and Chicago and only 38 miles from Galena, which is already established. Mineral Point can be as beautiful as any of them and there isn't any fudge."

Kat's biggest challenge would be to convince Roger and Edgar to share their recipes and names to give the restaurant instant credibility as she felt their reputation would help create enough positive momentum to get things started.

Kat looked at me and said, "When I got on that plane in Madison the last time and landed in Washington, I finally realized why people in Mineral Point lived so long. They simply don't have the pressure, bitterness and politics we deal with in Washington every single day. Hank, I don't want that anymore. I want to slow down, enjoy life and be with the person I love."

As I sat there and listened, I realized that the combination of the seven segments all blended together and the moment of mistrust faded as that word 'love' again erased my trepidation. There was no discomfort. There was no reticence. What had once only been a dream was becoming a reality.

Kat added that my last visit to Washington and touring her art studio led her to believe that IF and it was a big IF, we decided to make things more permanent, she could use the brewery as her studio and bring in other artist's works on consignment to cover the overhead.

"The top floor of the brewery could be turned into an art studio. The east end could easily be opened up to allow for natural light. The second floor could be converted into one or two loft apartments and the main floor could be a working showroom with the kiln back in the cave where they stored the beer."

"Do you think anyone would mind if I called it Polperro, after the fishing village in south Cornwall? Because of the stone and the wood upper floors, the building has so much potential."

I was impressed. Kat had done her homework and knew more about my little town than I did. She also had it all figured out regarding the business aspect. Between the hotel and the brewery, there would be apartments, a restaurant and showrooms. In other words, she was planning ahead, in case I finally realized I loved her. I asked why two different owners and Kat said the family's lawyers wanted to limit liability of one from the other.

Kat looked at me and said, "If we fail at one, it wouldn't affect the other".

I simply looked at her and shook my head. My free-spirited, artistic lover had a business sense about her I'd never realized. "Are Roger and Edgar still in town?" Kat asked. I shrugged. I had no idea.

"Can you find out?"

"That's easy, just ask Madge in the morning, but we need to be careful." I added. "Here in Mineral Point, there is a saying telephone, telegraph, telemadge! If you want everyone in town to know who owns the buildings, all you need do is mention it to Madge and I don't think you're ready for that.

"Not with the other plans I have," Kat added.

"What other plans?" I inquired.

"That's a surprise."

"I know! You're going to buy another building and open a gentleman's club like the Dangle Lounge in Madison and you're going to be the main attraction as the hootchie kootchie girl and the climax of the night's entertainment. Farmers will come from miles around just to watch you shimmy naked across the stage."

I was joking, of course, and added, "After California, Wisconsin was the second state in the union to allow nude dancing when the Dangle in Madison pioneered modern day adult entertainment in 1966. The Dangle was originally a piano bar that had few customers that mainly catered to the politicians from the Capitol a half-block away and dentists in the Tenney building.

I continued, "I don't know exactly where he got the idea, but one of the owners had a waitress who agreed to get up and dance on the piano and take her top off and it started a sensation."

"Let me guess, when it became a strip club, all the politicians flocked there." Kat inquired.

"You got it," I concurred as I looked at Kat and tried justifying why I knew so much. "The Dangle is one of the most famous bars in the country. The city doesn't like the Dangle to put it mildly and the politicians are publicly doing everything they can to shut it down as they consider it to be part of the anti-war, anti-establishment and counterculture of Madison."

Kat smiled at the hypocrisy as I continued, "They were the first bar in Wisconsin to go topless and then nude and actually won litigation using the First Amendment, which helped make them famous. Imagine, what James Madison would be thinking if he saw that his "freedom of speech was being used that way."

"If he was like most politicians, he'd be in the front row, expecting free drinks," Kat added. I chuckled as Kat then asked, "Have you ever been there?"

With the embarrassed look on my face and she knew I had. I justified my attendance by explaining that we'd gone because one of our buddies wanted us to go after his wake.

"His wake?" Kate questioned, incredulously.

"Yup! You think all farmers are old fuddy duddies. Charlie was one- of-a-kind and when he found out he had terminal cancer, he decided to do everything his wife would never let him do when he was healthy, like smoke marijuana, get drunk and rent one of those fancy skyboxes at County Stadium which we did September 12, 1965 to watch the Milwaukee Braves play their last home game."

"During the seventh inning stretch Charlie stood up and mooned the Braves as his way of saying goodbye." Kat chuckled as I shook my head and added, "We were all set to take Charlie to the Dangle to see Bonnie Ray from Santa Fe and Shakin Sharon, when he took a turn for the worse and couldn't go. He made us promise to go after his funeral. Ten of us rented a bus and went. We got rip roaring hammered and gave both girls hundred-dollar tips, compliments of Charlie."

Kat was laughing and then smiled at me with her wicked grin and said, "Tell you what, tonight I'll be your hootchie kootchie girl. I'll do a very slow, very erotic, strip tease and let you take off all my clothes and have me for desert if you want."

So much for the assumption that our relationship had moved to a less lustful plane! That night was, *'interesting'* to say the least. I grilled a couple of steaks and built a fire in the fireplace, while Kat lit some candles and we started drinking wine. I put some soft jazz on the good old turntable while we ate.

As we moved to the living room, I put on David Rose and his Orchestra's 'The Stripper and Other Fun Songs for the Family' that I owned, thanks to forgetting to send in the postcard to the Columbia Record Club. The album started out with 'Mood Indigo, then 'Night Train' followed by 'This Thing Called Love', 'Banned in Boston', 'St. James Infirmary', 'Soft Lights and Sweet Music', 'Black and Tan Fantasy', 'Harlem Nocturne' and finally 'Sophisticated Lady'.

Kat and I relaxed as we sat on the couch watching the fire and enjoying our second bottle of wine. As 'Sophisticated Lady' ended, I looked at her as 'The Stripper' began. Once you heard the tune and knew its association, there was no way you would ever forget. She immediately began to laugh as I covered my mouth as if surprised.

Kat rose and began to slowly do her thing, writhing and grinding to the music, while periodically slipping out of more of her clothes. As 'The Stripper" ended, Kat was standing naked in front of me and I profusely applauded, almost falling off the couch in laughter.

"Your turn!" Kat announced. If I ever wanted some quick sober-up medicine those were the words. I looked at her to see if she was in jest.

"You're kidding!" I exclaimed.

"What's fair for the goose, is fair for the gander" Kat replied. With that, the naked lady sauntered over to the turntable and inquired which track was "The Stripper".

I responded that it was the last one, hoping she was too drunk to hit the groove. Looking at me, Kat placed the stylus on 'Sophisticated Lady' and noted that it was to get me in the mood, as she came back to the couch and pulled me up whispering, "Give me a good show and I'll give you a VERY big tip."

I listened to 'Sophisticated Lady' and thought "What the

hell! as 'The Stripper' started, I kicked off my shoes to her delight and then my socks to boom, boom, boom. As the song hit the second bar, I began unbuttoning my shirt in cadence to each boom, while trying my hardest to swivel my hips. As my shirt fell to the floor, the music continued and I unbuckled my belt to the next set of booms and began slowly moving my zipper up-and-down to the beat of the slide trombone. Slowly, I let my pants slide down until I was standing in just my shorts while doing my darndest to be sexy, which would be really difficult sober and virtually impossible with all the wine sloshing around in my brain. Then, as the last stanza's of 'The Stripper' began, I pulled down my shorts to the hoots and whistles from one Ms. Katherine Johnson.

I stood there, totally exposed, as the music ended and the room went silent. Kat looked up at me and giggled her girlie giggle. We had both gone crazy! We had a little fun and created yet another one-on-one memory that we could laugh about, joke about and share forever. That night, we listened to music and watched the red embers slowly turn gold and then white as one-by-one they went out before our eyes as we huddled under the huge crochet cover Mrs. Gordon made as a 'someday wedding gift' before she left us. Empty glasses, once filled with wine, resonated to the sound of music and clinks to each other's happiness.

Two Aspirin and Call Me in The Morning – But Not Too Loud

The next morning, our heads ached, but it was all business as we walked up Chestnut Hill to the Rooster. After ordering her normal coffee and wheat toast, Kat brought up our Pendarvis lunch to Madge and how disappointed she was to learn the famous restaurant had permanently closed with the buildings being donated or sold to the State Historical Society.

Kat asked Madge if the owners had moved out as there was word they were thinking of relocating to Key West. Madge said they were still completing everything and periodically dropped by for afternoon tea. We had our answer.

After breakfast, we walked over to Roger and Edgar's house and rang the doorbell. Roger peeked out through the white lace curtains and smiled. Opening the door he said, "Hank and Katherine, if my memory serves me."

We both nodded in the affirmative.

"What a pleasant surprise! Come in! Come in!"

We obliged and went into the parlor filled with the knickknacks that had been on little shelves at Pendarvis.

"Is this a social call?" Roger inquired.

Kat took over and asked for assurances that what she was about to say would be held in the strictest of confidence. Roger had a funny look on his face but assured her he would. Kat reminisced on how much she loved Mineral Point and commended Roger for all that he and Edgar had done to restore Shake Rag.

Roger seemed grateful, even though he'd heard it a thousand times. Kat then outlined how she'd purchased the hotel and what she wanted to do with it, picking up where Pendarvis left off in terms of food and service, quality and ambiance and how her master plan was to help Mineral Point become an art colony.

Roger smiled, and I believe was honored as Kat continued. "It's going to be a risk, but I'm gaining the same passion for the area you and Edgar have and am willing to make the investment, but I need a little help."

I could see Roger's reticence building. He was tired and ready to move on. He and Edgar had put their hearts and souls into building up their business, and they had reached the end of the line. Like me with farming, the passion simply wasn't there anymore.

Kat added, "I'm not asking you to work. All I need are your recipes and the ability to note that we're carrying on the Pendarvis tradition."

Roger was initially gently shaking his head, no as Kat added. "You and Edgar would have final say on the menu, recipe's and promotions for the first year."

Roger continued to gently shake his head no and Kat added, "I'm willing to pay you $10,000 up-front versus five percent of the dining revenue on the entrées you were involved in during the first year."

I could see Roger's opinion changing as he noted, "I'd have to ask Edgar, and he's tired of all that we did."

Kat assured Roger, "You won't have to do anything except say yes and have final say on the food, advertising and promotion."

"Can I have a couple days to think it over?" "Most certainly."

"What if we say no?"

Kat was ready and pulled out the engineering survey and handed it to Roger while saying, "My consultants indicate that structurally, the hotel is in pretty bad shape and should probably be torn down. They also noted that the location would be well suited for either a gas station or some sort of budget motel."

I could see the pupils of Roger's eyes narrow. All he and Edgar's work near a low-end motel? Hardly!

Kat continued, "If you say yes, I'm planning on hiring the best restoration architects who would be challenged with sustaining the look, feel and integrity of Pendarvis and bring the hotel up-to-date structurally in terms of amenities. If what I have in mind works, it would simply enhance all that you have done."

The hook was in Roger's mouth and the meeting was over. Kat left the papers with Roger and we agreed to meet two days later.

As we were walking back to the Rooster I inquired, "You wouldn't really tear down the old hotel?"

"Of course not." Kat replied, "But he doesn't know that. Anyone who spent their entire lives creating what they did wouldn't want it sullied by some gas station or cheap motel next door. The only thing worse would be someone buying one of the cottages nearby and painting the sandstone white."

Two days later we met and the deal was consummated. Kat indicated that she had attorneys on retainer in Madison who would draw up the agreement, asking Roger if a corporate or certified check would be preferable.

As we were walking home, Kat said, "All I need now is someone in Mineral Point who can be my project manager. The hours would be short, the pay would be lousy, but the benefits – ahh, the benefits!"

"And what would the project manager's benefits be?" I inquired.

"Hmm, depending on the candidate, bi-monthly trips to the nation's capital to update the corporation on the progress and then, well, let's just say profound expressions of gratitude where the slogan 'anytime, anyplace and anywhere' seems quite apropos to me."

My eyebrows jumped as Kat's hand slowly slid across my lower back. She was seducing me, yet my security wheels were already spinning, as I added, "We need to keep this as quiet as possible and so I recommend putting a 'help wanted' ad in the Democrat Tribune and then you could 'interview' the candidates. If some retired farmer who's experience in plumbing, carpentry, electrical and HVAC happened to be amongst the finalists, well, perhaps, it would give him something to do and he could earn a little money and I'm certain would appreciate the benefits."

That afternoon, Kat went alone to the post office and rented a P.O. box as I put together the ad. We agreed that it should be as generic as possible and it read "Help wanted, part-time project manager to oversee a small remodeling project. Must have knowledge in carpentry, electrical, plumbing and HVAC. Submit resume to P.O. Box 331, Mineral Point, Wisconsin 53565."

Unbeknownst to me, Kat had already been looking for an architect with specific credentials, including old building restorations. As crazy as it was, she found one in Madison, with offices in the Frautschi building on King Street, just off the square and two blocks from the Madison law firm she was using.

I'd thought of my distant cousin's firm in Spring Green, but they were too big and too expensive for what Kat wanted to do.

"How did you know how to do all of this?" I asked.

Kat replied, "You need to remember, my father was a lawyer in New York before he got into politics and trusted no one. Our family's firm, got in touch with the law group in Madison and put the entire agreement together. When you have absentee ownership, people are always trying to screw you and you my dear, are the only one I want doing that."

The architects were given my phone number and called the next week. They wanted to tour the hotel. I agreed to meet them. Kat had been wise enough to put them on a flat fee instead of an hourly rate or they would have kept the meter running for the entire drive.

Two kids showed up with a Polaroid camera, tape measure and note pad, even though they had a copy of the engineering report. We spent the entire afternoon digging through everything from mouse poop to a dead weasel. They shook their head at the mess as we peered upward at blue sky through what was planned to be the dining room ceiling.

The kids seemed apprehensive of my abilities. I assured them that I was the project manager, lived in Mineral Point and was able to get them into Pendarvis to provide the look and feel that Kat wanted. I told them I'd have a complete written summary to them as soon as I talked with the owner.

They thought Kat and I were husband and wife. I was going to correct them until realized I sort of liked the idea.

Partridges and Pear Trees

One cannot even think of the 1940s in Mineral Point without looking beyond the tranquility of the hills and dales at the world and its turmoil. Beyond our respite of tranquility, the likes of Hitler, Mussolini and Hirohito set the course for the first half of the decade, even in our little town and the rest of the world, altering the course of its eventual destiny.

Too young for WW-I, I was deemed too old for WW-II. I would have gone had they allowed it, but I was farming alone and the kids were too young and so I was given a deferment. It wasn't as simple as it seemed. But then, when you're dealing with the government, whatever is?

The guidelines for deferment for farmers sounded like a math question from a college entrance exam. A farmer who lived on his farm and operated it alone was required to have at least eight milk cows. If both a farmer and his son lived on the farm together, 16 animal units were required for the man to obtain deferment.

By Feb. 12, 1943, in order to get the deferment, the farmer had to raise at least 10 animal units. By May 12, 1943, the farmer had to have at least 12 animal units and feed for the stock had to be produced on the farm where the resident lived. Since there was a variety of different animals on different farms, guidelines were often flexible. For example: For one milk cow there had to be three beef cows, four two-year-old steers or four feed lot cattle, 16 ewes or 80 feed lot lambs, a flock of 75 hens or either 250 chickens or 500 broilers, or 40 turkeys, or nine hogs while a breeding herd was not considered at all.

A typical example: If a farmer lived on a farm alone and had the following stock, he would meet the requirement of eight animal units and would be entitled to deferment. All he would need would be 2 milk cows with a value of two. Eighteen hogs raised for two more points. A flock of 150 hens was worth another two points. 250 chickens were worth one point. 16

ewes were also equaled one. With this, the farmer would have a total animal units of eight. All he needed to add was a "Partridge in a Pear Tree" and we'd have another Christmas song.

I'd always been a person who asked, 'why?'. With World War II, I posed that question only to learn that after suffering the consequences of World War I, which saw profound retributions demanded by the Allied powers with the Versailles Treaty, Germany suffered economically at a much greater degree during the Great Depression than America and the rest of the world did. This profound suffering allowed radical factions to grasp hold of power through the *Nationalsozialistische Deutsche Arbeiterpartei*, NSDAP, or National Socialist German Workers' Party, better known as the Nazi's.

The Nazi party formed in 1919 that took a small group of disaffected individuals and made them believe they could overthrow the German government and establish a new order under the leadership of Adolph Hitler. To expand his base, Hitler's strategy encompassed the tactic that his power could be fueled by dominance and the creation of enemies of the party and State. Enemies were identified first, within Germany and then based on any country, ethnicity, religion or orientation that differed from the Aaryn race that he symbolized as purity.

To ensure his longevity, Hitler and the Nazi's developed youth programs to indoctrinate and simply brainwash German children into believing that Germans had the right to dominate and overcome the "oppression" of those who didn't agree with their principles.

In March, 1936, against the advice of his generals, Hitler ordered German troops to reoccupy the demilitarized left bank of the Rhine River. Over the next two years, Germany concluded alliances with Italy and Japan, annexed Austria and moved against Czechoslovakia - all essentially without resistance from Great Britain, France or the rest of the international community, including the United States.

The U.S. was still reeling from the ravages of the Great Depression and was reluctant to fight again. Many Americans considered World War I to have been a terrible mistake, too costly in both blood and treasure and the American public was initially divided over whether to enter another international conflict. Interventionists, wanted America to enter the war on behalf of its allies.

The dominating Isolationists, wanted to avoid any war waged on foreign soil and this position was supported by the U.S. Congress even as Italy invaded Ethiopia, Japan conquered Manchuria and Germany rapidly began building up its military. Once Germany confirmed its alliance with Italy in the so-called 'Pact of Steel' in May 1939 with Hitler then signing a non-aggression pact with the Soviet Union.

On September 1, 1939, Nazi troops invaded Poland prompting Britain and France to declare war on Germany, and did so as America continued to look inward, more concerned with itself than the rest of the world. While still bound by the Neutrality Acts of the 1930's and campaigning for reelection on a promise not to enter the European conflict, President Roosevelt began seeking ways to assist America's allies which led him to propose a program called the Lend-Lease Act which Congress passed in 1941.

The Act allowed the president to ship weapons and other supplies to countries doing battle with Nazi Germany. Over the next four years, America sent more than $50 billion dollars of supplies to the Allies perceived by many as an unofficial declaration of war that enabled Britain to resist Germany until America formally entered the war at the end of that year.

This purchase of supplies assisted greatly in closing one of the darkest chapters in American economic and social history – the Great Depression. Hitler's Germany continued to expand. After ordering the occupation of Norway and Denmark in April 1940, Hitler adopted a plan proposed by one of his generals to attack France through the Ardennes Forest. The blitzkrieg ('lightning war') attack began on May 10th to which Holland quickly surrendered, followed by Belgium.

German troops advanced to the English Channel, forcing British and French forces to evacuate from Dunkirk in late May of that year. France signed an armistice with Germany one month later as German troops entered Paris for the first time with tanks rumbling past the Arc de Triomphe, down the Champs Elysees, to the Place de la Concorde, as French and allied forces retreated with the Germans meeting no resistance.

Many Americans asked why Hitler didn't destroy the city as he had done Warsaw and so many others. The answer given was that Paris was the center of art and artifacts and Hitler wanted everything, especially the museums to be intact in Paris to add to his own personal art collection, making sure that Paris proper was not bombed with the only bombing occurring on the city's outskirts at an automobile factory.

Within days, the French government surrendered and Hitler humiliated them by making them sign a new treaty in the same railroad car that was used when Germany signed their surrender from World War I.

The fighting was not over, with battles beginning in North Africa that same month, as Italy declared war on June 10th of that year. At home, high unemployment still carried over from the Great Depression, but agriculture and industry were beginning to rebound. Normal rainfall returned and farmers harvested large crops of corn, wheat and soybeans. "Thank you God" was whispered in many churches, including those of Mineral Point!

American factory production increased and farm prices rose. However, most European countries were cut off by German blockades, so exports went down, while America's demand for agricultural goods went up. The economy got yet another government boost as the Social Security Administration, created by 1930's New Deal legislation, sent out its first checks and banking and credit industries, now heavily regulated, regained the confidence of many Americans.

America had already begun readying its war machine in 1940 when Congress enacted the Selective Service Act, and the nation began the draft, including men from Iowa County and Mineral Point. More than 16 million men registered for the draft, which also allowed for conscientious objectors to be employed in noncombat work.

Congress authorized money to build planes and ships, housing for soldiers, and establishing new military bases across the country. The Alien Registration Act required that all aliens register with the government was signed as well. Hitler had hoped to force Britain to seek peace, as well. When that failed, he began his attacks on that country in June, 1941, followed by an invasion of the Soviet Union.

The debate concerning America's participation abruptly ended on December 7, 1941, when Japan bombed Pearl Harbor. On December 8, 1941, Congress declared war on Japan who demanded that Hitler declare war on the United States, as well. On December 10, 1941 Germany and Italy declared war on the U.S..

Hitler then shifted his central strategy to focus on breaking the alliance of Britain, United States and the Soviet Union. His plan was to force one of them to make peace with him in a war that would last until 1945 and would ultimately claim more than 50 million lives, including 400,000 Americans. 1,325 of those deaths were from Wisconsin. 34 came from Iowa County which was 30 more than lost their Iowa County lives during World War I.

In the earliest days of America's participation in the war, panic gripped the country. If the Japanese military could successfully attack Hawaii and inflict damage on the naval fleet and casualties among innocent civilians, many people wondered what was to prevent a similar assault on the U.S.

mainland, particularly along the Pacific coast. This fear translated into a ready acceptance by a majority of Americans of the need to sacrifice in order to achieve victory and overnight, Americans were ready and willing to take on the foes, regardless of what the sacrifice.

During the Spring of 1942, an American rationing program was established that set limits on the amount of gas, food and clothing consumers could purchase. Families were issued ration stamps used to buy their allotment of everything from meat, sugar, fat, butter, vegetables and fruit to gas, tires, clothing and fuel oil.

The United States Office of War Information released posters in which Americans were urged to 'Do with less–so the troops will have enough'. In a period of a few years, the country went from 30% unemployment and homelessness to sixteen million men and women directly involved in the war effort as the country went from a labor surplus to a labor shortage. Gone were bread lines, replaced by help wanted signs as women who formerly were 'housewives' went to work in factories doing 'men's work'.

Everyone pitched in! Food, gas and clothing were willingly rationed and no one cheated, that I know of. Communities conducted scrap metal drives to help build the armaments necessary to win the war. Meanwhile, individuals conducted their own drives, all of which were recycled and used to produce armaments as they purchased U.S. war bonds to help pay for the high cost of the armed conflict.

Men went off to war, while women found employment as replacement electricians, welders and riveters in defense plants, as men cheered them on. People in the U.S. grew increasingly dependent on radio reports of the fighting overseas. And, while popular entertainment served to demonize the nation's enemies, it also was viewed as an escapist outlet that allowed Americans brief respites from war worries regarding the wellbeing of the one in eight Americans directly involved in the war.

President Roosevelt created the Office of Price Administration in August, 1941. Its main responsibility was to place a ceiling on prices of most goods to prevent wartime price gouging and to limit consumption by rationing. Every Iowa County resident, including children, was issued a ration book, each of which had a certain number of rationing points per week. Meat and processed foods, vital for soldiers abroad, had high points. Fresh fruit and vegetables had no points. The first nonfood item rationed was rubber.

Because many of Asia's rubber plantations were under Japanese control, President Roosevelt asked citizens to help by contributing old tires, rubber raincoats, garden hoses, shoes and bathing caps. At one time, millions of discarded tires covered over one hundred acres at the Midwest recovery plant.

Supplies such as gasoline, butter, canned milk and sugar were rationed so they could be provided for the war effort and we were told to produce as much milk as we could and do so to help America win the war. Many people got three gallons of gas a week, farmers got more.

People stood in line for sugar, which was the first and last commodity rationed where the allocation was half-pound a week or half of what Americans typically consumed. Ann quickly learned the seven steps to converting sugar beets into sugar and we never used our ration coupons, giving them back to those who needed them more.

In 1942, Nazi leaders held a conference to coordinate what they called, 'the Jewish question' or the systematic genocide of Jews and other minorities that didn't fall within Hitler's concept of a master Aryan race. At the same time, more than 120,000 Japanese Americans, called Nisei, who were living on the West Coast of America, were moved inland to internment camps, including some for the duration of the war.

Sadly, although most were born in this country, the Nisei were designated enemy aliens who were required to obey travel restrictions, curfews and contraband regulations. Many lost their homes, farms and property during this time of internment in America, 'land of the free and home of the brave'.

In 1943, The U.S. Army activated the 442nd Regimental Combat Team made up of the 100th Battalion from Hawaii and Japanese American volunteers from mainland internment camps. Nearly 10,000 Hawaiian Nisei volunteered for military service and the, 100th Battalion fought in North Africa, Italy, France and Germany where they rescued the 'lost battalion' in 1944 and liberated the survivors at the Dachau Nazi concentration camp, proving that it is truly the content of character and not the color of one's skin that matters.

Dozens of other everyday items were rationed as the government halted production of cars to save steel, glass and rubber for war industries and stopped the manufacture of refrigerators, radios, sewing machines, vacuum cleaners, and phonographs. We were asked to dress warmly in order to preserve fuel oil for military transportation purposes.

The Terrill family switched back to burning wood from fallen trees and sharing some of it with neighbors, while trading ration stamps for things we could use. Scott and Jane were real young during the Depression, but had no idea of how bad things really were and so, they had no perspective. Every Sunday, when we came to town to go to church, we'd bring what we could in terms of rags, rubber, paper or metal that could help the government build airplanes and other equipment needed to fight the war. My how things had changed!

To fill the insufficient ranks of military nurses, posters and pamphlets urged young women to become a nurse. Once a woman was determined eligible, she would be trained for wartime and combat nursing including exercises in medicine, map reading, physical endurance and Army procedures. Over twenty Iowa County women volunteered and became wartime nurses.

By 1945, more than 250,000 women had served in the Women's Army Corps (WACS), Army Nurses Corps, the Women Accepted for Voluntary Emergency Service (WAVES), the Navy Nurses Corps, the U.S. Marines, and the Coast Guard. Most servicewomen were nurses who replaced men in noncombat roles.

During the war, the marines excluded colored Americans. The navy used them as servants. The army created separate black regiments including the Tuskegee Airmen known as the 99th Fighter Squadron who fought battles in North Africa, Sicily and Anzio and was joined by three all-colored squadrons known as the 332nd Fighter group. These brave men came home with 150 medals awarded by a country where they couldn't get a drink of water, ride in the front of a bus, eat in a restaurant or use a restroom simply because of the color of their skin.

The U.S. Treasury offered a series of war bonds citizens could purchase to invest in the country and, ideally, one's own financial future. A $25 war bond could be purchased for $18.75. The government would use the money to pay for military equipment. After about 10 years the bond could be redeemed for $25, a nearly 3 percent average annual return. Public school children in Chicago purchased $263,148.83 in war bonds and stamps.

The campaign concluded with a rally in Chicago's Washington Park. The war bonds they purchased were enough to purchase 125 jeeps, two fighter planes and a motorcycle. I guess Ann beat the gun, as we had a garden every year we were married while the government suggested that an alternative to rationing could be 'victory gardens', in which people grew their own food.

By 1945, some 20 million victory gardens were in use and accounted for about 40 percent of all vegetables consumed in the U.S.. Now those gardens all needed seeds and, sure enough, some of us realized we could grow sweet corn and sell the seeds to companies like Burpee's, which we did. The morning of June 6, 1944 became known as D-Day. The term was actually just an Army designation used to indicate the start date for specific field operations when 3,000 warships carrying 200,000 American and British soldiers crossed the English Channel and landed on the heavily fortified beaches of Normandy, France to begin a vicious battle against the German army and had no other meaning, yet will be remembered forever.

The infamous Battle of the Bulge began on December 16th as Hitler mustered 500,000 troops along the Allied front from southern Belgium into Luxembourg. In the bitter cold, the Germans pushed forward 50 miles, creating a "bulge" in the Allied lines. By the end of January, more than 76,000 Americans were killed, wounded or captured, with those who died buried in France, where they gave their lives for our freedom.

After considering all options, President Truman gave the order and on August 6, 1945, and the U.S. dropped an atomic bomb on Hiroshima, Japan. In minutes, half of the city vanished with about 200,000 people killed or missing with radiation affecting 100,000 more.

On August 9th, the U.S. dropped a second atomic bomb on Nagasaki with equal devastation. In September, Japan surrendered unconditionally on board the USS Missouri and World War II came to an end.

The war took a terrible toll in lives lost. It also changed America and Mineral Point in many ways. With the war, a revolution happened in American agriculture. All of a sudden, Iowa County farmers became much more productive, as it took less and less time to produce more and more food because we had better machines, new varieties of crops and livestock and pesticides, along with better irrigation techniques than ever before. That was the good side of farming. The other side was the reality that productivity on the farm grew because the government got much more heavily involved, both through direct payments and indirect support of agricultural technology research.

In 1940 the school milk program was initiated as a way to move surplus dairy products. While it helped, it was just one more way that the government got involved in farming. In 1947 the government came to general agreement on tariffs and trade which affected both the import price of finished goods and the sale of food products to other countries. Then the Federal Insecticide, Fungicide and Rodenticide Act was passed, telling farmers what they could and couldn't use to take care of weeds and critters.

The Agricultural Act of 1949 was passed, incorporating the principle of flexible price support and giving surplus food to the needy and, from then on, making money in farming meant you had to understand and manage government programs or you would lose. The government could either be your friend or foe; it was all up to you.

Fortunately, for Iowa County farmers, we were getting better at our jobs by using more and better technology and progressing at a faster pace than urban workers to the point that finally, after so many years we were all smiling once again. All Americans experienced two vastly different ways of life in the 1940's including those in Mineral Point.

After the Great Depression and World War II that placed strict regulations on the production of clothing, toys and entertainment, the new- found prosperity following the war, combined with the repeal of rationing laws and advancements in technology, enabled us to enjoy a more leisurely lifestyle.

During the war, with jazz firmly entrenched in American culture and those of us needing an outlet for some form of escape, we were introduced to dances like the Lindy Hop, Jitterbug and Jive. While orchestras had been the predominant music makers in the 1930's, the 19040's saw the birth of big bands whose music was accompanied by the syncopated rhythms of Benny Goodman, Duke Ellington and Glenn Miller.

Radio was an essential part of our life. I'd come in from the fields for lunch and listen to WIBA's 'Farm Hour' where they talked about the futures and weather and what this politician or that one wanted to control next. The kids would take over at night and listen to their favorite radio shows. While my parents had to trek into town on Saturday to learn the week's news, we quickly became accustomed to having it at our finger tips along with hour- long soap operas, cheering on the Badgers, listening to quiz shows and or concerts on the Philco. The world was shrinking and the word 'now' became even that more precise, finite and explicit.

As artists fled Europe, New York became the center of the art world and abstract artists, such as Jackson Pollock, experimented with new techniques, including abstract expressionism that inspired the entire creative community, including sculptors, poets, photographers and filmmakers whose art many people never really understood, including me.

At home, handsome crayon and watercolor paintings by Max Fernekes, such as one titled *Pendarvis Group,* took precedent along with Harry Knorr and his innate ability to take tree burls and make bowls out of them. Knowing the area, Harry had to look long and hard to find a burl to shape, realizing he only had one chance to make it right, knowing that a burl is simply a tree growth in which the grain has grown in a deformed manner to create an abstract, yet profoundly beautiful pattern. Normally found in the form of a rounded outgrowth on a tree trunk or branch that is filled with small knots from dormant buds, when carved, polished and stained, the form and shape of Harry's burls were gently formed to transcend function and become a natural work of art.

Both Harry and Max initiated the birth of Mineral Point as a true center for art and art lovers. I don't know if you want to call it art or not, however, after 1945, rationing laws ordered the trimming of beachwear fabric by 10%.

Designers introduced two-piece bathing suits that exposed the midriff, but covered the navel. Although the shrinking swimsuits were controversial among mainstream Americans, starlets and beach vacationing teenagers embraced the original version of the bikini and young men – make that most men - approved.

Perhaps it's a coincidence that in 1946, the first of the post war baby boomers were born and the generation that would rock the nation in many ways began as the sexual revolution started with the 'silent generation', amongst couples who didn't talk much about sex, but certainly participated in it. After fifteen years of depression and war, it's understandable that there was a desire to live life in the moment and enjoy it and accordingly, as couples were less likely to defer traditional restraints that had curtailed their inclinations in the past.

In 1947, President Harry Truman introduced what was called the Truman Doctrine. This was the an American foreign policy designed to contain Soviet geopolitical expansion that shifted away from direct American military involvement, to one based on appropriated financial aid that supported the economies and militaries of countries perceived to be threatened by communist take-over.

Truman felt that, "It must be the policy of the United States to support free peoples who are resisting attempted subjugation by armed minorities or by outside pressures." Truman contended that because totalitarian regimes coerced free peoples, they automatically represented a threat to international peace and the national security of the United States and it was more cost effective in terms of men and materials to support the countries economically, thereby creating domestic competition, than it was to go to war.

As a result of the Truman doctrine, countries such as Japan, South Korea and Taiwan were given financial aid and assistance in developing specific industries that allowed them to gain global footholds in such categories as electronics, automobiles, clothing and toys in direct competition with manufacturers within the United States. With this change, labels saying "Made in Japan", "Made in Korea" and "Made in Taiwan" began filling American shelves, initially with low-priced, labor-intensive products and then upscale items as well.

Because of the total devastation of most factories in all three countries, contemporary replacements were built with state-of-the-art equipment manned by personnel working at a fraction of the wages of their American counterparts. The net result was development of entire interrelated industries within the countries that didn't need imports of materials from the United States.

Beyond the American automobile, clothing and toy manufacturers, American television brands as such as Zenith, RCA, Quasar, Sylvania GE and Magnavox began competing against brands such as Sony, Toshiba, Panasonic, Samsung and Lucky Gold Star from these countries, eventually causing the demise of the American companies and loss of good paying jobs in America.

In 1948, a group of movie and television writers, producers, and directors were called as witnesses by the House Un-American Activities Committee and put in jail for contempt of Congress when they refused to state if they were Communists, beginning a time in our history that would become one of the darkest periods in twentieth-century American politics if you can believe that, particularly when there were already so many dark shadows to look at.

The popularity of big-band swing music declined after the war, replaced by a faster style based on improvisation. Some called it bebop. Other's called it bop. In either case, the music simply took the tempo and made it faster, while adding riffs designed to accentuate the melody. Popular jazz musicians such as Charlie Parker, Miles Davis, Earl Powell, Max Roach, Thelonious Monk, and Gil Evans came into play with modern jazz bands led by Dizzy Gillespie and Stan Kenton becoming popular.

While the rest of the world was in shambles, destroyed by war and in need of everything, America flexed its muscles knowing that whatever it made, whatever it grew, whatever it could provide could be sold somewhere and created the reference point from which all social, political and economic changes would be judged.

In ten years, Mineral Point transcended from a period of depression and despondency, fear and failure to one of dominance and enthusiasm. From hard times to good times, it all changed as frowns became smiles and fears became dreams, while the Terrill family prospered and life became good. While many made sacrifices, those who survived could simply take a deep breath and thank God by saying, "We made it!" as we looked forward to an even better tomorrow.

In 1949, Scott was seventeen and Jane fifteen and I felt like they were strangers. I'd spent all my time during the depression and war doing what I could simply to financially survive. Ann would go to their games and meet with their guidance counselors. I'd tag along for the Christmas presentations and fill in when I could, but running the farm all by myself was quite a challenge, first because no one wanted the milk you had and then I couldn't produce enough.

Sun up to sun down was spent taking care of the farm and then when all the cows were milked and it was dark outside, I'd come in the house, exhausted and try to help with the books, to keep things straight. I'd spend what time I could with the kids, but I know it wasn't ever enough.

We never took a vacation and really, the only time we did anything together, was when they were working on the farm. Our family survived the Great Depression and enjoyed to postwar good times, but my deepest regret was that I didn't spend more time being a better father and husband.

Thanksgiving

Kat gave me a choice, eating a Swanson TV dinner alone at home or coming to Washington for Thanksgiving. Hmmm! What a tough decision!

I made the travel arrangements and began mulling things over in my head. In our Sunday night conversation, I inquired as to the guest list and was told it would just be her and I. Annie would make dinner and we could just enjoy each other's company.

I thought about the dinner and asked Kat what she thought of getting her family together so that I could meet them. She thought it would be a great idea. I then asked her if we could invite another family to have dinner with us. She was a bit confused, as I didn't know a soul in Washington.

"Who do you want to invite?" Kat inquired.

"I was thinking about the Harris family," I replied.

There was a pause and then Kat responded that it was one of the kindest, nicest things she'd ever heard. I told her, it would be cool if we could have it be a surprise for Charles and Mrs. Harris particularly, if we could get their kids to come, as well.

Kat called the Country Club and asked if they could cater the meal as we both agreed that Annie could then enjoy her family. Arrangements were made for all the food to be prepared and two of Kat's favorite servers could be available for a midafternoon dinner, which would then give the servers time to go home to their own families.

Kat had the phone numbers for the Harris kids and offered to call them, along with her two boys, whom I'd never met. She called and all the kids thought it would be a wonderful way to see their parents and each other, as they had literally grown up together.

I departed on Monday for Washington, and Charles met me at the airport in the limo. Once again, I'd offered to take a cab, and it was refused. We arrived at the house and I put my clothes in Kat's closet.

A few hours later, I went up to change and my clothes had been moved across the hall. Geez! I guess the kids were the only ones who could change the rules.

Mrs. Harris was in the kitchen and I went in to say hello.

"Mr. Terrill, it's so nice to see you," Annie said as she was getting ready to bake pies for Thanksgiving.

"Please, call me Hank."

"I really can't do that, Mr. Terrill. It just wouldn't seem proper."
"OK."

Kat came home from the library and I shared an idea, why not have name cards for the table so we controlled the seating. We could say it was because I was so bad with names, which I am. Kat thought it was a great idea and we spent about an hour discussing seating for nine people. Besides Kat and me, there would be Charles and Mrs. Harris and their two kids along with their son Charles Junior's wife. In addition, there would be Kat's two boys, Will and Tad.

Kat informed Annie that we would be having guests and the total for Thanksgiving dinner would be nine. Kat wanted to put Charles and I at the ends and I said "No" as that would make us appear as opposites. I felt we should sit in the middle with me next to Charles on one side and across from Mrs. Harris, while Kat also sat next to Mrs. Harris and across from Charles on the other. Kat thought about it and smiled, realizing we were making a statement of equality and acceptance and ensuring there wasn't any familial herding at the table.

To my left, we planned to have Charlene, who was the Harris' twin daughter and attending Harvard law school. Next to her and on the end, we placed Tad, Kat's oldest son, who worked as an asset manager in New York. To the right of Charles, we placed Will, Kat's other son, who was an officer in the Marine Corps. To his right and at the other end of the table, we placed Junior as everyone called him, who was Charlene's twin brother, studying to be a minister in Atlanta, with his wife Marie to his right, who would then be sitting next to Kat.

Kat made small name cards which she put in a desk drawer and asked Mrs. Harris if she and Charles would like to join us for dinner. Kat reported that Annie, as she called her, was shocked. In all the years, they'd never had a holiday meal together. Annie was worried about cooking and Kat told her we were having the food catered so that she and Charles could enjoy the day.

As Thursday arrived, Kat called down to the Harris House and told Charles that three of our house guests were arriving at 9:00 AM at Washington National and asked him to retrieve them. Charles asked how he would know who they were and Kat indicated that she'd provided his pager number and the license plate for the limo and they would page him and they could meet up. Charles had done this before and thought nothing of it.

Tad was flying into Dulles and would rent a car, as he was going to stay a few days to see other friends. Will made arrangements to fly home on a military jet from California and would take a cab from Langley. Everyone was scheduled to arrive at the house by around noon.

Annie was down at the Harris house when we put the placards in the proper order. I smiled at Kat and she gave me a hug saying, "What a wonderful idea from a sweet, sweet man." I was humbled.

At 10:30, I heard the car in the entry out front and soon the front door opened and in walked Charline, Junior and Marie along with one VERY proud father. A few minutes later, Annie came running up the drive with her apron still on, smiling from ear to ear and full of profound joy.

"Lord, my prayers have been answered!" Annie exclaimed. "My babies have come home."

Just then the front door opened and Tad walked in with hugs all around, as I stood in the background, and allowed the love to be shared. As soon as the excitement slowed, Kat introduced me as her 'very special friend' from Wisconsin. I politely shook hands with everyone and felt welcomed.

We'd just completed the introductions when the door opened and Captain William Stinson walked in dressed in his Marine Corps uniform, which he was required to wear in order to fly military. The entire process of hugs and kisses began again, followed by a repetition on my introduction.

I could tell the kids enjoyed seeing each other. They literally grew up together with the only difference being Will and Tad went to private schools, while Charlene and Junior went to the public schools nearby.

We all headed for the sun porch and I became a spectator to life's changes and updates. Amongst the casual conversations, I was able the glean a few tidbits on the kids. Charlene, or Char as they called her, was in her last year at Harvard law school. I asked her if she'd ever heard of Dr. Daniel Terrill?

Char stopped in her tracks. "Dr. Terrill? THE Doctor Terrill, the first black man to graduate from Harvard law school?" I nodded in agreement as Char continued, "Dr. Daniel Terrill was of mixed race and therefore not considered black. George Lewis Ruffin is given credit as being the first Negro to graduate from Harvard Law in 1869."

"Doctor Terrill wrote the briefs for the Dredd-Scott case, but wasn't allowed to present them because he was a freed slave. For his efforts Doctor Terrill became the first black Federal Judge, which is also contrary to what history writes, where it says that Robert Terrell, was the first black federal judge, who graduated from Harvard Law School in 1884 and was appointed to the bench in 1910 or nearly forty years after Doctor Daniel Terrill."

I nodded and smiled, adding, "He was my cousin."

There as a frown on everyone's faces. "His father was my great, great uncle, while my great, great grandfather is the man who got Daniel out of slavery, sent him to Oxford and made certain he was safe in America."

Char simply shook her head, stating, "we've never been told that part of the story, only about his profound brilliance and legal expertise."

"If you have the time, I can fill you in on what I know. He was quite the guy."

Char enthusiastically nodded in the affirmative.

Junior and Marie indicated they met at Spelman College. Junior had a degree in sociology and Marie in chemical engineering. Marie worked for Coca Cola in product development. Junior got the calling and was attending the divinity school associated with the Ebenezer Baptist Church.

"Dr. King's church, if I'm not mistaken."

Junior nodded in the affirmative as I added, "I watched his speech from the mall on TV. Then, last year when I was here, I stood where he stood and could feel both the goodness and greatness of the man. His '*I Have a Dream*' speech should be required learning for everyone in America." I think the kids were shocked to hear that.

Will had changed into civilian clothes and had been somewhat in the background as I inquired, "Will, tell me about yourself, please."

Will was sort of shy and said. "I'm a military lifer. My current rank is Captain and I'm up for evaluation to Major next year. I've served two tours in Viet Nam and am currently assigned to Camp Pendleton.

"I have a son in the Navy," I offered. "I know, Captain Scott Terrill."

"I believe Scott's rank is Commander," I replied.

"No sir, Captain Scott Terrill. I've met your son who was transferred in from Hawaii about six months ago and is involved in expanding the Navy Seal program. I can't share any other information than that, but you can be VERY proud of Scott, Mr. Terrill."

I was both embarrassed and proud at the same time and wanted to quickly change the subject and turned to Tad and asked him what an Asset Manager did. He explained that his company managed the investments of specific clients including stocks, bonds, savings, real estate holdings, trust funds and foundations, including estate planning, taxation and government compliance to ensure the continuation of accumulated wealth for families.

It was a pleasant conversation, but what really caught my eye was the look in Tad's eyes every time he glanced at Charlene. Even oblivious me could tell there was something going between the two of them.

The gang asked about me and so I let them have it, probably babbling on too long. "I'm a retired dairy farmer from Wisconsin. A few years ago, my wife died, and I sold my farm to my brother. I'd never been anywhere and flipped a coin to decide between coming East or going West," at which time, I pulled my lucky quarter out of my pocket. "This coin brought me to Washington and, after seeing the sights and getting completely confused, I realized I needed more information about how our government did or didn't work and got lost in the Library of Congress. Some kind lady felt sorry for me and came up and asked if she could be of assistance. She found a book in one of the back corners that I was going to copy the pages I needed when she indicated that, for a dime a page, she could photo copy what I wanted to save. Well, it was the luckiest fifty-cents I ever spent, because that night we went out to dinner, had one of the best nights of my life and here I am."

As we were finishing our conversation, one of the servers came in and said that dinner was served. As everyone entered the dining room, they saw the name tags and took their appropriate seats. I think Charles, who had been silent, was at first shocked and then pleased to see that he sat next to me and across from Kat, realizing we considered him to be our equal. Annie took her place across from me, nodded and smiled. There was pure joy in her heart. She had been accepted.

I leaned back and asked Charles what his background was. He outlined that he went to Tuskegee and was trained as a civil engineer. With World War II breaking out, he volunteered and wanted to be one of the Tuskegee airmen. Unfortunately, his eyesight wasn't good enough and was assigned a desk job and here is what Charles said,

"One day Katherine's father walked in and everyone jumped to attention. I arose with the rest of the group as he came over and inquired about my job and my background. I respectfully responded, and Katherine's father asked what I thought of white people. I was shocked as no one had ever asked a colored man in the south what we thought of them before."

"I looked at Miss Katherine's dad and said, 'Sir, I've been taught to judge a man by the content of his character and not the color of his skin,' to which Katherine's dad smiled."

Charles continued as if he were reciting the entire event. *"'Where are you from son?' he asked. I indicated Vermont. He had a strange look on his face.*

'Vermont?' Yes sir, my father is a professor of geology at the University of Vermont.' I guess he was surprised, as most of the boys were from the south and didn't have an education."

"'Are you educated?'

"Yes sir, I have a degree in civil engineering. *'And they have you pushing papers'"*

"'Yes sir!'"

"'Are you thorough and do you pay attention to details?'"

"To the best of my ability, sir."

"'What's your name?'"

"Private First-Class Charles Harris, sir."

"'Well, Corporal Harris. You're done pushing papers. I need you as my liaison to men of color. Please report to your base commander and prepare to relocate to the Pentagon.'"

"I worked for Miss Katherine's father every day from then on in the military and achieved the rank of E-9 or Sergeant Major and served him in public life until his death nineteen years ago. He was my boss and my friend. We learned to trust each other and respect each other and get over our differences. When he had a problem or a worry, I'd give counsel. When he needed to let off steam, I'd pour the bourbon and we'd drink together. I was there with him when we went to the hospital to see his new daughter and I was with him the moment he died and never regretted a single minute of it."

"Civil Engineer?"

"Yes, sir!"

"Please call me Hank."

"Can't do that, sir."

"Understood."

As desserts hit the table, I took my knife and dinged the glasses for attention. As everyone quieted, I stood. "I'd like to propose a toast to family and friends and thank you for making me feel welcome. As you know, Ms. Katherine and I have become close and I hope today you feel like I do - that we belong together."

"After experiencing the tragedy of losing my wife, I thought no one would ever fill that piece of my heart again." I looked at Kat and raised my glass to her and said, "here I stand, humbled and honored to say to someone special - thank you for your goodness, kindness and generosity and for making me feel complete again."

There were tears and cheers. I almost wanted to propose, but felt it should be between the two of us just in case she said "no". In the end, the meal was a complete success with long-standing barriers broken and the question I was now certain I wanted to ask but needed to wait until she met my kids and they approved.

That night, I asked Kat if we could use Charles on the hotel and brewery projects to save some money. She said it had been a long time since Charles had been involved in anything other than maintaining the house and some family Washington properties.

"He's intelligent and bored and has a military sense about him that you don't find anymore." With that, Charles Harris became involved in making certain that what we were doing made sense structurally and on time, as he took care of all the logistical aspects concerning building materials and even scheduling the labor, saving us tens of thousands of dollars.

As we were picking up the empty glasses in the sunroom, I looked at Tad and caught his eye. "Tell me, Mr. Johnson, in asset management, do you also create corporations for your clients?"

A wry smile crossed his face. "How are we doing?" I asked.

"A little over budget, but nothing we can't handle. Especially now that Charles is on the team. He's one tough cookie!"

The next two days were spent learning more about the kids and having them learn about me, highlighted by me asking Charles if he wanted to get involved in the projects to which he responded like a little kid at Christmas. The kids politely listened to my stories and laughed at my corny jokes. What more could a man ask for?

Sunday morning I packed and placed the next chapter of 'War of My Brothers' on Kat's night stand. I said goodbye and gave Kat a kiss on the cheek as everyone stood there wanting to say goodbye. Charles drove me back to National for my flight home. The place was a madhouse, and we pulled into the VIP government area when I realized the limo had special government plates I'd never noticed before. Charles got out and opened the trunk and handed me my suitcase. With that, he extended his hand and as I shook it, Charles looked into my eyes and said, "Thank you, Hank!" making the entire trip worthwhile.

A Time of Innocence, a Time of Consequences

The years from the end of World War II to the end of the 1950s were dominated by several powerful changes in our lives. The first was the birth of the Cold War and the great fears it created. The Soviet Union, our former ally in the Second World War, became our nemesis and with it came the challenges and fears that bored deep within the psyche of every American man, woman and child.

One of the darkest moments in Wisconsin history can be traced to Senator Joseph McCarthy, who parlayed his inflated military record into political success. Elected to the Senate in 1946, McCarthy approached his reelection as an obscure member of Congress without any important issue or achievement on which to base his campaign.

Beginning in 1950, McCarthy began searching for visibility and, unsurprisingly in a time when anticommunism was a powerful force in national politics, presented himself as a scourge of disloyalty. In 1950, at a speech in West Virginia, McCarthy waved a piece of paper before his audience and claimed to 'hold in my hand' a list of people named by the Secretary of State as members of the Communist Party still serving in government.

Over time, the number of names on that list fluctuated widely and through all the years in which McCarthy raged through the political world, never once did he identify anyone who was ever convicted of treason or subversion. Sadly, McCarthy attracted devoted followers because of his aggressive political style, which made him seem to be a courageous, unpretentious figure, unafraid to attack disloyal elites.

McCarthy was not a leader of his party. However, until 1952, he was tolerated, even welcomed by the Republican leadership, since the party was committed to using the fear of communism to break the twenty-year Democratic lock on the presidency. However, after the election of President Eisenhower, McCarthy's tactics became an embarrassment and his claims of communist influence in the military, particularly enraged a president who had spent most of his life in the Army.

The Red Scare was visible in almost every area of American life. However, it was primarily a phenomenon of government and politics all hyped up by the media who takes mole hills and turns them into mountains. The entire communist 'threat' was produced and sustained by the government, even if it ultimately spread beyond government.

Anti-communism became official government policy not just in Washington, but at every level of government. Forty-four out of the forty- eight state governments in the United States passed laws between 1949 and 1955 designed to root out subversives and suppress communist activities. State and local courts engaged in remarkable excesses in pursuing and punishing communists. Even city and county governments became energetic in rooting out people they believed to be subversives. But it was in the federal government where the Red Scare developed most rapidly and decisively.

One consequence of the heightened red scare was the profound fear of the intensity of the atomic bombs and their incredible devastation which was so dramatic that we all were terrorized when we learned that the Soviet Union could attack and destroy America and our lives. We had never felt the direct pain of war and yet, even children were exposed to the realities of total annihilation.

Grade school children were shown films of compete devastation and taught to hide beneath their desks if an atomic attack were to happen. At night, kids said their prayers and prayed they would be alive the next day, not incinerated, mutilated or decimated, but alive. Gone was the innocence of being a child, replaced by an inner fear that today could be their last day. Whether they lived in New York, Los Angeles, Chicago or even Mineral Point, the pervading sense was one of oblivion, with the only sense of security being that if it were to happen, it wouldn't happen in our little town.

Day-to-day life in Mineral Point was, on the one hand, quiet and pastoral. Yet, under the surface, the baby boomers who were entering grade school, grew up during this time experiencing a gnawing fear and knowledge that, on any day and with little warning, their bucolic life could end as they were incinerated by an atomic bomb.

Our first actual encounter with Communism came with the Korean War that began less than five years after World War II. While much smaller and stature than the World Wars, it played an important role in changing America, and I need to outline what happened and its long-term consequences.

In 1910, Korea was annexed by the Empire of Japan and was considered a part of that country from that time on, including the entire Second World War. This meant that during World War II, the Allies needed to invade and defeat the Japanese in Korea as well as everywhere else in the Pacific.

At the 1943 Tehran Conference and 1945 Yalta Conference, Joseph Stalin and the Soviet Union agreed to join the Allies in the Pacific War and do so within three months of the victory in Europe. When Germany officially surrendered in May of 1945, the Soviet Union honored its pledge and declared war on Japan in August of that year, doing so three days after the atomic bombing of Hiroshima. Within weeks, the Red Army began fighting the Japanese in the northern provinces of Korea.

In order to honor the agreements of the Yalta Conference, it was agreed that the U.S. and Soviets would divide Korea into Soviet and U.S. occupation zones similar to that done in Germany and do so along the 38th Parallel. Joseph Stalin, maintained his commitment and the rapidly advancing Red Army halted their invasion at the 38th Parallel and awaited arrival of U.S. forces in the south.

The following month the Japanese surrendered south of the created border and the U.S. appointed a military governor who directly controlled what was now called South Korea.

With the surrender, the Soviets administered the northern half and the Americans administered the south.

In 1948, the occupation zones became two sovereign states. A socialist state was established in the north under the leadership of Kim Il- sun and the south under the leadership of Syngman Rhee. Both governments of the two new Korean states claimed to be the sole legitimate government of all of Korea, and neither accepted the border as permanent.

The Soviet Union withdrew its forces from Korea in 1948, and U.S. troops followed suit in 1949 upon which a large-scale North Korea backed insurgency broke out in the south. While the insurgency was ongoing, both sides engaged in multiple battalion sized battles along the border. North Korea's leader believed that widespread uprisings in the south had weakened the South Korean military and that a North Korean invasion would be welcomed by the South Korean people and began seeking the Soviet Union's support for an invasion.

Stalin initially didn't think the time was right for a war in Korea. However, by Spring 1950, his position changed as the Chinese forces under Mao Zedon secured final victory in China. The U.S. had withdrawn its forces from Korea and the Soviets had detonated their first atomic bomb, breaking the U.S. atomic monopoly.

Because the U.S. had not directly intervened to stop the communist victory in China, Stalin believed the U.S. would be even less willing to fight in Korea. With that conclusion, Stalin developed a more aggressive strategy in Asia, including promising economic and military aid to China.

In April 1950, Stalin gave Kim permission to attack the government in the South under the condition that Chairman Mao would send reinforcements, if needed. For Kim, this was the fulfillment of his goal to unite Korea after its division by foreign powers. Stalin clarified that Soviet forces wouldn't openly engage in combat and would avoid a direct war with the U.S.. Kim met with Mao in May 1950 where Chairman

Mao expressed his concern that the U.S. would intervene, but agreed to support the North Korean invasion primarily because China desperately needed the economic and military aid promised by the Soviets if they backed Kim.

The Truman administration was unprepared for the invasion as U.S. military strategists were more concerned with the security of Europe against the Soviet Union than East Asia. The administration was worried that a war in Korea could quickly widen into another World War should the Chinese or Soviets decide to get involved.

There was initial hesitance by some in the U.S. government to take part in another war. However, considerations about Japan played a critical part in the ultimate decision to engage on behalf of South Korea, especially after the fall of China to the Communists. U.S. experts on East Asia saw Japan as the critical counterweight to the Soviet Union and China in the region.

The Korean war began on June 25th, 1950 when North Korea invaded South Korea following clashes along the border and insurrections in the South, with the Truman administration still uncertain if the attack was a ploy by the Soviet Union or simply a test of U.S. resolve. The decision to commit ground troops was determined when a communique was received indicating the Soviet Union wouldn't move against U.S. forces in Korea, allowing the U.S. intervene without undermining its global commitments elsewhere.

In its three-year term, the Korean War was among the most destructive conflicts of the modern era, with approximately three-million fatalities consisting not only of military personnel, but thousands of civilian massacres on both sides representing a larger proportional civilian death toll than World War II with all of its atrocities. 36,000 American soldiers lost their lives of which 726 were from Wisconsin, including 637 Army, 80 Marine and eight Navy personnel of which five soldiers were from Iowa County. Beyond the loss of humanity was the destruction of virtually all of Korea's major cities, leaving the country in total ruins before the war unofficially ended in an armistice on July 27th, 1953.

In the end, nearly a half million Americans had been involved, and for the first time in American history, the U.S. didn't win the war. In fact, neither side actually won, and the war goes on to this day, since the combatants never signed a peace treaty.

At home, there was the feeling of uneasiness that comes in times of trouble, but the commitment, community efforts and sacrifices seen in the two World Wars simply didn't exist. Life in America was safe and secure and continued on. However, as in any war, young people were lured away from small towns and farms, either to enlist in the military or take jobs in the cities, including our two kids, who both left Waldwick for school to never return.

Times were good economically. The dramatic growth of affluence, which transformed the lives of many, but not all Americans, came about as the country emerged as the world's leading industrial power, where the demand for anything 'Made in America' exceeded supply simply because those in need were still recovering from the ravages of war that had shattered their ways of life. The average family income grew as much in the ten years after World War II as it had grown in the previous fifty years combined and the country saw a significant decrease in poverty from 30% in 1950, to 22% in 1960 and under 14% in 1969.

What caused this remarkable growth? One important cause was government spending, which was clearly the major factor in ending the Depression in the early 1940s. Government expenditures in 1929 were 1% of the gross national product. In 1955, they were 17%, with the bulk coming first from military spending until the end of the Korean War. As the war ended the focus shifted to social and infrastructure projects such as the interstate highway system and veterans' benefits that included mortgage and education assistance, government-sponsored research for the military and space and finally, farm programs and other sources of expenditures that continue to fuel the economy. Today, those expenditures continue to grow as we see that federal spending represents over 30% of the entire gross domestic product or GDP.

Another cause of postwar economic growth was population growth that saw the tremendous increase in the birth rate in the years after World War II that was responsible for increased demand and consumption in all kinds of things. It spurred economic growth as well.

The growth of suburbs after World War II was one of the greatest population movements in American history. Eighteen million people, representing 10% of the population, moved to the suburbs in the 1950s. The American population grew 19% in ten years with suburban population exploding by 47%, creating a vast new market and providing a huge boost to several of the most important sectors of the economy, such as the housing, automobiles, highways and a wide range of consumer industries.

Population numbers didn't follow the same track for Mineral Point. The 1940 census reported 2,275 citizens. In 1950 there were 2,279 and in 1960 there were 2,385 and now 2,305. In twenty years, the Mineral Point population has grown by a grand total of 30 people or just 1%, as young people left Mineral Point for larger cities like Madison, Milwaukee and even Chicago.

Many middle-class Americans in these years believed American people, for all their diversity, were becoming more and more alike and could expect to continue to do so in the future. Few ideas became more pervasive in popular culture than the sense that America was becoming a middle-class nation and a society in which everyone was already part of the middle class, soon to be or aspiring to become part of it. And there was some evidence in the accuracy of this powerful idea.

There was rapid growth in the number of people able to afford what the government defined as a 'middle-class' standard of living representing 60% of the American people. Home ownership rose from 40% in 1945 to 60% by 1960. 75% of all families owned cars, 87% purchased televisions, and 75% had washing machines.

Another major factor was the establishment of the plan to build the Interstate Highway system. President Dwight D. Eisenhower was influenced by his experiences as a young Army officer crossing the country in the 1919 Motor Transport Corps convoy that drove in part on the Lincoln Highway, the first road across America that required over two weeks to go from coat-to- coast. During World War II, Eisenhower gained an appreciation of the German Reichsautobahn system, which has become the Autobahn network that he considered to be a necessary component of a national defense system.

In 1954, Eisenhower appointed General Lucius D. Clay to head a committee charged with proposing an interstate highway system plan. Summing up motivations for the construction of such a system, Clay proposed a 10-year, $100 billion program, which would build 40,000 miles of divided highways linking all American cities with a population greater than 50,000 to be financed by a national gasoline tax.

In June 1956, Eisenhower signed the Federal-Aid Highway Act into law. Under the act, the federal government agreed to pay 90% of the cost of construction of Interstate Highways that were required to be a freeway with at least four lanes without stoplights or intersections and uninterrupted, high- speed roads.

Construction began, and the consequences were almost beyond comprehension. First was increased use of the automobile for interstate travel and suburban living and from that, the local reliance on the car for individual transportation. This has resulted in a myriad of changes such as fast-food restaurants, which not only brought low-cost meals and fast service, but changes in the nutritional make-up of the American diet that's evolved into higher levels of obesity, high blood pressure, heart disease and Diabetes.

The second major result was the shift in the transit of goods from rail to semi-trailers allowing for faster and more finite distribution and the beginning of the loss of social regionalization in terms of everything from the food we eat to dialects we speak, and social, political and even religious perspectives as American society has moved away from a series of regional areas to one that is national in scope, dominated by formula restaurants and formula retailers who have identical operations, offerings and policies who could then use the combination of economies of scale, convenience and television advertising to appeal to Americans.

The net consequence has been a homogenization of America where what you see at the exit of your nearest Interstate interchange is the same brand with the same products, the same look and same service as everywhere else in America. The regionalizing retail factors that formerly delineated one area of the country from another, along with the great southern migration brought on by air conditioning, have begun to see the regional differences in America rapidly disappearing.

The only victims of the Interstate System have been the small towns. Gone is the drive-through traffic that supported local businesses where travelers would stop to eat, purchase goods or simply enjoy the personality of the community through which they were traveling. Today's small towns, like Mineral Point, are no longer able to enjoy the fruits of the independent traveler. Instead, small town retailers must rely on repeat local business, while the entire community has become a destination-specific attraction that must compete with every other type of retail and entertainment venue for the time, attendance and discretionary dollars of the casual traveler.

The effect of all these changes has been a change in the American way of life in which today, Americans no longer believe it's good enough simply to subsist. Instead, they want to enhance the quality of their lives which is a basic right and material abundance is the way most Americans define their world, regardless of what the social, ethical, emotional or psychological costs are to acquire those material things.

In our town, farm equipment sales exploded in the 1950s as new tractors, combines, bailers, harrows and other equipment that would increase efficiency were purchased. Milk machines gave way to milking parlors that automatically transfer the milk directly from the cow to large refrigerated coolers for pickup by the transport company. Each phase has resulted in expanded capability. With each expansion, came the need for greater productivity and capacity. With every increase in the need for capacity came the demand for better ways to grow crops or acquire more land. Gone were the days of a few cows and forty acres, replaced by hundreds of cows and some farms nearing a thousand acres.

For the Terrill family, there were more immediate concerns, as it may have been for many of the 'traditional' farm families during this time. We were aware of the world events, but were more concerned with keeping both the family and the family farm together. In 1955, the two Terrill families lived off the production of our 335 acres from both farms. In addition, we were renting 90 acres of cropland near Jonesdale.

I was milking cows and growing feed, and my total net income for the year was less than $2,000 with Tom's not much more. Each evening Tom would drive into town to a feed mill to work for a few hours. Two days a week, Sue put in an eight-hour shift at a cheese factory. They simply needed the money.

We didn't complain. Accepting that a farmer is someone who likes to work and enjoys seeing stuff grow is what kept me on the land as long as it did. I guess the land is just like the animals, you've got to like them and pamper them to get the most out of both of them. When you're farming, you've got to live it all the time. Come rain or shine, hell or high water, you've got to be there.

I could have never made it without my wife. Ann was perfectly capable of getting on a tractor and discing a field if need be. She recognized her role, knowing and accepting that on a farm, she was both the helping hand and my business partner.

When Scott was born, I dreamed of him becoming a farmer, same as me, but also felt that he needed to find his own way and that's why college was so important. If he wanted to be a farmer, fine! I'd help him. It was important for him to make up his own mind, and he did. He fell in love with the Navy and is making a career out of it.

Scott enrolled at the UW in 1950 and joined Navy ROTC and never spent another summer at home. Once, I asked him why he chose the military and he said "I know what it takes to be a farmer. It takes a man who's strong, who can think and make quick decisions, just like a Navy officer. Farming's not for me, dad. I need the structure and consistency and that's what the military is giving me."

In 1952, Jane graduated from Mineral Point High School and decided to go to school in Oshkosh because they had a good Nursing program. After a couple years, she switched majors and got a degree in Elementary Education. She met Frank, who became her husband, a week after she graduated from college. They lived in Appleton for a while, with Frank working at some TV and Appliance store until he got a job with the post office delivering mail. Because of having terrible asthma, Frank was exempted from the military. As Frank's asthma got worse, they moved to Flagstaff, Arizona. I never got to know Frank that well and he didn't seem to want to get to know me.

1953 saw the introduction of television with WMTV Channel 33, and WKOW, Channel 27, broadcasting from Madison followed in 1956 by WISC, Channel 3. Television shrunk the world and brought entertainment to the masses and we all became reliant on it instead of our neighbors for information and entertainment. With television, any problem could be solved in 30 or 60 minutes and complex solutions resolved as well. Many comedies presented an idealized image of white suburban family life: happy housewife mothers, wise fathers, and mischievous but not dangerously rebellious children were constants on shows like *Leave It to Beaver* and *Father Knows Best.* These shows reinforced certain perspectives on the values of individualism and family — values that came to be redefined as 'American' in opposition to alleged Communist collectivism, I guess.

Westerns, which stressed unity in the face of danger and the ability to survive in hostile environments, were popular too. Programming tailored for children emerged with shows such as *Captain Kangaroo, Romper Room,* and *The Mickey Mouse Club* designed to appeal to members of the baby boom. The Mickey Mouse Club even had a series called 'The Adventures of Spin and Marty' that provided an idealized version of ranch life and then 'Adventures in Dairyland' with Annette Funicello that was filmed around here and had everyone in our area all excited to see a real 'movie star'.

Commercial broadcasting, meant the three networks presented advertisements that had one underlying message— you're not good enough, happy enough or successful enough unless you have this product or that service, all intended to make you better, happier, sexier than you already were. Gone were the days of sacrifice and doing without that had been part of the war effort, replaced by the never-ending subliminal message that more is better while materialism planted seeds of discontent that changed American society and made people dissatisfied with what they had when it was more than we'd ever had before.

The kids of the fifties had their own social structure including fashion and music with one of the most memorable fashion trends being the poodle skirt, which was a bright, colorful, long, swingy skirt that hit just below the knees. The fabric used was mostly felt appliqued with the image of a small poodle. I remember Jane coming home from Oshkosh and begging mom to make her one, as it was all the rage.

High school dances of the 50s were typically informal, school chaperoned events. The kids would remove their shoes and dance in their socks to protect the gymnasium floor. Combined with rock 'n' roll and the liberating feeling of removing their shoes while dancing, inspirited teens to shake, rattle and roll, giving way to a whole new style of dancing. The famous TV dance show 'American Bandstand' featured teenagers showing off their dance moves while judging music based on either the lyrics or the rhythm.

Elvis Presley and James Dean, among others, were the girl's heartthrobs. Both had sideburns that were about an inch below their ears. To catch the girl's eye, high school boys began wearing their hair long in what was called 'duck tails' with their shirt collars up and pants with buckles, half- way down their butts with the whole sleek look highlighted with a black leather jacket. Ann and I thanked God our kids were grown before the styles and attitudes changed. I don't think I could have handled it.

Now and then Ann and I would drive to Madison and go to either the Big Sky or Badger outdoor drive-in theaters. We preferred the Big Sky on the west side of town, because it was closer, but it all depended on what was playing. We'd go on 'buck night' when a whole carload could go for a dollar. We'd bring our own snacks as paying twenty-five cents for buttered popcorn seemed crazy when we had acres of corn just beyond the barn.

Because the kids were grown and gone, we missed out on the coonskin cap fad made famous by Fess Parker who wore one while playing the role of Davie Crocket in the 1954 Walt Disney series. Imagine a coon-skin cap that every boy in America wanted to wear that spurred around one- hundred million dollars in sales and began the whole idea of tying in 'must- have' merchandise with movies and music.

A new style of music drew rhythm inspiration from the blues and embraced themes popular among teenagers, such as young love and rebellion against authority. In the late 1940s, some country musicians began experimenting with the rhythms that led to the creation of a new musical form known as rockabilly that evolved into rock-and-roll.

I guess none of us 'old timers' understood why, but the theme of rebellion against authority, found in many rock-and-roll songs, appealed to teens. In 1954, rock group Bill Haley and His Comets provided youth with an anthem called 'Rock Around the Clock.' The song was used in the 1955 movie *Blackboard Jungle, which* was about a white teacher at a troubled inner-city high school that seemed to be calling for teens to declare their independence from adult control.

While young people found an outlet for their feelings and concerns, most parents were much less enthused about rock-and-roll, the rebellion and sexuality the music seemed to promote with many parents regarding music as a threat to American values. With our kids gone, we never felt that challenge and after the Charleston, swing and jazz, I liked the up-tempo format of rock-and-roll that saw the guitar come to the forefront instead of the brass instruments that had dominated the world of music for so long.

To their credit, this generation seemed to develop a greater consciousness than previous ones. Perhaps it was television that did it as the kids sought to define and redefine their identities that reflected their desire to rebel against adult authority, something we never thought of doing, or did just in different and not quite so obvious ways.

Even as the booming 50s meant so many advances in the quality of life, there was a growing anxiety among many young Americans who felt that their lives were too constricted by the staid culture of the era. It allowed for the emergence of a new counter-culture growing beneath the smooth surface of the decade that would explode in the 1960s critiquing American society and politics, bursting into the center of national consciousness in the 1960s and beyond.

That critique took many forms. Negroes demonstrated in Montgomery, Alabama and elsewhere, firing the first shots of today's Civil Rights Movement. The liberals struggled to reveal the persistence of poverty amid prosperity, and there was increasing resistance by women to the obstacles they faced in the workplace when they attempted to move out of their roles as wives and mothers. Finally, there was the growing concern about the environment among scientists who saw, much earlier than most Americans did, the dangers of heedless economic growth.

Another and ultimately more powerful critique of the middle-class culture of the 1950s came from feminism where the book *The Feminine Mystique* surveyed college-educated women who were married, had children and living in prosperous, upper middle-class suburbs and were living the 'dream' that the media portrayed affluent society as the ultimate in joy, happiness and satisfaction.

Here, the author found that behind this mystique, in virtually all the women she interviewed, was a fundamental sense of uneasiness, frustration and vague unhappiness that most women had great difficulty articulating that was embedded in the nature of the gender roles society had imposed on them. These women were intelligent, educated, talented and, yet, they had no outlets for their talents except housework, motherhood, and the support and companionship they offered their husbands.

While these were all in their infancy and came from different perspectives, they all had one common link in that they were directly connected to the white male culture of the time. Caucasian men began to sense a growing fear that the modern world threatened their autonomy, independence and authenticity.

Perhaps the clearest example of disenchantment with and alienation from the middle class came from a group of young artists who emerged largely from the middle class, but chose to stand outside the mainstream culture they held in contempt because of many of the fundamental premises of their own middle-class society.

These were the men and women who called themselves 'the Beats' or Beatniks who openly challenged the conventional values of middle-class America that included material success, social values and political habits. Many of them adopted an alternative lifestyle that emphasized rootlessness, anti-materialism, drugs, antagonism to technology and organization, sexual freedom and a dark, numbing despair about the nature of modern society.

Sadly, most of the Beats were in search of 'ecstasy', that they believed would come from some form of release from the rational world in which America thrived. As they evolved, they began to accept the premise that considered the culture repressive, making them seem frightening and subversive to many more conventional Americans. While this was their right, they attracted little attention from the American mainstream, except as objects of ridicule and contempt, particularly outside big cities in small towns like ours. However, the Beats existence was significant because they were the beginnings of the counterculture that emerged in the 1960s personified, eulogized and contemporized by the music of the times.

America in the 1950s had changed, and yet the changes were only the beginning. Seeds were sewn that would grow into entire fields of events, values, circumstances and social changes that would change the world, rearrange the world and make America completely different from it had ever been before or would ever be again.

Viva Las Vegas

Kat called when I got home for a follow up and said the week had been a rousing success, noting there was more joy in the house than she'd seen in years. She then popped the question regarding when she was going to meet my kids.

I hadn't been fully honest with her in that the kids and I really weren't very close. It was true that Jane moved to Flagstaff because of her husband's health. It was true I'd never been to visit her, even though Ann had on numerous occasions, simply because my four-legged bovine mistresses would never let me out of the barn. What hadn't been shared was the fact that after Jane went to Oshkosh to college, we never really met eye-to-eye on a lot of things and hadn't spoken since Ann's death. Ann raised her. Ann supported her! I was too busy trying to save the farm. I know, shame on me! As for Scott, it was the same thing. I was always too busy to be involved in his sports or supporting him. When he left for college, he really never came home and when he did, he was a stranger I really didn't know. I met his wife at their wedding and she seemed nice. I hope and pray he's being a better father than I was. If I could do it over, it would have been different and I wouldn't have 'assigned' my role to Ann and been there for him.

It was March, and I was getting anxious to do something. The reconstruction of the hotel was coming along with the normal snags and B.S. that contractors all seem to have. Thank God for Charles as he didn't take any crap from anyone and even though 90% of his communication was on the phone, the workers all knew that he was all business. We'd intentionally left the brewery alone. One project at a time was enough.

One Sunday night, Kat called and asked what I was doing for Easter. As usual, I had no plans and assumed she'd want me to come to her house. Instead, she asked if I wanted to go to Las Vegas. It sounded exciting to me! We made plans with Kat flying from Washington to Denver and me from Madison to Denver and then the two of us connecting and going to Vegas.

Having never been West, I was smitten by the Rockies and spent the entire flight from Denver to Vegas staring out the window and trying to take pictures with my Kodak, which I soon learned turned out terrible.

We landed at McCarren, and the glitz hit me. I certainly wasn't in Mineral Point anymore. Slot machines in the airport terminal and billboards everywhere with nearly naked ladies staring down at me. We hailed a taxi and Kat directed the driver to the Desert Inn which I learned was the swankiest hotel on the strip. There were other hotels that were more famous, but this was where the elite class stayed.

I was amazed at what I saw. Pictures of topless women and barkers on every corner trying to get you to see this show or that, including girlfriends for the night if you were into that thing. Most people were just wandering the streets before going in and depositing their savings at one of the gaming tables. Kat made arrangements for us to see Frank Sinatra and Rodney Dangerfield, whose jokes were a little 'different' than those I saw on the 'Tonight Show' to say the least.

Kat noted that deciding where to eat on the Las Vegas Strip was a challenging task given the number of truly great restaurants to choose from. At the best restaurants the meal was just part of the experience and she noted that the Bacchanal in Caesar's Palace, not only fed you, but gave you a massage as well. Kat let me know we would need to dress up and had made reservations well in advance and so I brought three suits and two sports coats and, for the first time in my life, had my shoes shined by someone else.

After Mineral Point and even Washington, I was simply overwhelmed by the dining options with several great French restaurants that had extraordinary food where I even tried escargot for the first time. Imagine, eating snails! Kat wasn't done feeding me as we ate in a world class steakhouse, some Italian joint with a little guy who played the accordion and even an American restaurant, as well. The best part, beyond the food, were the settings. Each restaurant had beautifully designed interiors that offered an ambiance that complemented the cuisine. Whether a selection of fine art or a romantic view, the Strip's best restaurants were out to give their guests a memorable experience.

We made our way gamboling from casino-to-casino, which Kat taught me meant hopping, while deciding the gambling was for suckers and losers. Even the penny slots weren't my cup of tea as I hate losing at anything. Besides Sinatra and Dangerfield, Kat took me to see Siegfried and Roy who were magicians with live lions and white tigers in their act, then to see some ventriloquist who was hilarious, and, finally to some musical revue with water and dancing and all sorts of topless ladies in thong bottoms with feathers and rhinestones everywhere.

"And?" Kat inquired as the show ended.

"I liked your version at home much better, especially the grand climax," for which I got a soft poke in the ribs.

Each night, after dinner and the shows, we'd end up in the bar at the Desert Inn and see these little guys smoking cigars with big bodyguards and blonde girlfriends.

One night as we were walking back to our room I asked Kat who they were and she replied, "Some old guys with SDS."

"SDS?"

"Short Dick Syndrome," was her reply.

I learned later who they really were and went 'yikes!'.

Speaking of little guys with big cigars, one night, we decided to eat in the D.I. Sky Room restaurant. We sat down, had a cocktail and ordered. A few minutes later, the Maître' D came over and told us we had to move. I looked at him, was offended and refused, believing you just didn't do that to people, as it was embarrassing.

This guy said that we either had to move or leave. I wanted to make a fuss, and show him some of my Minnie Point badass, but Kat said, "no" and so we moved. Needless to say, I was pissed.

As we were settling in, this little guy with a big cigar and two buxom blondes entered, with four huge bodyguards. The little guy and the blondes sat at one table, while two bodyguards took two adjacent tables, including our former spot, and simply watched the trio eat. Adding one and one together, I got the picture.

When our meal was done, we waited for the server to bring the bill. After ten minutes and no response, I finally caught the host's attention, and he came to the table. I explained we were done eating and would like the bill. He noted that it had been 'comped' for our inconvenience and the restaurant's apologies, which made the move from our original table seem all right. As we were leaving, I nodded and tipped two fingers in an informal thank you salute to the little guy, but he was too busy staring at the cleavages sitting with him. Ahh, Vegas!

Kat thought we should do some sightseeing, and so we rented a car and went to Hoover Dam. I don't know how she did it or who she knew, but we went on a personal tour deep down inside and learned all kinds of things. The weirdest fact was that it would take the Hoover Dam concrete 125 years to completely harden. It's 600 feet thick at the bottom and crews inserted 600 miles of steel pipes, woven through the concrete to significantly reduce the chemical heat from the setting of the concrete or it would have been a bit 'toasty' down there. I was nervous thinking about soft concrete and billions of gallons of water.

With the dam just outside Las Vegas, it was a quick trip. I took some pictures but was disappointed when I learned the water didn't gush over the top like I thought it would, but turned the turbines at the bottom, which created all the electricity for the gaudy lights in town.

That night, Kat asked if I'd like to see Grand Canyon. I said, "Sure!". The next day, we left early as it was 130 miles to the South rim. We got there, and I said, "Holy shit! That's one really big hole in the ground."

After taking somewhere around 20 more terrible pictures, Kat asked if I wanted to call my daughter Jane as we were only 80 miles from Flagstaff. I thought for a moment and then reluctantly nodded in the affirmative. We found a pay phone, and I called.

"Hello" was the familiar voice on the other end.

"Hi Jane, it's your dad."

 "Dad?"

"Yes, how are you?"

"OK," she said in a very hesitating manner. "Who died?"

 "No one," I replied.

"OK." Jane added, in a somewhat hesitating voice.

"Say, we're at Grand Canyon and my friend said we're only about an hour and a half from your house, do you think we could come and visit?"

There was a pause on the other end and then a reluctant, "OK".

"How about, we take you, Frank and the kids out for dinner?"

"OK," I heard in a polite response knowing that she was thinking, 'What in hell is this all about?'

"See you in a couple of hours," I replied.

We drove south on Highway 89, and I quickly realized Arizona was a lot more beautiful than I thought it was going to be. All I'd ever seen were Saguaro cacti from old John Wayne movies. Our map only took us to the edge of Flagstaff and we stopped at a filling station and I called Jane again, telling her we were in town and asking directions to her house. Fifteen minutes later, we pulled in the driveway and Jane came out.

"Sorry to come unannounced," I said and then introduced Kat, who nodded and politely smiled.

"Dad, I wish you would have given me more advance notice," Jane offered.

"This is my fault," Kat responded. "We drove from Las Vegas to see Grand Canyon, and that's when I realized how close we were to Flagstaff. Your dad has told me so many wonderful things about you, I just wanted to meet you in person." This was pure B.S., but I saw Jane softening.

"Come in, please!" Jane offered.

We entered the small but tidy ranch home and saw pictures of the grandkids I'd never met and one of Ann from the last time she visited, but none of me, as Jane added. "The kids will be home from school shortly and Frank will be done at four. I called him and told him you were coming. I'm normally not home now, but I'm just getting over a bad cold and have been home for a couple of days."

Shortly thereafter, two elementary school girls walked in the front door. After brief introductions, we sat on the couch and one of them asked, "Are you Grandma Ann's husband?"

I replied, "Yes".

"Do you live in heaven too?"

"No, God said I needed to wait here awhile before going to live with your Grandma."

"Were you naughty?"

"No, God still wants me to do things here, like come and meet you," which seemed to suffice.

Kat began asking the kids' questions about school, friends, favorite subjects and what they liked to play, their favorite foods and where they liked to eat. With that, the kids got comfortable and I saw Jane do the same.

I mentioned Kat was an artist, and the girls got excited.

"Can you draw us a picture?" one of the girls inquired.

"Sure," Kat replied. "Can you get me two pieces of plain paper?"

The girls ran and got the paper as Kat sat at the kitchen table and drew their portraits using a regular pencil. The girls were simply amazed, as was Jane.

A little after four, Frank arrived. He had changed very little. A little gray hair and paunch, but other than that, about the same.

I introduced Kat, and he indicated that news from Mineral Point was that someone had purchased the old hotel and was fixing it up. I concurred, knowing he'd only been to Mineral Point a half dozen times at most.

"You miss farming?" Frank asked.

"Not really," I responded. "Between the government and the daily grind, it can wear you down."

I was waiting for some snide remark about the government, but it never came.

Kat asked questions about the post office and Frank's duties. I asked about his health and he said the dry air was just what the doctor ordered.

As it neared 5:00 and the conversation was slowing, I recommended we eat as we had a long drive back to Vegas. Jane suggested an all you can eat buffet. I looked at Kat and she commented, "That would be fine, but we wouldn't get much time to visit."

Jane nodded and seemed reluctant to make any suggestions.

Kat inquired, "What about Josephine's Modern American Bistro?" "We've never been there" Jane replied.

Kat added, "I was reading a magazine in Las Vegas and they were mentioned as having the best Italian food in Flagstaff."

Frank had a worried look on his face, as I'm certain the bill would have been outside their budget.

Kat continued, "What's really neat, is that I earn points with my Diner's Club card and have enough so that we can all eat for free." Looking at the girls, Kat asked, "Do you like spaghetti?" They both nodded in the affirmative. Kat added, "I have two sons and they love spaghetti, too, especially taking it and sucking each piece into their mouth," at which she made the slurping sound and the girls laughed.

"Are they little kids like us?" one of my granddaughters asked.

"Oh no, they're both adults. One of them is in the Marines and you know what, he knows your uncle Scott."

The kids thought that was pretty cool.

Frank got out of his postal worker's uniform and into jeans and a checkered shirt. We agreed to drive separately so that we could leave from the restaurant and followed Jane to Josephine's, where Kat asked for a table on the patio. The hostess indicated they were all reserved and Kat took her by the side, said it was important, slipping her a $50.00 bill and asking her to check again to see if one couldn't be for us. Amazingly, the table next to the fountain opened up, and we sat down.

For the next hour, Kat asked questions and provided answers. I could see Jane melting and knew Kat was winning the battle. I simply smiled and hoped Jane approved. Our food orders were taken and Kat asked for three bibs. I think the waitress thought it was odd, but brought them anyway. Kat and the kids got spaghetti, and Kat showed them how to slurp the spaghetti. I really don't know who had the most fun or had the most sauce on their face, the kids or Kat. Frank, Jane and I watched as Kat cast her spell on the kids with all three having enormous smiles and tomato sauce all over their cheeks.

As we were nearing the end of the meal, Kat excused herself and went to the lady's room. I looked at Jane and said, "I'm sorry I've never been here before."

Jane nodded as if she understood.

"I want to see you more often and watch my granddaughters grow. Would you mind that?"

Jane looked at me and asked, "Would Katherine be coming with you?"

I looked at Jane and knew this was the critical moment as I replied,

"If you wouldn't mind."

Jane touched my hand and softly squeezed, saying, "Dad, she's simply wonderful. I want to thank you for coming and bringing her with you. I know mom would approve."

I wiped the tears from my eyes just as Kat returned.

"All set!" she announced. "Thanks to Diner's Club."

I knew better, but also knew it was the only thing to do. Pride has a way of getting in the way sometime. Once again, the woman I was falling in love with was showing dignity beyond reproach.

We stopped by the fountain and Kat offered to take some pictures with my Kodak of the family. I asked the waitress to come over, and we took one of all of us and promised to send a copy to Jane when we got home.

We walked out to the cars, and I looked at Jane and she at me. Jane turned and hugged Kat as Frank shook my hand and Jane said to both of us, "Please come back soon".

Jane looked at me and, with a tear in her eye, and said, "thanks dad."

My, how sincere gratitude can be a wonderful, wonderful present!

Pendleton

The drive back to Vegas seemed shorter and quieter. Perhaps it was because of the fresh memories swirling in my head, creating a gentle smile as I looked over at my sleeping friend. As we neared Hoover Dam, the lights of the city shone as if it were the middle of the day. I thought of the giant turbines whizzing down deep within the dam providing the power the city needed and realized that Kat had this all planned and it was simply wonderful.

While it was late for us, the slogan, 'the city never sleeps' certainly rang true as the real gamblers were crowded into the casino. I just shook my head as we walked through the masses where every player was certain they'd beat the house, even though the chips were stacked to always, and I mean always, be in the house's favor.

We went to bed and awakened in time for an early breakfast. Kat inquired whether we could go visit Will.

"Where is he?" I asked.

"Camp Pendleton" she replied. "In California?"

"Just north of San Diego. He wants to see us and introduce his new girlfriend."

"How long will it take to drive there?" I asked.

"We'll just hop on a plane. It's less than an hour's flight and they run every hour," Kat replied as I thought of John Kepler and the Greyhound from Madison.

"Sure, OK, why not?" I could add another state to my very short list of places I'd been.

Kat called the concierge and asked them to make reservations and then called Will. Kat recommended we pack an overnight bag and that way we wouldn't be rushed. I thought it was crazy to pay for a hotel room we weren't going to use and wondered why we just didn't fly home from San Diego instead of Vegas. Kat noted we had been 'comped' at the hotel which meant the room was free and so it wasn't costing us anything for the missed night.

In addition, we'd both purchased round-trip airfare to and from Vegas and it would have cost more to make the change than simply doing what we were planning. Once again, my rookie naivete showed through.

We caught our flight and, as the plane made its approach into the San Diego airport, I almost pee'd my pants when it looked like the plane was flying right between the buildings. My God, that seemed close!

Will was there in civilian clothes and had an absolutely gorgeous blonde California girl standing with him. Her name was Sydney, and she had the whitest teeth, and best body (I know, shame on me) I'd ever seen. Will was quite proud of his latest attachment. She looked like a 'keeper' to me. However, I couldn't get Kat's warning that "she was just another one" out of my mind.

It didn't take long to realize that what Sydney had in looks; she didn't have in smarts and I realized that when God was passing out brains; she thought he said trains and missed hers. Oh well, we all can't have everything! We drove north on what they called 'The Five' to Oceanside, where

Will owned a beautiful condo overlooking the ocean. It was spectacular! All white furniture with enormous windows and a fireplace. It made my little house in Mineral Point seem quite bland.

As we finished getting caught up, Will suggested we visit Camp Pendleton so that he could show me around. Sydney said she needed to go to L.A. as she was auditioning for some part in a movie and said goodbye. We drove separately back south, parked our rental car in a K-mart parking lot and rode with Will as we entered the base. I was impressed by the security and the fact that, even though he was in civilian clothes, the MP's knew who Will was.

After we passed through security, Will noted that there were around 25,000 Marines and sailors at Camp Pendleton. "They fall under the 'Blue Diamond' and can be especially proud of their heritage because the 1st Marine Division is the oldest, largest and most decorated division in the United States Marine Corps."

Will showed us where he worked and the training area and then told Kat that Brigadier General McConley wanted to say hello. I didn't know who the guy was until we got close to the base command center and saw his name on the plaque outside the building. The guy ran the place. Holy shit!

We walked inside and everywhere you looked there were MP'S and support personnel. After what seemed like five different doors and waiting rooms, we finally made it to the inner sanctum and met the General who was about my age and in as good of shape as me, arose. His broad smile quickly let me know he was glad to see Kat as he gave her a big hug and politely shook my hand.

As we sat on facing leather couches, the General called his secretary and asked if we would like some coffee, tea or a soft drink. We all agreed on coffee and the secretary departed with orders from the base commander which meant an urgent trip to the mess hall for someone.

I knew enough about the military to assume that Will should have been somewhat intimidated by the General. Instead, while polite, Will was just as casual as we were. Perhaps it was because he was in civvies, but there seemed to be more.

"Kat, I was so sorry to hear about your mother," the General shared. "Jean and I would have come to the funeral, but I couldn't get away."

"Thank you, Roger," Kat replied. "It was her time and she's with dad."

"I'm glad she's with him at Arlington. That's the least the government could do after all your dad did for his country."

"Thank you, that means a lot coming from you," Kat replied.

There was a pause for reflection that brought a soft smile to the General's face as he looked down at the carpet with the

Marine Corps insignia in it and then back at Kat asking, "Is Charles still with you?"

Kat nodded in the affirmative.

"And Annie?"

Again, in the affirmative.

"Great people! Simply great people! I never met a finer man than Charles Harris and I'll never forget all those times when he and I would be in the office and I could hear his laugh." The General paused for a moment and then looked at Kat and said, "You know, your dad was one of the greatest men I ever knew."

"Thank you, Roger," Kat politely said.

"I wouldn't be here today, if it weren't for him," as the General gently shook his head in reflection and admiration of a man who had 'opened the door' on his career.

"How is your godson doing?" Kat inquired.

The General looked at Will and said, "Well, he's still wet behind the ears and keeps chasing those starlets, but from a career perspective, he's doing fine. We've still got about eighteen months until he's eligible for promotion to get his oak leaf clusters. However, unless he totally screws up between now and then, he's set to become Major William Johnson right before I retire. I've made some calls and will make certain that he gets to do his time at the Pentagon after the promotion. Then, assuming he doesn't get caught in all the politics there, I've pulled in a couple of favors and he's set for a tour at Quantico before his next change in rank which is to my level. From then on, it's up to him. If he's half the man I think he is and one quarter your father, someday I'll be calling him 'sir'".

Will was actually blushing.

The General turned to me, and I became the focus of his attention. "Where are you from, sir?"

"Please call me Hank."

"Where are you from Hank?" the General inquired.

"A small town in Wisconsin."

"Which one?" "Mineral Point."

There was no reaction and so I added "close to Madison".

"Where all those leftist kids are?"

"Yes, General, but far enough away that we can stay out of politics."

I didn't want to get in any discussion of the war or politics, that's for kids to do and not old men sitting in a General's office.

Will added, "Hank's son is here on the base, sir."

"He is?"

Will continued, "Yes sir, Captain Scott Terrill."

The General's demeanor quickly changed, confirming,

"Captain Terrill is your son?"

"Yes sir." I replied.

"Does he know you're here?"

"No, sir. This was one of those spur-of-the-moment trips. Kat, I mean Katherine and I were visiting Las Vegas and decided to see Will."

The General called out "Ann" and his secretary came in immediately. "Call ops and see if Captain Terrill is available and have him report to me immediately."

"Yes sir!"

The General looked at me totally different. "Mr. Terrill, I don't know how to say this, but your son is one of the best soldiers I've ever had the honor to command. While he is Navy, his efforts in building the Navy Seal program have been nothing short of fantastic. What he's done, and in such a short period, is create one of the greatest fighting organizations in the U.S. Military. While Marines pride themselves on their discipline and tactical abilities, your son's Seal teams are exemplary. I'm honored to have him work with us here at Pendleton until they get their own training center."

Just then, Ann stuck her head in the door and announced, "He's on his way, sir. Should be here in about five minutes."

"Thanks, Ann."

For the next five minutes it was chit chat about farming and how Kat and I met and all the other things outstanding leaders talk. You can always tell an outstanding leader because they get you talking about yourself while the wannabe's only talk about themselves.

A few minutes later, Ann opened the door and announced that Captain Terrill was in the anteroom. The General took his fingers and did the reverse wave while nodding in the affirmative, indicating to send Scott in.

As Scott walked in, he saluted the General and was told, 'at ease' at which point the General said, "I think you might know these people."

Scott nodded at Will, whom he'd met, shook his head to indicate 'no' at Kat and then looked at me in total shock. "Dad?"

"Hi, son!"

"Please have a seat, Captain," the General offered, at which Scott pulled up the chair that had been adjacent to the General's desk, and like Will and the General was sitting only than three inches back..

"Care for some coffee?" "No, thank you, sir."

"It's a small world, isn't it? I had no idea that you knew Will, err, I mean Captain Johnson and his mother."

"I've only met the Captain a few times here on the base and never had the honor of meeting his mother." Scott replied.

"Well son, if you want to meet the daughter of one of America's genuine heroes, just get to know Mrs. Johnson."

"Yes, sir," Scott replied.

We spent the next few minutes sharing stories and then Ann stuck her head in to remind the General he had a conference call and that meant it was time for us to go.

We all stood and shook hands and departed. As we walked out, Will and Scott were leading the way and everyone, and I mean every single person's tongues started wagging.

When we stepped outside the command center, Kat looked at the two boys and offered, "Let's have dinner."

Scott took a deep breath while I was expecting a polite 'no'.

However, Scott was savvy enough to realize that this was an opportunity to meet someone who obviously was in high favor with the General and also learn the truth behind all the rumors about Mr. Will Johnson.

It was agreed that we would meet at seven at Rainwaters on Kettner in downtown San Diego, which was famous for great steaks and only ten minutes from the airport. Kat called and told the boys we were on the 11:00 PM flight back to Vegas.

The dinner went much better than I expected with Will and Scott initially talking 'shop' with Kat then working her magic such that stories were told about each other to where everyone was comfortable and the laughter began. As dinner was ending, my watch said 9:30 while we were all joking and having a wonderful time, and I hoped some space between father and son was finally being closed.

Kat excused herself and went to the lady's room. Will excused himself as well, sensing Scott and I needed a few minutes alone. I looked at Scott and wanted to apologize for the surprise. He noted that it was a pleasant surprise, and that Kat was everything Jane said she was, noting that Jane called while we were driving back to Vegas the night before, simply raving about the wonderful woman she had met.

"Can I ever make things up to you?" I asked Scott.

"Dad, one thing I've learned over the past few years is how hard it is to be a good husband and father. I know now what a struggle the farm was. I didn't know then. Do I wish you would have been a bigger part of my life? Yes! But, today, I'm in the same boat. My job means being away from my family and leaving Kaye to be both mother and father, and I've ended up just like you."

"You're much better than I ever was, son."

Scott shook his head 'no' and added, "Dad, without the work ethic you showed me, I would never have made it and I thank you for that."

"What do you think of Kat?"

"Are you kidding me? She's incredible, dad. Mom would be so happy to think you found someone as wonderful as she is."

That was all I needed - approval from my kids and I got it!

"The Three Bars"

Our flight was on time and we arrived in Vegas at 12:20 AM and were in bed a little after one and asleep by about 1:05. It had been a long day! Our flight to Denver the next day wasn't until 3:00 and so we had a leisurely breakfast and then packed and went to check out.

I hadn't spent a dime gambling and still had my lucky quarter in my pocket. Between Kat, her kids and mine, I no longer felt I needed any luck and stuck the quarter in what was called a progressive slot machine in the hotel lobby. I pulled the handle, hoping my quarter would bring good luck to someone else. The wheels spun and then there was one set, then two sets and finally three sets of triple bars, all with the number seven in them. Lights went off and bells rang, and I honestly thought I broke the machine when three employees came running over to me.

"Congratulations!" "Huh?"

"Congratulations, sir, you've won the progressive jackpot!"

I must have had a weird look on my face as I asked, "what does that mean?"

"Look up at the flashing sign, sir."

I looked up and almost fainted. At first, I couldn't fathom the numbers as people around me were cheering and then it came to light. My lucky quarter earned $47,316.75. My God!

Kat came over and looked at me and grinned from ear-to-ear saying. "You won! You won!"

I thought it would all come out in quarters and wondered how in hell I could carry that many on the plane. The hotel personnel asked me to follow them and we went to a small room where they took my picture and made me sign some papers allowing them to use my photo in advertising and then issued a check for $35,487.14 after Uncle Sam took his cut.

Kat and I headed for the airport and made it to Denver, where we said goodbye - Kat to Washington and me to Madison. I handed her an envelope that I'd been carrying the entire trip. It was the next chapter of "War of My Brothers".

She smiled, knowing that it was my way of saying "see you soon". "I'll need a few weeks to write the last chapter and hope I can come and see you."

"Can't you get Irving to speed it up?" Kat replied, referring to my IBM typewriter.

"Let me see what I can do!" as I pulled her in and gave her a very long, very passionate kiss.

"Make it a brief chapter, ok?" she whispered as she pulled back and looked at the terminal door as it was about to close.

"I will," I nodded. "I promise." And with that, she was gone.

I watched her plane take off and then walked through Stapleton to my gate and stood there. Thoughts and memories of the past few days cascaded through my mind, filling me with the warmth that only comes from contentment. I'd seen Las Vegas, Hoover Dam, Grand Canyon, my daughter Jane, San Diego and son Scott and won the Progressive Jackpot on the slot machine with my lucky quarter. It couldn't have been any better. Well, yes, it could have been - the money could have been tax free! Tee Hee!

As I got on the plane and headed for Madison, I thought of the decade that had just ended. My God, there was so much to write about. As I got back to Mineral Point, my mind was fervent with ideas and I began typing. Without sleep, I began and for nearly eighteen straight hours I wrote and wrote and wrote, wanting to finish what I'd begun, while trying to figure out what I was trying to say.

<u>*Peace and Love - Man*</u>

By the middle of the 1950s, most of us had jobs that paid well, life was good, and we expressed satisfaction with our lives. Even though the threat of the cold war hung over our heads, it had been acclimated to and life went on. We taught our children what were called middle-class values - a belief in God, hard work and our country.

The 1960s started off as the dawn of a golden age for most Americans. On January 20, 1961, John F. Kennedy became president. His confidence that, as one historian put it, "The government possessed big answers to big problems" seemed to set the tone for the rest of the decade. However, that golden age never materialized. By the end of the 1960s, it seemed as if the nation was falling apart.

The first profound and obtuse challenge to our sense of personal security began on October 16, 1962, and lasted for nearly six weeks. All Americans were attuned to the devastation of a nuclear holocaust from the way it had been presented to everyone from elementary school children to adults as a horrific act of inhumanity that meant either instant death or long- term cancerous debilitation.

While we had become acclimated to the cold war between the United States and the Soviet Union. Sadly, it escalated into an international crisis with American deployment of missiles in Italy and Turkey that were matched by Soviet deployments of similar ballistic missiles in Cuba in what was termed the Cuban Missile Crises. In a few short days with President Kennedy on TV and newscasters literally whispering about a nuclear war, everything changed as America and the world came the closest ever to escalating into a full-scale extermination.

Through the act of God, cooler heads prevailed. However, for nearly six weeks we all were exposed to the threats of annihilation that took what cultural naivete that remained and smashed it to bits with cold, hard reality representing the point when America lost its last grasp of innocence.

Perhaps it was then that the young changed course when we all finally realized we weren't omnipotent and isolated from the problems and challenges or the rest of the world. Perhaps, all the innocence and dreams that so many continued to cling to rang out on Friday, November 22, 1963, with the blast of a rifle that sent President Kennedy to his death.

So much of what people believed in expired and with it, the underbelly of social ugliness leapt up and into our souls. The years of depression and wars had been frosted over by the good times of the fifties and yet, so many other elements from the past converged on America to change it, re-arrange it and totally and profoundly take what had been and make it incredibly different.

Not only did Kennedy's death demonstrably mark the end of the age of innocence for America, it created what so much of our world has become today, a nation of exploiters who take the smallest nuance, expand upon it, create an issue and then reap its bounty. While the assassination riveted all of us to our television sets for the very first time, it also showed those in the broadcast industry that a total news format could not only exist, but thrive.

Instead of the newspaper or 30 minutes of daily TV news, we're becoming a nation and a world of nonstop global information. With this, the demand for immediate information gratification began as we no longer found it tolerable to wait for the morning edition. We needed to know 'now'.

While forever news has been both good and bad, the reality that the media needed to satisfy 24 hours of content, instead of 30 minutes, began a downward spiral that has yet to reach bottom. Stories that we once would never have been aware of became national headlines repeated over and over and over again and again and again, until every minute detail is drummed into our heads. Events, circumstances and situations that reflected the abnormal are now propagated until we all believe that they are the norm to where with each passing year, our beliefs and values, our concepts and elocutions, are being devastated to a point that the core beliefs in our culture, society and our way of life are being eroded and degraded to a level of dissatisfaction, disarray and disbelief.

In 1965, five years after the FDA's approval, 6.5 million American women were taking birth control pills, making it the most popular form of birth control in the U.S. social mores began to change and with it the interaction between men and women where, for the first time in history, women began to examine sex as a form of recreation instead of procreation. Suddenly, the risk was gone and without the risk, the entire subject of casual sex became a topic of not only national discussion, but another form of expression, followed by breakdowns in the stigma against premarital sex and living together.

You now had a generation that was liberated and it wasn't long before there was no more delineation between being "good" or "bad" as virtually everyone began interacting and doing so to the point that intimacy became of foregone conclusion. For the first time the belief that there could be no consequences took hold as the baby boomers broke through one more barrier that had constrained them, thereby differentiating themselves from their parents and grandparents while creating one more reason why the decade was so profound.

While sex was on the brains of so many and consequences seemed so small, nowhere was it more prevalent than in the world of fashion. Women's clothes became more revealing as they have become a statement towards liberation with the removal of bras as a testament to the belief that women earned the right to express the social freedoms previously enjoyed only by men.

Even in the small towns like Mineral Point, girls began appearing in public in miniskirts and skin-tight, bellbottom, hip hugger jeans or hot pants with their torsos barely covered, all designed to entice and yet frustrate men of all ages as part of the Women's Liberation Movement, as much a sign of rebellion than a fashion statement. 'Showing it all' has become the new trend, and the former demure days have gone flying out of the door.

Out on the farm, things are also changing. Between 1950 and 1970, the number of American farms declined by fifty percent, as many farms either consolidated or were sold in a period more dynamic than in any other time

in our history. With this consolidation, the number of people on farms dropped from over 20 million in 1950 to less than 10 million by 1970, while the average size of farms went from 205 acres in 1950 to almost 400 acres by 1969. At the same time, productivity has increased – farmers are producing even more food per acre at a cheaper cost to consumers and doing so on roughly the same amount of farmland than ever before. I guess I'd been a part of the trend as Tom's farm increased to over 700 acres and the head of cows he milked to 150.

One of the principal causes of this consolidation has been specialization. Today's large farms aren't replicas of smaller ones on a bigger scale. The economic realities that have allowed a farmer to grow has also forced him or her to change the operation and specialize in a few cash crops. In 1900, 98% of all farms had chickens, 82% grew corn for grain, 80% had at least one milk cow and pigs. Last year, only 4% of America's farms had chickens, just 8% still had milk cows, and only 25% were growing corn. Of the seventeen major farm commodities, the average farm in 1900 produced five of them; in 1992, the average farm produced less than two.

So, what promoted consolidation? One reason was the four wars where each war strained the supply of farm labor which in turn pushed farmers to mechanize. Second, farm machinery manufacturers made consolidation possible and were finally reaching their potential, after being hampered by the Depression and material shortages of World War II. In addition, as equipment became larger and more specialized, it also became more expensive to the point you really can't afford to have part-time equipment used only to generate part of your income. Tom and I saw the handwriting on the wall and had invested tens of thousands of dollars in a new machinery and one milking parlor. We then planned our two farms to plant, cultivate and harvest crops with the highest efficiency. We weren't geniuses. We simply had no choice except to raise as much of the crop that uses the investment as possible simply to maximize our return on investment.

Another huge reason has been the advances in agricultural research where increases in knowledge and technology have actually forced farmers to consolidate simply because it takes a lot of time to keep up with the newest information in any area. Farmers like Tom and I have begun to concentrate only on the research that pertains to our own specialized operations.

Land in farms peaked in 1950 at 1.2 billion acres. Today, tillable land has dropped to just under one-billion acres. That means American farmers are producing more from 20% less than they did twenty years ago. Most of the lost farmland is being converted to suburban and urban sprawl. However, the most important subset of land devoted to actually raising crops has actually remained relatively constant. This means that farmers have converted other land from pasture or marginal lands into cropland and are making the land productive by installing irrigation systems, conservation practices or fertilizers and pesticides.

Government policies, declining farm labor, improved and enhanced technology and larger more expensive equipment have all led to larger, more focused farms. There's nothing inherently wrong with increasing the size of farms, but intentionally or unintentionally, the increase in size has resulted in fewer farmers and therefore fewer customers for the shops and stores in Mineral Point that has served as a detriment to the wellbeing of our community.

Socially, the time of hope and innocence began to evolve into a time of anger and violence as more Americans have begun to protest and demand an end to the unfair treatment of black citizens, while many more have begun to protest and demand an end to the war in Vietnam and still more protest and demand full equality for women. These three social, political and ethical challenges are defining who and what America has become – a country that favored white men, whose government no longer respects the intelligence of the masses, replacing it with rules and regulations, laws and acts designed by white males for the good of white males, allowing them to retain and sustain the power and structure we allowed them to build.

Today, many young Americans question these beliefs. They feel that their parents' values are not enough to help them deal with the difficulties that confront them and their belief in the government has begun to erode simply because they believe that the government does not believe in them. First college students, then high school and finally elementary kids have rebelled by letting their hair grow and wearing unusual clothing as their dissatisfaction is strongly expressed in the music they listen to and the anthems by which changing values are being exemplified.

Newton's third law states that for every action there is an opposite and equal reaction. This law applies not only to physics, but economics, sociology, politics and life as well. The Great Depression resulted in the development of economic, social and political structures designed to protect the masses from themselves and created America's first threat to success and our first 'ism' - socialism, where for the good of many, that put limits upon the success of a few.

While the ideal world had everyone sharing in the effort and reward of the system, the net result of growing socialism has been a limitation on individual reward through mandates, limits and controls. While this has tremendously assisted the overall well-being of our aggregate society, it's come at the expense of lowering the reward for effort levels invested for those fortunate, talented or lucky enough to succeed as big Government has replaced big Business in America. Socialism became the first "threat" to our personal achievement and to America.

The second 'ism' that continues to face many Americans didn't come from within, but is still an incipient threat to our well-being and that is Communism. While, other than the six weeks in 1963 we haven't been directly exposed to its wrath, we've been emotionally bludgeoned by the threat of nuclear war, forcing millions to take part in air raid drills down to the innocents - small children trying to hide their bodies and souls beneath their desks, all the while having flashbacks of the devastation they'd have seen from films of the American atomic attacks on Japan.

The battle between the United States and the Soviet Union has our country attempt to prepare us for nuclear war while trying to convince us that someone might survive. The net result is a profound sense of angst that permeates lives and innocence burning an incredibly powerful image in people's minds, hearts and psyche, leaving everyone feeling as if there's no secure future. Young people today subconsciously believe there's no long- term existence. They sense that tomorrow will truly never come or, if it does, it won't be as good as today, as they all feel and understand that total oblivion from a nuclear warhead was less than 30 minutes away.

Children of the sixties have had it better than any generation the preceded them and yet, they also represent a time when a generation has never had it any worse. With an era filled with so many different aspects of social, cultural and political change, that it's almost impossible to comprehend, none reflect the growing changes more than the Viet Nam War brought to our homes in living and dying color. Our battles in Viet Nam have made us challenge our government, our leadership and all authority and have taken us from being a people who trusted respected and obliged those in control, to one who challenges, disregards and simply disobeys those who have established the system to their benefit.

As the relationship between citizens and authority is waning, there are reactions on both sides. Some of it good and some of it bad and to where a few rogue police officers have gone beyond their bounds to acquire testimony and admissions through coercion, pressure or threat to the point that the government had to determine right and wrong, good and bad when it came to police power and did so with the 1966 Miranda rights, set by the

U.S. Supreme Court to supposedly prevent self-incrimination. This ruling states that, prior to the arrest or questioning of a person suspected of a crime, a person has certain rights based on the Fifth Amendment of the Constitution including remaining silent, representation by a lawyer and the knowledge that anything they say may be used against them.

Where the genuine change comes into play is that if the accused person confesses, the prosecution must then prove that they were given their rights before a decision of guilt or innocence can be determined. In passing this decision, the United States established the rights of citizens while putting limits on law enforcement where, once again, the actions of a few became mandates for all, in a society that's come to canonize the individual as it demonizes the institution, and doing so time and time again.

In the end, today's success is being measured as an antithesis, where bad is good and good is bad, victory means defeat and our social heart and soul is being shredded into thousands of pieces, each representing a life, a thought and an intention, well meant, but gone asunder. Compound this with the social revolution that is bringing about action without consequence in a liberated world and the table is set for profound modification of our own definition.

Today's Women's Liberation Movement has come about based primarily on the social concept of feminism that consists of a range of social and political movements, along with ideologies aimed to define and establish the political, economic, personal, and social equality of the sexes. Feminism incorporates the position that societies prioritize the male point of view, and that women are treated unjustly within those societies. Feminist movements are campaigning for women's rights, including the right to: vote, hold public office, work, earn equal pay, own property, receive and education, enter into contracts, have equal rights within marriage and be awarded maternity leave.

Feminists have also worked to ensure access to legal abortions and social integration, and to protect women and girls from rape, sexual harassment, and domestic violence.

When you're a farmer, you don't have time or resources to be a Chauvinist. There was always too much work to be done. While there might have been structural and social limits in big cities and big companies, it has never really existed on the farm and yet, men have been accused of treating women different and holding them back when many of us didn't have any clue what these feminists were talking about simply because we knew that without our wives we couldn't exist. One reason I gave up farming is that I couldn't do it alone. My business partner and partner in life was my wife, Ann, and when she departed, I simply couldn't continue on.

What an incredible time this decade has been! A period of revolution - social, political, ethical, sexual - all intersecting at one point we call 'now' where young adults are in their most formative state. At the point, many of the post-war baby boomers stand, sincerely believing that Newton's Law does not apply to them as they take everything and push it to the limit.

These really are times of intense excitement, fear, frustration, fornication, experimentation and revelation and we all truly believe we are important and can 'change the world - rearrange the world'. For us, their parents, I don't think the kids can even imagine the times of distrust, disbelief and fear. For those generations who will come after these kids. I believe that this decade will be a period filled with stories and acceptance of what was and what is and the realization that these are times that truly changed the world - opening many doors, good and bad, that had never been opened before.

When I was a child, I remember traveling to Madison to cheer our boys on as they left for battle in World War I. When I was middle-aged, I remember the sacrifices we made with our victory gardens and rationing to help in the war effort of World War II. Today, as our soldiers return from Vietnam, they're spit on and called baby killers, when all they've done is serve their country by doing what they've been ordered to do. Gone is our sense of patriotism and national pride! Gone is the feeling of love, devotion, and that sense of attachment to a homeland and alliance with other citizens who share the same sentiment.

While we fight wars around the world in the name of peace, inflated nationalism in America continues as we promote ideas and movements in the interest of our country. Behind the rhetoric lies a subordinate aim of nothing more than gaining and maintaining our own nation's self-governance and economic well-being, regardless of whether our form of government, social structure and economy is right for the nations we try to persuade, conjure or force to follow our rules.

If our structure was perfect and ideal, then it might be fine. However, when you have so many issues, so many problems and so many ways that individuals demean, degrade or debase the premises upon which our country is supposed to be based, how can we justify what we profess when we can't even achieve those goals here at home?

As the events of the past ten years have evolved, I wonder, has our country entered a realm of Jingoism where our nationalism has developed into a form of aggressive and proactive foreign policy, such as our country's advocacy for the use of threats, actual force and monetary regards, in efforts to safeguard what it perceives as its national interests? America does not have all the answers when the goal of most people is to simply live in peace and security, with the hope that the world will be a better place for their children.

We must look inward and ask ourselves, "If we're all God's children how can we sincerely believe that groups of humans possess different behavioral traits because of their physical appearance and how can we divide people based on the superiority of one race over another?" In some cases it's apparent, in others, it's simply hidden beneath a cloak of abject prejudice, discrimination, or antagonism simply because they are different. We talk of the United States of America and, yet, our past and current history doesn't see it that way. Today, we build concentration camps called 'projects', designed to consolidate and discriminate whether or not we want it called that.

White or Caucasian people make up a little more than 10% of the world's population and yet we control so much more through different social actions, practices or beliefs, all supported by political systems where different races are ranked as inherently superior or inferior to each other, based on presumed shared inheritable traits, abilities, or qualities. At its extreme was Adolph Hitler. However, if America is truly the land of the free, shouldn't it be that all people have the same opportunities to achieve? No one should be given more. However, no one should be given less, simply because of the color of their skin.

Sadly, I see that the future will evolve and today's demonstrative 'we' generation will become tomorrow's 'me' generation - uptight, selfish, materialistic who will be much like their parents, except more cynical. As the snow quietly settles upon their temples, I wonder if what they did really made any difference. Are they any better? Is our world a better place in which to live? Are their children any happier? Again, Newton's third law will prevail. Again, we've witnessed a society that changed, incorporating a new sense of purpose, values and dynamics that's established what's right and what's wrong for all of us to strive for.

I wonder if, as the final decades of our final century of this millennium come into play and the outside threats that had pervaded our society, our government and our psyche began to subside, will we begin to live without the focused external threats that we've become accustomed to? Instead of tranquility, will we find ourselves embroiled in the largest, most incipient threat to our existence ever - a pervasive enemy so powerful and so dynamic as to shake our social order and threaten our virtual existence.

This threat is so powerful, and yet, so pervasive that it will challenge our social, political, economic and even religious foundations, shaking them as they have never been shaken before - threatening all that we've cherished for eleven generations, challenging our values and goals, redefining who, what and where we stand in recorded history.

This 'ism' is profound and yet evasive - elusive and yet so blatant that it stands before each of us day after day. It will question who, what and where we are in our existence, redefining our concepts of accomplishment and success and narcotizing the entire populous into following the rhythmic beat of its drummer.

This 'ism' is more profound and more pervasive than all that's come before. It's more threatening and potentially more damaging than all that we've faced. It has the ability to simply destroy the way of life for generations to come and do so in a manner that will leave the populous divided and defeated, unable to achieve any form of social peace and welfare. This 'ism' has started from within - an economic model that we export around the global village we call earth. This 'ism' is materialism - the acquisition of 'things' for the sake of ownership.

In 1899, Sebastian Spering Kresge opened a modest five-and-dime store in downtown Detroit, Michigan that changed the entire landscape of retailing when he began selling everything for five and ten cents. The low prices appealed to shoppers and allowed him to expand to eighty-five stores by 1912, with annual sales of over ten million dollars. He was followed by a cadre of competitors as other retail entrepreneurs copied the idea with such dime store chains as Ben Franklin and H.L. Green joining the fray.

Even with the wars and depression, Kresge stores could always offer families products at prices they could afford. In 1950, a man named Sam Walton opened his Walton's Five and Dime in Bentonville, Arkansas. Story is that Bentonville was chosen because Sam Walton's wife, Anna, liked small- town living and he could take advantage of the different hunting seasons the area had to offer.

By the 1950s, and more people with cars and televisions, the introduction of shopping centers including the Madison East Shopping center on East Washington Avenue took place. While the stores on the square and State Street were only open until five except on Monday nights and closed on Sunday, Manchester's and the other stores in the shopping center stayed open every night until nine and were not only open on Sundays but had parking right outside their doors. This wasn't happening just in Madison, but all over America, and it was apparent that Kresge needed to change if it wanted to continue to be a leader in the growing competitive retail environment.

In 1962, Kresge's opened the first K-mart discount department store. By 1966, there were 162 Kmart stores and 753 Kresge stores, all competing for the consumer's dollar, enticing people with their "blue light specials' to buy things they could easily do without if they really wanted to, but justifying them because of their low price. That same year, Sam Walton opened his first Walmart Superstore in Rogers, Arkansas. What was different between K-Mart and Walmart was the fact that K-Mart focused on the suburbs while Walmart had a strategy of owning multiple stores in small towns where the competition came from small independent retailers that he had competitive advantages over?

With so much to buy, another major change took place when BankAmericard went national in 1966 to become the nation's first licensed general-purpose credit card while a group of California banks formed the Interbank Card Association and issued the nation's second major bank card called MasterCard.

Walmart recently went public and continues to grow, buying more and more of its products from overseas where products cost less to manufacture, allowing them to march through small towns and eliminate the family-owned local retailers, who simply can't compete on assortment, price or advertising.

I can't blame the retailers. Somewhere in the 1960s there was a change in what people thought as consumers and as a society. Gone was the concept of want, replaced by the belief that something, everything, was a product or service people needed. Before credit cards, easy money and "blue light specials", we all had wants which were simply things we desired but could live without. Living on the farm, we wanted electricity and indoor plumbing, but we got by.

A need is something necessary to survive. If used to be that if you could survive without something, then it's not a need. People have forgotten that the key thing to remember in making a choice between wants and needs is not only about their comfort right now, but also about their future survival and quality of life.

In one generation the bar has been raised concerning every single element within the basket of our existence, making each of us longing for more and larger items to maintain what we perceive to be a "basic" style of life. Such things as single car garages and one-bathroom homes are beginning to seem quaint when, just 50 years ago, cars, garages and even indoor plumbing were beyond the reach of many.

Our accumulation of physical things has transcended into our basket of accumulated experiences where elements such as vacations have become expected and items as innocuous as children playing soccer and baseball have become organized "experiences" that connote different degrees of acquisition.

Today, our world is becoming one of "packages" such as packaged homes that meet certain socio-economic criteria based on income, lifestyle and age, to packaged experiences, also based on the same set of criteria. We're becoming a meringue society where there's a great deal of fluff, but little or no substance. We live in huge homes with rooms we never use, next door to people we hardly know that we never talk to. We press a button and the garage door opens and take our children to soccer or football or ballet as we jabber to someone we hardly know, never realizing that our occupants are also strangers in our lives, simply social appliances used to measure our social credibility factor, married/divorced, big house, two children, two cars, one dog, ain't life great!

Once again, Newton comes into play. The cost of the extreme is the extreme cost. We'll continue to run our economic race, always uphill. We'll find ourselves over-extended financially to the point that many Americans are past due on their bills and we make the only available sacrifice we can...we give up precious time to sustain our 'dream' world and our 'dream' existence - now working more than any other society on earth, now more hassled, now more frustrated, now more lonely, isolated and more emotionally devoid of the spirit we aspired to.

Our short-term costs are profound - lost time, lost energy, lost senses of accomplishment, purpose and well-being. Our long-term costs are pathetic, social strangers who have brought that isolation and loneliness into the area that deserves our highest sanctity, our family! Gone is the sense of being special. Gone are the redundancies that only come from repeated encounters at the breakfast and dinner tables interspersed by social solitude as everyone ponders their 'other' lives. Gone are those quiet moments when people gathered around each other only for the sake of each other, replaced by harried schedules where strangers meet in the name of tradition.

And what's the result of this insanity? We're all aware of its persuasiveness and yet we find that it has defined the concept of success and simply moved the bar even higher, eradicating yet another slice of what was once 'middle class', simply moving them to lower middle or upper middle, depending on whether you are a two-income professional or two-income blue collar family, defining our roles by where we shop, what we drive, and even where we vacation.

We all clothe ourselves in a 'persona' that hides the real spiritual self and do so out of position, definition and protection so that those on the outside can't peer within our heart and soul, unless we really, truly want them to.

In this decade, violence became the norm. Not only in terms of demonstrations but events such as the 1968 police riot in Chicago, during the Democratic National Convention, the murder of Martin Luther King Junior and Bobby Kennedy as he was campaigning to win his party's nomination for president as the talking heads of non-stop news never cease reminding us, challenging us, scaring us that our world is worse than it really is, simply to get us to keep on watching so that their ratings go up and with it, their rewards.

I've often wondered why so much has happened in such a short time. It would be difficult to go back and piece together all the different parts of the puzzle that made everything happen as it did, and hopefully, I have given some insight into why.

I guess you would have to look at the sociological impacts of the Great Depression, the World Wars, post-war baby boomers, television, birth control pills, the cold war and the threats of nuclear holocaust, Viet Nam, race relations, women's lib and even the Interstate Highway System and then try to connect the dots to see how each has affected our existence, expectations and relationships with each other. It could be done, it wouldn't be easy, and in the end, it probably isn't necessary because we're here and that's really all that matters.

Having said that, I still sincerely believe that you can trace many of the events through our music of the time and see how this form of communication not only reflected upon, but helped perpetuate the upheaval that we all created, participated in, and survived. The decade began with folk music consisting of basic melodies accompanied by guitars where the lyrics mattered. The decade ended with rock-and-roll being splintered into different directions, including folk rock, traditional rock and heavy metal, each trying to grasp enough straws of relevancy to be important.

Just think about these few things   all this happened in these ten years...'Peace and Love'... recreational drugs... recreational sex micro-mini skirts... Love-In's.... Love Children... Hippies   Flower Children   Public Nudity... Living Together..... Woodstock and 400,000 people. Expanded Families.... Psychedelia..... Hendrix.. the Moody Blues.... Joplin, Jefferson Airplane.... Cream.... Ritchie Havens..... The Doors.... The Beatles, Hare Krishna.... Hair..... Topless Bathing Suits.... Mod...... Black Like Me, H. Rap Brown.... Eldredge Cleaver.... Malcolm X.... Selma, Alabama.....Viet Nam... We Shall Overcome   Civil Rights.... Afro.... Viet Cong.... Joan Baez Draft Dodgers.......'Make Love Not War'...Bobby Kennedy & Reverend Martin Luther King and 'One small step for man, one giant leap for mankind'.

In one decade, each of those people and concepts were introduced, accepted or rejected, and became part of the normal set of values by which all people are now being judged.

As I look back on this time, I wonder, is this the America men and women fought for? Is this the America we dreamed about? Is this the America we truly want - a group of strangers marching to the beat of different drummers who we seek out happiness through "things" instead of beings?

What an incredible time! A period of revolution - social, political, ethical, sexual - all intersecting at one point called "now" when so many young people were in their most formative state as they took everything and pushed it to the limit.

'War of My Brothers' has hopefully outlined the battles against all forms of negative change and extremism that resulted in the social, political and economic challenges I've witnessed, participated in and in some ways regret. Life used to be so simple and now its pace is such that it has escaped gravity and begun to accelerate to the point I fear no one will ever be happy or satisfied again.

All anyone should ever want out of life is to be happy. When the challenges of war, depression and social upheaval came to the front, we all did our best to recognize the 'War of My Brothers' and pledged that there would always be something we could change to create a sense of happiness by sincerely making others sincerely feel wanted, needed and loved.

On June 25, 1967, the Beatles presented a song that was broadcast globally to over 400 million people that really says it all.

Love, love, love

There's nothing you can do that can't be done Nothing you can sing that can't be sung

Nothing you can say, but you can learn how to play the game It's easy

Nothing you can make that can't be made No one you can save that can't be saved

Nothing you can do, but you can learn how to be you in time It's easy

All you need is love, love Love is all you need.

Mineral Point, Wisconsin, is a small town filled with people who know each other, love each other and share this thing called life. All the fancy homes were built over 100 years ago, and the pace at which we live is much slower than you find elsewhere. There's an innocence and purity that can easily be found simply by putting a smile on your face. There's love and laughter that echoes off the hills that surround our little town. There have been scoundrels and yet, for the most part, most of us are good, honest, sincere people who have retained something you don't find elsewhere and that is we truly care for each other.

While the world had changed and cities grown, our town stays pretty much the same. I think most of Mineral Point's residents have lived through good times, bad times, happy times and sad times and yet, they have sustained a dignity that comes from knowing they're happy with what they've got and really don't need much more. A gentle smile! A warm handshake! A simple nod makes up for the helter-skelter and the faster pace that others equate to happiness and that's why I'm proud to call it home.

Hello Again...Hello

I read my typed manuscript on the 1960s and hoped it wasn't too 'political' and walked up to the post office and mailed it to Kat. That Sunday, I awaited her call. Seven o'clock came, and the phone didn't ring. I was concerned. By then I knew it would be a sleepless night. The next morning, I went to the hotel we were re-building to check on progress and no one was there. I drove up Shake Rag and it, too, was silent. I was tempted to go home and call Kat that night, but felt I'd better not.

The following Sunday night, I sat by the phone, and it didn't ring. At nine, I called Kat's number and there was no answer. I became worried. Was the spell broken? Had I done something wrong? All I needed was something. No one deserves to swim in an abyss of unanswered questions.

It was now over two weeks since we'd separated in Denver and I was forlorn. Finally, I called the Library of Congress and inquired about her and was told that no information about employees could be shared. I really didn't know what to do.

I needed to know and flew to Washington, staying at the Marriott across from National airport that night. The next morning, I went to the library and looked for Kat and she wasn't there. I went to the information desk and inquired and was told that she hadn't been to work since we were in Vegas. Now I was really concerned.

I took a taxi out to McClean and arrived at the house. The gate was closed and locked and no one answered the bell. I had no idea what was going on.

I was about to leave when a neighbor saw me and came over. "Can I help you, sir?" she asked.

"I'm a friend of Katherine Johnson's and I'm concerned. I've been trying to contact her for the past two weeks, but to no avail," I responded.

"Mrs. Johnson and her driver were in a horrible car accident and she's in the hospital."

"Oh, my God! Is she OK?"

"I'm not certain, but I do know that her driver was killed."

"Charles?"

"Yes, I think that was his name."

For the second time in just a few years the same terrible news echoed in my heart and soul as I whispered to myself, - 'Oh no, not again!' Someone I truly cared for has been involved in a tragedy.

"Do you know what hospital she's in?" I inquired.

"Sorry, I don't"

"What about Annie, her housekeeper?"

"She took her husband's remains back home." I closed my eyes in disbelief.

"How do I find out which hospital Katherine's in?" I asked.

"Sorry, I don't know."

I went back to the hotel and began calling all the police departments. There had to be someone who'd know where Kat was. Finally, on the fifth call, I was told that Katherine Johnson was in intensive care at Bethesda Naval Hospital.

I took a taxi to Bethesda and asked to see Katherine. I was told that she wasn't allowed to see any visitors outside her immediate family. I looked at the nurse and tears began rolling down my cheeks. I explained that I'd come to Washington to propose and the nurse just shook her head and said she was sorry, but it was hospital policy.

"Can you tell me how she's doing?" I asked.

"Sorry, I can't do that."

"Has anyone been to visit her?"

"Sorry, I'm not allowed to share that information."

"What can you tell me?"

"Not much!"

"Can I send her flowers?"

"Not in ICU!"

"What can I do?"

"Pray!"

Nothing has value until its gone, and I was afraid I was losing the woman I now knew I truly loved. As I turned and was about to leave, one of the best things I'd ever seen walked through the door. It was Tad with Charlene at his side.

"Tad, I didn't know! - What happened?"

"Mom and Charles were broadsided by a truck. Charles didn't make it. Mom's in pretty bad shape. We're just on our way back from Charlottesville and the funeral."

"They won't let me see her." I noted.

"Let me see what I can do," Tad replied as he turned and went to the nurse's station. A few minutes later, the head nurse arrived and had a discussion with Tad.

Tad came back and indicted that they were working on getting approval so that I could see his mother. He warned me that things weren't looking good. Kat had been a coma with a broken left leg and ribs, punctured lung, ruptured spleen, neck injuries and a fractured skull.

A few minutes later, I was allowed in the room to the chorus of beep, beep, beep. I looked at Kat and saw the bandages and tubes. My heart sank as her lifeless body lie still. They had to put a tracheostomy in her and insert a breathing tube. Her head had been shaved and was bandaged, and she was in traction. My God!

I went to her side and took her hand without the IV and placed it in mine. I looked at Kat and whispered, "Heh lady, it's Hank. It took me a while to find you, but I did. I came to tell you I love you. I came because you're the most important thing in my life and I can't live without you, simply because you complete me." As I looked at the expressionless face, whose eyes were closed and listened to the beep, beep, beep, I thought I saw a tiny tear in her right eye and it gave me hope.

Tad returned to New York, giving me the keys to the house and permission to use of Kat's car. Each day, I'd drive to the hospital and sit, wondering if she would make it. Each day, I prayed Kat would return to me. Each day, I realized that I couldn't go through what I had before. I visited every afternoon, watching and waiting simply to see if Kat would slowly make her way back to reality and me.

I realized the few clothes I put in my carry-on wouldn't be enough, and I also needed to let everyone in Mineral Point know what was going on. I called my brother Tom and Sue answered. I told her what happened and Sue was distraught. "Not again!" she said.

I asked her if she and Tom could go to the Rooster and let Madge know, realizing that all of Mineral Point would be aware within two days. I then asked if she and Tom could go to the house, pack some of my clothes and ship them to me and then go to Madison and get the Chevy at Truax Field as it made no sense leaving the car there for what appeared to be an extended period.

Sue said they would. As an after-thought, I asked her to eject the audiotape in the car and send it with my clothes. For the next five days, I spoke the same words. "I came here to tell you I love you. I came here because you're the most important thing in my life and I can't live without you, simply because you complete me." That fifth day saw my clothes and the tape arrive. After dinner, I went to Radio Shack and bought a small portable cassette player and what the clerk called 'ear buds', knowing there was no way Kat's head could handle regular headphones.

The next day, I went to the hospital and made certain it was OK to put the earbuds in Kat's ears and began playing the music Kat had listened to on our drive from Chicago. There appeared to be a soft smile on the former expressionless face, or perhaps it was my imagination.

On the seventh day, as I held her hand, I played the music again and there was a gentle squeeze. On the eighth day, I walked in, placed the ear buds in Kat's ears and her eyes opened, if only for a moment, and she softly smiled before nodding off again.

I had plenty of time between visits and needed something - anything to take the worries away. Finally, I made my way to a bookstore where I bought some books and spent my time reading. One day, I made my way out to Kat's studio and saw her drawing of me. It was signed, 'with love – Kat'. It was then that I broke down and cried. It was then that all the fear that had built up inside me was released. It was then that I fell to my knees and begged God to let her live.

Because of the massive injuries, healing was a slow process. They kept Kat sedated as the pain would have been intolerable and yet as she would come to, if only for a moment, she would smile and nod before drifting off again. Gratefully with each day, a little more of the woman I loved reappeared.

One day, I went to visit and her room was empty. For an instant, fear reviled my body as I thought I'd lost her. Gratefully, she was deemed well enough to be moved to a regular room, and I knew the time had come that she was coming out of the woods and back to recovery. She still couldn't talk and was in a great deal of pain, but would look at me with a gentle smile and beckon me to her side where I'd hold her hand until she dozed off again.

They say that recovery isn't a linear progression but a series of steps where one step can be small and the next profound. After what seemed forever, the tracheostomy was finally closed and when I arrived she was propped up in bed. I went to her side and held her hand and she squeezed it. Her throat was too sore to speak, but she tried simply mouthing the word 'sorry' as I stood and shook my head 'no'.

Kat mouthed 'Charles' and I repeated the same movement, simply communicating 'no'. Her lower lip protruded and I could tell she was sincerely sad and then her eyes closed and my visit was over.

The next day there was a gentle smile. Kat looked at me and mouthed 'thank you'. I looked at her and thought, 'for what?' The room had filled with so many plants and flowers it looked like a flower shop. As she dozed, I looked at the cards and was surprised to see that several were from Army Generals, two Cabinet members and even one from Richard and Pat Nixon. I wondered how Kat knew the President and why she would ever want to move to Mineral Point.

Perhaps the time of recovery was what we both really needed as we got to see a different side of each other and sensed that what we had was more than infatuation. As she was laying there, I looked at her and asked if she heard what I'd said while she was still in a coma. She looked at me with a soft, gentle smile and whispered, 'I felt you, Hank! I felt your goodness and generosity. I felt your humility and compassion, but above all else, I felt your love and passion for life that's what made me want to live.'

The next day I arrived, and Kat was sitting in a chair, which made me happy. I looked at her and inquired if she was going to join Will in the Marines?

She whispered "why?" as I responded her crew cut was actually quite attractive, to which she raised her right hand and closed three of her four fingers and smiled while flipping me the bird and I knew she was on her way 'back'.

It was then that I offered her a poorly wrapped present to which I said, "I brought you a gift." Carefully and with a slight smile on my face, I handed her a box which, I believe she thought was chocolate. When she opened it, she realized it was a copy of the book she'd copied the pages from at the library.

"Could you please explain page 189?" I asked.

With that, Kat slowly opened the book and saw a small piece of paper that repeated what I'd whispered so many times, *"I came to tell you I love you. I came because you are the most important thing in my life and I cannot live without you, simply because you complete me."*

Tears welled in her eyes, allowing me proceed with what I'd wanted to do since the very first time we'd met. I moved to the side of her chair and knelt down on one knee and said, "Katherine Johnson, when you're better, will you marry me?"

Kat looked at me with a forlorn look and shook her head 'no'.

I was devastated until she simply whispered..."Do we really have to wait until I'm better?"

The Waldwick Series: The ten-book series spans nearly 200 years and are independent yet intertwined in several ways including, characters, location and thematic objectives that examine current social issues from different perspectives. Regardless of the time period or the characters in question, the core component - judging people by who they are instead, of what they are, remains paramount.

Waldwick addresses the subject of physical, social, economic and political oppression in the 1800's. Set in Cornwall, England, Virginia and Southwestern Wisconsin, *Waldwick* frankly discusses what one family was willing to do to overcome oppression, as told through the eyes of the narrator, George Terrill. *Waldwick* then summarizes what happens when the oppression is removed and opportunity arises. Integrated into the story line are actual events and people and how the main characters are affected by their existence and their interaction with these people and events. Above all else, *Waldwick* is a love story ... love of the land, love of one another and the love of freedom, woven in a tapestry of acceptance, tolerance and justice. *Award Winner*

War of My Brothers examines America of the early 20th century and how and why it changed as seen through the eyes of Hank Terrill, great grandson of George Terrill from the original Waldwick. Ride along as Hank witnesses World War I, the Spanish Flu, the 19th Amendment, that gave women the right to vote, the Great Depression, World War II, Korean War and Viet Nam and how life changed, people changed and those who govern changed, as well. Experience the traumas of life and the joys of the living as you thank God that it didn't happen to you.

The King of Hearts has been reviewed as *"ambitious, extensively researched and deeply engrossing"*...a story that traces the actual Terrill family through 60 generations as it learns the consequence of wealth, power and prestige over 700 years only to have it all collapse around them. Using a blend of magic realism, lyrical prose and imagery *The King of Hearts* weaves a complex tapestry of a family's history from 65 BCE through sixty generations. Beneath it all, the book is about friendship and the deep, mutual bond between people based on trust, support, and genuine connection that goes beyond just companionship—it's about understanding, loyalty, and being there for each other through life's ups and downs.

Little Spirit Based in contemporary Wisconsin, *Little Spirit* examines the concept of eminent domain and the taking of land and dignity, first from the Indian's perspective and then today, as seen through the eyes of George Terrill IV a descendant of the original George Terrill. Using flashbacks through a 94-year-old, blind, Ho- Chunk Indian elder, named Great Grandfather, George learns about the feelings and challenges of the Ho-Chunk nation and the taking of their land and also how contemporary America hasn't changed that much in terms of citizen rights.

Driftless revisits George and his wife fifteen years into their marriage. Reflecting on the challenges they face when their marriage becomes mundane while examining the profound question of which is worse… having nothing or everything. As the mystery of the Forest is revealed *Driftless* examines the consequence of technology and the power of special interest groups to control the status-quo for their financial gain, while addressing the issue of individual rights in time of personal need, where the one thing all people have in common is … time!

The Hayflick Limit addresses the challenges of parenthood, while discussing a person's rights to live and die. When affected by an incurable malady the question becomes *"Would you choose five-to-seven years of normal mental acuity, at which time you would abruptly expire, or risk everything and allow for the slow, gradual decline with hope that a different, longer-lasting cure might come along?" The Hayflick Limit* addresses the role of government in establishing the validity of the Hippocratic Oath?

Let Go examines the consequence of bullying as Melia Terrill is affected by the verbal onslaught and her commitment to the only friend who has shown her the beauty of acceptance for who she is. The books examines the perks and perils of extreme wealth, the solitude of loneliness and frustration of achieving one's goals only to realize that all dreams can become nightmares when one risks everything for perhaps nothing as it delves into thoughts, emotions, joys, sorrow and consequences of being a captive of one's own past and fleeting fame.

Survivor...How Death Saved My Life looks at the consequence of an altered set of priorities and how it can take a near-death experience to "right the ship". Totally immobilized for six days, George Terrill examines his life and it's mistakes and vows, if he survives, to make things right. *Survivor* addresses the psychology of fear, the challenges of being told you have less than a 5% chance of living three hours and what you think about when you sincerely believe you're going to die.

Greed is a thought-provoking literary tale of ambition gone awry, exposing how the pursuit of wealth can fracture family relationships. This intense novel, explores the intricacies of human nature and the pursuit of meaning. It serves as a critique of modern society's obsession with wealth and status that challenges readers to reconsider what success truly means, making this book not just an exhilarating journey but a profound reflection on the human condition.

And/Or Using Newton's Third Law as a lens to explore relationships where every action sets off a chain reaction, *And/Or* journeys in ways no one can predict or control while asking difficult questions about resilience, identity, and redemption. As such, it ponders deep philosophical reflections and existential questions by drawing sharp connections between science and human nature, asking such profound questions as...Is it possible for a person to truly recover from betrayal? Can love survive after it's been broken? And when one loses everything, what's left? *And/Or* is a gripping, thought-provoking read that will linger long after the final page.

Disclaimer: This book is a work of fiction. Some events and experiences detailed may be true and have been faithfully rendered as researched by the author to the best of his abilities. The information in this book is intended to provide helpful and informative material on the subjects and events addressed and written as an interpretation of his learning.

The author is a descendant of miners from Cornwall. There's a town called Mineral Point, Wisconsin, where his childhood was filled with magical moments and marvelous memories. There's also a village called Waldwick that remains nearby and is the birthplace of his grandmother and mother. There are many Terrills living in the area who are his relatives and the author hopes and prays that he's done the family name justice by what he's written, for they are the kindred spirit upon which our country was created. There's no reality to the names used, as they are all of consequence.

If the tale he weaves meets your fancy and your interest is piqued, the author highly recommends visiting the wonderful area just southwest of Madison, Wisconsin. The scenery is spectacular and is only exceeded by the honor, dignity, and warmth of the people who reside there. While the story begins the tale of art in the city, many visitors are surprised to find that there are over twenty different artists with studios residing in this small town.

The author has written this book as a tribute to those who continue to live in Mineral Point. Once you've visited, you'll never forget the goodness and easy smiles that will come your way. For some, the experience reinforces the value of integrity and honesty and the joy of acceptance that only comes from an open heart and a profound sense of decency that is now emanated with each breath they take.

www.ingramcontent.com/pod-product-compliance
Lightning Source LLC
Chambersburg PA
CBHW070309310726
48976CB00005B/1637